I0655076

2050

Gods of Little Earth

A Future History

Volume 1

2050

Gods of Little Earth

A Future History
Volume 1

by J. Zornado

The Merry Blacksmith Press
2014

2050: Gods of Little Earth
A Future History, Volume 1

© 2014 Joseph Zornado

For information, address:

The Merry Blacksmith Press
70 Lenox Ave.
West Warwick, RI 02893

merryblacksmith.com

Published in the USA by The Merry Blacksmith Press

ISBN—0-69234-194-3
978-0-69234-194-0

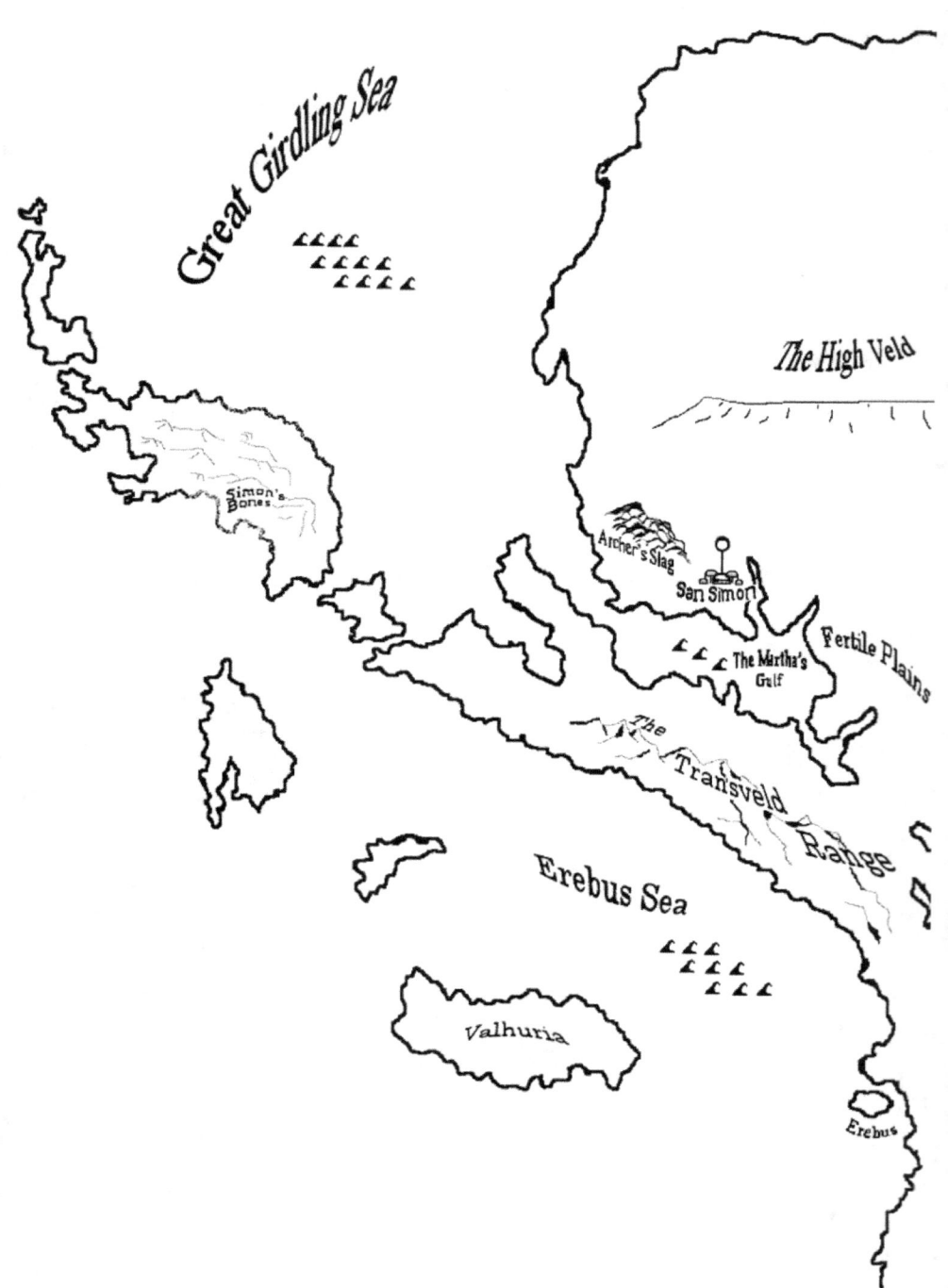

AkiGazi Land

Gazi Peoples

Badlands

Vilb's Hill

Ubernakia

Spire Massif

Lake Vost

White Sea

Little Earth
2050 a.s.

Prologue

There is SIMON who in Little Earth is called Blessed, and the oNe, and World-KIller, and the GreAt God, and He came into the world as the Ancients fell and He fashioned a Little Earth from the frozen wastes of Antarctica at the bottom of the Ancient's world. He raised the Arclight and He raised His Great City and He called it the Seventh Realm.

After the Blessed Simon came upon the land and took it as His own, the lesser gods banded together to contend against Him and out of jealousy and spite they plotted together to cast Him down and steal His Power of M, and they did. And it is a great mystery for on that day they scattered Simon to the seven corners of the Seven Realms, and Simon's face disappeared from the surface of the world.

And on that day the Four took the Little Earth into their own hands and used what Power of M they could master to re-make the Seventh Realm, and they tore down what Simon had built up and put their own works upon the land, all but Simon's Great City and His Arclight—these things of Simon the gods took as their own.

For in their hubris the gods decreed that the Seventh Realm would become a Little Earth where immortals reigned over the children of the gods. The children of the gods would work to tame the land and draw a new world from the ashes of the old, and the gods would look on the work of their children and take credit for their accomplishments.

Always the Four sought to claim the greater power of Simon as their own, but Simon had hid it from them when the Four overmastered Him. And so the Four were forced to contend among themselves for that portion of the Power of M each desired, but none of the Four were contented. They chafed and bit at one another in vengeful greed until finally they turned their minds to making war against each other. Because of war all they turned

1

their hand to took seed only to fail, and finally, the Arclight of Simon failed and the long day grew cold and the long night grew dark and Little Earth stood upon the edge of ruin.

Even as the gods despaired of ever finding where Simon had hidden the Power of M, Vilb Solenthay set out on his Pilgrimage to the Great City in search of the truth about why his world was dying. Of his companions, and how he met them, and who they were, and how he found his answers and embraced his fate, more follows in this record. Little did Vilb know that he would become an ember to ignite a great conflagration across the Seven Realms.

> To know the gods of Little Earth
> Pilgrim needs a second birth.
> Go seek The Martha about her Son.
> (for His is the name for our Destruction)
> Next Lord Qir, who blinds the just,
> Then Quadros Prang who feeds his lust,
> Last is Azo who serves The Martha's trust.
>
> What deed provoked the Four against the One?
> Simon, Simon, where have you gone?

– The BooK of M

The Necrophage

The Gods give it all into your hands. For you is the skin, and the flesh beneath the skin, and the bones beneath the flesh, yea, even to the marrow. They give it all into your hands. Take it and be filled.

– The Book of M

I

It was nearing midnight and a glaring summer sun circled in an otherwise empty, arid sky. Vilb Solenthay sipped carefully from the mouth of his water skin, tied it off, pulled his cowl down lower over his brow and began to scramble hurriedly over the rocky terrace. He was anxious, excited, but committed as he approached the edge of the plateau. He was further north than he liked to be. Beyond where he stood, west, and below lay the Ubernaki Badlands, a place he did not go but in sorest need. He had heard something as he hunkered down, hoping for the biting wind to calm. Voices, men, and by their tracks he could see that they carried some burden. He hurried along and caught a glint, a shining star on the horizon, flickering, as if calling to him, and then it dropped into the badlands.

All of this he could tell for those who had passed made no attempt to hide their passing. Desperate men, no doubt, on a desperate deed. Careful to disguise his own passing over the loose sand, he paused for a moment and then in the next he was scrabbling over the plateau rim and dropping into the first ravine he had not visited in many suns—it was too far out, too far from water.

Simon protect me.

Down he climbed, the withering sun on his back. Shadow up ahead, and rest, he thought. Suddenly his foot slipped and Vilb battered a hand lunging to catch himself. He cried out and the sound of his voice startled and unsettled him. He paused, crouching, his back to the sun. He sucked on a bleeding, already purple knuckle and wished he could tend to the wound properly but he felt a strange urgency to move forward, even though forward meant further from his hill, from water, from shelter.

Simon protect me. Deliver me from evil.

He prayed to Simon against infection, rose to his full height and continued on, slowly at first. He praised Simon as he made his way down into the ravine, thanked The Martha every other breath for the good fortune that had guided his feet thus far, and yet, at the same time, prepared himself for bitter disappointment. Was it a trap? Villager boys out to skin the old hermit-gen? They had tried before. But this felt different—he was too far out, and as far as Vilb was concerned, the tracks he had seen confirmed that this was no cruel trick.

Vilb was hungry. All the time. His tall frame had withered over the suns until now he was all lank and no shank. He chuckled and a dry, raspy sound rose from his chest. He would starve to death if the growing season failed again, he thought. A full season of sun. No cloud. No rain. Even the fresh water spring in his hill trickled pathetically, where once it flowed and echoed off the grotto's walls. Little Earth was drying up.

He would not be the only one to starve, he thought, but this was little consolation. Those in the Ubernaki village would fare no better. Savages. Flesh-eaters. Vilb shuddered as if to give power to his rejection though a part of him knew that had a bowl of properly seasoned flesh been placed before him at that instant, he would have fallen upon it without restraint.

But there was no flesh before him, and there had not been for many circles of the sun, and, he reckoned, for many long nights as well. Perhaps he had changed. Perhaps he had left the past behind. He watched himself shrink, wither, a shaken man, ancient before his time, yet there was honor in this, he thought. Honor.

Then why were the gods not favoring him? Where was The Martha's bounty? Was it so wrong to want to eat when hungry? All he wanted was something fresh, something that dripped down his chin when he chewed. He shook his head as if seeing a point he missed. How was this a sin? He could not remember his arguments against the eating of flesh. Not a single point came to mind. Many suns, many seasons, countless circs, of meditation and discipline seemed to fail him and all he could feel was his stomach aching and rolling over in need. He slipped again as he climbed and cursed himself. It was simply disastrous to lose one's footing for a slip might lead to a serious injury, and an injury this far out meant death was very near.

Just get there, he thought. Understanding was what Vilb sought in the desert. His practice sought nothing more and nothing less. The true gen saw through to the truth, to the origin of truth. Is that not where the name gen came from? He wasn't sure, but he liked to believe it. The seeker of origins. Confusion and desire destroyed his discipline. Unfortunately, Vilb knew that he was far from achieving his goals and his mad dash into the ravine confirmed all such negative appraisals of his slow and often disappointing development. Flesh. Dripping down his chin. His stomach moved again and urged him on.

Just get there. Just get there. He scrambled on. The long light made him thirsty constantly and this season was particularly harsh. He could never get enough water into him. He woke up dry. He went to sleep parched. He drank all that his spring offered and still it was not enough. Like all the others in his village, Vilb dreaded the slow setting of the sun and the coming of the long night, but lately he felt a dissembling nostalgia for the starry sky and the cool, blackness. Anything to get this sun off his back. Even the long night.

He was thirsty, he was hungry, he was tired, and he was much further from his home than was wise. He stopped and looked around and his stomach made a fist. "Yes, yes. You're this far," he told himself, "but we both know that you won't sleep unless you see for yourself." Another prayer to Simon, for faith, and for the emptiness that He promised, for the great silence of Simon to fill Vilb's mind and for a moment he had recaptured his calm and serenity. In that moment he saw himself climb up and head for his hill, drink from his spring, gather his roots. He had been hungry before and would be again. All would be well.

But the moment passed, and as if released from a grip, Vilb's weight shifted forward and he found his sure-footedness once again. He quickly scrambled over the edge of a terrace and dropped onto a boulder, dropped deeper into the ravine, and into the chill of cool shadow. Shadow and water demanded rest, but not this time. A hunger fever was suddenly on him and it felt as if his many suns of training in the desert had taught him nothing—had all been self-deception. He felt drawn by the hand of other forces, other desires which had come before him and usurped his will. He was a grain of sand carried by the desert wind into his fate.

Rocks skittered down the escarpment at each footfall and he grunted and hissed at himself to trust his guided feet, for they seemed to step where they would.

Martha guide me… be a light unto my steps. Guide me, guide me. Just then he stopped, paused at a wide channel cutting off his path. He looked down. It was a short leap across, madness in this low light but he had no alternative. His eyes struggled to adjust to the shadow, but he did not wait. His feet carried him on. He leapt easily and landed lightly, leapt again down to an outcropping, and then another, and then a short drop to a sandstone terrace that ran a goodly way up the ravine towards his goal. From there it was one more jump to the shadows of the ravine floor, even cooler now, and up ahead he began to spy his goal and his heart pounded as if in response.

Breathing hard, catching his wind in ragged pulls, he filled his lungs with one great breath and held it in and listened. His throbbing heart made it difficult to hear.

Listen. *Listen.*

He squinted, breathed out and took another deep breath and held it. At first nothing. He crouched, closed his eyes and waited. Above him he heard a murmur of wind as it slipped across the plateau far above and down into ravines, crevasses, alcoves and blind valleys of the badlands, like a whistle and a moan. And then below him he heard a scitter of spherule over boulder choke followed by another. Was that a footfall? Voices? Waiting, holding another deep breath, and there it was again. He could not believe his luck, if that's what it was. He had followed hardly any track, only his instinct once he dropped into the ravine. But he heard what he had heard.

He was not alone. He exhaled and slapped his thighs but then quickly restrained any further outburst. Just get over there, he thought. It's waiting for you, praise The Martha. She wants you to live. She wants you to eat. Thank you. Thank you. In spite of his excitement he moved cautiously and remembered The Book of M: good fortune exacts a price commensurate with the intensity of one's desire.

So Vilb prayed against desire even as he moved towards his desire. Madness, he knew, but it was the madness he knew. He mumbled words all his own, a made-up incantation of childhood lessons half-learned, mostly forgotten, an Ubernaki spell against desire that Vilb had adapted from sheer need when he decided that he could no longer eat the flesh, could no longer live the way his village lived. And here it was. He was hungry. And there was something fresh to eat. He could smell sweat now, other than his own, and… blood.

There were times in the past when he believed that perhaps he had, finally, mastered his hunger, that he was larger than his craving. But now, here, this circ, the craving seized his mind and body and he could taste the memory of flesh on his tongue and he wanted it. The voice inside of him, once him now not him—not dead yet—demanded that he eat the flesh, that it was not too late, that he might yet restore himself. Did not the Ubernaki priests invite and command it to be done? Were they not The Martha's vicars on Little Earth? Did they not themselves respond to the Power of M and the Arclight itself ? Yes, they did, but on this point Vilb shook his head in a vain attempt to wrestle free from this most pernicious argument. He would be sorely tested this circ should he find the body, if indeed there was one to be found. But he could smell it. Others were passing somewhere above him, leaving the body behind. Desperate deeds done by desperate men. The body must be diseased. Or worse, possessed, Vilb thought. It was the only explanation for this most unusual disposal.

• • •

The far side of the ravine was in shadow and still too distant to pick out detail, so he looked down to the narrow floor, mostly talus and ancient outwash, and then, thoughtless now, to the east. His feverish thoughts had passed and he could think, at least for a moment. From where he stood Vilb could see where the southern wall of the ravine gave way to a view of a desiccated valley beyond. And beyond that, in the far distance, a serrated horizon line separated the green sky from the red karst of the valley. He spat and muttered an oath—wasting his water no less—turned and headed north up the gorge towards what he was sure now was a body—probably an Ubernaki, or perhaps an unfortunate Gazi had wandered into the village and been stoned for some real or imagined offense. His belly growled.

Could be AkiGazi. Vilb shuddered at the thought. They threatened to eat up the entire east of Little Earth. It didn't matter at this moment. Flesh was flesh, skins were skins.

A breeze wrapped around him for a moment, filled his srapi, and he smelled the flesh and blood of the newly dead.

New skins.

Thanks be to Simon.

Of course no meat, he told himself.

That's right, he thought. Just skins. And bones. He'd been praying for skins and bones for the last three seasons, and now, finally, his prayers had been answered.

Yes, of course you're hungry. Get there. See it. Touch it. Then you'll know.

The sling at his side hung heavy off one hip and he used it as a balance and a ballast as he danced across the gorge towards what appeared to be a kind of natural catacomb in the side of the valley. He was close now and in another moment he was there standing before an escarpment riven by rifts and crawlways.

He nodded. It made sense. Tombs. A canyon of tombs. And there were many, long unused though. He had been here before, many suns past when water and food made long treks possible. Even then he had managed to scavenge only a few meager bones in a leather hutch, almost useless to him except as fine needles, and some were so shaped that they were useless for any task except to look at, and this he occasionally did, for in the long night they carried with them a faint, emerald glow as if in sympathetic response to the Arclight which shone from far off San Simon.

The Power of M, he thought. Or not. Just bones. And ragged, tattered skin too old to hold water.

He kept them nonetheless, for they had a strange attraction and seemed to—at least at first—represent a gift from the gods and a blessing for his decision to leave the village and enter the life of the solitary seeker.

But fine needlework was for another age. This circ his was a more basic need. That was almost twenty suns past. There were many hundreds of openings in the walls all around him, and the thought of climbing to each one, of forcing himself inside, well, it was simply too much.

A wave of exhaustion weakened him. Was it worth it? He could die trying to find out. His right leg instinctively thumped against the water skins hanging from his waist. Uncomfortably light. Vilb sank down and crawled to a shady spot to rest, to listen and, with luck, to sleep. The body would keep.

II

When Vilb awoke, the sky was a richer green than before and the sun had dropped below the valley rim. Still, it would be a long while before twilight. This circ he must squint. He rose and stretched and took in the ravine wall before him. He had slept on it and woke up more confident in his plans. If he could find it, the body would make at least one, perhaps two large water skins. That would make five all told in his possession, a goodly amount, enough to take him thirty, thirty-five circs. It could make the difference. Perhaps that was Simon's purpose. Perhaps he would make the Pilgrimage after all. Water skins. Bones. But no meat. He sighed heavily.

How am I to make the Pilgrimage if I'm starving?

He had no answer. He was trapped between two absolutes in his mind: his commitment to take the Pilgrimage to the Great City and his renunciation of flesh. He shook his head. Perhaps the two could not co-exist? Perhaps relaxing his vow against flesh might allow him to achieve his larger goals?

Devil's logic, he thought. No. He would not give in to it. He looked around suddenly, a chill taking him, half-expecting to see Quadros Prang swooping down on him all wings and fire.

Nursery stories, he reminded himself. There is no Quadros Prang. There is probably no Simon or The Martha for that matter. Or Azo or Master Qir. There are no gods. Just wind. Sun. Thirst. Hunger.

But The Book of M was handed to the Ubernaki Meson by The Martha herself some two-thousand suns ago, at the beginning, even before the gods raised the Arclight and transformed the Seventh Realm into Little Earth. There were Ubernaki eyewitnesses.

Yes, but The Book of M is our only source for these stories, and a few family tales. Perhaps it's only myth. Legend. Perhaps the world would be better off if it could forget the gods of Little Earth and solve its own problems and not wait for Simon to return.

Vilb shook his head to drive out the blasphemous thoughts. Forgive me. He believed. In spite of himself, he knew,

if only because he heard things, understood things, dreamed things, remembered things that could only come from the gods themselves. It's why he left the village enclave to begin with, and it's why he planned for so long to take the Pilgrimage in spite of the fact that no Pilgrimage had set forth for San Simon in over five suns. He would. He would bring The Martha's blessings back to her people in the east.

• • •

But he had not nearly enough skins for the trek. No, not nearly. And if he meant to go this time, to really head out and cross the plains as a Pilgrim, a gen Pilgrim no less, he would need more skins.

The rain no longer fell. Most of the springs on the plateau near his hill had gone dry, or ran brackish and foul, and now, two circs from home and at least two circs from known water, he began to worry. He knocked his knee against the two water skins hanging at his waist as if to prove to himself that he would, indeed, die of thirst if his luck did not change soon.

"It should be here, right around here," he said aloud. The sickly sweet odor of sweat and blood was in the air and it was unmistakable. A surge of energy filled him.

He climbed down from the boulder and scrambled up through the talus and began to make his way towards the nearest, most accessible terrace on the catacomb wall. Something told him that the Ubernaki, had they been the ones he had heard the circ before, would not have climbed high or hard—they were at heart a lazy people and would have wanted to dispense with what was almost certainly a desecrated body as quickly as possible.

The catacombs were rarely used anymore besides—no body these circs no matter how unholy could be wasted. Even so, what he smelled must be the remains of an Ubernaki casting out, and this quickened his pulse. He or she who was cast out was entombed with all of his unclean things. With luck, praise Simon, Vilb might find water skins, tools, srapis, anything the village considered unclean and dangerous would have been disposed of along with the body. There was not the fuel to burn them nor the body as there once was and it would be his gain—he scrambled forward in the hopes that a treasure trove of tools, skins and food awaited him.

What if the body was possessed... made unclean... by... Quadros Prang?

Suddenly Vilb laughed out loud. Two small feet protruded from a cavity made by a seam in the cliff face and any and all fears left him. It wasn't even a proper tomb, even by Ubernaki standards. Vilb clapped his hands and clambered on as quickly as he could towards the feet.

. . .

Vilb loved the dead for they were quiet and unquestionably generous. Some of his most profound insights had come in conversation with a body, even decayed the dead made for striking and often witty conversation, but it had been ages since he had found one imminently usable. Mostly bones he found now, closer to the Ubernaki village, the remains of what must be AkiGazi raiding parties falling upon the hapless and the hungry.

New skin and bones. The wealth. It was almost too good to be true. The tools he could make. The bone loom might even get fixed this time around. One, two, perhaps even three water skins, with luck, but he knew he shouldn't be counting, not yet. He needed luck and some skill. He stood over the feet.

I renounce the craving for the flesh—
and shield the weak from it and all
Manifold forms of desire.

Give me the strength to do this deed.
Simon. Simon. Where have you gone?

"Be *gen*," he said softly as he dropped to his knees, breathless. His hands, trembling, went immediately to the naked, white feet protruding from the dark fissure. They were small. A child's feet. He took them in his hands and the warmth and softness of life shocked him. He dropped them as if he had been bitten. Not dead. Not dead. Fresh things to eat. A shiver of anticipation coursed through him. His sling and his two water skins he untied and laid down carefully as he crouched low and peered into the black hole.

The Martha is with me, he thought. This circ She is. Perhaps. But where was Simon? The old hermit clapped his hands and pulled at the ends of his chin whiskers.

What are you waiting for? Get it out of there. His stomach growled.

"Yes, yes. Be patient. It seems that I am the patient one around here. Let me keep my own pace." Nothing could undermine his exuberant pleasure at the find. The Martha's grace. True, it was the small body of a child. Softer bones. Fewer skins. But nevertheless. A find. A true find.

You will want to eat it.

Vilb went cold. He would have to kill her, perhaps. If she wasn't near death. He rose to his feet, bent at the waist, the small feet between his legs. Warmth and softness—life—in his hands. Was he prepared to kill for his meal? He pulled hard on the feet. The body had been cruelly wedged within the rock. It must be almost dead. No killing would be required. He tugged hard, and managed to expose the legs, the bloody torn srapi. He rose, took a breath, bent down again and grabbed the waist and pulled hard until the upper torso gave way and came sliding out as Vilb fell backward. On all fours now he crawled to the side of the body and took it in. The arms were up around the head as if shielding the face from something, but once free of the tomb they fell away. An involuntary moan erupted from him when he saw the bloodied, misshapen face.

A pang of guilt and pity for the child overwhelmed him. Ubernaki justice had not changed since he had left the village. "You were cast out," he said, sand in his voice. He stood up. The face had been brutally beaten. The srapi was soaked with blood.

May Simon return and crush the Ubernaki under His Marbled Feet. One stinging tear came to his eye and he fell back on his haunches. Confusion filled him as a mix of desire and memory and, yes, strangely, sorrow for this strange child.

"But your people have, once again, given you the skin and bones you need," he heard himself say out loud.

Yes, yes, that's true enough. But such a small body and such soft, soft bones. One skin, no more than one. Such a small, soft body, he thought, and just then a nauseating pang of hunger racked him.

You need to eat. All that you've been through. You're almost ready. Feed yourself. The voice this time in his head gently pleading: *Pilgrimage. Think of the Pilgrimage.*

"Skins and bones," Vilb spoke aloud, his voice shaking, uncertain, teetering on an edge. "Simon. Simon. Simon. Simon." He pounded his ears. But even as he pounded and prayed he knew the soft flesh would be too much for him. He would eat of it, take his fill, renounce his vow. And why not? How had it served other than to reduce him to a state of emaciated longing? It was unnatural. The Book of M said as much. Take the flesh, yea, even to the marrow. Take your fill. And now this, a soft, warm body only recently dead—but not even dead yet. A feast. A great blessing.

But before he could consider what to do next the small body rolled over onto its side and vomited. Blood washed over the parched stone.

Finish it and take what you need. On his knees again Vilb listened as well as he might to the child's breathing. It gurgled and bubbled in its chest with a fantastic urgency. Without debating it any further with himself he put the child's head in his lap and forced its jaws open. The stump of flesh that was the tongue twitched in a pool of blood at the back of the throat. Vilb took a deep breath and his eyes watered. It was a girl, maybe nine suns, maybe ten, her tongue had been cut out.

He groaned.

"Oh bloody hell," he shouted, thoroughly upset now. "Either help me or leave me be." He put the girl's head down gently and rose to his feet. He opened his reath hutch and withdrew a small pouch.

You don't have to save her. Stop and think, would you? Hear me for a moment. Just a moment. Use the gifts the gods have bestowed upon you. Vilb's hand searched the sling for a salve he brought with him on long treks. It protected his lips from the sun and helped to heal small wounds. It wasn't much but it was all he had.

One quick slit and it's over and then one, maybe two new water skins. And enough meat for the Pilgrimage.

"Enough!" Vilb roared. The tears were pouring down his face now as he took her head in his lap. The nose was smashed, her eyes were bloody, perhaps gouged, and thick layers of coagulating blood covered her chin and neck. Vilb tried to open her mouth but she had clenched her jaw shut with the strength of the dead, only she was not dead. He set her head down softly and returned to his sling to retrieve three bone dowels from the reath hutch. He gently forced her teeth apart and forced a bone bit between her back teeth. She gagged and moaned and writhed with unexpected strength. Next, he poured the salve into her mouth and onto the ragged flesh where her tongue had been.

"This will help the bleeding and help the wound to heal cleanly," he said softly. He poured some on his own knuckle, but to what end he could not imagine.

You don't have to do this. It's only an Ubernaki piece of waste, and it's nearly dead. Help it die.

The girl screamed and tore her head out of his hands, turned her face away and spat out the bone in her mouth. She swooned from the effort and went still. "Easy. Easy. Go easy little one. That's right. I know. I know. Sleep now. Yes, good."

As she lay there passing in and out of wakefulness he washed her face carefully and applied salve to her closed eyes. Her chest was a bloody rash of stab wounds and each of these he washed and covered with sulfur he kept for his own scrapes and injuries. It was wholly inadequate, but it and the salve were all that he had. Through it all he wondered how it was that she had survived so many wounds.

An emerald hue seemed to emanate from her skin in spite of the clotted blood that covered most her body. Her head had been shaved, no doubt for the casting out, he thought. He held the child and even bloodied and beaten it was the face of unbroken morning and he handled it with reverence while he washed and tended to the wounds that ran along both cheeks, and across her forehead. His dwindling water supply was suddenly of no concern to him. One of her ears had been badly torn and so he wrapped a long strip of cloth around her head to bandage the wound. Her chest rose and fell more quietly now and the blood no longer flowed from her mouth or other wounds.

Vilb dribbled what remained of his water into her mouth and decided to wait and to watch. Perhaps she might still die.

We can only hope.

He would wait here and see what the midnight sun had to offer them. Vilb closed his eyes and slept.

III

When Vilb awoke the sun had cleared the cliff wall to the south and shone full into the ravine and this seemed to enliven the girl. She still lay flat on her back, but her breath had deepened and calmed.

"There's nothing else to be done about it. I will carry her to the hill."

You're mad.

"What else can I do?"

I can't help you.

Well, then, Vilb thought, and he bent down, gathered his things before lifting the girl carefully and slinging her gently over his shoulder. She coughed heavily and vomited blood down his back when her head went over. Still bleeding? How could she lose so much blood and yet live? With no other way he began climbing down to the ravine floor and up again to the other side. The going was slow and treacherous and he fell to his knees any number of times as he moved through the loose talus. Before too long though the ravine wall down which he had climbed the circ before loomed off to his right, and above. One more long climb and he would be on the plain and on the level path to his hill.

Food at home, such as it was. And water. His right knee knocked the now empty skins.

Though he tried to climb he could not while carrying her. He went the long way around at that point, as there was simply no other alternative though it might prove disastrously far. It had been suns since he had seen the Pilgrim Stair. It was the long way, but the only way possible with her slung over his shoulder the way she was.

If a Pilgrimage was on the Stair, Vilb might have to wait circs for his turn to climb up out of the valley and onto the Ubernaki plain to the east. He had seen it many times, Pilgrimages overloaded with baggage and people and ridiculously heavy things found along the way, and then they came upon the narrow stair and had to descend slowly into the badlands beyond their plateau, and it slowed them to a crawl. Squabbling often erupted over what would be left behind, and often a Pilgrimage's first death occurred then, and the Stair was only three circs walk from the village, but it was a crucial three circs. Vilb had collected up many of his greatest finds at the top of the Stair and at the bottom—thick, heavy sleeping mats woven from fibers; srapis, one of which he was wearing now, complete with cowl, pockets, even a stash of bone needles sewn into a pouch. He had found the finest spoons he had ever seen, four nestled together, bound by a fine, tough line, each with the name of the Ubernaki village Meson engraved on the handle. The Mesons didn't eat off of just anyone's bones. Shards of bowls he gathered together, the hard-fired stuff so rare these circs, one occasionally came down on a soft patch of sand. He found only one whole bowl once, a priceless cistern for him in his cave at home. He had found bundles of fuel for fire, so rare in the Ubernaki valley, Pilgrims let fall for fear of falling themselves. Bundles of food, mostly jerky only the way the Ubernaki could cut and season it, often left by the way side in the rush to lighten the Pilgrim's load. Most often beads and baubles fell, the heavy weight of vanity jettisoned as a Pilgrim met the first true challenge of the Pilgrimage, and chose, rightly so Vilb thought, to let it fall and climb on the less encumbered.

But as the Pilgrimages became less and less common, Vilb struggled to maintain his own stores, which, he came to realize, became increasingly more difficult. Water skins especially. They wore out when not properly filled and became parched and hard. Like his own body. Drought meant split skin, yet what was he to do? His were old, and though lovingly cared for he'd lost two from splitting in the past three suns. Wretched bad luck.

Vilb looked up the Stair and shuddered. One man could make the climb in a half-circ with good luck and an open Stair on his side, though even an experienced climber slipped and fell on the sections of the Stair exfoliated by wind and weather. It was said the gods fashioned the Stair into the cliff wall for their faithful to find them in the west, but if that were so, it had been a long, long time since any hand or craft had seen fit to tend them. They were nothing short of treacherous. Even so, Vilb had climbed it dozens of times, took pride in the doing of it, and even a few times with an ill-balanced trove of treasure. He could make it.

Late that circ the sun rode low around to the northern rim of the sky and again he made it to the Ubernaki plateau and the Pilgrim's

Gate. The spring there had long since dried up, much to the dismay and disappointment of misinformed Pilgrims in the past, and so he pushed on. Between the top of the Stair and his hill he had once left a hidden depot of stores and it was not far off now. If it remained intact and unmolested, there should be enough scroggin for the two of them should the girl awake. Water, on the other hand, would be a problem until he reached his hill. Still, the girl was not a heavy burden and he knew the plateau intimately. He had made it. From his depot, his hill was another long-circ's walk, easy enough with a full belly. He felt stronger, wind-swept and clean somehow. He was hopeful enough to make a penance for his earlier weakness in the face of his hunger. Vilb mouthed his prayers as he strode across the arid deflation towards his self-made oasis.

> *I renounce the craving for the flesh—*
> *and shield the weak from it and all*
> *Manifold forms of desire.*
>
> *Give me the strength to do this deed.*
> *Simon. Simon. Simon. Simon.*

Vilb made it to his hill even as the sun began another circle. He lay the girl down in the antechamber and had only enough energy left to drag himself to deeper into his cave and collapse on his mat in fatigue. He was too tired even to eat or drink.

· · ·

Vilb awoke in the gloom to the sound of shrieks and he sprang up from where he lay and stumbled, half-asleep, towards the sound. It took a moment but then he remembered his journey and the girl.

What had he done bringing her here? His sense of triumph, of moral purpose, had completely abandoned him. He knew he could not kill her and therefore he knew he would not reap the harvest of skins or flesh had he desired it in the first place. The shrieking went on and filled the cavern. It unnerved him. Rather than rush to her, he made towards the spring, kneeled down and pressed his face against the damp stone so that he might sip and slurp as much water as he could hold from the trickling stream. And still the shrieking. By the gods. What could he do? She had been cast out by the Ubernaki. For good reason? He held only contempt for his people and did not fear them, but should some young men learn of what he'd done he might very well suffer the consequences of desecration. Not good for the reputation of a gen.

The next moment the shrieking stopped but the quiet did little to settle Vilb's mind.

Vilb moved about the branch work of his cave, really a system of caves within the funglin that rose above the Ubernaki plain. Without reason he found himself shuffling from chamber to chamber, checking his stores, his bone loom, again back to the grotto for more water—a trickle of water this circ, a good sign all things considered. He took the time to drink his fill. He ate. His stomach settled and his head cleared. He felt refreshed for the first time in circs. He washed the desert from his face—and then stumbled through the large chamber where the girl slept and into the light of the cave entrance hidden beneath an overhang encrusted with crystal.

Behind him, back in the cave, his home for nearly twenty suns, the place in which he had mastered his loneliness, renounced his desire and sought Simon in the desert, in which no company had ever come welcome or unwelcome, a child who would not die moaned and whimpered in her sleep and threatened to spoil all that he had achieved. Strange, he thought, it was only now that all that he had achieved became obvious. The girl's presence had at least demonstrated to Vilb all that he had, and all that he was now deprived of. Yet even as he wanted to return to the simple silence of solitude, an aching longing filled his breast with surprising, breathtaking power. A hunger no less powerful than his first circs without flesh came over him with a double fury, and its potency surprised him and it was made worse by the shame he felt for his weakness. That the hunger could still rise in him so powerfully after holding it in check for so long, all of this humbled Vilb, weakened him and left him unsure, vulnerable. He lay down next to the girl to await her awakening and drifted off again to the sound of her steady breathing.

• • •

You have been chosen.

Vilb lurched awake and looked around. He'd heard a voice, but it was not a voice he knew so well. It came from outside him, or had he dreamed it? Sunlight from the cave's small opening brightened the antechamber where he lay next to the girl. Beside him she lay panting, her face bathed in perspiration, eyes open wide in horror. Suddenly she screamed and her hands began to flail before her as if she fought for her life. Then a voice came from her, fierce and shrill.

"I am the desolation of the land," she shrieked as her hands fought wildly with the air. She rolled over clumsily onto her knees and tried to stand. Shocked by what he had heard it took a moment for Vilb to reach out and press her gently to the mat.

"No, no, no. Lay down. Lay down." She fought against him for a moment, but then as if suddenly hearing him and obeying, she lay down quickly on her back, her eyes open, bulging, unblinking, and her breathing quick and shallow.

Had she spoken? How had she spoken? He lay there next to her and waited for the screaming and thrashing to erupt again but she remained quiet, if tense. The quiet, however, began to unnerve him as much as the screaming had earlier, for as she lay there panting, her eyes remained opened wide with horror and her head had turned to the side so that it seemed that she was staring at him. All of this was too much to bear so he turned his back on the girl and tried not to think of her bulging eyes staring at his back.

You have been chosen. Vilb turned to face the girl, his mind resisting what his senses were telling him. His mouth hung open with an unspoken question.

He strode away and paced the far side of the chamber but still he felt her eyes on him. He couldn't bear it any longer and he retreated deeper into his cave. What did it mean? That she could speak? And what had she said? Chosen? For what?

As if to flee, yet with nowhere to hide he stepped deeper into the cave, into a storage alcove, into a gloom, and removed a screen that covered a rift and let a shaft of light into the chamber. There against the wall rested his Pilgrim's pack, perpetually prepared except for what he used each circ. Vilb unpacked it as if he did not trust the one who had prepared it, though he himself had done it just before his last scavenging trek. He carefully unrolled the mat, inspected it thoroughly and then rolled it again tightly and tied it off with sinew. Spoons he had, his favorite item though he never used them, though he thought that should he ever reach his destination— the Great City, San Simon—he might have a chance to eat as the civilized ate, or, better still, trade them for something more useful. He opened the reath hutch and inspected its contents. There were over a dozen tools, some shaped like long needles, others as hoops with one gap that might receive and join with other tools, like some kind of bone puzzle. He had fondled them all at one time or another, and even joined two or three, but always when he did the tools would become stuck together as if welded, and this so unsettled him that he feared that he might damage them in his attempt to take them apart again. This time he had no such plan—only to inspect and be sure they were all safe and accounted for. Which they were, except for the fact that the hutch glowed with a preternatural intensity that he had never seen before. Frankly, he assumed that the emerald hue he was accustomed to was really a reflection of the cave, or of the Arclight's influence in the high sun of the long day. But this… this glowing emerald was something new, and something undeniable. He closed the hutch quickly and secured its ties. When he lifted it to pack away it felt heavy, far heavier, as if something in the floor of his cave pulled at the bones inside.

Vilb took a deep breath. This was most unseemly and disturbing.

Without much attention he came to his three water skins. Still only three. He stowed his pack neatly and stood up, a fog thickening in his mind. From the antechamber where the girl lay he heard her speak in a calm, resolute tone, as if it were a village Meson announcing harvest time.

The gods are calling.

In consternation Vilb returned to check on the girl. Her eyes were still open, still bulging with her recent ordeal, fixed on something unseen in the half-light. Perhaps there was another in his cave? Quickly he moved, and quietly, from opening to opening, chamber to chamber, climbing high into the cave ceiling where someone small might hide. But no. The two of them were alone.

Vilb knelt down beside her and the girl stared into the horror of oblivion, or into the nightmare eyes of her murderers, or both. With nothing left to do, Vilb lay himself down beside her again to wait, to listen, and sank into a shallow, fitful sleep.

Waking dreams haunted him all through his restless fugue. Images appeared and he saw things that he had never known before. An unfamiliar voice spoke along with the images and called each one by name. Snow. Ice. Cold. Glacier. Frozen. You have been chosen.

What did it mean? What was he seeing? Chosen? Chosen by whom? Vilb did not want to be chosen, not really. His life was simple, if spare. Yet he understood it, and in very short order his understanding of his life seemed to be scattering to the wind. He longed for his hill and his cave and his bone loom and the simple problems of food gathering, the mortar and pestle, the weaving, and when to risk a small fire. And water skins, always water and water skins. The elements of his life seemed like old, familiar friends he had never truly appreciated until only now, and he felt it all slipping away at precipitous speed.

Again he heard the stentorian voice coming from the girl's body and it startled him to full wakefulness.

It is time for progress, Pilgrim.

What on Little Earth could it possibly mean?

IV

Late the following circ the girl began to mumble in a small, child's voice utterly unlike the voice Vilb had heard before. Her eyes were closed too, and this gave Vilb a feeling of great relief for some reason. She slept again, but now it seemed to be the sleep of the living and Vilb too finally rested more soundly than he had since he first began pursuing his now vanished prize in the catacomb. He was there, standing over, when she awoke again much later.

"This is scroggin—it's just tea-rice and nut paste," he said. "Eat it if you can, though it may be… difficult. It may not be what you're used to, but it will sustain you." The girl lay on her back unmoving except for her eyes. She fixed them on him. "I am Vilb… of Solenthay," he said, uncomfortable with her stare, her presence. Using the pretense of offering her a sip of water, he broke his eyes away from hers, rose and turned away.

"Are you the Healer?" the girl asked suddenly and as she spoke Vilb let fall the water skin he had gripped in one hand by the neck. A few precious gurgles later and Vilb had scooped up the skin and quickly tied it off.

"You have no tongue," he said involuntarily as if to remind her, and himself, of her injury.

"You are gen?" she asked, and her voice piped like a child who did not know whip or lash. "Only gen would live out here, separate from the world, busy thinking all circ about Simon. Busy thinker thinking simple thoughts of Simon. Do you think your thoughts of Simon all circ long?" It was almost a song she sang, yet she mocked him it seemed. He shook his head, nonplussed by the irrational impossibility of the moment.

"I…" but he didn't finish. He felt himself go slack and his tongue worked silently in his own mouth as if to remind himself of what a tongue was and how it moved.

"The gen wear almost nothing, yet you wear the srapi, and sleep on Ubernaki mats? I like your whiskers." Vilb stopped himself from tugging on the ends of his beard and folded his arms across his chest.

"How is it that you can speak?" he finally managed. "You brought me here? Where are we?"

"I live in the hill above the Pilgrim's Stair. I brought you here after... I found you."

The girl looked at him for a moment and her eyes danced and shimmered.

"Excellent," she said. "Our Pilgrimage has already begun."

"What?"

"Master Qir told me you would come."

"Master Qir... told... you? He told you what?"

But the girl did not respond. Instead, she picked up the bowl of food beside her and began to eat hungrily, shoving the food into her mouth with lithe, steady fingers. Vilb's face hardened.

"How is it that... that you speak?" The girl ignored him, set down her empty bowl and reached out for the water. Mindlessly he handed it to her and she took a deep draught, returned the skin back to him, lay down on her side and went immediately back to sleep.

The girl's speaking was not possible. He had seen her injuries, by Simon, and he had treated them. He had no such skill—no one in Little Earth, save perhaps the gods themselves, had the skill to heal such wounds. But she sat before him alert, speaking, dare say, mocking. And what of Master Qir? The child believes the gods speak to her? Perhaps now Vilb was beginning to understand why the Ubernaki Meson had decided to resort to a casting out.

Vilb was restless and alert when the girl awoke next.

"I'm hungry," she said as he cautiously approached her. She extended her empty bowl mutely. He took it from her without a word, filled it with scroggin and handed it back, fixing her with his gaze as if owed an explanation that was, finally, forthcoming. It was then that he took in the girl's smooth, glowing face and its delicate hue of emerald. Her eyes too were green, and her hair like no hair he had ever seen before—rust colored, like the sunset, or a cliff wall of red rock cast in twilight. The circ before it was matted, blood soaked and nearly black. Her face was riven by three long, ragged cuts, a smashed nose and blood encrusted eyes, and in spite of the sulfur, the pus had begun to seep in the wounds, especially around her torn ear, but now... look at her now. Whole. Completely. She had a glow of health about her that Vilb had not seen for… well, never. It was uncanny yet Vilb felt intoxicated by the energy of vitality that seemed to charge the very air around the girl.

"You know who I am?" she said. Vilb filled again her empty bowl and shook his head dumbly. She eyed him, expecting a response.

"An Ubernaki child I suppose," he said finally. She filled her mouth with food and it sprayed out as she spoke. "Or a devil sent by Quadros to ensnare you?" Her eyes lit up and she grinned and chewed. Vilb shrugged.

"No," she said, swallowing a mouthful.

The Arclight is failing. There. Her face had not moved yet he heard the words as if they had come from her mouth. Vilb shook his head again, his mouth slightly open.

"I found you… dead… up at the Catacombs. They… they cast you out?"

She chewed and swallowed and then she nodded.

"I am the scourge of the land," she said flatly, and then took a long drink. "I am the desolation of M." She gulped down another mouthful of food as Vilb stared back at her, speechless.

"But you may call me Prav."

Skins and Bones

The Hidden One who is called Simon the Mighty Earth-Killer calls to you and bids you make Pilgrimage to His City. Yet beware of false gods who do battle against Him and who wage their war with voices and visions of deception. If you lose your way even then heed Simon's call, for He has not forsaken you.

– The Book of M

I

"I have seen more than two hundred sun rises," Prav said, and her face looked strained and tight for the first time, a deep crease in her brow left Vilb with the feeling that perhaps there was something to what the girl said. "I've wandered the east of Little Earth for over forty of them."

"You are a child," Vilb said nevertheless, asking as much as telling, shaking his head yet more uncertain than ever. "You are nine or ten suns at most." He was incredulous.

"But it is true. I have looked as I do now since I was a child. I have seen much of the east of Little Earth, have been cast out by Gazi tribes twice, escaped a third Gazi tribe just as the AkiGazi came upon them, and then wandered until the Ubernaki Gatherers found me in their fields. Only recently, after Selantha died, the Ubernaki cast me out, but that was not my fault. Master Qir did that."

"Master Qir? Did what?" Vilb had not had proper conversation for a very long time and the girl was proving difficult to follow. It was as if The Book of M had come to life and the miracles of the gods were more than mere myth.

"Killed the Teacher, Selantha. Do you want to hear how it happened?"

"No, not really. But I am interested in learning how you," and he gestured to her mouth while leaning in close to see into it,

"… you seem to have grown a new tongue… and…" Vilb gestured to her face, ear. "You know."

"No matter. I will be telling you about your dream, though."

"Your dream?"

"Your dream. You know, yes?" She smiled at him as if he were withholding information merely for her enjoyment.

"*Gen* do not dream," he stated boldly, though he certainly did, but the girl didn't have to know that. Is that all he was, it suddenly occurred to him. Just a crazy old hermit? The thought lightened him for a moment. Perhaps there was, after all, no fate, no gods, no destiny, no purpose and no point. He was but gen in name and his purgatory in the desert nothing more than self-proclaimed grandiosity. He took a deep breath and felt instantly better. Yes. He was mad, as mad as the ones he'd left behind in the village. They were all mad. The girl was mad, driven mad perhaps, or madly driven, it did not matter. At that instant Vilb felt sure that she would have to go and that he would return to his scavenging happily, content with three water skins. Perhaps even a Pilgrimage on his own terms some circ, but without the pompous trappings of religious zealotry. Yes, that settles that. He smiled but said nothing more to the girl. It was quite simple, after all.

"Well we'll see about that," Prav said, as if challenging Vilb's unspoken reasoning. "Let me tell you about the dream."

Vilb began slowly. "Prav is it?" and the girl nodded, sitting up now. "I cannot keep you here," he said solemnly, expecting an outburst but prepared to contain it and escort her to the bottom of his hill.

The girl nodded and looked around.

"Yes. I do not wish to live in a cave."

"Nor do I want you here. I can return you to the village if you like." She stared at him dumbly, all affect having drained from her face. Vilb immediately realized what he had said. "I don't mean… perhaps some other village? Or, well, I'm busy. Very busy. With my preparations. I cannot feed you and take care of you, and water skins. I have three, you know, only three and it is difficult to keep them filled as it is."

"Preparing" she said, her voice flat and humorless, and Vilb, relieved that she seemed to understand, went on excitedly.

"I prepare for Pilgrimage," he said and nodded. He was, at last, getting through to her.

"Yes. So do I. It's just as Master Qir said. I will tell you some of the dream as we walk. It's a long dream. Two thousand years the world has been sleeping." She shook her head as if she couldn't believe what she'd said. "A dream within a dream. The Ancients dream us, you know. It goes back to them. To the past, before Little Earth."

Vilb was caught off guard. At every turn he felt ensnared by the girl's words. "Walk where?" His head was spinning again. The child's ingenuous clarity confused him and her miraculous healing remained an unanswered question.

"On Pilgrimage." She walked her fingers across the cave floor in front of her. "It's a long walk."

"On… I… but… you."

The girl nodded as if she understood what Vilb had not managed to say. "Yes. You must take Simon's Path." Now she dropped her voice to almost a whisper. "Pilgrimage is only the beginning. That's only the start. We'll travel with the Healer. To the Fourth Realm." She paused, her eyes wide, as if to let this fantastic news settle in. Vilb looked at her as if she had told him they would be traveling to the moon. "Yes," she said, and nodded, seeing his amazement. "It is a fantastically long journey over the sea. To the Fourth Realm. To Levinthal. He must be stopped and only Simon can stop him." Her voice dropped to a hush and she leaned in close as she finished. "Only Simon."

"The Fourth Realm? Over the sea?" Vilb felt his old confidence returning now that the girl had revealed the true nature of her madness. "I do not believe in children's stories," he announced with conviction. "There is only Little Earth, only this," and he looked around at his cave-home.

She eyed him intently, silently, until he had to turn his face away and she went on, only this time more sternly. "And I will tell you about the fall of the Ancients and how it's all happening again, right here on Little Earth." She looked up at him with a withering stare but Vilb was having a hard time keeping up with her.

"You see? It's always happening, again and again." She seemed suddenly pleased with him. "But we mustn't accept that as a foregone conclusion, no we must not." The girl wagged her finger as she spoke and Vilb had the strange feeling that he was caught in some child's game and she was lecturing her doll.

Vilb stared silently back at her. He felt a powerful urge to sweep the sand from the floor, to roll his mat, to be busy and to distract himself in the hope that when he returned she would be gone.

"First we have to go to the Great City, you and I, and restore Simon. Before it all freezes... again." Her face clouded over and seemed deep in thought. "Quadros Prang won't like it one bit, but that's too bad," she said thoughtfully, and then fell silent.

"The Pan-Archer? Restore Simon?" Vilb sank slowly to his haunches, the wind out of him and his strength suddenly gone. "Freezes?" He knew this word, but only from the dream he said he didn't have. He rubbed his forehead hard in the futile hope that this gesture might clear his mind. It didn't.

"Before that I need to sleep a bit more," and with that Prav smiled with such warmth and openness that Vilb's heart melted unexpectedly. She lay down and was, it seemed, asleep as soon as she closed her eyes. Vilb watched her for a moment and could not help reaching out and stroking the girl's forehead as if he had done it a thousand times before.

II

The Pilgrims' Procession was beautiful to behold. Even from a distance they were colorful and noisy. Pilgrims wrapped themselves in banners and colorful tapestries and covered themselves in shining bits of stone so that they glistened and shimmered in the sun and the light played off of them and made them visible across the plain for long distances.

Walkers all, and they had elaborate and well-designed packs in which they carried the most incredible storehouse of goods. An entire pack industry existed in the Ubernaki east, for the Pilgrimage had been ongoing for generations, and the packs had grown progressively larger and heavier.

Vilb had studied these packs and fashioned his own, smaller and lighter yes, but adequate for his own needs. It took him five suns to scavenge all of the bones he needed for such a thing, but when it was done he felt as close to Pilgrimage as he ever had. But then his pack had remained in his cave, an empty frame, a skeleton without sinew, muscle or flesh.

Perhaps wisdom would come of his time on the hill after all, and then he would laugh and call himself a fool. Yet now, just now, his pack stood filled again and ready, and the girl had suddenly appeared in his life ranting of Pilgrimage, and he found himself making ready to leave, yet it felt like some kind of sand storm and the dust had yet to settle in his mind. The girl said the choice was plain. Stay and slowly starve or pursue his fate.

He laughed a bitter laugh. His fate. He thought he was pursuing his fate for these long, lonely suns as a gen.

Still, he could not deny the girl's presence or her strange power over him.

Vilb tugged at the ends of his beard and turned on Prav. "What about you?" he demanded of the girl. "Are you even ready for such a journey?" Only five circs had passed since he had found her in her tomb. Since then she had spent her time eating and sleeping. Hearing the question Prav sat up and watched him move around the chamber in agitation.

"Master Qir sent me to find you. Or one like you. You will do."

"One like me? What does that mean?" Vilb asked, suddenly offended by what he'd heard. He shook his head but the girl remained silent. "Even so," he went on, mollified by her seeming indifference to his offense, "I would like to make the Pilgrimage before I am too old. But you are a child and the way will be difficult. Few will help us if we travel together. Children are forbidden to travel. Are you ready for such a journey? Any procession we meet—and we're unlikely to meet any these circs—may be cruel to us, and we may die along the way, alone."

"There is no death for you and I. That blessing Simon has prepared for others." Vilb was speechless for a moment, but his mind, it seemed, had already been made up, as if for him. The time had come, as he had always hoped that it would, yet unaccustomed to surrendering to the freedom of the moment, Vilb bound himself with the familiar cords of doubt. "Let me warn you," he said, as if announcing a great secret. "I don't believe in the gods, at least not in the way that you seem to. They are guiding ideals, warnings in story, points upon which to meditate and to become absorbed by." The girl sniffed in response but offered nothing more and Vilb let the matter drop for the moment.

V̇ilb moved nervously around his cavern not sure of what to do with the things that he would be leaving behind. Travel light, he told himself, and so he planned to carry only what he usually carried on his walkabouts, and he and the girl would gather the rest of what they needed on the way. Water, however, remained foremost on his mind. Even if he had enough water skins, which he did not, filling them would probably prove to be difficult. As it was, he had only three, perhaps enough for one to make the long walk to the Gate, but certainly not enough for he and the girl to go far beyond.

"Have faith," the girl said, as if hearing his thoughts.

He slung his skins around his waist and promised himself to rectify the problem at the earliest opportunity, though what this opportunity might look like he had not the slightest idea.

On his back he secured his pack, the rolled sleeping mat and below that his sling. He had almost decided against carting along the reath hutch, for it had grown even heavier, weighing almost as much as a filled water skin, much to Vilb's dismay.

The girl, however, had interceded.

"The Martha will be pleased by your faithfulness," she said.

Vilb nodded. He understood penance. Very well. He did not care to part, and perhaps lose forever the strange ossified bone, more jewel now than bone.

"You seem to know something of these tools," Vilb said, and lifted one out of the hutch and showed it to the girl, but she shielded her face with both hands. "No, no, not yet. Please," and she fell back as if to avoid the heat of the high sun.

"Very well," Vilb said, and left it at that.

Of food he would bring everything he had which would last them to the Gate, but beyond that they would have to scavenge from the land. Yet another difficult challenge, for the land was parched and drought stricken. The wild greens and roots were fewer and farther between as sun after sun of drought dried the lotic paths that once criss-crossed the eastern plateau. Fuel would be almost as difficult a question as water, though perhaps slightly less necessary. Vilb packed the tiny amount of bramble he had hoarded in his travels and bound it together and carried it on his back beneath his pack nonetheless. The well-timed fire had heartened him at many crucial times in treks past, and this time would be no different he mused.

Last were his remedies. Powders, ground minerals mostly, some herbs, roots, his beloved marrow-wite salve. All of this would fit within his sling, along with the reath hutch, though the collection of bones was as heavy as everything else put together.

Leave it behind, boy. It's dead weight. The Martha be damned. It's your back. The voice of reason had returned and Vilb nodded in response to his thoughts.

Yes, it was heavy and Vilb set it down and compared what he was carrying without it packed, and was even inclined to leave it, at least for a moment. The Book of M's chief remonstration for Pilgrimage was pack light. Even so, Vilb disliked agreeing with the voice for some reason, reasonable as it seemed to be. There was something vaguely humiliating about it when it made sense to him. He felt handled, somehow, manipulated. In fact he usually made a point to ignore it and to set out to prove it wrong whenever possible.

Vilb picked up the hutch, dropped it in his sling and hung the sling around his shoulder. He would bring it. Just then he turned and there, watching him and smiling, stood Prav. Vilb dozed and recalled having dreamed of Prav's smiling eyes over him, singing softly to him, and promising him that together they would restore Simon. Vilb awoke calmly and opened his eyes in wonder.

He rose and packed once again for his journey, and once again he came to the reath hutch and without thinking put the heavy package in his sling.

Fool of a gen! Carrying stones is what kills most Pilgrims!

Vilb packed on. This circ was the circ.

Though the sling was heavy, his pack was light and for this he was grateful. Perhaps they could make it after all. Or not. Returning Pilgrims were an exceedingly rare commodity. One story told of a group of Pilgrims that had made it back to their coastal village over the Girdling Sea in something called a boat. Fantastic though improbable to the extreme. Whatever a boat was, it went along with other miasma of confused conceptualizations about the west, the Great City. According to local myth he had heard many suns before at the foot of the Stair, the returning Boat-Pilgrims became the village council of which one was immediately made Meson. Countless bountiful seasons followed their return. Vilb swelled at the thought but was immediately cut off by the girl's call.

"Are you ready in there?"

"I was just asking myself the same question."

"And?"

Vilb paused to reflect and realized that he was prepared—well-prepared as far as he could tell. The suns of shamefully procrastinating had, suddenly and quite unexpectedly, taken on a new significance. His pack looked good, Vilb nodded quietly and then called back to Prav. "I could be no more ready than I am right now. We can fill the water skins along the way. I know of a spring." Vilb felt almost ebullient, like a boy about to set out on a hike in the rain and he remembered when he saw his father high on a hill waving down at him, calling to him to stay? To follow? Vilb was never sure, but he felt keenly the distance between himself and his past—perhaps Pilgrimage, perhaps this journey, might be a way for Vilb de Solenthay to close the gap between he and all that he hoped to be and do in this life.

Maybe now. Maybe this time.

Prav broke into his reverie. "There's a procession coming up the Stair as we speak. If we cut across the plateau we can join them before the sun begins another circle. It's a large group, almost one hundred."

"No. There hasn't been a procession that size for, well, almost five suns."

Prav shook her head. "There's one this sun. Right now. I heard about it… when I was… with *them*. And besides, Simon told me." Prav's eyes danced with emerald light.

"Yes, well," was all Vilb could manage. *Kill her now and be done with this madness!* screamed an angry voice inside him and Vilb fought off an impulse to grab the girl's throat in two hands and see if he could squeeze the life out of her. "Dear gods," he said aloud and stepped back, suddenly overwhelmed by the vehemence inside him, but Prav was already ahead of him and safely out of reach. This desire will pass, Vilb thought. A good long walk is exactly what he needed. Still shaken, however, he advanced hesitantly to the mouth of his cave.

"Yes. Come on," Prav called back and Vilb strode ahead with more energy because it sounded as if she had already left the cave. As he trotted after her he looked back, thought of what he might have forgotten, hitched his pack and once again adjusted his sling over his shoulder.

Water, he thought. Water.

Prav had climbed quickly down Hermit Hill and he could see her gazing west over the plain. Vilb trotted to catch up to her sustained pace.

"Do you plan to run the entire way little one?" Vilb called out and he heard not so much his father, but his Ubernaki Teachers in his own voice. Prav ignored him.

"Then tell me this. How do you know about the procession on the Stair?" He wanted her to stop and wait for him.

"I told you. I just know." She called back but didn't slow her pace.

"Look at you. You have nothing. No water skins. No sleeping mat. No fuel. What will you eat?" Vilb felt the need to gall, to shame, to vent his fear. She was too fast for him yet he was in his element. Sand and sun he knew. Walking, he knew.

"I told you not to worry about this. Simon will provide. I have been out on the land before."

"What if… what if…" but Vilb sputtered and then quietly laughed to himself. We shall see.

"There is no what if," Prav snapped back. She stopped and turned finally. "We go," and so saying she set off towards the sun riding the rim of the southern sky.

"We need water," Vilb cried out as she jogged off before him. "And skins!"

IV

When the sun was almost behind them they had covered nearly five thousand strides, and still Vilb could not catch up with the nimble-footed girl. He tried to close the gap through the stony wastes but she pulled away in spite of his experience. His lips were dry and hard and already cracking in the heat and the wind. He slapped his skins by his side. He counted them. Again. Still only three.

You let the girl rush you. Fool. But it's not too late.

The arroyo ahead of them marked the end of the plateau and the drop down the Pilgrim's Stair and up to the other side, beyond which Vilb knew less well. It had been green here once, covered with scrub brush that hugged the ground as if protecting itself from the wind. He and his father had made a camp here when he was a boy long ago, near a spring. Now, however, only desert greeted him. The dark line of the Spire Range loomed across the canyon—and somewhere at the foot of a hanging valley sat the Great Gate that lead to the White Path into and through the Spire Massiff.

He tripped and fell but retained the presence of mind to turn and fall on his left side in order to protect the water skins.

A snap of a broken bone sang out when he landed.

"I hope that wasn't me," he said to the desert.

Suddenly Prav was there standing over him.

"I could take you now," she hissed. In her hand was a shimmering white blade. Vilb rocked so that he might turn over and so rise but Prav, standing just out of his arm's reach, darted in, pushed him down and backed off again.

"Just stay there," she said.

"What are you doing?" Vilb called out angrily.

"I'm saving you. You desert loners pride yourself on your ability to get three skins out of what most can only manage two."

Vilb rolled over onto his stomach and as he did Prav threw herself on his back and put the blade to his throat.

Vilb held his voice steady and spoke to her as if she had asked about their progress. "Up the western side and we should come to what they call the Pine Stands, though I do not know how it comes by its name. It's column after column of stone. My father called it a forest, though I'm not sure what that means. Beautiful really, and then, we should come to the spring," Vilb said carefully, penance in his voice. "There is an outcropping that marks the water. Drink all that we can now and we will fill the skins once we arrive there."

Remorse and despair overwhelmed him. He was far from home, perhaps too far to return with the water in his skins, and still a very long walk yet from the Gate. And why was this child-thing threatening to spill his blood? His head ached with the backwardness of the world. She had lost her mind, of this he was now sure, and for this she had been cast out of her village. Her tongue, he had decided, was only injured in a botched attempt to cut it out and had healed quickly because of his quick action in applying the salve. Her body had healed, as bodies do, he had decided, though her mind remained broken. And she had tricked him and meant to murder him out here in the wastes.

Then why are you out here with her?

Vilb struggled to his knees, his wind suddenly gone, his mouth parched and his throat coated with dust yet still the girl clung to his back, the blade and his throat. How had she recovered from such grievous injuries, and so quickly? Why had the village cast her out? And what of her bizarre and blasphemous stories? Was she mad or something worse?

"Something worse," Prav said from behind. "What?" Vilb looked around.

"Thinking again, Vilb?" Prav asked.

"Yes," he said flatly.

"I can help you with that," she said. Her words did little to comfort or reassure. "It only requires you to surrender."

"Surrender?" *She has tricked me, trapped me.*

"I can cut the voice out of your mind," she whispered in his ear. "Once and for all."

"What?" Vilb's head felt light.

She's mad. Shake her off of you and take her skins!

"I can cut the voice out of your mind once and for all," she repeated. "It is not you that speaks, but a distant… god. One who thwarts you and keeps you from The Martha's will. Do you seek to do The Martha's will?"

"I have always… The Martha."

"Yes, good," and with this Prav reached into Vilb's sling and withdrew the reath hutch.

"What are you doing?" he demanded weakly but his strength had suddenly left him and he was on all fours. Prav slid from his back, took up the tool Vilb called the needle from the hutch, and in one swift move plunged the finger-long, slender shimmering emerald spike into Vilb's right temple and then all lights went out.

. . .

Vilb awoke refreshed and energized.

"What did you do?" he asked quietly. Prav sat beside him and when he spoke turned and smiled at him.

"They listen, all of them, and some of them are strong enough to... speak to you. Some even can... well, they want to... take your body for their own."

Vilb rubbed his temple. It made no sense except that he felt so much better. Alive, really, for the first time... in his memory.

"Who listens?"

"The gods," Prav whispered.

Vilb coughed, incredulous. "The gods?"

Prav nodded, her face grave now.

"Which, who?" was all Vilb could mutter.

"Levinthal. In the Fourth Realm. He has become very strong because of Quadros Prang. He uses you, contends with The Martha for control..."

"Of me?"

"Of Little Earth. Of the Greater Earth. All of the Seven Realms."

Vilb shook his head. He could not deny the sense that he had been somehow released from a claim on his mind. But a Greater Earth? Seven Realms?

"I do not understand, but I am grateful for what you have done."

. . .

They made the Pilgrim Stair, down and then up again the other side in two circs, and then walked for much of the next circ and had come to a series of blue hills crossing a grassy, scrub covered path. Finally the dust had subsided and his mouth, throat and eyes had recovered somewhat. Here the spring should be, he remembered, tucked in between the blue foothills and a rocky outcropping to the west.

"Do you see it?" Prav shouted from well ahead.

"Here!" Vilb shouted back and pointed and then began to stumble. His water skins were nearly empty and they slapped lightly against his side as he walked. All but falling, he made it to the bottom of the hill and up into the outcropping where a massive limestone up-thrust came into view. He listened intently, held his breath, waited, again, but still he heard no sound of water.

Vilb grunted, exhausted now, the heavy fatigue of the journey settling in. His temple throbbed where Prav had skewered him.

"We will trade at the Gate for water skins," Prav said as she approached him. "Do not worry." Her voice was soothing, comforting.

"Trade? You must be joking." Vilb croaked. "With whom? With what?" He sat in the dust and closed his eyes.

"Yes. Trade at the Gate. With Pilgrims."

"If they exist.

"I've seen them."

"Impossible."

"I've seen the dust on the horizon. They're coming to the Gate from the southeast."

"That's where you saw the dust? Probably storms."

"No. It's clear now. It's the Procession. I'm telling you."

Vilb sighed and allowed himself to consider the possibility.

"What have we to trade?" he asked hoarsely.

"I don't know. Me perhaps?"

"You?" He opened his eyes now and looked up at her.

She was standing before him and they were now eye-to-eye.

"You?" Vilb said again. He did not understand.

"You would rather die then?"

Vilb shrugged, glowering now and unsure. He felt suddenly more alone than he had ever felt in his life. Whatever or whoever the voice was, it had been a part of him, company of a sort, and now there was only the empty, desolate silence of his mind.

She eyed him until he had to turn away to escape her gaze.

Prav lowered herself into the shade of a boulder and kneeled.

"It's quite simple. You need water. Now," Prav said from behind, but he wasn't listening to her.

"I'm a fool," he said. "I failed." He let his chin fall to his breast.

"No," Prav said. "My plan will not fail."

Vilb was confused by the audacity in the child's voice. "My plan will not fail," she said again. "Look," and she pointed south east and to the horizon and there a star seemed to have fallen from the sky and glittered in the distance. "They come, and they bring water skins and water, shining things and banners. Later they will suffer, but now they can be taken advantage of quite easily."

"You would take advantage of Pilgrims?" Vilb asked.

"Are you as stupid as you are proud?" She stepped around in front of him, fists on her hips, her face on fire, her eyes lit up by the sun behind

Vilb. She had wrapped herself in one of the coarse srapis she had found in his cave, the cowl pulled tight over her head, circling her round, still plump face, her red hair a ring of fire around her face. She looked small, yes, but fierce and dangerous too.

"Your fear is faithlessness, it's arrogance," she said, and wagged her finger at him. "Your blindness is not all the fault of the gods. You keep yourself blind. It suits you." She looked at him for a moment.

"We are just beggars," Vilb said and dropped his head. "No. For the procession you must be a Gazi father and I will be your daughter. My mother has already died on the way. Killed by AkiGazi. We narrowly escaped."

"What? What are you saying?"

"Where is your mind? Wake up. We need a story and I am giving you one. This is our story: You will play the Gazi man. Gazi men are weak. You're perfect. I will play the running child, and we will play the Gazi family on the run and alone in the desert. They will be taken in, you will not resist when they seek to barter your life for my skin and bones, and you will become a member of the procession."

" I hear but I do not understand," Vilb said dully.

"You do not need to understand. You need merely do as I tell you. Act as if you were a Gazi man responsible for a child two-skin. Can you do that?"

"No," Vilb said, and he raised his eyes to meet the girl's. "I won't do it. I refuse."

Prav turned on him fiercely. "That is not acceptable!" she declared, and then, just as suddenly, she melted before him.

"Simon needs us. He depends on us. He needs one like you." She was pleading now, tears in her eyes.

Vilb hunched, silently, his head in his hands. "You are mad," he said.

"Yes," she said. "Yes," and unexpectedly she laughed. "I will play your mad goolak daughter-two-skin."

"You have had more time to prepare," Vilb said.

"Yes. I agree. This may be a stretch for you. Your time alone with Levinthal in your brain has made you soft and slow- headed."

"I prefer to think of myself as peaceful and contented."

"Yes. Well. Can you do it? It requires a fire inside that… I am not sure you can manage." Prav paused and looked at Vilb and he met and held her gaze.

"You underestimate me."

He suddenly stood up and raised himself to his full height. He looked down on Prav as he spoke. "I will join the Pilgrimage. I will trade your skin and bones, all in one, or one bone at a time if need be, and I will play Gazi father to you, and treat you as I was treated, for that is all that I know."

Prav smiled. "Let it be now."

"But I warn you again. I do not do this for Simon, or for the gods, or for, as you say, some unknown god you call Levinthal. I do this for you. For your kindness to an old hermit and for quieting my mind."

Prav smiled again and Vilb reached out and stroked her chin absentmindedly. He shook himself in the next instant and straightened up, adjusted his pack and sling and shook the dust from his srapi.

"We still have a long walk before us," and he shook the water skins. "We have hardly any water left."

Prav stood beside him and looked towards the rising dust on the horizon. "My plan will not fail," she said.

After a period of rest they continued walking, hungry and parched. Vilb's mouth had gone permanently dry and his lips, cracked early on, now bled in spite of the salve that he applied. Even so, he remained silent and steadfast. The present crisis had simplified his thinking and made matters painfully clear for him, and for this he was grateful. They must reach the procession or die and no internal debate would change that. League after league their pace quickened and when the last of the water had been sipped from the skins, the sun had circled low on the horizon. By the time they made camp and prepared to sleep, Vilb realized that the Gate would be in reach the next circ.

"Finish the water in the skins," Prav said.

"It's already gone."

"Good. We're there. The last of the procession has just arrived at the foot of the Gate. After sleep we will walk in the shadow of the Spire Massif."

"It will be good to have the sun off our backs," Vilb said. "We will join the procession once they have a chance to circle, but I fear something has happened to them on their journey." Prav grew thoughtful before speaking again. "That might work into our favor even still." She shrugged as if answering her own thoughts. "They will make camp for a few circs, maybe more, and there is water." Prav looked out over the distance as she spoke even as Vilb took in the serrated line of peaks and valleys that towered to the south and west of them. He took in a deep breath and sighed. There was now no turning back.

"We shall see."

The Last Pilgrimage

And I will build for you a great White Path, and on this path from all corners of the east you shall come and flock to Me and I shall bathe you in the light of the Arclight. You will dream dreams and have visions and grow wise, only to return to your homeland and replenish your people. So sayeth Simon.

– The Book of M

I

By the back light of the midnight sun Vilb and Prav came upon the first foothills of the Spire Massif and climbed up from the desert plateau. From a rounded crest they paused, caught their breath and overlooked the perimeter of the Pilgrims' encampment to the south, well below them. From here it appeared to be a small circle around two small fires burning wanly. The Pilgrims had made camp at the foot of a hanging valley, its two sides like two arms set to embrace them, and shield them from all but the worst storms. Above and beyond the Pilgrims' camp rose the Twin Horns, two towering peaks that rose above and beyond the rest. Between the Horns snaked the White Path through a deep saddle running west to the lands beyond.

Vilb felt a horror and a thrill when the shadow of the serrated ridge of the Spire Massif fell upon him. It rose like broken, jagged teeth from the lower jaw of a dark mouth.

"They say the mountains are the bones of Simon's body," Vilb said hoarsely.

"Not these," snapped Prav. "The Bones of Simon are much further west." She looked up at Vilb. "Maybe you'll see them some day, some *circ*." Vilb repressed a shudder. It was all too unreal, yet here he was. The Gate, the formal opening of the White Path to the Great City was, from where he stood, only a dark line in shadow, but he knew it was an ancient arch of stone that marked the true beginning of the Pilgrim's path. Climbing over the Massif appeared to be impossible yet Pilgrims had been travelling this way for nearly two thousand suns, the promise of the fertile plain and the Light of Simon had always beckoned the stalwart Pilgrim onward. That, and a strange compulsion, the calling it was called in The Book of M. It could not be explained, only experienced. Was he experiencing the calling?

"It was easier," he said, thinking out loud. "What was easier?"

"I was thinking about the Pilgrimage. Trying to imagine what it was like when the Path and the Gate were newly raised, when Simon walked the Little Earth in great strides, when the water flowed in rivers and the mountains were covered with … ice." He used the word, though he did not understand it. It came from his dream. Ice.

The girl made no sign that she heard him. She pointed to the ring of Pilgrims in the distance.

"We will wait here until evening prayers and then make our presence known. Remember: you are dying of thirst."

"How could I forget?"

"See the two there? Guards. That's unusual."

"Where?"

"There!" Prav thrust a finger into the distance. Vilb shook his head, trusting that the girl's eyesight did not lie, for he could not see so well. "I hope they will join the camp as soon as the company circles for prayers. When that happens, we go."

"Why do they have a guard?" asked Vilb. "I have never heard of such thing."

Prav ignored him again. "When we go, stay back. Let me go first." With that Prav leapt up and began to make her way quietly down the northern flank of the foothill and quickly disappeared from view.

Vilb waited a moment and then sprang after her, exasperated and not a little terrified. When he reached the bottom of the hill he could hear the entire company of Pilgrims singing. They were yet a long way off, but their voices carried, and the sound of their evening prayer brought him back to his own past with the village. It sounded like a huge procession, far larger than Vilb had ever heard tell of.

Vilb had to jog along to catch Prav and so by the time he had come upon the outer edge of the encampment he was breathing heavily and allowed himself to fall to his knees in case anyone had seen him. Up ahead he spied the girl about to break the perimeter of the camp. Vilb felt a sudden surge of panic of the unprepared. What was she leading him into?

Then, even as his heart raced, the Pilgrims lifted their voices in one last chorus and the song rang out over the foothills and came tumbling back down upon him as it made its way to the Massif and back again.

Oh Simon, Guide us!
Blessed One, Earth-Shaker,
The Martha's Son
Our Restoration
Fill us with the Power of M—
Light of the Archlight,
Oh Simon, Guide us!

The song ebbed, the echoes subsided, and then one last voice cried out. "And may Simon bless the Meson!" Cries of support, though no unanimous roar, echoed around the circle.

Vilb crept up beside Prav just as she turned and whispered to him. "That will end shortly. By the end they will curse the Meson and death will find them."

When the sound of the last voices died away Prav leapt up.

"Now!" she cried and with that was running forward as fast as her short legs could carry her. Exhausted, unsure and still a bit stunned by it all, Vilb rose hesitantly and stumbled after her, and one after the other they covered the last few strides and broke through the perimeter and into the Pilgrims' circle. Stumbling into camp was easy for Vilb. His exhaustion was real, and desperation hung heavily on him. When he crashed into the center of the ring of Pilgrims he fell to the ground where Prav already lay, breathing heavily and moaning. "A child!" a woman screamed and the crowd began to murmur and rumble like a distant storm about to strike.

Then another cry of fear went out: "AkiGazi!" A dozen Pilgrims approached Vilb and the girl. The midnight sun was well behind the Spires and it was clear that the Pilgrims had a difficult time discerning who it was in their midst.

"No. Not AkiGazi..." A tall woman dressed in the black tunic of the Meson's house came near and bent down over the pair. "Look at those srapis."

"Maybe they killed and took them!" Angry murmurs. A young man spoke as the ring pressed in close, curiosity overmastering their fear apparently. "What do you think, Quarter-Meson?" Vilb looked up and met the gaze of a stone- faced young man. He pointed at Vilb as he spoke. "That one has some strange way about him though."

Should he rise to his hands and knees, Vilb wondered, or just lay there dying?

The Quarter-Meson, a tall, striking woman with a face of flint and eyes of green stood over him, her hands grasping the lapels of her robe.

He had seen her before but when and where... he could not recall. Vilb was dumb struck though and thought her wind swept, chiseled features beautiful. He stared at her as well as he might even as he feigned distress.

She raised a hand and spoke with the deep, resonant voice of calm confidence. "Do not fear, my friends. These two are not AkiGazi. He is one of us by the looks of him. Probably a gen or some other wanderer of the badlands. Return to your prayers and calm your minds. Simon is with us." She turned to the young man waiting on her and spoke so that only he, she thought, could hear. "But I have never heard of a gen travelling with a child. This is not good, nor can it come to good."

"A gen could help us," said the stone-faced man. "They're holy men."

The words "gen" and "not AkiGazi" raced through the company. Vilb thought maybe one hundred had gathered around him, or more, or less. It was difficult to make out from where he lay.

"Water. Get some water!" another man shouted, and others as well, and the water skins came quickly. Vilb allowed himself to be revived slowly.

"Move the wild one into the tent. Stake the two-skin outside," the Quarter-Meson said, and Vilb felt rough hands grab his wrists and ankles and he surrendered willingly as they carried him into darkness.

▌▌

While most of the procession rested or slept or prayed, the Quarter-Meson, who the other Pilgrims called Oneira, and two elders sat together in the Quarter-Meson's tent and waited for Vilb to recover his strength. Pilgrims had brought generous amounts of food and water and he felt refreshed and encouraged, though guilty for his part in what he considered a dishonorable subterfuge. When he could he sat up and looked around. A small oil lamp burned and threw smoky shadows against the tent walls. Prav was nowhere in sight and Vilb immediately feared that the child had already been put down.

"I am Oneira, the Quarter-Meson of this Pilgrimage," the woman said to Vilb.

One of the Pilgrim elders spoke up breathlessly. "Was it AkiGazi?" he asked, and Vilb recoiled instinctively.

Oneira raised her hand slowly. "Please, Vek. Let this Pilgrim take his mat. We have all night to discuss the AkiGazi."

She turned again to Vilb, patience in her voice that did nothing to hide the desperation in her sea-green eyes. "When you are ready we need to hear your story. Our lives may depend upon it."

Vilb remained silent and fixed his own gaze on the ground before him. He wanted to ask about Prav, but this would only raise suspicion. He had to wait and play his part as the lost Gazi father.

"Who are you and what are you doing out here?" the one called Vek demanded.

"I know nothing of the AkiGazi," Vilb said, looking at Vek. "And I... we... came to be here the same way as you. The Martha has called and the hope of Simon leads us."

"We?" Vek repeated, and his eyes went wide. "Quarter-Meson!" Vek turned on the woman in anger so much so that Vilb thought he might attack her at any moment. "These blasphemous misdeeds must not stand. They will not stand. No wonder the AkiGazi terrorize us! No wonder the Power of M is nowhere to be found among us!"

"Be silent!" Oneira said quietly, but there was granite in her voice and Vek calmed down. "You stir up too much fear." She paused and looked long at Vilb. "Other villages have... other ways."

"May Simon protect us," said Vek and he said it in such a way that he did not hope for or expect protection, but rather, something else. Something decidedly not of Simon.

"Where is my two-skin?" asked Vilb cautiously. "It is safely staked," said Oneira gently.

"Bring her to me," said Vilb, hoping that Ubernaki customs had not changed since his time in the enclave.

Vek let out a hiss and leapt to his feet.

"She's mine," Vilb said. "She... travels with me." Oneira nodded as if understanding.

A long, uncomfortable silence ensued. It was now that Vilb took in the two others in spite of the shadowed nether gloom of the lamp lit tent.

Oneira was tall and broadly built, like the mountain range behind her. Her skin was the Ubernaki color of translucent jade, lighter than most, like Vilb's and the girl's. Her hair was wound tight around her head and bundled at the top and wound by sinew and held in place by a fine white comb. She came from the Ubernakis who lived on the coast, by the Girdling Sea. She wore the bronze collar and the purple srapi of the House of Meson and in her hand she carried the Meson's Trumpet, a bronzed long bone from the leg of a past Meson.

At least Vilb knew that some, perhaps many, of the ways of the Ubernaki had not changed since his time in his own village. But Oneira was from the coast and Vilb's village was a desert enclave, not far from the Stair and the Plateau.

Vek was a different story. He was from a desert enclave, of that Vilb was quite sure. The desert srapi Vek wore loose about him was exactly the kind Vilb wore, only Vek's was once red, the mark of his position in the village hierarchy. Around Vek's eyes wind-driven lines of age gathered, made more intense by worry and fear. Vilb felt that he was in the presence of family when he looked at Vek, and the feeling unnerved him. Under no circumstances, Vilb thought, would he follow this Ubernaki man. He stank of flesh eating and filth and all cruel things common to the Ubernaki.

Oneira, on the other hand. To her he might gladly and willingly submit and become one of the many Pilgrims who called her Quarter-Meson. There could be no one better to travel with than this woman, he thought, though he realized his determination was rash and impulsive, yet he felt relief to be in the hands of one so used to leadership. Her feet seemed rooted to the ashen soil. And her eyes. Vilb had seen those eyes somewhere before, though he knew it to be an impossibility.

"Bring the child in," Oneira finally said and Vek protested, hissed, stamped his foot, but she said nothing, waited for his storm of indignation to pass, and called to one of her own guards outside the tent.

"Bring in the child," she said, and in another moment Prav stood before them while the guard pounded a stake into the earth to which she was tied. The leash was too short to allow her to stand up straight and she was not permitted to sit. Vilb, Oneira and Vek took up three points around the girl, equally distant from one another as well. A few other figures hovered in the background, watching in the darkness.

"Thank you, Meson," said Vilb and he watched the woman flinch when he gave her this obvious sign of respect.

"She is Quarter-Meson," barked Vek.

"Vek will not let us forget our positions in the hierarchy," said Oneira quietly, though not without some bitter restraint.

"We thank him for that."

"It is the only thing that separates us from the AkiGazi, the Gazi and all of the rest of the backward talus of the Seventh Realm," Vek said defensively. Vilb peered at him cautiously. He was a dangerous one, this one. A zealot.

"The AkiGazi look to expand their grazing territory," Vilb said calmly. He had reasoned as much when watching them all through the last three long nights from the top of his hill. AkiGazi had come all the way to the rim of the Ubernaki plateau, though only in very small numbers, and always as wanderers. Vilb had met them, tried to talk with them but they could not exchange words and they headed west quickly after their meeting. Scouts, Vilb thought then, and now.

"They will take the entire east," said Prav quietly.

"No!" Oneira exploded. "Do not speak again! Ledge!"

She called and the guard entered.

"Take it back to the stake outside!" Vek shouted.

"Please, Meson. Be patient," Vilb cried. He waited and held Oneira's gaze. "This is no child," he said finally. Oneira finally nodded, waved the guard off and quieted Vek with a look.

"Speak," said Oneira.

"A goolak," Vek hissed. "As I suspected."

Oneira stiffened, slowly lifted the Meson's Trumpet before her and spoke. "Speak out of turn again and I will call for judgment and the hewer-stick." Vek balked and his face went pale. "You will be silent," Oneira said as she made one last gesture with the Trumpet.

"The child is not a *goolak*," Vilb protested, a calm reassurance in his voice though he himself was not so sure.

"I am the desolation of the land," Prav said quietly, though it appeared that only Vilb could hear this latest outburst.

Vilb turned to Oneira: "Meson?"

Oneira paused before speaking, and when she did she spoke slowly and deliberately. "We knew of our peril when we set out on Pilgrimage, but our hearts were set on the journey and the hope of Simon. Yet just before we made camp a band of AkiGazi took seven of us." Her face twisted into confusion and she appeared harried as she spoke. "It's unheard of! AkiGazi this far south! And the creatures that carried them have left all of us horribly frightened. The Pilgrimage is in ruins. Most have already decided to return to the village once they have refilled their water skins here."

"Creatures carrying AkiGazi?" Vilb said. "I hear but I do not understand."

Oneira turned to Prav. "I have seen her face before. While we prepared for the procession, while assembling at Vek's Enclave. Those that have been cast out have never returned. How is it that you are here?"

"I am the restoration of M. I am the desolation of the land," she said, her voice a whisper.

"So I have heard," Oneira said dismissively. She turned to Vek and called for Ledge to return. "This is no goolak. This is something else," she said.

"I have undergone the casting out and I do not wish to undergo it again," Prav said.

Vek hissed, genuinely disturbed. "Can you tell us of the AkiGazi?" Oneira asked quietly.

"And these strange beasts that carry them? What are they?" As she spoke she invited Ledge to join the ring and he sat down. He was built exactly like the Quarter-Meson, sea-blown eyes and striated hair, though his was flaxen rather than bronze.

"The AkiGazi are hungry. Like us," Vilb said as he moved to his right to make room for Ledge and to remain equally distant from the other three. Oneira remained where she was, however, and so when Vilb moved to his right, he moved closer to the woman. She had taken him into the procession, Vilb thought. "They abandoned the gathering way long ago," he said finally.

"How do you know this? Who are you?" Oneira asked. A genuine fear had crept into her voice.

"My name is Vilb de Solenthay. I come originally from the Desert Quad Enclave, though I have not lived among them for many suns." He could not help but tell the truth to Oneira. He wanted no lie between them.

"How many?" she asked.

"Twenty... twenty-one," he said and Oneira nodded.

"Go on, " she said.

Ledge interrupted. "You have told us nothing. What of the AkiGazi then? Why do they..."

Ledge seemed unsure how to proceed.

Vilb cut him off. "A madness drives them," he said.

"They're spreading over all of Little Earth. They take and eat all that they can from everywhere. The Gazi, the Ubernaki, all have become their... fertile valleys."

Vilb looked long at Prav until he caught her gaze for a moment and he held it as long as he could, took a deep breath and placed his palms to the ground before him.

"I can tell you," whispered Prav. "I was there. I can tell you."

Ledge rose but Oneira waved him back down. Vek had pulled his knees up and buried his face between them in silent protest.

"What can you know?" the Quarter-Meson asked. Was it a genuine question or merely a dismissal? Vilb could not tell, and Prav did not care. She used it as an opportunity to speak, and perhaps Oneira had intended as much. Something of this nature had almost certainly never happened before, but it felt as if sink holes were all around them and they marched blindly in the dark and fell in. Any light would be welcome.

"Drought wracks Little Earth. The Arclight is failing. The coastlands and the fertile valleys in the east and the north die of thirst. The grasses have turned to dust all across the Plateau, and the fruits of Simon wither on the remaining vines. The Gazi and the AkiGazi, and now the Ubernaki suffer, and it will go on. Quadros Prang will see to that." At this Prav choked and pulled at her collar. Oneira motioned silently to Ledge and in a moment the girl was free and kneeling more comfortably on the ground next to her stake.

Ledge set a bowl of water down next to her and bowl of scroggin. Vilb bit his lip and waited while she gobbled the food down and drank the bowl dry.

"When the AkiGazi began to dwindle, Joto and his Sumio Enclave drove south from their homeland, deeper than they had ever traveled. It was a desperate effort—certain death awaited them should they fail to find food and water by the time their own supplies were gone."

"It was Joto, they say, who found the first of the underground tunnels. There he met Quadros Prang."

"The Quadros Prang? In the flesh?" Vilb was incredulous and Vek looked at him as if surprised, though not offended, by Vilb's disbelief.

"Yes. The story says that Joto's first flesh came from his brother. When Joto's brother died in an accident Joto decided that he would not burn the body of his brother into ash. Why should the dust and stone eat the flesh, for the roots and nuts and water stored in his brother's body would be lost, and in those starving times this seemed like madness to Joto. Instead, Joto ate the body and converted his brother's death to life for himself and a few of his men."

"Joto and his small band then re-entered the world with new eyes and found that the world was full of flesh. Since that time the AkiGazi have sustained themselves on the flesh of the hunt. Until recently."

"Go on," Oneira said quietly.

"They hunt the Gazi, capture some, put down the rest. In this way they have reduced the Gazi peoples to a memory, all except those who live in the droves maintained by AkiGazi Drovers."

"But why do they attack us? How is it that they've come to our lands?" asked Ledge.

"While the Gazi and Ubernaki dwindle, the AkiGazi have managed to swell their numbers, and now they have many more mouths to feed and so now travel to the far corners of the east and north of Little Earth to hunt."

"How is this possible"? Oneira asked.

"It was Quadros Prang. He gave them the *vasalur*, and the grass that does not wither. Quadros vies with The Martha. He destroys all that she builds."

"What is *vasalur*?" Vilb asked, strangely moved.

"That's what they call the man-things that carry the AkiGazi hunters on their backs. They can run fast and far on little food or water. They were once Gazi Peoples."

"We were all once Gazi Peoples," said Oneira ruefully.

"That is exactly what The Book of M teaches us," Vek said disdainfully. "It is more than possible, likely in fact, that the Gazi and the AkiGazi come from the Ubernaki."

"If that is so, then I fear for Little Earth," said Vilb.

Prav went on. "These man-things carry the AkiGazi tribes great distances, even to the furthest lands of Little Earth and now we have become their fertile valleys, and they harvest all that they can while they can."

"They eat Ubernaki?" Ledge said, still absorbing what he had heard. "But who are they to set themselves apart and bring death to us?"

Vilb sputtered with indignation. Could the fools not see it for themselves?

"What troubles you?" Oneira asked him.

"Your men trouble me," Vilb said impulsively. "This... this world troubles me. How can you not see it? The Ubernaki are flesh-eaters."

"That is different," Vek retorted, and waved Vilb off.

"They call themselves the Sons of Quadros," Prav said, undeterred. "The remaining Gazi People are thin and spread far, and have learned to avoid them. They believe that they have lost The Martha's protection. When necessary, they fight and kill to save their own lives yet they die and The Martha does nothing. Master Qir, however, does not sleep. He moves and he tries to wake us, to save us."

Vek snorted, unable to contain his indignation. "I do not believe in the tales of the gods, nor do I believe that we sleep," said Vek, all but exploding. He turned to Oneira. "Please, Quarter-Meson, let me speak. I can be silent no longer, and if I risk the hewer-stick. So be it."

"Then speak if you must," said Oneira.

"There is only this," he said slowly, methodically, and as he spoke he pounded the ground with his fist to make his point. Vek paused and looked around though careful not to let his eyes fall upon the child. "Each of us must bring our minds into harmony with the reality of this life. This, this earth, these… " and here he looked all around him, "these tents, and bones, and… and all that we call our own, our lives, all of this is Simon. Nothing more. No magic. No Power of M. These are all stories that give shape to our faith, but our faith can be grounded only in the earth, the sky, the wind." Vek paused to gather his thoughts. "Beware superstition," he finally said. "The tales of the gods of Little Earth are nursery tales, nothing more."

"And you know this? Then why do you go on Pilgrimage?" asked Oneira, almost pleading, and this moved him to retrace his steps.

"I claim nothing for myself," Vek said finally, a shadow of humility passing over him. "I only state the truth and announce the hope in which we all share. There is power in the Great City, of some kind. The Arclight does shine in the long nights. We have all felt its power. Perhaps… we can… bring some of that power back with us?"

"Power?" Vilb said quietly. "What hope do you have in power? You mean the Power of M, and so you contradict yourself, my friend Vek. You cannot be a disbeliever in Simon and still hold to the Power of M." But even as he spoke Vilb could hear that in Vek's position there was the shadow of his own uneasy faith.

Vek stood up suddenly. "Quarter-Meson, I think our decision is all but decided for us. The Pilgrimage must end and we must return immediately." Oneira's jaw dropped slowly. Clearly this was unexpected. The Quarter-Meson recovered herself and looked long at Prav, and then Vilb and then she rose and brought a bowl of nuts and berries and a full skin of water to the girl. "Rest and eat and drink," she said, "and then the two of you may tell us more when you can."

III

The sound of shouting voices and a howling wind startled Vilb from a sound sleep. The sun had come around and lit the sky from the east and the tent glowed inside with a warm, ambient light and for a moment Vilb thought he was back in his cave, but the shouting continued and he remembered where he was. He stood up and rubbed his temple and wondered suddenly what Prav had done to him in the desert. His head ached dully though otherwise he felt refreshed and well-watered. He wiped the sleep from his eyes and looked around and his gaze fell upon the girl, Prav. She stood in the tent opening, her hand shielding her eyes. The flaps whipped and the entire tent thrummed with a great gust of wind.

"It's Vek," Prav shouted over her shoulder to Vilb. "The wind makes it hard to hear, but I think he's leading them back. It's not safe for us here anymore." Just then Ledge strode past the girl and into the center of the tent. His face and hair were now coated by wind-driven ash and still Vilb could see the signs of distress on his face, in his shoulders. His gray srapi of the Meson's Guard he had wrapped tight around his thick frame.

"You must leave us now," he said to Vilb. "Head northeast of camp. There's a crest there. We will meet at the base by the Chert Portico. Go. Now!" Ledge rushed out even as his words hung in the air. The tent flap whipped violently in the wind.

"We go!" Prav said, and she was already strapping water skins to her waist and grabbing the bowls of uneaten food.

"Grab those water skins!" And for an instant their eyes met and Prav smiled and Vilb understood. Had this all been a charade to gain water skins?

"They belong to the Quarter-Meson," Vilb said, but grabbed one nonetheless. He lifted his things and prepared himself. Now he had four.

As if blown by the wind Prav appeared before him, grabbed the front of his srapi and with surprising strength pulled him down to his knees so that they were now eye-to-eye.

"Pick up those water skins!" she commanded and Vilb found himself tying the remaining water skins together with his own. Okay, five now.

"Come on. This way." Prav had already lifted the back wall of the tent and slipped under when Vilb turned to follow.

Once safely away from the encampment and almost to the top of the crest Vilb looked back towards the camp. The procession had all but disappeared into a cloud of wind-swept dust.

"Now what?" Vilb said, shielding his eyes with one hand while holding a corner of his cowl over his mouth and nose with the other.

"Find shelter and wait. Ledge, Oneira, perhaps a few others, may join us soon enough."

"If they do not?"

"If they do not then we go on and pray for Simon's help."

"Hah!" Vilb laughed involuntarily. His own lack of faith startled him.

• • •

Vilb and Prav laid low among the ruins of the portico while the dry, biting winds poured down from the Spire Massif and excoriated the land.

"It is time to talk of the dream," Prav said.

"I have no dreams." Vilb carefully took a drink from one of his water skins and kept his eyes on a shattered corner of what was once probably the portico pediment.

"Impossible," Prav said flatly.

"I am telling you that I do not dream."

"Then do you eat?"

"Of course."

"Do you breathe and sleep?"

"Do not mock me, two-skin." Vilb could see from the corner of his eye that the girl was taken aback by this, and, frankly, Vilb too was startled by his own vehemence. Had anyone asked him last sun about children he would have had an open and large response, about their salient natures and the importance of future generations. But now, when faced with one, when confronted by his own desire, he found it difficult to control his disdain, his fear.

"All of Simon's children dream."

"Gen are dream masters," Vilb said, though he himself did not believe it. Prav laughed outright and fixed her gaze on him until a look of recognition came into her face. "There is a sleeper in you, in all like you."

"In Vek? And Ledge?" Vilb asked, meaning to be spiteful and difficult, but his question sounded in earnest even to his own ears.

"Yes. Vek is you. And Ledge. All just a marker off from the original design. Variations on a theme. Gone to seed. The entire east of Little Earth. A garden gone to seed."

Vilb did not understand and so he laughed but without humor. He reflected for a moment then, and took a breath. "I do feel something, like a… split. Within me. Whatever you did to me in the desert has quieted my mind, but it has not… unified it. Is this not the way all men," and at this he paused, "all of us experience this life?"

"No," said Prav flatly.

Vilb shrugged and closed his eyes, let his head rest on the boulder behind him, and breathed deeply.

"It is true, I have dreamed," he said finally.

"Yes."

"Yes, the same dream, many times."

"Yes."

"It is a dream of wind and blinding white dust that buries Little Earth." Vilb paused, his eyes still closed. "I am never long without this dream."

Prav watched him as his brow furrowed and his eyes worked furiously under his eyelids.

"Go on," Prav demanded but Vilb hesitated feeling suddenly exposed and vulnerable and, if the truth be told, foolish. His dream had long become a part of the background, like the long day and the desert and the unending search for food and fuel. To focus on it now felt like a disturbance and that in disturbing the dream, he might awaken it.

"Yes!" Prav cried, as if in answer to Vilb's thoughts. He eyed her with a sidelong glance of annoyance.

"Please do not do that again."

"My apologies, Master gen. Say on."

Vilb took a deep breath and nodded.

"I dream of my father," he began, as if reciting his lessons from boyhood. "I dream of the wind and the white dust that buries Little Earth. The… ice… is deep, so deep that it fills all valleys and razes every mountain. In my dream my father strides through this ice and it rises only to his knee and he too is white, but polished marble, living stone, and he could walk to each of the Seven Realms in a circ."

"But you do not believe in the Seven Realms," said Prav dryly.

"In my dream I do."

Prav nodded. "You dream of Simon as he first was." "What?" Vilb opened his eyes.

"He sleeps but soon the One will awaken and be restored and the Four will tremble and the guilty will be punished, and there will be war between the Realms. I have had the dream as well, but many times, and in many forms, and unlike you, I have surrendered to His Mind… surrendered to Simon long ago."

Prav stepped closer to Vilb. "Close your eyes again. Keep your eyes closed. I am going to touch you."

"Uhhhh," Vilb groaned, unsure for a moment, but before he could muster any real challenge Prav stepped close to him and turned her palms out, towards his face, and placed one on each of his closed eyes.

He sat up, tense, as if ready to push her away at any moment.

"Shhh," she said. "Do not talk. Breathe in and out. Feel yourself breathing. Good. Yes." She pushed firmly against his eyes. He struggled a bit against the pressure on his face.

"I will not hurt you," she said. "Trust me." Vilb breathed a heavy, ragged breath that shook him as he exhaled. "Regard your thoughts as wind-driven clouds. With a clear mind see your eyes turn and look inward, back, into the darkness of your own mind."

"Yes," Vilb said, and suddenly he felt exhausted and sleepy.

A curtain between his waking mind and his dreaming mind seemed to fall away and a vision opened to him, within him. "I see a great inland sea surrounded by seven shining towers that climb to the sky," he said breathlessly.

"Yes! You see the Great City of the Ancients. The Fourth Realm. Levinthal is there."

"Lev-in-thal," Vilb said slowly. He knew that name and suddenly Oneira's green eyes flashed before him and somehow he knew Levinthal, Oneira, Prav, Vilb—pieces of a mosaic that had yet to come together as one.

Prav released him and stepped back and Vilb lifted his face, eyes wide with wonder and fear. "Who is Levinthal?"

"He is the master of the Fourth Realm," said Prav, nodding.

"Where in Little Earth?"

"Not Little Earth. The Fourth Realm is of the Greater Earth, that which Little Earth is only a part of. It is beyond the Girdling Sea."

"Beyond?"

"Beyond beyond. Our home."

Vilb was shaking his head now, over-full with information of a sort that he had no way of comprehending, and as in other instances when he had found something difficult to comprehend, rather than take one step at a time through what was new and strange he plunged his mind into a fog and felt safely lost there, the mists of confusion abrogating him of all responsibility.

"When Oneira and the rest of the company join us I shall have more to say about the dream. Believe me, I need you to hear it, but not yet." She paused for a moment and then went on. "The Book of M tells us that Simon wielded the Power of M to fashion Little Earth, yes?"

"So The Book of M records."

"Well then," and now Prav leaned in as if wary of being overheard, or as if drunk on root wine. "Does Simon have the same nature as the Power of M or is Simon... something else? I mean, did the Power of M make Simon or does the Power of M come from Simon? And if so, is Simon greater than the Power of M? Or is it the other way around? Or are they one and the same?" Vilb simply stared at the girl, silent, bewildered.

Prav threw back her head and laughed, her cowl falling away and her long, red hair falling out. She appeared thoroughly delighted and then, just as suddenly, she stuck her tongue out and laughed again.

IV

When the others from the Pilgrimage had finally joined them the girl had dropped into a dark mood. Only two Pilgrims out of the ninety-three at the encampment had followed Oneira and Ledge. Only two others? This had troubled Prav greatly. Why only two? She had, it seemed, hoped for a great many more.

One of the Pilgrims had been especially troubling to Prav as far as he could tell. She became morose and irritable, frightened even, and he realized that he had never before seen her truly unsettled, that is, until now. Since the time the four had joined them, she had remained tight-lipped, had dropped to the rear of the group and allowed Oneira to guide them up over the moraine and to the White Path beyond the Gate. For their part, the two new strangers followed in a trance and paid no attention to either Vilb or the girl.

When the group reached the Path Vilb looked back, disappointed that he had not passed under the Gate, the stone arch erected almost two-thousand suns before by the First Archer of the Great City of San Simon, Azo. Azo was, according to The Book of M, one of the Four who loved the children of The Martha and as a boy learning his lessons, Azo was a personal favorite of Vilb's. The Martha was loving kindness, yes, and all things good and green in the world, but Azo was dazzling depicted as he was in a flowing pearl srapi and an arrow in one hand, a horn of plenty in the other.

A long time ago, Vilb secretly prayed to Azo for guidance, for his decision to become a gen, for Azo and The Martha were aligned and were two, yet One.

It had been long since he had learned his lessons. But now, to hear that the AkiGazi claimed Quadros as their savior? It all came back to him. The Book of M depicted Quadros Prang as a god, yet a demon at the same time. Could he be both? As a boy he was too afraid to ask and so he remained perplexed. Teacher called it a mystery.

What of now and this age-long drought? What of the eating of the flesh of one's tribe? Why the fear and loathing of children? How had things come to be this way? It was the most obvious, pressing question on Vilb's mind and now he realized that he had made no progress in answering it these many suns.

It was precisely the unknowability of the past that frustrated him. So many myths. So many stories. So many possible meanings. Vilb had no answers to even the most rudimentary of questions. Why did the Four turn against the One? And where had Simon the Great God gone? Was there ever a Simon in the first place or was that too only a part of a child's story?

Some Simonologists argued that The Book of M clearly implies that the gods were Ancients who came from beyond and made Little Earth in their image, and that the gods lived before Simon if something so bizarre and irrational could be contemplated.

Was there a before Simon?

And if the gods did exist, where were they now? Had they left Little Earth? Vilb rubbed his temple. He let his questions go for the time being, if only to ease his aching head, sipped on his water, and followed obediently behind the others. The small procession walked in silence up the rising White Path that stretched before them on its way up into the hanging valley between the Twin Horns of the Spire Massif.

The Millennial Palm

When the gods saw that the long night was not good, for the
seeds would not grow in the night, they dug deep into the stone
and touched the Power of M. From it they drew the Arclight and
placed it atop the Great City, and it burned there so that the seeds
The Martha had planted in Little Earth might grow, and they did
grow, and the gods were pleased.

– The Book of M

I

Vilb had made the trip to the Great Gate once before, as a boy with
his father, but the Spire Massif he had never crossed, nor even dared
to set foot on the path beyond the ancient archway. And now that he and
his pitiful company were on their way the range—and what Pilgrimage
truly required—overwhelmed him in its sheer, seemingly insurmountable
scope. The path they walked was not a path at all in the true sense of a
path. Once beyond the archway they soon began to find their way choked
by hills of talus, boulder and other detritus from the mountain sides, and
only climbing over it, or wending their way between the larger masses,
allowed something like forward progress to be made. From a distance the
path appeared to be a wide winding trough that cut through a series of
aretes that rose and fell, each higher than the last, until, finally, the Horns
themselves stood on either side and between them, presumably, the White
Path rode the saddle. Like sentinels guarding their way to the west, the true
gate to the west was the Twin Horns, Vilb realized, and the pass between
them was a very long, hard way.

Even the slight grade up the valley beyond the arch had left him short of breath and stooped, and now this picking his way over loose slump and slide reduced his resolve, though at each boulder he found a way up and through. Yet all he could think about were his hands, dreadfully desiccated, the skin painfully cracked. It seemed now that the hopes for a successful Pilgrimage were all but ruined and their ridiculous procession appeared to him as a party of lost fools. At the next appropriate moment he planned to confess his weakness, give up his pride and skulk quickly back to the Great Arch, and then, as food and water allowed, home to his hill. Why had he ever desired anything but his solitary hill, its cool grotto, its dazzling oolites, encrusted stalagtites, the crystal walls that shimmered in the long night's full moon light? Vilb could almost hear the water trickling over the smooth stone of his grotto spring. There he had water enough and the soothing shadow, and the aloneness that only now he realized he had come to require.

"Should we rest?" Oneira asked as Vilb caught up with her. She had stopped to wait for the rest of the company, many of whom were far behind Vilb. In fact, he and Oneira had far outpaced the others. Was she tired? Vilb couldn't discern any fatigue in her at all.

"The way gets steeper up ahead I think, and the others are too far behind." Vilb turned and waved to the group behind until they each acknowledged him, and then he sat down wordlessly and continued to brood.

What if they did make it through the Massif? What then? The entire Pilgrimage would take, even under the best conditions, until the middle of Twilight, and should they meet any trouble on the way—should the journey take longer than they anticipated for instance, and this seemed more likely now than ever—then the night would fall and find them foraging somewhere between the Massif range to the east and San Simon perhaps still far ahead of them to the west. What then? What of food and water?

Indeed, if the Arclight had already failed west of the Spire Massif, or even dimmed, then conditions there may be no less hostile than here. The thought of a stricken, starving west had never crossed his mind, but now it did and his head was spinning.

And what of the AkiGazi?

Even as this thought came to him he felt as if he needed to lay his head down for it had become a heavy burden to him and it took all his remaining strength to hold it up. The others finally joined him and Oneira even as he lay there trying to catch his breath. The others made a small camp between two large boulders not far from where he lay, and he turned and watched them as they dropped their burdens and lowered themselves to the soil. All except for Prav. The girl hung back, hovered at the edge of the ragged circle the Pilgrims had made. She stood there, her fists hanging down at her sides, her arms rigid and a scowl on her face that Vilb found impossible to read. Perhaps it was the mood he was in, but when he looked at the girl he felt a cold terror bead on his back and brow.

It was into this that Oneira spoke suddenly.

"I cannot lead you," she said. "I have already failed the Pilgrimage." The others remained silent and after another moment Ledge, one of few who had remained loyal to her, responded. His head was between his knees as he sat on a rock. He did not lift it to speak, though Vilb thought he sounded in earnest.

"You must lead us," said Ledge. A long pause and no one else spoke. "We have no one else."

"I will not lead while you remain with us," Oneira responded, and this caused Ledge to raise his head. "The others, the young men here who have joined us from the procession, Vek and the other called Vansom, and Vilb and the child two-skin..." she paused and turned to look at the one called Vansom. "Do any of you wish to lead?"

Vansom was a young man with brazen bronze curls and could have been the brother of Vek. He was hardly more than a boy, just out of the Quarries, just recently called out from among the three-skins and the Teachers to join the lowest strata of the Quad Enclave, but it was a strata favored by the Meson, and of that he was proud. The long, white face and the grim arrogance characterized those that had survived and been called out to join the Enclave leadership. To be considered for such a privilege the child, even as a two-skin, had to demonstrate that it was morbidly confident in its own strength and perfectly willing to use it against the other twos, and yes, if need be, even the older three-skins, going so far as to help put down and dress, season and dry, dozens of skins each sun. If this pleased the Teacher, (or as just as often happened, ended up in the death of he or she who would rise in the Enclave) then one's chances of hearing the Meson's Call had significantly increased. Vilb shuddered at the things he had done to survive as a child-skin and then later, as a member of the lower strata Enclave. There were other ways to please the Teacher, thought Vilb, other ways to please, other ways to obey and so invite the Meson's Call. Vilb shuddered.

"I will not lead," declared Vansom blithely and waved Oneira off. Though they had never laid eyes on one another Vilb knew Vansom even as he had recognized Vek. It was the knowledge of self-recognition once again and Vilb recoiled at what he beheld. A powerful feeling of loathing and distrust, woven with fear and judgment, enveloped him. Vilb found that he hated Vansom. Next to Vansom crouched yet another figure, an older man, older even than Vilb.

Ledge looked up at the figure crouched beside Vansom and then up at Oneira. She seemed perplexed by the appearance of this stranger and shook her head silently as if to acknowledge Ledge's silent question.

Oneira spoke up first, still the Quarter-Meson after all. "Who are you, Pilgrim? I don't recognize your face."

"I do not know you either," agreed Ledge. Vek shifted nervously behind both the stranger and Vansom. "I thought that you and he were together," nodding towards Vansom. The crouching stranger remained silent, his face down, his hands and fingers working hard at some invisible weaving.

"Speak up," Ledge said. The stranger mumbled something. "I cannot hear you. Speak up." Vansom folded his arms across his chest. He seemed to be enjoying the tension of the moment. "I am afraid to tell you," the stranger finally managed.

Vansom shook his head in disgust.

"Who are you?" Oneira said. "What village are you from?"

"I cannot say," the stranger replied.

"You must say," said Ledge, and he rose to his feet. "We cannot travel with you as a stranger. Who are you?"

Oneira raised her hand. "Easy, Ledge."

"She knows," the stranger said, and his hand shook like a tremor across the plain, his arm began to shake, and then his whole body took up the temblor. The stranger pointed towards Prav.

"By Simon!" cried Vansom, and he shoved the stranger hard with the heel of his foot, knocking him roughly to the ground. At this Prav strode forward and stood before the old man.

"You hurt me!" Prav cried, and she marched forward, her fists up and she stood over the stranger who lay on his back shivering. His hands were limp on his chest. "You hurt me!" Prav cried and she stamped her foot, and her face was squeezed tight and the tears began to flow down her cheeks. "Get up!" She screamed and she kicked the stranger in the ribs and waited for him to respond in some way. Meanwhile her hand darted into her srapi and then out again and in it she now held her short, white blade.

Vilb lurched to his feet sensing that blood would be spilled. He had never recovered the blade from the girl and now she held it over the heart of the stranger who lay passively under her gaze.

"You!" Prav screeched, took a step backward and swung her right foot with all the might of her body and kicked the stranger in the ribs again. The old man groaned but did nothing to protect himself. Rather, he seemed to be offering his body to the girl's rage.

Oneira rose to grab Prav from behind but the girl spun and slashed fiercely and drove Oneira back even as the girl stepped to the other side of the stranger's prone body.

"What is going on?" demanded Oneira.

All of the group was now standing. Oneira held Ledge off with one hand gesture. Vansom seemed amused while Vek remained nervously behind him. Vilb felt confused and suddenly sorrowful that violence had found them so soon. He knew that it would be sooner or later, for it always did with the Ubernaki, but this was unexpected. Did it have to be this way? Was it inevitable?

What he did next he had no explanation for, no conceived plan, no vision of the outcome. He simply walked forward, crouched beside the trembling, prone stranger and spoke quietly to him.

"You are Ubernaki?" Vilb asked him.

The stranger nodded and without turning his head, spoke.

"You are the hermit on the hill," the stranger said. "I know of you. I have seen you. Gen." Vilb nodded.

"We're all gen," the old man whispered and grimaced, or grinned. Vilb nodded again, though he did not understand.

"Enough!" Prav screamed, and in a fury she fell on the stranger, lifted the blade high and prepared to plunge the blade into his chest except that Vilb put a hand up and knocked her thrust off course. The exquisitely sharp blade sank deep into the old man's right shoulder and this moved him to action. He was not ready to die after all. Leaping to his feet, he clutched the blade handle and pulled it out with a groan and let the blade fall to the ground.

No one moved. Prav stood petrified and closed her eyes and this so surprised the others that they stood and watched, desperate to find out what the mad child would do next.

Another moment of silence passed and then Prav raised her right hand, palm forward, and faced the stranger.

"I am the abomination of the land. I am the desolation of M," she said, her voice shrill and high, like a child's when in a confused fury, only Prav did not seem confused.

"What is going on?" pleaded Oneira to no one.

"I am sorry!" the stranger yelled, his contorted single brow and bulging eyes a leading edge of some inner avalanche tearing through his mind.

A convulsion shook the girl and from her palm something emerged, though of substance Vilb could see none. Even so, the space before her palm became white, distorted light, and in the shape of a ball. It quickly passed from Prav's palm to the stranger's chest and as it passed through him he fell over limp, apparently dead. The ball of distortion did not stop, however, but continued on towards Vansom at a steady, even rate which gave him ample time to dodge out of the way only to watch the distortion pass through the boulder he had been leaning against. The ball of light passed through the center of the stone and shattered it, and still onward it traveled across the moraine until the sound of breaking, falling stones could no longer be heard.

Oneira moaned quietly. "We are the playthings of the gods."

Ledge reached down and picked up the milky white blade.

Prav, meanwhile, remained still and silent as if petrified.

"The girl… took that from me," Vilb lied. In a moment he had his reath hutch out and stowed the white blade beside the other tools, now shining with a speckled emerald light.

"Why did you not tell us before?" Ledge exclaimed as he caught sight of the hutch and its contents.

"What do you carry?" Vansom whispered, all sign of smug humor gone from his face. Even Vek leaned forward to gaze at Vilb's strange tools though his attention never left Prav for long.

"Please forgive us, Healer-Meson. We did not realize,"

Oneira said to Vilb, and bowed her head deeply.

"I… I found this. Long ago," Vilb stammered as if trying not to lay too strong a claim on what he had, up until now, always considered his by right of discovery. Yet now the tools seemed like a heavy liability. "In the catacombs," he said. "Long ago." His voice trailed off weakly.

"The Power of M," said Oneira solemnly. "We are truly blessed."

"Or truly cursed," said Vek, and he shot Vilb a dark look.

Vilb packed his hutch and placed it back in his sling as if hiding a shameful family secret that, though he did not understand, he felt the need to hide.

II

Prav had curled up into a ball and slipped into a reverie. She rocked and moaned quietly with her eyes open but rolled back into her head. The old man, according to Vek, was one called Rifter, and he lay in a death-state with his legs twisted under him, gray eyes open. All disfigurements of fear on his face were gone. His forehead was smooth, and his jaw relaxed, as if ready to shout a friendly greeting.

"Both of them are far gone," Oneira said.

"The gods stalk and dog our every step," Ledge said, his voice ringing with the high-pitch of fear.

"What else could explain what we have just seen? If I am right, then we are marked for death. You say she is your daughter, hermit?" Oneira turned on Vilb, a hard ferocity in her eye. Her look accused Vilb of bringing a curse of evil and destruction along with him and for this she wanted satisfaction.

All of the old terrors of the Quarry Teacher suddenly loosened his knees and he wobbled.

"When I found her she was... well, she had been injured most grievously. The casting out that you spoke of. I found her in the catacombs after the four had... completed the ritual."

Vilb was rattled.

"And her injuries?" asked Oneira.

"She recovered. Quickly," Vilb spat out, unsure of his role in all of this.

"She's Millennial. The tongue proves it if nothing else," said Vansom. "Any decent casting out does the tongue. It's one of the first things. That one there," Vansom said, pointing to Rifter's body. His amusement had given way to high- seriousness, but a smirk lingered at the corners of his mouth.

"He did it to her. He told me on the climb up here. At least that's what he said. He's on his way to the Great City to seek forgiveness." And at this last detail Vansom let loose a short, barking laugh.

"What else did he say?" Ledge demanded, apparently impatient with Vansom's lack of obsequiousness.

"Just what I said, nothing more," Vansom said. "If this Prav is Millennial—a gift from the gods like you think she is, then he and the others who took her to the tombs did so for good reason, and you know it," and now he fixed Oneria with his gaze. "You know why they cast her out?" It was a question so subtly posed that the answer was clear, Vansom knew it, and Oneira knew that he knew it, and so she gave ground in a small retreat.

"I do know," Oneira announced matter of factly. "Prav killed Selantha."

Vansom clapped his hands and laughed silently.

"Who is Selantha?" asked Vilb.

"The Enclave's High Teacher and second to the Meson," declared Vek, skulking in the shadow of a large boulder.

Oneira turned back to Vilb. "Can the reath hutch be of any service to us, Healer-Meson?"

Vilb shook his head and backed off. "I am no Healer-Meson. I am a gen, and the reath hutch... I do not understand how to use it. I'm not even sure what a reath hutch is."

"But it came to you?" Ledge asked.

"Yes, in my first sun as a gen."

Ledge and Oneira exchanged a long look.

"You are the Healer-Meson then," Oneira said.

"How can that be?" Vilb protested.

"You have the hutch," Oneira said.

"I realize that, but I do not understand what it is or how it works."

"Read your Book of M, my friend." This from Vansom.

"We shall see," said Oneira looking from Vansom to Vilb. "What should we do about... her?"

Vilb waved Oneira off. "Leave her. I think I can manage her." He turned away, trying to hide from the others a rising feeling of responsibility for the girl, or whatever she was, in spite of what she had done to Rifter.

Oneira shook her head. "And when she wakes up? If Vansom is right, then Rifter," pointing to the dead man at their feet, "participated in the casting out."

Vilb nodded and turned his back on Oneira. "She was torn everywhere." He folded his arms.

Ledge interrupted defiantly. "How could this be the same two-skin? How could anyone survive such a thing?"

Vilb turned and advanced on Ledge slowly. "She was a bloody mess when I pulled her out of the cliff. How she healed I do not understand. I thought perhaps it was my efforts, but I do not think so."

"Perhaps it was your efforts," Ledge countered.

Vilb said "No," and paused as if listening to some distant voice more important than Ledge's. "Rifter may not be dead,"

Vilb said suddenly. He crouched and removed the stricken man's srapi in a flustered storm of hands and cloth. Once his chest was exposed Vilb put his ear there, closed his eyes and listened.

Vilb knew about the heart—he had seen enough of them while a boy in the Enclave, and he had studied his own as well as he might, cowardly and weak though it was, though so much like Rifter's that they may have been one heart, though in Rifter's body it was not beating, neither was it entirely silent. A whispering went on in the fleshy walls of the chambers of Rifter's heart, and the blood pooled there as if waiting in vivified anticipation for the next command. No, Rifter was not dead so much as waiting for what was next. Vilb felt his temple throbbing and next heard a humming and the humming grew in his mind until he had to swallow it down into his own core and the inner-most void within him opened up, and the void permeated all that he was.

Vilb shook himself as he lifted his head up and looked at Oneira. "This is not death. Hand me my sling." Oneira lifted the hutch from the sling and brought it to Vilb. He looked long at it.

"Can it help?" Ledge asked.

"I do not know," he said, but in fact he had an intuition. Vilb took the hutch from Oneira, put it down carefully and laid it out so that he might examine the contents. His hand moved over each one as if listening, and then, as if led by the tool, he reached down and lifted out one of the small, delicate bones no longer than his smallest finger, and placed it in Rifter's navel.

Next came what he called the Pin. It had a hoop at the top that fit neatly over the first tool and when Vilb put the two tools together, they began to glow with a preternatural green light.

Vilb felt the hair on the back of his neck and arms rise up and the very air around them seemed to vibrate and crackle like the heaves before a lightning storm.

Rifter's chest heaved and he inhaled suddenly.

"Look!" Oneira whispered. Quickly Vilb snatched the tools back and returned them to the hutch. "The Power of M has been here," Oneira said with awe in her voice. Vilb put his ear on Rifter's chest and then lifted up again and shook his head in wonderment.

"I do not understand," he said, but he was smiling.

"What if the child-thing poisons him again?" Vansom asked. "How can we stop her? Perhaps we should leave her here while she sleeps?"

Just then Prav rose to her feet.

"What do you want from us?" Oneira asked suddenly as the girl took a step towards them. "Why are you here?"

The girl looked stricken. She put her hands out, palms up, as if preparing to catch a heavy burden, and she moved towards them.

"He hurt me," she said, and the tears began to fall again.

"I wanted… I wanted to hurt him. Like he hurt me." She was sobbing now, heaving, silent things that dropped her to her hands and knees. She began to wretch and gag. It was too much for him so Vilb stepped over to the girl and put his hand on her back. She turned away violently.

"Don't touch me! Don't ever touch me!" she screamed, and her face twisted in rage and her eyes blazed with molten heat.

"Prav," Vilb said, and his voice was a calm twilight breeze.

He reached out again, this time his palm up towards her. "We won't hurt you. None of us will hurt you, nor do we want to hurt you. You are safe. We will keep you safe. I promise to keep you safe."

The girl rose to her knees, and Vilb met her gaze and it was as if they were seeing each other from a great distance. The girl threw her shoulders back and dropped her chin to her chest as one last shudder racked her. She took another deep breath and just as suddenly as the emotional outpouring had manifested, it withdrew even more quickly and disappeared behind the now placid shield of the girl's face.

The Reath Hutch

Other voices may call to you and lo, visions may arise before you. False prophets will wander your lands, but trust in none other than Simon in whom you have your life and light. From Simon and His progeny the Power of M will appear and deliver you from thirst, yea, even from the bitterest of ends.
– The Book of M

I

For three circles of the sun the company walked doggedly up the ascending path that cut into and through the leading edge of the Massif. All the while the Horns loomed overhead, growing larger, but somehow, no closer. For a time the path had evened out and they made quicker progress, but as the serrated crest rose over them the path grew narrower and once again choked with boulder. By the end of the third circ since setting out from the Gate their pace had slowed to a crawl and they were reduced, once again, to scrambling over boulders two and three times their height.

"Could we have missed the path?" Vilb asked.

"No. Impossible," Oneira said. "We have to push up and over this. The Twins are there," she said and pointed up at the sky between them that suggested the promise of open spaces beyond. "The path runs through a col further up. We will come to a descent soon, this circ or perhaps the next. Water and grass and *trees*," she said as she heaved herself over a boulder.

"Trees?" said Vilb.

"Yes. *Trees.*"

Oneira shrugged, unable to explain. Vilb tried to imagine such a thing as trees but had no felt experience to associate with the word.

"Of all the works of Simon *The Way of the Pilgrim* describes them as one of His most beautiful," she said.

"I do not know this book," said Vilb

"It is ancient, almost as ancient as The Book of M," she said, and turned back to the climb. "I am surprised you have not heard of it."

Oneira paused in her climb and looked back. The others were behind and so she paused. "It was a gift from The Martha long ago, when it was said the gods wandered Little Earth and enjoyed their creation. You must think I am mad."

Vilb shook his head. "I expect Pilgrims to believe in their Pilgrimage, in the hope of the gods."

Oneira nodded and resumed climbing.

"It wasn't always this difficult," she said. "At least according to *The Way of the Pilgrim*."

Vilb settled into a morose and dejected mood as he heaved himself doggedly over another boulder. The sense that they were hopelessly lost, or worse, on a path that lead to certain destruction, had grown in his mind since they had set out three circs before.

Oneira climbed further and faster than the rest of the company—anxiety drove her perhaps. She moved as one who hoped to find the end at the beginning and so avoid the struggle of the journey which is, Vilb thought, always a struggle with doubt. In the journey. In oneself.

When almost out of sight Oneira suddenly appeared at the top of a crest, turned back to the others and waved. She shouted that she had found the path. Just beyond her it became easier and began its gentle descent into the valley between the Twin Horns.

The others, including the revivified Rifter and a quiet, docile Prav climbed with renewed hope and finally joined her at the top of the crest. Vilb stood off from Oneira, unsure of this latest development.

"Look!" she said, and her breath came in ragged gasps.

"Just look," she gasped, and pointed into the valley. It was a level, blue strip in the western distance at the foot of the

Twins. The others gazed silently.

"I see no trees," Vansom said flatly.

"Perhaps you do not know what to look for," Rifter said, a careful rebuff in his voice. A quiet antagonism had grown between the two of them ever since Rifter's recovery and his refusal to side against Prav. To

Vilb's surprise, only Vansom, armed with sardonic humor, continued to doubt Prav while Rifter became, of all things, her staunchest ally going so far as to carry the girl up over the most difficult stretches of the path. Vek brought up the rear and remained silent, sullen, and on guard. Even so, Ledge, Oneira and even Vilb were happy to keep Rifter between them and the girl. Apparently Oneira put her faith and blind hope in the goodness of the gods. Vilb was not so sure. In fact, he was less sure in the goodness of the gods than ever before, in spite of what he had witnessed between the reath hutch and Rifter. Was it truly the Power of M? Had the gods worked through his hands, his hutch? Vilb had grave misgivings about the whole matter, but said nothing. The others had taken heart and had chosen to believe that, indeed, the gods were guiding them, but not all of the others were so sanguine in their faith.

"Don't trust Simon," Vansom had said their first night after Prav opened her Palm against Rifter.

"Shh," hissed Ledge. "Not now. Not here." If there was an Orthodox among them, it was Ledge. His devotion to the gods, to Pilgrimage, to Oneira, was complete.

Vansom barked back. "Do not shush me you simple- minded gray cloak." Vansom wore the purple srapi, as Oneira did and commanded all of the respect accorded the strata of the Meson's House. Vilb had long since forgotten about the social niceties of the Ubernaki, but now he remembered how deeply the Ubernaki accepted the reality of the strata. It structured every social relation from birth onward, and as a result the colors of the srapi became a feature and a function of the mind, as if the rocks themselves were ordered in a descending stair of importance and power, and though Vilb no longer believed in the strata, he was glad to see that he had inadvertently found at the base of the Stair—and since taken to wearing—the purple srapi. He had long since burned the brown srapi he had begun his hermitage with many suns ago. Ledge, on the other hand, wore the gray, only one strata above the brown and so obedience and servitude was sewn into his habiliment.

Prav on the other hand threatened to make unreal the strata every time she and Rifter caught up with the rest of the company. Rifter wore the gray, but on his back rode Prav. A bizarre and unsettling sight even for the hard of heart. This child two-skin, or whatever she was, wore the purple—pilfered from one of Vilb's caves. He had not marked it at the time and only now realized for the first time how unsettling the girl in purple must be for the others.

At the same time Vilb's situation was precarious at best, for they had mistaken him for a Healer-Meson, and though he denied it weakly, he wore the purple and this, more than any denial, was evidence of his position. It was a clear-cut crime against the strata, and if they were in Ubernaki territory he had no doubt that Ledge and Vansom would set aside their grudge and do their duty in regards to Vilb. Best not to let that happen, he thought, and remained silent, for now.

Oneira caught her wind, but slowly, and so she was still doubled over, her hands on her knees and she gulped air. "No, there are no trees," she finally managed, "not yet. But down there the way is more clear. Just climb down, and then, through," she said, and made a motion with her hand to indicate a graceful, speedy journey ahead. "The trees are beyond. And the grasses. And the water. And soon after Lake Vost, Simon's Great Way Station. There we will sit by the water and recover our strength. The gods have not abandoned us."

"What about that path?" Prav said suddenly from the rear, and she pointed up to where another narrow path continued not west but south and climbed away from the Twin Horns and higher into the Massif foothills.

"No," Oneira said, her face glowing with a light fever brought on by exertion and thirst, or perhaps madness Vilb thought. "We are almost through. I am certain. This way down and in a few more circs we..." but she could not finish. There was a pleading look in her eyes as if someone in need was calling to her and she must go to their rescue. "The Light of Simon," she managed finally. "I feared that I would not live to see it."

Oneira turned and began moving quickly down the path only to leave behind the hesitant company. She disappeared from view in a few moments as Ledge, breathing heavily, managed to catch Vilb's eye and they exchanged worried looks.

"This is not right," Prav said from the rear.

"I agree with the child," Rifter called out immediately.

"The way is too easy too quickly. We have not yet reached the path that leads us to the valley."

"And how would you know?" Vansom shot back.

Ledge turned to Vilb in Oneira's absence and then Vansom turned too and it seemed that they were all now waiting for his instructions.

"Someone must go and fetch Oneira," Vilb said suddenly.

He grabbed his sling and bolted down the path before Ledge could respond.

With waning strength Vilb stumbled as quickly as he could over the stony path and for a time he made good headway and the blue streak of the valley below appeared just before him. A moment later, however, and the boulder choke filled the path and he had to walk more slowly, picking his way, twisting an ankle and cursing Oneira mildly under his breath even as he marked consciously his desire for her. He had felt it from the beginning, and now that she was out of his sight he felt her absence keenly and wanted only to find her and walk beside her again.

Just then Vilb came to a fork in the path and he paused. He could hear Ledge, Vansom, Rifter, the girl and Vek coming up from behind, so he waited for a moment and considered the way. To the right the path became a narrow, even road that descended gently through a gulch and appeared to lead down to the valley. To his left the path climbed and continued wide, but rough and uneven. In her state Oneira almost certainly rushed down into the gulch, but from there he smelled a fulsome stench rising occasionally into his face. He would not go down that path but he feared Oneira may have.

To his left another path narrowed to an almost impassable width and turned back upon itself and headed not west but south, and up into a steep climb and looked to be a short hike to the top of a shoulder. Perhaps from there he might see below, into the reeking narrow, or perhaps, further beyond.

Both possibilities intrigued him, for even as he thought of Oneira, the thought struck him that from atop the shoulder he might see the glimmer of the Arclight. He had never seen the Arclight during the long day, and only its ambient green diffusion illuminated the long night in the Ubernaki east.

The climb up was steep and difficult. Committed now, however, he dropped to his hands and feet and crawled on until he reached a shoulder of the ridge, and from there he could, indeed, see into the narrow below. Oneira was nowhere in sight. Perhaps she was below, hidden by the deep shadow. He stared hard, but to no avail even as he scrabbled closer. He was breathing heavily and loudly now, so much so that the others surprised him when they appeared from behind, winded and disgruntled. Vilb managed only a moment to peer into the far west, but could discern no sign of the Arclight over the Great City. They had still far to travel.

▌▌

The thought of the flesh-hunters had not come to him for circs, consumed as he had been by the Pilgrimage and the strange company he found himself in, but now the thought possessed him completely. They were here.

"AkiGazi," said Vilb vehemently, and they all understood what this meant and dropped to the floor of the narrow path and pressed themselves against the rock. If the AkiGazi had Oneira, then they would almost certainly be looking for more, Ledge whispered. The AkiGazi knew that Pilgrims never traveled alone into the Massif.

Vilb risked raising his head and looked up the path as it climbed above the shoulder to the ridge's peak, and he realized in a panic that he had nowhere to go if another band of AkiGazi should suddenly descend upon him from above, and he began to scramble backwards on his hands and knees as quickly as he could go, a terror welling up inside him.

"Quickly," whispered Vilb, and pointed with his head that the others were to backtrack.

They crept backwards until they came to where the escarpment rose up and hid them from the narrow gulch below and so were less exposed, though they remained vulnerable to anyone coming up—or down—the path. Vilb was breathing heavily and so they paused there in order to catch wind. Vilb's heart pounded in his chest and at each deep intake of breath he exhaled Simon—intake—Simon—intake—Simon—intake—Simon, and so on until he had calmed himself down and breathed easier.

When in doubt, call His name.

"One of us," Vilb said through his breathing, "must go back up there and see what can be seen, but carefully. It's a dangerous climb up, and you may have to climb down some ways in order to find what you're looking for." Before any debate might ensue Ledge moved up the path.

Still on his stomach, he crawled back up the way they had just come and eased himself around the edge of the escarpment, to the very edge of the path, and then over. He disappeared head first, clambering into the gulch, and soon only his feet were left and they too followed the rest of him until only the sounds of Ledge scrabbling over loose stone testified to his presence.

The sun slid behind the southern peaks of the Massif and cast them all in cool, long shadows before Ledge returned, but finally he did return and he was covered in thick dust, his eyes bulging. There could be no mistake, he said. There were many figures and some movement below, and a fulsome stench.

"It's an AkiGazi trap. The path narrows and at the far end they've choked it off with a slide. Probably their own doing. There's no way through it. Oneira ran right into it. It's as if they knew a Pilgrimage was coming."

"Did you see her?" Vilb asked desperately.

Ledge let his head fall between his shoulders and Vilb's heart sank. "She's… I think she's with them. There were others down there, and they had them trapped where the path opens up between two narrow openings on either end. I saw large things in the shadows—perhaps what they call vasalur?—and maybe some Gazi," and here he dropped his voice, "and I think some Ubernaki Pilgrims… from… our procession."

"Our procession?" Vansom blurted out and Ledge nodded silently.

"How did they get here so fast?" Rifter asked.

"Vasalur," said Prav. "We cannot wait here. We have to keep going."

"Yes, I agree," said Vek from behind. Vilb turned. This was unusual. "They know these mountains," announced Vek from behind. "They must have other ways through, ways we do not know."

"Vasalur," Ledge said with disgust in his voice. "They give off an unholy stink. And there is a spring, I'm almost certain. When it quieted down I could hear the sounds of water. Faint, but I'm certain of it."

"But did you see Oneira?" Vilb demanded again. Something told him that Prav was right, that they had to keep going, that they were taking too long, but he would not leave Oneira behind. It was as if he had left her once and had learned this lesson, and would not leave her again. Though it made no sense, the feeling was palpable and one that he realized he could not and would not ignore.

Ledge shook his head. "No. It was in shadow. But she must be in with the rest. I heard a lot of voices and excitement.

It must be so." Ledge's face was drawn and distraught and Vilb felt a hopelessness seize him. "Now what?"

"We have to get out of here. They are certainly out looking for the rest of us," Prav said.

"Where is Vek?" Rifter asked suddenly. All three of them looked down the path from where they had climbed. Prav spoke up.

"He's gone to find the AkiGazi," she said smugly.

"What? Why would you say such a thing?" hissed Ledge.

Though humiliated by the silent, brooding Vek in countless petty ways since being thrown together, Vilb could hear that Ledge was prepared to defend his own people—however smug he may be—against the blasphemous words of a strange and dangerous child-thing dressed in purple no less. Surely Ledge must believe that the company had all but asked ill fortune to fall upon them for tolerating the girl's presence.

"Vek is Vansom's man," Prav went on, "and has no intention of going any further with us than the Spire Massif. Vek is waiting for Vansom back at the Gate."

This was obviously too much for Ledge. "You are mad," he hissed, and moved towards her as if to strike the girl. Vilb turned to Vansom.

"What of it?" he asked, gravel in his voice. "Is this true? What do you know of Vek?"

Prav held Ledge's gaze even as Vansom spoke.

"You believe what you must, but I believe Vek has merely headed back for the Gate. How could he betray us?"

"He worships Quadros Prang, that's why," said Rifter.

"And you are now a believer, is that it?" Vansom shot back.

"One little sleep and a dream and you know the gods, do you?"

"We do not have time now to discuss the whys and wherefores of Vek's religious imaginings," Vilb said impatiently.

"What can we do for Oneira?"

"We have to get down there," Ledge said. "But I don't know what we can do against the stone they have used to block the gorge.

"Yes, I agree," this from Prav, and Vilb felt the girl asserting herself and he felt strangely comforted by the gesture.

"I want to go to the top of this path," she said and without further debate she scrambled ahead, climbing over Vilb in the process, and took the lead with Rifter, silent and close behind.

Without another word Vilb decided to follow the girl though he had no clear sense of what they hoped to accomplish. Still, moving forward towards Oneira was, at least so far, better than remaining where they were.

They climbed, slowly, careful always to stay back from the edge of the precipice. Vilb set off after them in the hope that Ledge would, finally, follow and in a few moments Vilb heard the others scrambling over the stones behind him. They climbed the path and rose with it as it wound gently around the far side of the ridge, until at the southern end of the ridge the path dropped off suddenly to a sheer drop into a gulch below.

"Who fashioned these stairs?" Ledge wondered aloud.

"AkiGazi stairs," Prav declared, though how she knew

Vilb did not understand. The girl leaned over the edge and peered into the valley below. "They drop down to the gulch floor on the other side of the AkiGazi camp."

"When did they have time to carve such stairs?" asked Ledge, fear and disbelief in his voice.

"Perhaps they camp here only when they suspect a procession is on the way," Vilb offered, though from the looks of things it appeared that the camp had been in place for some time, probably suns, and quite probably many suns. It made sense, though he still didn't understand why the AkiGazi had come, but that they had come was incontrovertible even to Vilb's tentative awareness. He had seen their fires on the plateau not long ago. Perhaps they had been in the east for much longer. Perhaps they had been collecting up Pilgrims for as many suns. The thought sent a horror through him.

Was it an extended hunt?

This was a possibility. The vasalur provided a long reach for AkiGazi hunters. Perhaps drought explained it after all, Vilb decided. Yes. Perhaps drought had driven them south to more fertile fields. Was it merely hunger that drove the AkiGazi so far from home, in such a desolate and forsaken region even in the best of times, here, in the shadows of the Spire Massif?

"We have to climb down," Prav said firmly, "and be careful on these stairs. The AkiGazi are not masters of stone work."

With that she dropped to her knees and let her feet over the side to the first step, and then slowly down the rough-hewn rock feet-first, her face towards the escarpment.

Vilb ventured a panoramic glance all around him before he began to climb down, so rare and stark a view he had never seen. Looking west, the round disc of the sun rested in the saddle between the Twin Horns, up-thrusts of jagged obsidian guarded the west from all but the most desperate travelers. To the east the foothills of Spire Massif tumbled into the plateau and moraine and talus and trough melted away into the flat line of the eastern plateau beyond.

And somewhere to the east and north was his insignificant hill.

He slung his pack and wound his sling tight against his body, dropped to his knees, onto his stomach and slithered backward over the edge and to the first step.

Into the gloom they dropped and finally reached the floor of the gulch. There it was cool and still, the air fresh for the first time since coming upon the AkiGazi, and Vilb felt tempted to push on, to leave the flesh-hunters—

and Oneira—behind, and head down the open, even path before him. He looked at Ledge but he showed no signs of such thoughts. "We must move the stones," Prav said, staring into the shadow.

"Do not be ridiculous," Ledge hissed and Vilb nodded.

"Perhaps if we signal to her Oneira might be able to climb over."

"If we move the choke we can recover Oneira and the AkiGazi's vasalur. If we did," Prav went on, anticipating angry rebukes, "they could get us to the fertile valleys of San Simon in ten circs rather than sixty. But first we have to move the boulders."

"Enough of this madness!" Vilb cried. "I do not want to hear you speak again. Do you hear me? You must be silent. Silent," he demanded, and moved towards her. "I would sooner ride you than one of those foul creatures. Even now their stink makes me sick." Vilb looked around wildly, his hopelessness besting him.

Prav grabbed Vilb's srapi and pulled him down so that he had to kneel in order to avoid falling over onto the girl. She brought her face close to his. "Vilb!" she cried. "Wake up!" She slapped him hard across the face and the power of the blow toppled him onto his back, his legs twisted painfully under him. He felt hurt and surprised rather than angry, and he brought a hand to his stinging face. She moved forward and tried to place one of her palms against his temple, but he pushed her away and scrambled backwards.

"We must hurry!" the girl pleaded. "Do you not yet understand? This is the work of Quadros Prang. He is searching for all like you," and at this Prav looked from Vilb to Vansom. "He has already seduced Vek and no doubt has heard, or will hear shortly, that the reath hutch has been found and is coming to him even now." She paused and waited for her words to sink in and then she went on quietly. "Quadros Prang seeks to destroy the gods, and Little Earth, and all of Simon's children."

Vilb remained silent, still dazed by the force of the blow.

"Move the boulders if you can then," Vilb managed coldly while massaging his jaw. "And do not strike me again." Prav, once child-like, now behaved as if she were an adult of significant experience, and the shift in her character bemused and astounded Vilb.

"Step back, the four of you, far down the path," she commanded, and she backed them up twenty paces and then turned and walked towards the boulders. Rifter hesitated until Prav gave him a reassuring pat on the hand and said something quietly to him that only he could hear.

"Come on," Vilb whispered to Ledge after Prav was almost out of sight. "I am wondering that she may be able to do this. Remember Rifter?"

"I am almost certain that she cannot do it," Ledge grumbled along with Vansom. "You go and let me know what happens."

Vilb nodded silently and followed Prav at a distance. The girl had already made it into the narrow corridor of stone and he could just make out her small figure leaning against a particularly large boulder at the base of the pile.

He squinted into the gloom and crept closer. It appeared as if the girl was speaking to the rock as she leaned against it, and then she dropped to her hands and knees and began to dig along the base of the heap. Vilb moved forward quickly and was soon by her side.

"What are you doing?" he whispered.

"I am digging a trench" she said, her small hands working feverishly in the hard soil. "What did you expect?"

"I... I don't know." Vilb cocked his head back and surveyed the pile to the highest stone.

"Hey," Prav whispered. "I am waiting for you."

"What?"

"You must move the stones," she said. Vilb looked up again.

"No," he said, laughing quietly and shaking his head. "You have the... the," and he waved his open palm at her. "You know."

"The Millennial Palm," she said. "Yes, well, it may suffice, though to conduct such power would certainly kill me and I am not prepared to die. Not here, my friend. You are the one who must conduct the Power of M."

Suddenly angry, Vilb crouched next to her.

"Before you say anything," she said, "open the reath hutch."

He eyed her suspiciously until curiosity overmatched him and he withdrew the heavy hutch from the bottom of his sling. Carefully he untied the sinew that bound it and then spread it open before the two of them.

"The *remains*," she said solemnly. "These are what Quadros Prang seeks, and you and your... family history. The Martha too, but she can only wait and hope that you find her."

Vilb did not understand. "What history? Whose remains?"

But Prav shook her head. "We do not have time for a history lesson. Now, you must channel the Power of M."

Vilb stood up as perplexed anger surged within. His face became a caldera of seething confusion and fear. He had had enough of this girl's madness.

Prav, on the other hand, seemed unperturbed. She had returned her attention to digging a furrow across the path and along the base of the dam of stones even as Vilb churned and sputtered over her.

"Very well," she said. "I'll be as brief as I can. The gods, each in their own turn, greatly seek this thing you carry. All seek it, yet all fear it for it is the key to Simon's Restoration. At one time long ago these bones belonged to her. They grew within her, because of Quadros… and The Martha hid them with her children in the hopes that they would never be found, or that if they were, she would control them. Master Qir has sent me and others like me to aid The Martha in her exile and to thwart Quadros Prang's plan. You and I are a part of an endgame that comes long before us. We are puppets, you and I. The servants of the gods." And still the girl's hands worked the ground drawing pictures.

Vilb stepped closer and rubbed his temple and Prav made no sign except to keep digging and talking.

"Master Qir is willing to aid the Restoration of Simon, though it means quite probably the destruction of the Four and the Power of M assumed by the One we call Simon. With it He will draw together and heal Little Earth—or destroy it in His wrath. A great scouring is feared, for Simon is almost certainly not pleased with the gods. Will you serve Him?" And still her furrowing hands scraped at the earth.

"Serve who?" Vilb was thoroughly bewildered now.

"Simon, the Lord your God!"

Vilb shook his head, dumbfounded. Madness and myth, he thought, a legend that should have been forgotten would not die.

"Look here. All along this furrow I want you to take out the *remains* and lay them end to end."

Vilb looked at the glowing tools and the freshly dug furrow and shook his head. "These are weaving tools, nothing more." Vilb backed up and sat on his haunches, pulling at his beard and knocking two red stones together. "What… what do you want from me?"

"Not my wanting," she said, and Vilb remained still. Prav stood up and moved quickly before him, grabbing his srapi so that she was gazing into his face. Before he could ward her off she pressed her palm against his temple and he felt an explosion in his brain that momentarily stunned him, left his head cleared, absolutely silent, black, with only his awareness floating bodiless and empty, in a great silence.

"There," she said and stepped in close to him. "Listen."

She placed one hand on the back of his head and the other over his chest. "Do not speak," she said, her mouth close to the top of his head, and then she knelt down, still holding his head in her hands, and whispered into his chest something he could not make out, and then she drew a long emerald needle from his temple.

Vilb took a deep breath, rose to his feet and staggered.

It was then that the voice, as if making up for prior absences, exploded in his mind.

Destroy the girl! Save yourself!

Vilb felt a splitting ache over his left eye.

She is the abomination of the gods! Do not let her lead you to the demon Prang! Take the hutch and flee!

No response rose up in him. Vilb held his head in his hand. He could feel Prav standing close by, and he opened his eyes to take her in. She appeared to him as if she were a distant image seen from afar, without definite limits or boundaries or detail. Waving, reflecting, almost transparent. Yet it was Prav, a series of glowing rings circling her, emerald light shone from each and bathed her in an iridescent, sea green. He reached out to wrap his arms around Prav but she stepped away and avoided his grasp.

"Vilb," said the girl quietly. "Oneira needs you. Help her. For the love of Simon."

The ground spun and pitched beneath him and Vilb felt his stomach lurch and twist. A wave of nausea sickened him and he vomited. The girl dribbled cool water onto his face, his burning forehead, his acid mouth.

"I do not know anything," Vilb croaked.

"Open the hutch." Prav's face had come back to itself, round, glowing, a slight emerald tinge to her cheeks. Her green eyes now appeared like two obsidian points, reflecting nothing. She held her place and no longer wavered, and Vilb moaned and waited for a particularly intense, stabbing pain to pass through the center of his chest.

Prav was standing over him now, her face stern, but not unkind. "You are no one. You have not been chosen. You are one of many, any one of which could have found the hutch, could be with me now, just as I am one of many, any one of which could be with you now. The timing is all, do you see? We are not special. We are not chosen. We are pawns. We do as we are instructed to do."

The girl made sense, but Vilb's suns in meditation had taught him that every proposition might be turned on its head and made equally true. "Yet what we are doing now happens to us, now, in this time," Vilb said, his mind grinding on in spite of it all. "This makes us... chosen, special. Time. This moment." He rubbed his temple.

Prav threw her head back and laughed. "As you wish!"

Vilb rose to his knees, still one hand across his chest. Sweat and soil seeped into his left eye. He breathed quickly in short, shallow bursts. The hutch lay before him and he took a slower, deeper breath and reached for it. His hands, in spite of their shaking, carefully untied the sinew binds. He felt feverish and light-headed.

My son, my son, do not do this deed!

"Ignore him," said Prav. "The voice in your mind seeks only to abuse you and use you for purposes other than Simon's Will."

"Levinthal?" Vilb asked tentatively and Prav nodded.

"He meddles in the work of the gods, though he is no god himself, yet he seeks the Power of M but do not let him have it!"

"Oneira," said Vilb, and the hutch was open now and he extended his palm over the tools. Not satisfied with this, he placed both hands over the tools, palms down, just above them. His hands began to tremble more violently and he spread his fingers wide. Beads of sweat broke out on his forehead and his breathing became louder.

"I cannot do this!" he exclaimed suddenly. "Whatever happened was not of my doing and now I am supposed to call on the Power of M, but I cannot. I cannot." Vilb dropped his hands and lay his head back down on the stone.

"Perhaps what you say is true," Prav said. Of course it's true, he thought. "Perhaps we should move on, leave Oneira and the others in there to whatever fate Simon has prepared for them. Gutted and skinned I would imagine. Not unlike what your tribe does to the dead, eh?" A look of judgment so harsh and withering came from her that Vilb felt as if he had to shield himself from it or suffer some horrible consequence.

"I do not eat the flesh!" he retorted, his eyes narrow and sheathed. He waved her away weakly.

"I think you do," Prav said and walked back into the narrows. "Back to Vansom, then," she said. "Perhaps he can open the hutch and draw on the Power of M. Or perhaps Vek and his AkiGazi might find it useful. They each, like you, are attuned to the *remains*."

"Wait," he called out. Not Vek, thought Vilb, and certainly not Vansom that Ubernaki gray-cowl. "Come back," he said weakly, and in a moment the girl was standing over him, her arms folded and on her face a peculiar look of satisfaction and expectation.

"Do not think," she said.

"What would you have me do then?"

"Surrender."

"To... to..."

"To the Power of M. You must surrender."

"I do not understand." He sounded pathetic, even to his own ears.

"Oneira does not need you to understand. She needs you to call upon the Power of M!" As if anticipating Vilb's actions before he knew what they were, Prav backed off a few paces even as Vilb lifted himself to his feet, the reath hutch spread out before him. It was then that thoughts of Oneira rose up within him and he felt a tenderness and a longing for the woman, a sadness for his isolation, and a desire for her strength and familiar beauty to be beside him. Together they could make the Pilgrimage.

Vilb's eyes fell on the needle, a long bone except for a loop on one end large enough to put his thumb through. He found it in his hand before he could remember having picked it up and he placed it without second thought on his chest, the loop over his solar plexus, needle descending down. He then lifted the next tool most like it, only this had two thin shafts connected to a larger loop—the tweeze he called it—and he linked the loops together and placed them pointing upwards, the sharp points coming up to his throat. The others he linked in a ringlet, his hands knowing precisely how to form it, and he placed it on his head like a crown. In each hand he held a scallop-shaped bone tight against his palms.

"I have no idea what I am doing," he said.

• • •

"Bury them. Bury the dead. That's it. Yes. Good." The girl was excited, pacing back and forth. "Do it. We're almost done." Vilb shook his head, still unconvinced. "Hurry," she said. He looked down at the girl, moved to one end of the furrow and began to push the loose soil with his foot. In a moment he had covered the length of the furrow.

"Stand on the loosened earth," Prav said, "and place your palms against the largest stone." Vilb nodded and did as he was told without complaint. A strange feeling had come over him, as if he were large, larger than the stones before him, and at the same time he was the stones that blocked his way.

The line of light was no wider than Vilb's smallest finger, but there it was, a shimmering, green glow around his hands that began to pulsate, and then suddenly it blazed white and it seemed that his hands and the stone had become fused into the blazing whiteness. At the same time a deep thrumming filled the air and resonated up through his feet and into his body. His hands and knees felt as if they had rooted themselves to the ground, or, really, had become the very stuff of the ground.

All around his hands the glowing spread forward and back along the ground and up into the lowest, largest boulders of the barrier, and then these too began to glow white hot. The pile of stones shifted almost imperceptibly, and then there was no mistaking what happened next. The stones began to slump, incrementally at first, and then with gathering speed, into a molten slag of its own melting. A blast of blinding heat knocked him backward and he shielded his face as he clambered away on all fours.

"The Power of M!" the girl cried, transfixed by the blazing, molten gap that had opened at the foot of the barrier. Vilb could not move without tremendous effort, made all the more difficult by the white heat that poured out of the molten ground. He swooned again and dropped his head to the ground and waited to be consumed.

It was then that a vision took hold of him, a waking dream, but one that he had never experienced before.

In this waking dream he could see Little Earth from high above and below him was the Arclight and the great stone city of San Simon, raised by the Power of M long ago. It was a vast work and it angered him and he came down from the sky a massive figure and knelt down and pounded the Great City with a massive fist and smashed the works of the gods until nothing was left but a reeking abyss. Into this hole he channeled the sea and the waters rushed in.

In the next instant he strode to the east and saw that his body stood taller than the Twin Horns, and he knew then it was not he who walked the land but Simon Himself, the living God of Stone filled with a towering wrath, and even to the core of the world His rage reached and found fuel and drew the inner fires of Little Earth into Him and through Him and his gaze fell across the sea to the Fourth Realm.

Three strides carried Him from the heart of Little Earth to the coasts far to the Gazi east. He smashed with one foot the Spire Massif and shattered the Twin Horns to their roots as he passed. With a hand He scooped out another vast pit to the north, where the AkiGazi homeland once was, and with his other he dug a channel to the Girdling Sea and caused a cataract to sweep the north and to scour Little Earth clean, perfect and lifeless and then He brought back the cold and buried the land in ice and He saw that it was good.

"**D**evilments and bedevilment!" Vilb muttered and went on muttering as he came to himself. He felt a strange and powerful sense of betrayal left over from his vision. He was afraid as well to open his eyes for what he might see. When he did finally open them, the bedeviling light and heat had passed, the air was cool and the shadows had returned to the gulch floor. Where the massive wall of stones had rested the way was now clear, the ground now a smooth, smoldering surface of igneous blackness shimmering with emerald.

"Great power," the girl said from above him, obviously pleased.

Vilb rose to his knees and waited for his equilibrium to return. He felt a trickle run down his left cheek and his left ear felt clogged and sodden. He wiped at it. Blood. "You want my skin, is that it? "

"Perfect power," she said in response.

Vilb heard a voice call out from deeper into the canyon.

"Here!" And then another. "For the love of Simon!" It was Rifter's voice. Vilb could see him coming towards him, and he held the unconscious Oneira in his arms. Another woman followed.

"She sleeps," Ledge said. "An AkiGazi poison."

Vilb turned and looked for Prav. His head was light and he felt as if his feet were having a difficult time remaining in contact with the earth. "I do not understand what has happened," he mumbled and looked for Prav. Perhaps she might understand his vision, his dream, his terror. But Prav was with Rifter filling water skins at the AkiGazi spring.

"Is there anyone else?" Ledge called out to Rifter and Vansom.

"One of the AkiGazi. A young boy. I hit him hard with a rock. He's there." Vansom pointed to where the boy's body lay, tumbled like a collection of loose sticks.

"Get him. We need him. Any others?" said Prav.

"No. They must have fled when... the stone began to... melt. They left three vasalur behind."

"Good. Go and invite them to join us," Prav requested, but it was more than a request. It was a claim on leadership. In a few moments the group had recovered all that they could carry from the AkiGazi encampment and were setting off down the open path for the Twin Horns. Two of the vasalur allowed Rifter to sling the unconscious AkiGazi boy and the sleeping Oneira across their backs and they quickly headed down the path. They were large beasts that walked on all four. Their forelegs and hind legs looked curiously like the arms and legs of a man, only longer, thicker, stronger. Their large heads had elongated faces, small eyes and small mouths and protruding noses, and their skin was white, drained of all color, and it was not they who stank, but the refuse in which the AkiGazi camped. Rifter lifted Vilb to his feet and moved on while Vilb lingered to the rear and paused on the now hard and cool surface of the gulch floor.

Where were the remains? He turned his palms up and carefully regarded his hands. They had become almost like stone. His fingers moved as before, and his skin was as before, yet not as before.

"Dear Martha protect me," he said, and he shuddered.

The once pale green tinge of his palms was now the color of the rusted stone all around him, almost orange with flecks of golden sunlight dancing along the length of the lines that crossed his palms, and he felt himself as a substance both heavy and light.

As he raised his eyes and lowered his hands to his sides, Prav was there. "Now you must be careful to never let them touch the earth," she said. "You carry the seeds of a new world," and she smiled as if pleased beyond measure.

"I do not understand," Vilb managed. "I… you… what is this? What am I… carrying?"

Prav looked up at him and for the first time he saw a sadness gather around her eyes. He felt himself held there and carried for a moment before she broke away.

"I am the desolation of the land," she said quietly. "I am the scourge of M." She held out her palm as if to have him inspect it and he felt his hand drawn to it and expand as if it were a water skin suddenly over-full and ready to burst. "You carry the means and I am the end." With that she headed out after the others leaving Vilb alone, perplexed beyond measure, exhausted and thirsty. He had a long struggle to catch up with the light-footed girl.

IV

Not until they stopped did Vilb dare to come upon the company, shambling through the group, most of which had thrown themselves to the ground, too exhausted to make camp. Prav had a strange power over all of them. Her will kept them marching faster and farther than any single one of them would attempt. Vilb moved towards Oneira and sank beside her. Prav was curled up nearby in a ball beneath a boulder. Vilb crawled over to her and stroked her forehead. The girl breathed quietly, already deeply asleep.

Oneira nodded and smiled wanly at Vilb. She was finally awake. He took her hand in his. "All that I prepared for no longer exists," she declared quietly. "We are a grotesque procession. The Gazi, the AkiGazi, Ubernaki, the vasalur, a dead man and… and," but she could not finish even as she gestured towards Vilb, or the girl, or both. Her voice died out, the contempt too much to hide in her state of exhaustion.

"And you? Who are you?" Vilb sat beside her but released her hand. Oneira turned away from him.

"I have not the slightest idea. Who am I?" She was angry, indignant. A light flared up in her green eyes and Vilb's heart beat harder. "I am at a loss, utterly, as never before. I know nothing about anything. All of my former knowledge has become useless." He took her hand in his again and held it. It was dry, weathered, sculpted by wind and sun and stone, and it was warm and it was living.

Vilb exhaled sharply. "Prav believes that Little Earth is dying. She tells me that the cold is coming. Only Simon can save us, but first we must save Simon."

"Cold?" asked Oneira, ignoring all the rest.

Vilb thought for a moment how to explain. "Like a dead fire. Ashes. Void of light and heat. But the whole world."

"Death is cold," Oneira said, nodding.

Vilb nodded. "The Arclight is fire. The sun is fire. What would happen if the fires were cold. Soon the air and the land will become like the gray, empty ash after the fire. Cold."

"I do not know," Oneira said, but she had turned to him and was listening.

"The cold will be everywhere, and there will be nowhere, nowhere any of us can go to escape it. It will slow the blood, and then flesh will die. Like stone. This will take only a short time, and then Little Earth will be as lifeless and barren as it once was," and Vilb added quickly, "according to the girl."

"But you believe her? You believe that you will save Simon? What blasphemy is this?"

Vilb did not have the heart to speculate with her about who he thought he was, or Simon, or the other gods for that matter. It was too much to put into words.

"I don't know what I believe," he said finally, quietly, and he gripped her hand more firmly and placed his other on top of it. "But I feel ready to do anything."

"What do you mean?"

Vilb looked up and nodded. "Indeed it seems that Simon does speak."

"But do you believe it?" she asked. "Has *He* returned?"

"I do not know," Vilb said, and he dropped his head and pulled up his knees, a painful self-consciousness having come over him.

"You don't believe what?" she demanded, but he had stopped listening to her as a realization dawned on him slowly.

"I've got a long journey in front of me," he let out softly, as if not to damage the idea. Oneira let out an unwilling moan and then recovered herself. "It is all nonsense," she said, and let out a burst of hysterical laughter. "It is all stories meant to tame children!"

"I know. I know. The other Seven Realms exist beyond the Girdling Sea. The future. The gods. All stories." Oneira rose to her feet. "What does this word mean? The future?"

"It means... many sleeps from now." Vilb paused and tried again. "It means to think about the long day to come after the long night." Oneira looked down at him and took in the sleeping Prav as if deciding.

"You are mad," she said quietly. "And I am sorry for you. I am. And I am sorry for all of us. Life on Little Earth is difficult. Dust. Drought. It all makes life even more difficult. The AkiGazi do what they must to survive, yet they make life difficult as well, and then there are other unknown things. Sickness. The gods." She moved to go, dismissive now and distant.

"Don't," he cried. "I cannot go on without you! Already I have come to rely on your strength." He grabbed her for a moment by the shoulders, then released her and grabbed at his own ears. "I am losing my mind, yes!" he cried, fell to his knees and grabbed at her srapi. "Yet do you not carry that same madness within you? Is it not madness to deny what you have felt, what you have seen, and what you continue to see in your dreams?" He rose up and strode away, turned quickly back at her, pointing: "How is it that we can have similar dreams? You and I, and the rest of us?"

"This proves nothing. Everyone has similar dreams. It has always been this way." She shook her head.

"But why?" Vilb stabbed a finger towards her. "Why do we not all have our own dreams? How is it that we are all so... so..." but words left him and he came up short, his hands open before him, empty, but shimmering gold and orange.

"That is not a real question." Oneira turned away again and silence fell between them.

Oneira began to pace before him, slowly at first, and as she walked she sighed deeply and spoke.

"I know that the AkiGazi worship Quadros Prang. I know that flesh eating in the east has become the way of life for generations of our people. I know that this was not always so. Why have things come to be this way? I fear the gods have forsaken us."

Vilb reeled backward for an instant. The Question. It was his. And now he saw that it was hers as well. Why have things come to be this way?

Oneira talked as if she were stunned. Here eyes went wide, staring at the ground near the sleeping Prav. "The AkiGazi pray to Quadros. We know this. They seek power, domination in his name. For Quadros. Against The Martha. Our spies—Vek, who may have been one of them—tell us this."

"But what does it mean?"

"The AkiGazi have enslaved the Gazi peoples. Quadros Prang grows the grasses that the Gazi eat. The AkiGazi eat the Gazi." A perfect food chain. The AkiGazi wish to domesticate the entire eastern population of Little Earth and expand into San Simon. Quadros Prang will be Lord of Little Earth. So we have heard. They say…" and here her voice dropped to a deeper bass, "he visits them. He floats among them and He teaches them and He protects them and they learn to thrive in the small circles of the high sun. They are hungry too. We hear much of this. And where is The Martha? How can she allow Quadros Prang to do this to Her children?" Oneira dropped next to Vilb, her face twisted in agonized confusion. She looked at Vilb, her eyes pleading and the moment was new, yet familiar, unique, yet ancient and somehow Vilb knew that he had known Oneira, if only in some dream he could not remember having had. Her lower lip trembled and for a moment it seemed she was about to sink into him, but in the next her eyes closed and she straightened herself.

"We have to go forward. I don't know how I know but I know that time is running out. We must get to the Great City. I have to believe that the gods, at least The Martha, will hear our prayer."

Vilb looked into Oneira's face and beheld a churning sea of pain and confusion. She shook her head. How could he go back? Yet what did it mean to go forward?

"Let's follow the girl to the plains beyond the mountains. Lake Vost is not far and perhaps we will see, you and I, what Pilgrims of old beheld. Yes?"

"I'll follow you to Lake Vost," she said finally. "At least to there. The others, I'm afraid have already left us."

He leaned towards her. "What is this life?" he whispered, and a smile threatened one corner of his mouth.

"Weeping… dust." She looked back down the path to where the others rested, her eyes wet and shining. She trembled.

Vilb nodded. "But nothing more?"

"Voices," Oneira said finally. "Voices in my head."

The Hanging Garden

I

Vilb crouched down low at the top of the sand ridge that overlooked the long, straight Pilgrim's path. Before him the wide road flew like an arrow into the west and, in some places, shone a pearly white as he had heard. Perhaps dust had settled on the road, or perhaps the stone had crumbled in places and lost its luster, but Vilb could discern no dark patches of vegetation. He had hoped that there might be some indication of the fecundity of the gods beyond the Spire Massif, but not yet. He sighed deeply but took heart in the fact of the path. There it was. It was real. The gods, then, too. Mustn't they be real as well?

What other fearful power could have made such a path? Vilb's heart throbbed. Only the Power of M could make a path so unflinchingly straight and wide—this had to be the work of the gods.

"Yes," said Prav suddenly standing behind him, as if hearing his thoughts. "This is the work of the Ancients, those who gave birth to the gods. The Martha's highway they called it, but her highway ends here. She could never finish her way to the east. Not as she had hoped. It's all a great failure, you see. You and all the rest of her children. But still she hopes for your return. She waits for it. She waits for one like you."

Like me, Vilb thought. But not me. He shook his head, nonplussed by the girl's strange insights.

Further still, to the south and west a dark shadow interrupted the flat desert glare. "Lake Vost," said Prav. Vilb nodded. He'd heard that The Book of M recorded the greatness of the Lake and the grandeur of its acropolis, first devoted to Simon, then razed and rebuilt to the Archer of the Great City after Simon's Scattering.

Vilb groaned and felt his stomach move painfully inside him. Something down there filled him with trepidation yet now more than ever there was no going back, yet going forward felt as if he were falling into oblivion.

"Why have you brought me here? Why have you done this to me? To her? To the rest of this Pilgrimage?" Vilb turned on Prav and felt a fury rising in him. He picked up a handful of earth, rubbed the dust between his palms and moved towards the girl. She stepped back slowly, both palms towards Vilb.

Just then the wind gusted and he shivered. Cold. Yes, cold, Prav's voice echoed his own mind. And so it begins.

A small, dawning realization, an intuition really, for he had no experience to verify, only a feeling, a sense, but what he sensed he knew to be true as if he had lived through it once before. If this were just the beginning, his srapi would be no comfort soon. He shook and felt bitten by a series of chilling gusts that passed quickly, leaving him suddenly spent. He shivered and his teeth clattered against each other.

Vilb shuddered as another gust whipped his srapi. "I don't understand," he cried into the wind. It was more of a plea than a declaration. Prav stared at him, a smile curling the edge of her mouth.

"You will. Soon. I promise you." Prav moved urgently towards him and grabbed his elbow. As she gripped him a painful jolt surged into his arm and from there through to the tips of his fingers until in another moment his toes tingled and the muscles in his face popped and jumped with spasms. In the next instant he felt warm and clear headed. His anger and fear left him just as suddenly as it had come upon him. The wind quieted and Vilb felt as he always had before. He looked at the girl with a mix of gratitude, awe and fear.

"I will call the others up and we will continue."

"To Lake Vost," Prav said. "But I warn you. The gods wage an elemental war for Little Earth and Lake Vost may be held by the enemy."

Vilb let his head fall.

"Which enemy?" asked Ledge as he came up from behind.

Vansom was there. Prav would say no more and Vilb could only wonder if she meant AkiGazi, or worse.

"Worse," she said, and slipped over the ridge and began her descent.

II

I t took the company three more circles of the sun to clamber down out of the mountains and into the foothills, and there they found a narrow path that allowed easier progress and from there they made rapid progress over the last foothills of the Spire range. By the fourth circ the girl, Oneira, Vilb and the others were moving almost at a trot. The vasalur seemed impervious to fatigue though the AkiGazi boy strapped to its back did not survive the trip over the mountains.

"It is just as well," said Vansom, hearing the news of the young man's death. "His flesh may be our best hope." Vilb shuddered and let the company do as they had always done with the bodies of the dead.

• • •

An urgency was upon them all, for fear of hunger, thirst, cold and AkiGazi drove them on. Three circs west of the Spire Massif and at last they crested what proved to be the last foothill and looked down upon a wide plain of scrub and yellow grasses. Vilb gasped at the sight. He had not seen this from above. So much vegetation, even desiccated and wind tossed, he had not found for a dozen suns and the fragrance of the growth filled him with a renewed sense of hope. In spite of their rag-tag procession, they had made progress, and now the vegetation promised water. Perhaps he might risk a little hope after all. Perhaps the Fertile Plains were still fertile.

Even as he let his mind wonder about such things Prav stopped as they reached the crest of the last hill and the great western plain opened below them. She pointed and Oneira gasped. "What is it?" Vilb asked.

"There," she said, and the others gathered around. Beyond the plains of grass there was what appeared to be a field of rich green vegetation. The path would take them directly towards it, for it seemed to block their way, running far into the east and to the north.

"It is a forest," said Prav, and her voice was filled with wonder and confusion. "This was not here before." "Before when?" Oneira asked.

"Before, when I traveled to the east from San Simon." "How can one so small and young have traveled so much of Little Earth?" asked Ledge, incredulous.

"She is not a child," whispered Vansom into Vilb's ear, well back from where Prav stood facing west. "She is a goolak, or worse." Vilb shook his head and stepped out from between the vasalur's white flank and Vansom's hissing.

"Worse," said Prav flippantly, apparently overhearing Vansom's remark, yet she seemed ultimately unconcerned by his words, and she turned and faced Vilb. Oneira stepped up beside him.

"Quadros Prang holds Lake Vost," she said flatly. "To go forward is to fall into his hands, and to go back is to be overcome by AkiGazi. We have only these two choices before us."

"How can you know this?" cried Vansom. Prav shrugged. "Can we not go around this... forest?" asked Ledge. "The Great City is still a very long way. Perhaps..." but his voice died away.

"There is no other way but forward or back," said the girl, finality in her voice.

"I cannot go back," said Oneira. "I promised my people that I would bring back the help of the gods. I cannot go back empty handed, and I will not be captured by... anyone... again."

"I will not go back either," said Vilb, and at this Prav smiled.

"Good. That is good. What of the rest of you?" asked the girl. Ledge hung his head but finally spoke up. "I will not leave the Quarter-Meson."

Vansom spat and Ledge gasped at his waste of water.

"I will not go further and I will not go back," said Vansom resolutely.

"What of you?" asked Prav again, and the company turned and looked at one another, unsure of who she was asking, but Vilb finally understood that she was looking at the vasalur and expecting to be answered.

The beast pawed at the ground and shook his head back and forth as if made uncomfortable by the girl's attention.

They stood that way for many long moments until Vansom said, "It is only a beast," but his voice rose as if he were asking a question. Vilb looked to the girl and back to the vasalur.

"Very well," said the girl, and she turned to Vansom. "He will bear you where you wish to go. Perhaps you might find the edge of the forest and meet us at San Simon. Or perhaps you might find his people in the north. Or your own beyond and behind us."

Vansom hung his head, shamed by this sudden and unexpected act of generosity.

"Very well. I will go back and warn our people," he said, speaking directly to Oneira. She nodded silently, accepting his words but giving them no more than the barest acknowledgement.

• • •

The procession parted and the girl, Vilb, Oneira and Ledge moved forward towards the forest. As they advanced Vilb could feel the air growing warmer even as the blue of the sky deepened. Above them the low riding sun burned with an emerald halo as he had once seen it as a boy. For a long circ they walked, but finally Vilb's heart raced when he spied the top of some great temple rise from behind the forest. He had almost forgotten about Pilgrimage, and here before him was one of the first, great signs of its reality. Here was the palace and the gardens of The Martha, the Pilgrim's Way Station of long past. He hadn't dared to hope that a place for the weary, dirty, thirsty Pilgrim yet existed in these drought times. But even then he checked himself. The girl had said that Quadros Prang now held power here. But what could such a thing mean?

The fragrance in the air struck Vilb most profoundly as they approached the forest-garden of the gods. The stink of life and death accosted his nostrils and made him gasp. It was heavy, he felt saturated by it and he wrung his hands against his srapi as if to wipe them dry. But they would not dry. It was familiar, yet unknown, this strange odor, this close grip of wet and smell and decay. The vegetation of the Ubernaki plains had never supported anything so... so fertile, not even in the growing seasons. It was nauseating and exhilarating and befuddling all at once.

They trotted over a gentle incline and descended towards the green wall of the forest-garden. It was a massive wall of leaf, vine, bark and bower, and it rose up before them high over their heads. It blocked the way completely, for there was no way into the thick growth and apparently no end in sight in either direction.

All except the girl approached as close as they dared. It was more than a forest, rather, it was a great hanging canopy, the living suspending the living in a great tangled fecundity that left Vilb gasping, sputtering and laughing with amazement. He peered in and caught glimpses of open areas, cool shaded glens, and he thought he heard the sound of water running with power and volume. Vilb edged in closer, the only thought in his mind to rest against one of the many living pillars that held up the garden and made the shade. The damp odor of the vegetation was no longer making him gasp. It seemed to be the most delicious breathing he had ever done. What was that stuff he was breathing before? Could it be called air? His entire body seemed to expand, the flesh on his arm seemed to gain buoyancy. His chest expanded and remained more upright.

Next to him Oneira gasped and mumbled a prayer to The Martha. Ledge was running up and down the length of the forest-garden wall, his eyes wide in wonder.

"It's true," Vilb said at last. "Do you see?"

"I see... this." Her hand trembled as she gestured towards the impasse.

"The gods are real," was all Vilb could say.

"You see now, you see," said Prav. Sure and confident. She was pulling at both of their hands, leading them down the garden wall.

"Listen," she said, and she giggled. It was a strange sound to Vilb's ears, not one he had ever heard before, and he pulled his hand away. "Listen," she said again and clapped her hands together quickly. Vilb heard it too, somewhere in the dark greenery, it was the sound of voices. He shuddered.

"Is He here?" Oneira whispered. Ledge strode up, breathless.

"Can we enter?" he cried, and a fey mood seemed to be upon him.

Prav had run up ahead to a dark opening in the garden wall.

"There!" hissed Vilb.

Oneira stopped, suddenly terrified. "I do not want to go in." She looked around for a way to escape but quickly surrendered for there was no way back and no way forward. Ledge ran ahead to catch the girl and Vilb began after him but stopped short and looked back at Oneira. She had fallen behind and was not moving. He looked quickly round again to Prav and Ledge who were making fast progress towards the opening and he felt the urge to keep up.

"Are you not tired?" Vilb cried out, hoping that she would come towards him, but she remained still. He turned back towards her now but he found it increasingly difficult to walk away from the forest-garden until he had to stop and rest, so difficult was the attempt to walk back towards Oneira. Still ten strides separated them.

"I will not," she declared to him from a distance and her face had become hard as stone.

Vilb's face twisted as he wrestled with the desire to bolt ahead and leave her there. He bit his upper lip. "You will not?" he repeated. He breathed hard to catch his breath. "But why not? Please. I need you to protect me. Who am I but a foolish man? You are the leader of the Pilgrimage."

Her face softened for a moment. "I was," she said. Vilb shook his head and he reached out to her.

"The Pilgrimage remains. Don't abandon it... or me... now. Please."

Oneira shuddered. "He is there."

To this Vilb had no response. At this moment the gods seemed inconsequential to Vilb. Before him was unimaginable life tickling his nostrils, thrilling his lungs, and the sound of a torrent of water all but intoxicated him. Who was Quadros Prang? What were the gods, after all?

"Please!" cried Vilb, and he knew that this was his last request. He would leave her here if he had to choose between the forest-garden and the stone woman. Perhaps Oneira realized this as well, for she moved towards Vilb. "Very well," she said, and strode past him towards the girl and Ledge, standing at the edge of the forest-garden, looking in.

III

Vilb and Oneira began to trot because Prav and Ledge had stepped into a dark opening in the forest wall and had disappeared from view. Together now, hand in hand, they ran to the forest and paused for an instant, looked at one another, and plunged into the same dark opening, a living corridor of some kind, and plunged headlong into the dark. Before them the light shone, a soft golden light shimmering through a mist, and they laughed in amazement and moved forward at a run. In the next moment they were in a glade, the sun beaming down through vine and leaf, beside them stood Prav and Ledge.

Before them, standing in the center of the glade a figure stood bathed by golden light and falling water. He was massive in scale, amber in color, and appeared to be made of stone, for he was seamless. Vilb pulled up short, wiped the dripping hair from his forehead and laughed in response to his shock. It was as if a marble statue had suddenly sprung from the earth to mark the way.

The figure was twice the height of Vilb, and many times stouter. "I am Methodius. I am here to serve you," said the massive figure, and he bowed low. In the next instant the massive figure stepped forward and dropped to one knee before Vilb. He looked him in the eye, and Vilb thought he saw a strange meekness settling around the stone cheeks and eyebrows. He was a warrior of some kind Vilb realized. He wore some kind of armor over his upper body, leather boots laced high to his knee, and leather seemed to wind round his hips, yet all of his garments were also made of stone, and a seamless part of his body.

"Greetings to the Pilgrims from His Most Holy Highness, His Excellency the Pan-Archer. He invites you to break your fast in this place." Vilb stared. His mouth fell open. He reached out towards the living statue to feel for himself what it was. Methodius took one step back and Vilb's hand missed and Methodius continued to speak. "The fruits will restore you. The water will sustain you. The Power of M is heavy in the air here. When you are rested and well-recovered you will join His Excellency. He awaits you in his palace. With this Methodius rose to his full height. "I am at your command." The figure bowed again, turned and bid them follow. Vilb, Ledge and Oneira stood speechless, dumbfounded.

"Lead us on," Prav declared. The girl stood beside Vilb and looked up into his face. She took his hand and together they walked on, following the glowing figure moving down a forest path.

It was difficult to know precisely, but Vilb felt that Methodius escorted them south and west through the garden. At times the air was close and thick with moisture and decay, and so dark that it seemed to Vilb that the long night had come suddenly, yet in the next moment a glade opened the sky to them, and the rain fell as a gentle mist all about them, and the grass was wet on his feet and tears filled Vilb's eyes and he wept with joy at the feeling on his skin.

Methodius moved slowly, but even still Vilb and the others had to trot at a steady pace to keep up. For a circ and more the company walked yet Vilb did not grow tired. In fact, he grew stronger as they proceeded, and at this he was amazed. It was as if the air itself gave strength. The small company did not finally stop until they reached the edge of the garden and stepped beyond into a columned portico. To the west what could only be Lake Vost appeared as a blue expanse yet rippled, moving, glistening in the late circ sun. Vilb had only heard of lakes and seas as a child and considered them as real as he did the gods. Real yet not real, at least not for the likes of him. Yet now he beheld both the great Lake Vost and one of the servants of the gods. He had never imagined the look, or the smell of so much water. He laughed a great laugh that quickly became a sob, which he choked back quickly.

"You see, now, don't you?" said Prav, her voice twinkling and unfamiliar. "There's more." Prav pointed west and Vilb set off after Methodius.

Methodius led them across the portico and up a long step, like a hill of marble, Vilb thought. Once at the top Vilb gasped and Ledge and Oneira moaned. Before them was a massive glowing white dome resting atop a vast columned acropolis itself resting atop a sprawling stepped base that rose up out of the blue water.

"A god-made mountain," Oneira whispered. The scale of what he witnessed left Vilb breathless and reeling and he struggled to keep up. It was actually two domes. Atop the first dome was a second, smaller crowning dome lifted high above the first by a colonnade. Atop the crowning dome a spire rose and atop the spire a green fire, like a star, burned brightly.

"It is the Power of M you feel," said Prav triumphantly as she hurried forward. "Come on!" She bounded and lept ahead of them.

Methodius stopped before a stone path that led west towards the palace while a spur went north ending immediately at stairs and above them, another portico. It was a gate that led back to the forest-garden. Methodius turned and cleared the path for the company. "The Lord invites you to rest now, and recover your true selves in His garden," and he pointed up the stairs.

Prav ran ahead without pause, up the dozen stairs, two at a time, across the portico and into the shade of the garden. Gone. Like that.

Vilb looked at Ledge and then Oneira yet said nothing. Where could they go but forward? A moment later the burbling sound of water just ahead was too much to bear. Vilb could no longer restrain himself. The fragrance of strange fruit ran riot in his head. His stomach lurched and bid his feet to move, and even as Oneira called to him from ahead, Ledge ran past him towards the garden gate. Vilb staggered up the stairs of the portico and across, prepared for anything, if only he could eat and drink his fill.

IV

Before his eyes could adjust to the shadow his hands and nose led him forward. He plucked the first fruit he felt from the vine that found his hand. He pulled hard, brought it to his nose and inhaled. A swoon came over him and he laughed and devoured whatever it was in its entirety, rind and flesh, seed and stem. Tears flowed freely down his face and he laughed and cried in rapturous joy.

He put in his mouth anything he could touch. The leaf was sweet and tender, the root rich and aromatic. The soil was alive with the living death of decomposition and teeming with worms. They too were fat and tender and plump with living juice. He had never seen worms like these in the east, nor so many in his life as was in one small patch of earth at his feet.

Murmuring springs filled the air with a life-assuring babble. Here I am, said one, and beyond it, another, and deeper into the garden, yet another, and so on until Vilb had lost Oneira and the rest of the company and found himself in a clearing. There was no sun only a crepuscular, shining roof above. Without second thought he lay down beside a spring he called his own and it seemed to him then that the whole world was a garden and his life, up until now, had been a horrible, dreadful nightmare. It was here he belonged. He gathered water as well as he could in his hands and doused his face riotously.

Water. It was all he could say. It was all he could think. Water. He drank and he wept and he drank and he wept again.

Whistles and cries could be heard in the shadows. Birds, Vilb remembered. There was a thing called bird here once. Birds and worms. He sucked pink flesh from his teeth, laying down, his face in the shade, his legs in the sun. He heaved a heavy sigh, belched.

He thanked The Martha, remembered Simon, and blessed even Quadros Prang from whom, he assumed, his good fortune came. No demon could work such wonders, he thought. Quadros Prang deserved his love no less than the other gods, and now, perhaps more.

Vilb drank and spit and bathed. And he wept for the pools of water he found as he explored the garden. Finally he slipped gently, quietly, into a shimmering pool and his entire body was enveloped by the warm embrace of the blood of life.

He was in the water.

Water was all he knew and all he needed to know. He had forgotten everything by then and had no idea how long he had been in the garden. Circs? An entire season? A full sun? A long night? Anything could be true, so intoxicated, so enraptured he had become.

When Methodius finally reappeared to escort him to the palace, Vilb was as a stupid child awakened in the middle of sleep, unaware, lost and utterly docile. Had he seen this towering white statue before? Or was he an amber-gold? And when? Surely it meant him no harm? The white creature ushered him through the garden and out onto the stone floor of the temple's portico. It was cool on his feet and he blinked stupidly in the waning sunlight. He shaded his eyes and looked back at the garden with longing. Standing there he found that he was with two other persons dressed like he was dressed, standing alongside another towering white escort.

Vilb hardly recognized the others, and it took a few moments for him to remember their names. They returned his stare with their own blank looks.

"Oh-ni-ra," Vilb said slowly, pointing at her and she nodded as if grateful for the reminder. The waters, the shade and the vine had restored her, Vilb thought, and her eyes and skin shone like a polished seeing stone. He took her hand and they walked in silence behind Methodius and Ledge.

They walked across the portico, down the steps and into the gathering twilight of the desert floor. Soon the garden was behind them and Vilb's feet touched the scorched soil of Little Earth once again. In that instant he felt his life come rushing back to him, coursing up through him from the soles of his feet to the crease in his brow. It hit him suddenly. He turned and headed back to the garden gate but Methodius put one large arm around him and forced him back onto the path wordlessly. There was no going back. At least not yet.

And then a voice burst loudly in his mind. Not the intuition of Simon or the teachings of The Martha, but his old self, the oldest self he knew.

Do not be fooled by this seduction. Take no other gods before me. You are my servant.

But all he wanted was water and to taste that pink fleshy fruit again. Vilb could not restrain a little whimper and he turned again for the stairs that led to the garden temple but Methodius did not let him pass and Oneira kept hold of his hand.

"This way," Methodius said and soon they were at the lake shore, and then beyond it, walking on the water towards the dome.

Vilb soon realized that the lake was not a lake at all, at least not where they walked. Beneath them, just under the surface of the water, lay a white stone path that spread between the shore and dome though bluer waters gathered on either side of the path.

Above them Vilb could hear a humming and could feel it in the stone at his feet. His gaze was drawn upward and he watched as the upper dome's crown turned slowly and came to a stop as if watching their progress.

"His Excellency awaits within," declared Methodius when they had successfully crossed the blue, sun speckled lake. Vilb felt a sick horror arise in him now, a harsh and painful contrast to the bliss he had only recently left behind. He whimpered again.

Before them rose a series of steps, each one as high as Methodius. For Vilb it was like staring into a smooth, white cliff face.

"There are stairs for *you* this way," and with this Methodius led them to an opening in the first step in which was carved a series of smaller ones. These he could manage, and so they made the climb to the top of the first great level.

Once at the top of the stair Vilb could see the dome swelling above the colonnade and cornice. They marched across the marble plain and came to the next massive rise. Up again. The main structure was ahead across yet another marble plain, the dome high above.

The dome blocked out the sky and they walked in deep shadow. Methodius softly glowed ahead of them.

"Where are we going?" Vilb finally asked. He was tired and wanted nothing more than to go back to the garden and sleep.

Finally Methodius stopped, pointed through the colonnade into the darkness under the dome and spoke.

"He waits for you."

Quadros Prang

Now after The Martha heard the words of the other gods, she repeated them in Simon's presence, and Simon said to her, "Go and utterly destroy those who would betray Me, and wage war against them until they are utterly vanquished."

– The Book of M

I

Where was Prav? As her name came back to him, her face and all that had passed between them, then it was Vilb remembered. He cursed himself under his breath. Missing were his pack, his skins, and what of the reath hutch? All gone. He turned his palms up and regarded them—gone was the curious glow left by the remains as he had experienced them in the Spire Massif. His hands looked positively ordinary and with this realization his heart skipped a beat and his knees grew wobbly beneath him. The dread of his own death swept over him and with it, a profound sense that he had failed. But who had he failed? The Martha? Simon? It seemed preposterous. And then he knew. Prav. He had failed the girl. How, he did not know, but he felt it in his bones. He turned and looked at Oneira desperately hoping that perhaps she had thought to collect up his things, only she too was empty-handed. A deep despair hollowed him and he stumbled again and had to lean on Ledge to catch himself.

Methodius led them on now, guiding them into a great cavernous space under the dome of the palace. They were in the deepest shadow and the air was charged, as if a storm were overhead. Every hair on Vilb's body stood on end.

"What could he want with... us?" whispered Oneira finally, her voice shaking. Vilb shook his head. He was at a loss. Was this the fate that befell all Pilgrims from the east?

"Perhaps he may still let us return to the garden," said Ledge, but even he did not believe it.

Oneira squeezed his hand spasmodically. "Do you believe it?"

Vilb did not know. By the light of Simon! He knew nothing! He walked in the dark through this life, and now the depth of that darkness was utterly laid bare to him, and he felt small and hopeless. He wanted to scream, but he clenched his jaw and swallowed hard on his frustration and fear.

"No," he said finally, and there was grit in his voice. "I do not believe we will return to the garden."

The amber light of Methodius moved inexorably on before them and except for his form, all was dark. Vilb craned his neck and looked up, but above him was only night.

"Dear Simon, deliver us from evil," whispered Ledge breathlessly.

Vilb nodded, reached out for Oneira's hand and held on to it. She was trembling and only barely able to move forward.

"I do not think the gods can help us here," said Vilb.

The light of Methodius grew brighter and larger before them and in the next moment Vilb realized that the figure had stopped, turned and was waiting for them. He had a strangely placid, almost pleased, expression on his face and his eyes all but beamed at Vilb.

Methodius bowed his head and spoke: "His High Holy Excellency will see you now." Suddenly Vilb felt the stone at his feet move and push towards him and his stomach dropped into his knees and he gripped Oneira's hand and Ledge reached out to him for fear of being knocked to his knees. The air rushed past them and sang in their eyes, and though Vilb had no previous experience with such a feeling, he felt almost sure that they were moving up at a tremendous rate.

"What is this?" he called out, utterly bewildered. He reached out for Oneira's hand.

"The way to Quadros," answered Methodius, and no sooner had he spoken than the feeling stopped and he was blinded by the light of the naked sun. Methodius ushered them forward as they blinked and shuffled along, one hand up shielding their faces. When Vilb's eyes adjusted he could see now that they had somehow traveled up and were on top of the large dome and inside the smaller, crowning dome. A strange buzzing filled the air and it vibrated Vilb's chest and it set his teeth to chattering. His flesh tingled and his heart pounded inside him.

Methodius led them forward to a dais surrounded by some dozen large stairs, large enough for the legs of Methodius or those like him to ascend. On either side of the dais stood another massive stone figure, but white rather than amber, and motionless.

"Your majesty," said Methodius, kneeling before the foot of the dais. His head was bowed.

"For once you serve us as we demand," croaked a voice from above. "We are generous and we will reward you for your service."

"The Aegis serve the Power of M, your Excellency."

"Rise then and stand by," said the voice above, and then and only then did Methodius rise and stand guard behind Vilb, Ledge and Oneira. Except for the figures—had Methodius called himself Aegis?—there was only the dais, the stairs atop an ebony floor polished like a seeing stone. Vilb looked down at his feet and saw his own pallid, drawn face staring back at him. He reached up to touch his beard, his hair which remained standing and waving in the air. What a ghastly sight. He was bones and skin and srapi and almost nothing left of flesh, or light or life remained in him. Had not their time in the forest-garden restored him? Apparently not. Apparently it had drained the meager resources of his body and he stood now and beheld a loosely jointed bundle of sticks held together by he knew not what power. The sight unnerved him, but less so than what he saw when he looked around at the edges of the domed space. Figures lined the perimeter, naked figures, figures that appeared to be Ubernaki, Gazi, AkiGazi, each with their distinctive hair and skin color, each motionless, frozen in some pose of life, but they did not appear to be alive. There were dozens, many dozens circling the dais, and some were not posed in living postures at all, but their torsos had been splayed, or cut transversely, or limbs were missing, torn from sockets, or cleanly cut. Many had their bodies laid open for inspection, or for what other purpose Vilb could not fathom.

He shuddered even as Oneira let out a low groan and Ledge hissed something unintelligible. They had seen it too.

"You are admiring my collection," said the voice from the dais. "They all do. I am quite proud of it." In the shadows that enshrouded the dais, at the top of the stairs, Vilb could see movement and then the crowning level somehow slid forward and loomed out over the stairs and seemed to be on the verge of falling and crushing the three of them. Vilb leaned back instinctively to avoid being crushed and he felt a massive hand support him from behind, holding him upright.

"How long I have waited!" the voice from above cackled.

"My waiting makes me worthy. My waiting purifies all that I have done." It was almost a song he sang, though the sound of it made Vilb's flesh crawl.

It was a stone chair, a Meson's throne, only larger, polished obsidian of the blackest ink and it slowly fell from the sky above them as if riding on invisible hands. In the next moment the stone chair descended, dropping directly before the three stunned figures, and remained there, as if tethered from above, though Vilb could see no such tether, and could in no way imagine how such an imposing stone mass could be suspended. In the chair, staring now into Vilb's face, there was another face, and it spoke to them.

"Welcome, friends," said the figure, more bone than flesh it seemed, and its mouth hardly moved as it spoke. "Quadros Prang here. Forgive me… my appearance. I have not been well these past two thousand years," and at that the figure seemed to shake and Vilb realized that the emaciated figure was laughing. Vilb's mouth hung open in speechless wonder.

Quadros Prang was nothing more than a pile of old sticks, tossed into the corner of the throne. Moreover, the throne was much too large for Quadros Prang's shrunken figure and its dimensions served to reduce him even more. His head fell heavily to one side and it appeared as if the narrow neck had not the strength to hold it upright. His was a figure of perfect ossification, and this Vilb understood perfectly, for the desert of Little Earth hardened all and reduced all living flesh to dust, all bone to stone, and Quadros Prang seemed more stone than flesh, all except his bulging, blue eyes. They were flesh, and wetness, and need, and they were in earnest, of that Vilb was certain.

"You are most welcome, my friends," said the figure once again, and seemed to wave an arm to gesture at them, though the figure did little more than rustle the purple fabric loosely gathered around his body.

"Are you the Lord?" Oneira asked, her head bowed. The figure shook and it sounded to Vilb like skins drying in a whispering breeze. He was laughing again.

"Yes my dear, I am the Lord, your Quadros." He laughed again.

The throne began to move and to circle the three of them.

Vilb found that he could not turn his head, nor raise his arms, nor make any move whatsoever.

Quadros took them in as he made his first orbit. "The bitch botched the whole thing. Again." He turned his chair to Vilb and came as close as his chair would allow. Quadros spoke quietly into his face. "Things haven't been going so well in the east, eh? That's my doing. I hope you've enjoyed it. We're no longer on the same side, you and I. I am going ahead without you, and if all goes well, you'll be dealing with me from now on."

"To who?" Vilb found his voice, though it only croaked. "Who, your... your Excellency?"

"To whom, boy. Whom." He turned his chair and floated away, only to turn again and face them from a distance.

"He is in there, listening. That can't be helped," rasped Quadros, "at least not yet. But soon. Soon." The chair was moving again, towards them and he rode up close to Vilb and dropped low and looked up into his face.

"Not bad, really, not too terribly bad." Quadros remained staring at him like that for long, uncomfortable moments. Vilb listened as the ancient figure's breathing rasped in and out.

Here is a god of Little Earth.

Far from awe, Vilb felt a gorge of anger rise up in him, a strange desire to reach out and smash the figure, to trample him under his feet.

Quadros Prang laughed as if in response.

A fine dust came from the breath of Quadros and it hung in the air all around them. A sea of dust particles filled the air all around and Vilb watched, momentarily mesmerized.

Suddenly and quite without warning Vilb exploded with a sneeze and his body broke the invisible bonds holding him for an instant. His right knee bumped against the throne of Quadros and sent it rocking backward gently. A jolt surged through the leg that had bumped the throne and the muscles up and down Vilb's right leg went into spasm.

Quadros began to shake, as if a spasm had taken hold of him as well. As the old man's body rattled, flecks of spittle, or perhaps dust, sprayed from the dark crevasse of his mouth. Quadros was shaking with yet another fit of laughter. He drew his throne up close to Vilb and stared into his face. Vilb stepped backward instinctively and felt Methodius immediately block his retreat.

▌▌

"I hate to admit it, but she did good work once, long ago, all things considered," the old man croaked. "Eh, Methodius?" "Indeed, Master, the Easterlings appear most sound in spite of everything."

"Don't worry my friends," croaked the old man, apparently to Oneira now. "Your herd is safe and so is Martha's... bag of tricks... I meant to thank you for that, my boy," said Quadros as he turned to Vilb. The old figure patted a bundle beside him.

"What?" was all that Vilb could manage.

"The *remains*, boy, the remains," Quadros said.

The chair and its passenger began to circle the three of them again and Vilb felt as if he were somehow being unwound from the inside.

"What do you think, Methodius? Which of them shall we add to our collection?" Now he stopped before Ledge. "This one has more flesh on his bones, but... something tells me he's not quite right for the collection."

Ledge could only stand silent, bound by invisible bands.

"And you..." Quadros said, approaching Oneira. "You look too much like her, and that won't do. That won't do at all." And now he came before Vilb. "I have many like you, she favored your type, for obvious reasons, but you seem... different. I'll keep you here and add you to my collection." Quadros paused as if thinking. "You, my boy, you. Yes. You please me."

The old man shook again with laughter.

"I do not understand," said Vilb, his voice hoarse and barely above a whisper.

"Yes, I know. It is the state of things in this menagerie. It's not how I would have planned to remake the world, but I was not consulted now, was I? Indeed, I was not. So you are in the dark. And soon, Little Earth will be in the dark, but no matter. Eat and drink for tomorrow we die, eh my boy?" Quadros laughed and his frail voice took on a strange, raving power.

"You die, to be precise. I do not die. I cannot die. To be sure, I have wished for death on more than one occasion, on many occasions in fact. Longed for separation from this mortal coil, to melt and thaw as it were, but there is no death for the cursed gods of Little Earth. Only life everlasting. Lonely, cursed living that goes on without end." At this Quadros collected himself, paused, and looked again at Vilb and the others. "I am a prisoner of this body—thanks to Mother Martha, her simp Azo and that betraying backstabbing sycophant. Master, they call Qir. Oh please."

His voice trembled now and his whole form seemed to shake along with it. "Now that I have the promise of a new body here," and his eyes grew wide as he spoke, "and the Power of M in my hand..." his voice trailed off and he seemed to lose his way in the thicket of his thoughts. He tapped his withered, bony hand against the stone of his chair as if tapping out a rhythm. "Never give up on one's dreams, boy," he declared finally after a long moment of silence. "That's the lesson learned here. That's what I've come to see on my end. Even if it takes two millennia to exact revenge, to win your prize, never give up on your dreams. Never give up!" Prang began to hum some strange tune that Vilb could only marvel at.

Quadros moved in as close as he could possibly get to Vilb, and then leaned in as far as he could move his frail frame and he brought his face within a hand's breadth of Vilb's. The eyes of Quadros were red-rimmed and wild, bulging and wet, and Vilb could discern the pulse of the ancient figure's heart beating behind the blue iris.

"I have them here," whispered Quadros, staring into Vilb's eyes as he spoke, but it was as if he spoke to someone else, and not to Vilb, as if his gaze passed into and through Vilb to reach some part of him that was not him. "He had the remains, had almost become entirely fused with them, but I soaked them out of him, soaked every last one and now they are mine. Checkmate, I think, my dear, dear old friend. Yes, I think so. Finally. And rest assured. Soon enough I am coming for you."

"What?" managed Vilb.

"What?" mocked Quadros. He focused on Vilb for an instant. "Know thyself," said Quadros disdainfully. "It's job one of any living, thinking being." With this he spun his chair around, found a new position and leaned in close again. "I have the keys here, right here in this room. Think on that, my friend. And a body. She tried to hide them from me, but here they are. You know what that means. The whole em-frame installation will be coming back on-line, and soon. That I can guarantee. After two-thousand years!" Quadros stared as if expecting an answer but Vilb remained silent, utterly befuddled.

"You're the handiwork of Mother Martha, my boy. Gone to seed, though, to be sure. But enough of that. I am not here to give you a history lesson. You have read your Book of M, of that I'm sure, otherwise you would not be here, the dutiful Pilgrim, so please, let me come to the point." Quadros Prang's throne spun suddenly around and moved away from Vilb and came to the foot of the dais, spun around again and faced the three of them.

"Two thousand and fifty years, my boy. I have waited that long, with her betrayal against me, and the rest of the out to destroy me, but they are fools and to the patient goes the prize." Quadros's voice trembled. He seemed lost in a fey reverie. "Long years… long years. Long and empty and lonely years. They left me to wander, to rot in a cell, to live the life of the undead with no one. Alone. They called me cruel but they are cruel. Living cruelty that will not be allowed to endure. Of that you can be sure. She will know. Oh yes, Mother Martha and her minions will know all about this moment, to be sure. And Qir, pah!" Quadros tilted his head and pitched his voice into the far reaches of the chamber. Its power and resonance surprised Vilb, for it rang out and carried far beyond what he would have thought possible given the size and condition of the figure in the chair.

"Help me to my new body, Methodius!" croaked the old man, and in the next moment the Aegis strode from the perimeter of the chamber holding a bundle wrapped tightly in white fabric. Methodius lay the bundle before the throne, unwrapped it slowly, his massive hands almost too large for the task, and then backed away silently.

Between Quadros and Vilb lay the motionless body of the girl, Prav. Vilb gasped.

"Thanks to you, my boy, you brought her to me. It's beyond you, my boy. You may blame Mother Martha. She made you do it. Like salmon, or the homing pigeon—but you do not know what I am talking about. These are things from the Ancient world, my past, yet you are that past. You return to spawn, to the Great City, to see Mother Martha. I simply cast my net and caught each of you as you swam my way. And here you are. Qir's little terrorist—his living booby-trap—and you... you, my boy are the real prize. The remains are the keys to the kingdom. I am grateful to you. You will have a prominent place in my museum, commemorating this disastrous episode in human history known as Little Earth. An "ark" she called it. Their grandiose grand-standing knew no bounds. Ah well. So be it." With this Quadros went quiet and hovered over the girl's body.

"Help me once again, and for the last time," said the old man to Methodius, barely louder this time, but the Aegis had lost all his iridescent glow and seemed to be nothing more than ornate statuary. "Why will you not help me, my friend?" pleaded Quadros, a sudden pathetic desperation in his voice, and still there was no response.

The old man grunted and if Vilb did not know better he would have thought Quadros sounded afraid as he spoke. "My Aegis and the millennial palm naked together in this way, have come into conflict. You my boy, you may help an old man gain his reward. Come. You may help me." He appeared frail, pathetic and vulnerable." At these words Ledge lurched forward and moved towards Quadros.

In that same moment Prav lept up beside Quadros, jumped into his throne, snatched up a bundle from his lap and leapt lightly to the floor. Quickly she withdrew a few paces and lay the bundle down and flung it open and hurriedly withdrew two shimmering amber pieces—the twin leaves Vilb called them back home, flat shapes intricately carved from what could only be the two sides of an infant's tiny skull. The leaves glowed softly in her palms now and she bounded towards Vilb and placed one in each of his palms and closed the fingers of each of his hands around them.

His closed hands glowed with a golden light.

Just then Vilb heard the old man croak unintelligibly to Methodius, but the Aegis did not respond.

"It's mine!" bellowed Quadros, his voice now filling the air all around him, and Vilb felt a wave knock him back into Methodius's frozen figure. "They are mine! They belong to me!" Another wave pushed Vilb across the floor, stunning him momentarily.

"Cheater Qir!" Quadros declared, and he moved in towards Prav and Vilb, Oneira and Ledge each scurried behind an immobile Aegis. "Dirty stinking rotten filthy cheater!"

Quadros's anger knocked Prav to the floor. "You ungrateful brat! Tell your master that our armistice is at an end!" Prav crawled towards the open remains while Quadros in his throne bore down on her. "You can't do that!" Quadros shrieked now, desperate and disconsolate. "I have spent everything to find them and they are mine!"

Not knowing what else to do, Vilb snatched the girl and together they circled Methodius's frozen form keeping the Aegis between himself and Quadros's circling throne. Where could he go? How could he flee? He side-stepped again and was knocked to the floor by an invisible hand.

"You are inconsequential!" Quadros bellowed at him.

Prav held her palm out towards Quadros.

"I am the desolation of the land. I am the scourge of M," she said, her voice, sure and clear and as she spoke the floor shook and Quadros in his throne crashed to the floor and went sliding backward into the darkness.

Vilb looked at Oneira and she seemed to understand. She scrambled to the hutch and slid it across the floor to Vilb.

"Make a circlet around your temple, like before," cried Prav. "Around you, end to end touching, and your throat. Yes, that's it."

Vilb had a vision of the melting stone in the valley of the Spire Massif. He scrambled to his knees and quickly drew the remains towards him. His hands shook as he worked fast, fearing Quadros and another fray. First one, then another.

He scooped each one up. Could he hold all of them at once?

Eleven pieces, there, now, in his hands. What would they do in this place?

What do you want them to do?

Prav cried again, and Vilb's hands trembled. He had to loop and link end to end just so, and it was delicate work and not to be rushed. Just then the floor vibrated and Vilb saw from the corner of his eye the black light of the throne of Quadros.

An invisible blast hit him and knocked the remains out of his hands and onto the floor. He scrambled after them and began to arrange them around him, each one touching the other on the floor first. Each part of the remains had a light of its own, yet as the remains each made contact with another, the whole glowed more intensely until Vilb held a ring of amber light in his hands.

Vilb rose to his feet, now wearing the remains and as he stood they sank into his flesh and his head and upper torso glowed and shone in the shadowed chamber. Quadros groaned as his chair crashed again to the floor with a heavy thud of dead weight and slid to a stop not far from the dais. "How could you do this to me?" whimpered Quadros.

Prav jumped up and down with glee. "You've disrupted the EM-field! He's going to be very angry with us!" Vilb heard her voice as if from far away, for she and the others were outside him now, outside a place that for Vilb was calm and blissfully quiet. It felt precisely like the warm embrace he had experienced while bathing in the garden—delicious to be in the water, and now here it was again, only warmer and more penetrating. He surrendered to it and felt that he would soon become the light.

"Not yet!" cried Prav, and the girl's voice served to awaken Vilb as if from a dream, and he opened his eyes and found himself still in the chamber, Oneira, Ledge and Prav looking up at him with expectant, desperate faces.

Prav grabbed Vilb's hand and Oneira grabbed Ledge, and together they followed as the girl led them towards the dais and then around it to the other side.

"Come on!" cried Prav. "Stand right here," she said, and they huddled together and in a moment they were falling, falling, and in another moment they were running through the dark of the great dome to the light of the long setting sun.

"What happened to... to... Quadros?" Oneira asked. "The Power of M," the girl said. "It's deep below us."

They reached the sunlight. "This way," said Prav and they moved as quickly as the still stunned Vilb could manage. They had not gone far into the light when Methodius appeared and made further flight impossible.

"Quadros Prang has grossly underestimated the Keystone," said the Aegis triumphantly, now on one knee before Vilb. "When he can he will retreat for the Great City. We must get there before he does."

"But you serve Quadros!" cried Ledge.

"I serve the Power of M and the Aegis await the Restoration of Simon," said Methodius solemnly, and in so saying he placed one massive white hand over his chest.

"Yet you serve that thing in there!" Oneira retorted angrily.

"As a slave of power," said Methodius and he paused and looked down at Vilb. "You are the Keystone."

"I am... what?" said Vilb and he turned on Prav. "I do not seek to be... what? A Keystone?"

"I do not understand!" cried Oneira.

"The other gods work against Quadros," said Methodius, and he kneeled and bowed his head before Vilb. "Master Qir has not been idle these past two millennia. The Great Mother is not powerless either. Even Azo in his prison makes his power felt. Beyond that, they say, in the other Realms, other forces struggle for the fate of Little Earth." At that Methodius gazed long at Vilb. "But now Little Earth is failing. We must visit The Martha in her exile. She will tell us how the Keystone must proceed."

"I... me... The Martha?" Vilb stammered.

Methodius waved him off. "We have no more time for explanations." Methodius lowered his voice. "It is the hope of every Pilgrim to have an audience with the Great Mother, is it not?

Vilb turned to Oneira and she to Ledge.

"A hand larger than our own guides us, it seems," she said. "We can only go on." Vilb looked at Prav. The girl stood beside him as if lost in thought.

"I cannot go any further with you," she finally blurted.

"What? But you must!"

"I am the scourge of M. I... I cannot explain it to you. Just go. Go and be what you are. Go!"

"Please, Keystone. We must go now!" said Methodius.

"Follow him. Trust him. Go now!" Prav echoed and Oneira and Ledge pulled Vilb along after Methodius. Vilb felt a sadness rise up in him and gush forth as Oneira and Ledge followed Methodius into a doorway that opened up in a massive column. Vilb stumbled along and then stopped, turned and looked back at the girl. His eyes were wet with tears that he could not understand.

"When will I see you again?" he called out. It is all happening too fast. He choked on a sob. In another moment Oneira was pulling at him, Ledge was urging him onwards, and they were racing to keep up with Methodius as he headed headlong down a stair well and into more darkness.

"Look for me in the Great City," he thought he heard Prav shout, or perhaps not. A door had closed between them.

The Great City

I

Methodius led Vilb, Ledge and Oneira underground and to what he called the Archer's Great Way. It was a wide, paved tunnel lit by the light of the paving stones themselves. Once well underground they mounted a large platform, a slab of polished marble, white, yet flecked with gold luminescence, and this they reclined upon as it carried them vast distances in a short time.

"We will come upon the City from underneath, and reach it before Quadros Prang," declared Methodius, and then he spoke no more, but stood stone still at the rear of the marble platform as they traveled. Vilb could not be sure how long they traveled, for the light never dimmed, nor did it ever grow brighter. Many times he dozed, and they ate their remaining food, but as before, a powerful thirst plagued them, for they had lost their water skins. Yet even as Oneira and Ledge complained of their thirst and Vilb agreed, he realized too that he did not feel thirsty, nor hungry either. The remains perhaps, had left some lasting change in his body, but as to that Vilb simply could not be sure how, or even if, it had truly happened or if he had simply imagined it.

When their transport finally stopped after an indeterminate time, Methodius finally moved again and he did so silently and swiftly. He led them away from the Archer's Great Way and down a narrow tunnel that climbed endlessly up and up, and then turned and climbed yet another, even narrower tunnel, all lit by the same strange white stone, and then to a doorway, a staircase, and up many stairs until Vilb felt that his legs would simply no longer carry him, and then they finally stopped.

In the next moment he led them through an opening, up another flight of stairs and they were outside in the growing twilight of the long day. Vilb looked at Oneira and Ledge.

"Shall we see the sights?" Vilb asked wryly to no one. Ledge shot him a dark look though Oneira pretended not to hear him. They both looked around anxiously and wrung their hands as if in pain.

They stood before a structure with a flag that hung dolefully in the still air which read, "Casimir's Apothecary." From here Vilb looked down the wide road, more like a paved flume than a road, Vilb thought, as if a regular flood flowed down this way to some distant low point in the City. They had come to the surface far from the great heart of it all, far from everything except gray stone of which everything as far as the eye could see was assembled. And not artfully, at least not according to Ubernaki standards which, Vilb had always thought, were not terribly demanding. Yet here, in San Simon, the heart of Little Earth and the source of the Arclight he had expected, well, more. Low slung granite boxes lined the way, occasionally a makeshift column leaned precipitously this way or that. Pathetic.

"Like home," Ledge said, his voice rasping from thirst and disuse.

A fulsome mist hung in the air, lighter here than before when they had first emerged from underground, but no less noxious. Between coughing and gagging fits Vilb was able to recover his wind only to then gag and retch again, and then breathe, and then gag, until slowly his lungs began to grow more accustomed to the City's atmosphere.

"Why does it smell so... so much like... filth?" he finally managed, but Methodius ignored him. It seemed to Vilb that the stink did not touch the Aegis though the white figure had taken on a decidedly deeper amber tinge since they had arrived in San Simon. Ledge and Oneira both remained quiet, though he could sense that Ledge was growing ever more anxious, like an animal who was provisionally aware of the slaughterhouse nearby.

"You there!" said a voice from behind them, and the three turned to see. An old beggar had appeared beside them stealthily, separating from the few stragglers hanging about. Otherwise Vilb and the others were invisible, mixing in with the others in the City, themselves dressed in what might otherwise be called srapis, even down to the color schemes, though Vilb had no idea if the hierarchy of color in San Simon was the same as it was in the east, yet he suspected as much.

It is a little world.

The beggar was a portly fellow with a red, bulging face that looked as if it had been excoriated by the wind one too many times. Small pockets of flesh were missing in his nose, forehead, chin, and even one ear was only a remnant. He wore a srapi too, the brown, and Vilb felt a certain disdain for the man automatically rise up in him. He is just a brown.

"I'm Bagnus by the by, friend and loyal servant to The Martha," and as he spoke he reached and grabbed at Vilb's sleeve as if to keep him close. He pointed back to where they had come, and a sudden break in the mist revealed the Citadel rising high above, a black line of crenellation, spire, and dome against the pale sky. "We're north of it now." Vilb looked behind him and took it in. The great wall appeared as a thick, black line that girdled the mountain at its middle. Above it the squared geometry of the Citadel rose on a stylobate that seemed fashioned from the mountain itself. The entire peak had been turned into one massive complex, a fortress, a seat of power. How deep did it dig into the mountain beneath?

Above it all on a spire thin and delicate and impossible to trace to its end, rose the Arclight. Or did it hang from the heavens? It was impossible to tell. High in the pale, hazy sky the emerald light shone, though the sinking summer sun made it difficult to discern except for a green, obscured halo. But at the center, if Vilb squinted and looked just askance his target, there he could see it, a jewel in the sky. Who could forget the power of the gods living beneath such a mystery?

In another instant the Citadel disappeared from view but Vilb had the sense that visible or no, the Arclight rode above them, watching, and it understood the Pilgrims, knew about their long journey and shone down on it benevolently. All of this would have been precisely the sense Vilb had hoped to experience except that he felt far from illuminated. Rather, he felt more in darkness than he had ever felt on his hill in the east.

"Look it here," said Bagnus, and he nodded and pointed back towards the City, down the road and north. "See there?

That's the main way in and out of this quadrant. That's where we're going." Vilb turned and saw a wide avenue, unevenly paved in granite, still more flume, and on either bank the City plain spread out to the horizon.

"Where has Methodius gone off to?" asked Oneira, and Vilb and Ledge turned quickly around in response and flung their heads around in desperate search, but Methodius was a hard figure to miss.

"Aye, he's gone. I'm taking you the rest of the way," said the old beggar.

"You... know Methodius?" Vilb could not manage to gain his bearings, and now this latest upset threatened what fragile equilibrium he had managed since leaving Lake Vost and Quadros Prang.

"Aye, and a few others like him. They hang about the City. And under it mostly. Some serve the Citadel guard. They're harmless, like cockroaches. Most of them are asleep."

"Cockroaches?" asked Ledge. "What is cockroachers?"

"Cock-roaches. Bugs," said Bagnus. "Infestation, or that's what most people think of them around here. But The Martha knows different, so I do too." Bagnus paused before going on.

"Let him go. You'll see him again, I warrant. That I surely do."

An occasional figure in a gray srapi—Bagnus called them cassocks—dashed across the broad thoroughfare, but there were few people about. It felt to be nearly deserted.

"The Purps call this road the Pipe. No wonder. Look at that beautiful road. Almost as nice as the one's up on top, except the mess that goes down, sometimes every day. That's where the stink comes from, but things sweeten up when the water goes through. A good hard rain washes it clean."

He pointed to the far horizon. "Beyond the hill there you get to the wilderness, desert mostly to the north, and there you can see the mountains to the west. Most of San Simon looks like this, like the quadrant here, all except the Southern coast, where you come up. They call it Temple Row. That's where the Purps have their places, there and at the Citadel proper. The rest of this," and Bagnus spread his hands as if to embrace the rest of San Simon, "is for the likes of us. Gatherers mostly, and those that feed us. And then there's the guard," and Bagnus lowered his voice and his brow contracted. "They have their own quad up behind Distribution and Petrification. Food is what that means. The food comes in from the fertile valleys, and everywhere else it seems nowadays, and goes out from there to the Citadel. What's left then comes to the City and lately we've had more food than even we can eat," and Bagnus slapped at his distended middle. "Food and spine everywhere. That's my only worry about our plan. So much spine around that it's not worth so much these days. I can tell you more later but we have to go in and see Casimir."

With that Bagnus stepped past the pillar to which Casimir's ragged flag was fastened and waved for them to follow as he disappeared into a low-slung stone structure exactly like all the other stone structures lining the road, north and south, and on both sides. How could one ever navigate such a place, Vilb wondered. Bagnus came to a tattered weave that served as a barrier, and pushed through.

"Follow in, follow in," Bagnus called over his shoulder. "Hello, Bagnus," a voice cried out as they entered. It was
dark inside except for small square patch of light coming in
through the back wall. "You need more pouch already?"

"That's Casimir," Bagnus whispered to Vilb, turned and shouted into the dark. "Casimir. How is business?"

"As well as it can possibly be, given the circumstances. Who is this you have with you? Looks like a... a Pilgrim. Two, no three Pilgrims." Vilb's eyes adjusted slowly to the dark of the shop, but even so he spied Casimir's illuminated shape moving from behind a counter and towards the three of them. In another moment he stood before them, in his hand a small bowl inside of which a small green flame suddenly flared to life. It lit the shop with a clean, emerald light. "I am Casimir and this is my place." He was a tall, lean man with only whispers of white hair clinging to the sides of his nearly naked head. Vilb had the strange sensation that he was looking into a seeing stone, only one that made him look older. Casimir peered intently at the three of them, his gaze lingering on Vilb.

Vilb felt it to be a look bereft of malice. "What's your business here, friends?" Bagnus interposed himself enthusiastically.

"Aye, I've brought these greenies from the east here on business," Bagnus said. "I thought that you might be able to help him with his troubles." Vilb could see that Casimir, though he wore the gray cassock, was not from the City. He was much taller and thinner than Bagnus, thin and wiry in fact and unlike any other gray cassock he had yet seen. A well-kept gray beard gave him the look of a Meson.

"Methodius brought us," Vilb said, and added more loudly and perhaps with more force than he intended. "To see The Martha."

"Shhh!" hissed Bagnus, gesticulating wildly. "Bartholomew is about and he serves the Pan-Archer and you know who that is I'd wager, if Methodius brought you. The old QP doll in his chair. We see his likes now and again. If he looks at you wrong, shfftt," and Bagnus made a strange sound and pulled his finger across his throat. "You're a goner, and it's Bartholomew's doing, or one like him. Just to let you know, by the by. Bartholomew's been up and down this part of the road today asking about strange Pilgrims. It's been an unusual day indeed." Casimir stroked his gray whiskers and reflected intensely for a moment and nodded.

"You'd better follow me," he said, and he disappeared into the rear of the shop.

"You ready?" Bagnus asked, and Vilb, Oneira and Ledge looked at one another.

"For what I do not know," replied Oneira, and Vilb turned to look at her. Her face appeared drawn and haggard, thin and wan, and so did Ledge's. Yet there was a strange light in her eyes that he had seen before, perhaps in others, or perhaps in a dream. He took her hand and stroked it gently.

"I feel as if we are riding a storm. Sooner or later it must blow itself out, no? We will finally arrive and know the place? For the first time?" Vilb tried to lift the corners of his mouth into a smile, or perhaps a grimace. He turned to Ledge.

"You, my friend, and stranger, have no commitment to any more of this than you set on yourself. I fear that what we have seen will continue to plague us."

"Lead on," Ledge said, and Oneira nodded quietly, squeezed Vilb's hand and sighed.

"Lead on then," said Vilb, and waved Bagnus before them.

"But first my friends and I need water."

"Aye, water," said Bagnus, "follow me," he said, and he scuttled away to fetch what he could in Casimir's dark shop.

Once refreshed, they stepped through the back portal of the shop and came into another room with shelves and tables and containers and pouches and ancient things made of wood.

"These are his remedies," whispered Bagnus, and he indicated all of the small containers that filled the shelves. "He told me that he has roots and powders here from the furthest corners of Little Earth. Even the east—those life-sustaining roots that grow out there. You eat them, I'd wager, or you wouldn't be here now, eh? How he comes to it I'll never know. Casimir is a wonder." Bagnus moved down a corridor and lightly fingered the skins and bowls and cups and other strange artifacts while he hummed an indecipherable tune. "Look and see here," the old beggar said as he passed. "Ubernaki skulls."

"Ubernaki?" said Vilb, genuinely surprised. "How do you know that?"

"Like I said. Pilgrims come from all over to die here.

Casimir sees a lot of them before the end." Bagnus kept on, now descending a staircase. "Not so many from the east these days. Hardly any really."

"Quadros Prang," said Vilb, but Bagnus pretended not to hear.

Casimir appeared before them breathlessly and waved them forward and then turned and he sped off into a dark doorway which led to stairs, and now they were heading down again, down under the City, only this time the stone work was black and unfinished, and dark. Only Casimir's green flame illuminated the darkness and they followed behind him as quickly as they could, for the Apothecary moved quickly. Countless paces later they were all breathing heavily in the dank, still air of the tunnel when the bobbing flame up ahead suddenly stopped and Vilb heard Bagnus fall into Casimir from behind.

"Please excuse me," Bagnus said, and he bowed. "Just stay close," Casismir said quietly.

Just then the air around them grew cooler and Vilb breathed easier. They set off down a tunnel that dropped precipitously, came to a stair, dropped again, and then led straight away for such a great distance that Vilb thought that perhaps Casimir had lost his way. Surely it was time to eat, or sleep? The dark disoriented him, but there was something more to the tunnels, especially now at these depths. His hair stood on end and he felt the muscles in his face begin to twitch and dance, as if pulled in all directions at once. Like the palace at Lake Vost.

Oneira whimpered behind him, perhaps fearing the same. "We're almost there," Casimir said from the lead, and he stopped and turned to Vilb and the others. "Are you ready to trust The Martha? This is no small honor she bestows on you. Remember who it is you speak to. She is one of the Originals, one of the Ancients, the Great Mother Herself and one of the gods of Little Earth. Do you understand?" Vilb could hear the promise of violence in Casimir's voice and felt sure that the Apothecary would make good on any threat when it came to protecting The Martha.

"Who does The Martha serve?" demanded Ledge. "Do she and Quadros Prang toy with us? Is that what the gods do? Do they mock us and use us?"

Oneira put a hand on Ledge's arm to quiet him and Vilb felt a pang of jealousy.

"I understand your fear, my friend," said Casimir calmly.

"But do not fear The Martha. She is that which is served and serves no other."

The stone itself began to glow around them and dispelled the dark, at first with a shimmer of color, as if the long night's aurora had been taken captive and made to shine here on the dark tunnel walls. Vilb reached out to touch the shimmering surface and it was smooth and warm. Casimir turned and led them down a narrow way, descended even further and the shimmering darkness turned to a warm, golden light, and Vilb could see quite clearly now, as if an unknown gauze had been suddenly removed from his eyes. The air was fresh and the walls were a smooth amber opalescence.

"We're down near the sphere now," whispered Bagnus to no one. "The Mother is near, very near."

It was then that a few figures came from behind, or from before, and then dozens more streamed into the tunnel, from heretofore hidden passages and overlooked passageways. A stream of red cassocks pressed in on the three Pilgrims yet of the three the figures in red wanted to reach out and touch Vilb.

At first he thought it was an accident of the tunnel pushing them together, but then it became more obvious, and more distressing, when a large group of red cassocks approached and each in his or her turn crowded around in order to grab his srapi, touch his head, caress his cheek.

"What do they want?" Vilb called out.

"Forgive them, friend," said Casimir. "They have heard about your coming."

"What have they heard?" Vilb asked, incredulous.

"That the Keystone will lead The Martha out of this place."

In the next tunnel the way cleared of red cassocks and the three Pilgrims were able to make their way to a wide, white antechamber with rounded walls and ceiling and a strange silver floor that an ancient memory in Vilb's mind called, "metal." Casimir put his fingers to his lips and then gestured for them to sit down and wait. "The Martha will be with us as soon as may be." Casimir dropped to the floor and Bagnus quickly followed. Vilb reached out and took Oneira's hand and they sank down together and waited even as Ledge remained standing.

A moment later a voice announced, "Our Great Mother."

Vilb's heart leapt in his chest and he felt suddenly ill-prepared and pitifully small. He had loved The Martha, or at least his idea of her, but having seen Quadros Prang Vilb knew that his previous love represented nothing but a delusional fantasy. But did he really want to know the truth?

Before he could contemplate an answer he intuitively knew that She was here, in this room. He could feel her, or what must be her. His hair stood on end, his whiskers danced and his scalp itched maddeningly. Inexplicably, however, a feeling of calm serenity came over him. Oneira seemed to breathe easier as well though Ledge continued to breathe heavily. Here was a place of safety. Here was perfect connectedness. A warmth spread from his chest to his extremities and his mind calmed and now he had no desire other than to bow and offer himself to The Martha. Tears sprang into his eyes and the need to purge himself of himself was strong.

"I just did as you taught me, your honor," Bagnus said quietly, answering a voice apparently that Vilb did not hear.

"We came as quickly as we could," Casimir said. "The Keystone."

"The Keystone," repeated a voice that resonated like a deep well and at the bottom only sadness and suffering and depth that interminable mourning brings. Vilb knew then that this could only be the voice of The Martha.

"So you have finally come," the voice said and Vilb knew she spoke to him.

"It was an accident," confessed Vilb. His eyes were cast down. He released Oneira's hand and put his own together before him as if in prayer. "I do not know what I am. Please help me, Great Mother." He moved to his knees, as did Oneira.

"Please help us, Great Mother," she said.

"How is Quadros?" The Martha asked.

"He is… frustrated, Your Honor," said Vilb, his forehead against the floor and it sounded as if the voice before him was quietly laughing, though there was no mirth in the sound.

A light emerged in front of Vilb and in the light The Martha revealed herself.

"Rise and let me look at you," she said. "I am pleased with all of you. It has been a long while since my children from the east have come to see me, though I admit, I am difficult to find in these dark days."

She sat before them wearing the red cassock of her followers, its cowl tossed back. A red weave she had wrapped around her neck and head as if to hold it together, so fragile, so ancient her body appeared to be. Her face was the emaciated visage of the dead, a milky marble skull covered in a flesh that had contracted around the bone and become one with it.

So much like Quadros.

"I am not yet past my child-bearing years," she said, and she lifted her chin and locked Vilb with her gaze and Vilb did his best to meet it, though there was something horrible about the sight of her. Her left eye was a clouded tumescence with a wandering, sea-blown iris mesmerizing in its own right. It moved as if in search of some suitable subject upon which to fall, while the other eye was no eye at all. It was all socket, the hollow lined with silver and encrusted with flecks of illuminated emerald gems.

Her hands were long and thin and, like the face, a petrified fusion of flesh and bone. This was The Great Mother Martha.

He caught sight of her left hand and noticed that it lacked a fifth-finger, or that most of the fifth finger was nothing more than an ancient polished nub. In spite of the warmth around him, Vilb shuddered. How had it come to this? Had she really lived for so long? Had she come from the Ancient World to be the god of this one?

"I am sorry for leaving you for so long, my children. Quadros as you know has interrupted a great many of my plans, and the east, all the Gazi seed I planted over the millennia have been left untended for far too long.

I am sorry. You must know that I never intended for it to come to this." She paused as if to consider her words. "But I was not unprepared. Even now Quadros squanders the Arclight and the Power of M to stop me, but you have finally emerged together as the Keystone."

"Because of the remains? What are the remains?" asked Vilb, and The Martha coughed.

"Yes, well, quite right my child, but we do not use such puerile terms here."

"Beg your pardon, ma'am," said Bagnus.

"What do you remember? Of... of what you carry and who you are?" She asked them both this question but did not wait for their answers. Behind him Vilb heard Ledge shuffle and move almost imperceptibly to a position left of Vilb.

"I am old," she went on. "And weak. And now I am forced to hide. Here. In this place. My defeat is only surpassed by the shame I feel. Surely you must understand this? I have nothing to offer you. Only Quadros moves with power now. He takes all to himself. Even as Azo and I rot in his prisons. Quadros positions himself for the final move."

"It is true," she whispered, and her face, if indeed it could still be called a face, shifted, perhaps softened. "Quadros even now wields the Power of M. It's our worst fear realized. Where is Master Qir when we need him?"

Vilb's eyes lit up at the mention of Master Qir. Did The Martha not know about Prav? The Martha went on. "And judging by your expression you believe Simon's Restoration is our only hope. Yet... it means my destruction." She raised her voice now and her eye flashed. "I see now that Levinthal remains as arrogant and self-righteous as ever. Have you no shame, boy? In coming here and raising the memory of my shame?"

Vilb sputtered, taken aback.

She raised a white hand and pointed over Vilb's left shoulder. Just then Casimir lept behind Ledge, grabbed him from behind and slit his throat with a milky white blade. He dropped the body with a thud to the floor and the seeping blood drained away through cracks in the metal floor.

"He was sent to destroy me," said The Martha, fatigue and sadness in her voice. She looked at Vilb once again.

"The Fourth Realm. Chicago. Levinthal rules you and I am sorry that I could not protect you from his... incursions into your mind. Into all of the east. He is a plague upon us."

She paused and sighed before going on. "As far as what you are, know this then: you are a wild sequence generated from outside the field. I have tried to control you, but others have discovered your pattern and have interfered. To obey them is to destroy me. But to destroy them you must save Simon, and in His Restoration is my destruction."

Vilb and Oneira remained silent and not comprehending.

"I see that you are without guile," she said, and a warmth flowed from the light before him once again and he gazed at her glowing face.

"There must be Restoration," she said quietly. "Without it we fail. But first you must remember. You must feel the past." She lifted a thin hand and made a gesture to her attendants in the shadows around her. "Take them to Azo. Quickly."

Azo

I

Azo was an old man, more skin than bone, who sat alone in a cell of ebony stone, from floors, to walls, to ceiling. He sat atop what appeared to be a heap of ragged fabrics of different colors, scraps really, illuminated by a preternatural green glow that had no source, unless it was the figure himself. But as Vilb grew accustomed to the light of the cell it became more obvious that Azo's eyes glowed with a verdant, preternatural green and this lit the figure's face with a lurid light more of shadow than illumination. It was as if the srapi he wore had grown over time, or that the man who once wore it had shrunk and lost himself in the unwinding of his robes. His face reminded Vilb of The Martha's ossified visage of too much bone covered by not enough flesh, though as to that Azo's appearance left Vilb with the sense that he had once—and could perhaps still—walk among the living.

"Forgive the inhospitable surroundings. I am not my own person these days." Azo gestured at the walls of his cell. "I am trophy of Quadros, denuded of my power. He keeps me here and I stay, by agreement. In this way I protect Martha. But first things first my friends. I am glad to see you, glad that our mutual friend Bagnus has defied the Pan-Archer and brought you before me. Quadros is lazy in his power, undisciplined, greedy and impatient—though we have tried to teach him the virtue of restraint, of patience..." and at this Azo's voice trailed off. "But we have failed. His greed takes him away from the Citadel for long periods, and so you have come."

"Can you not escape?" asked Vilb impulsively. "Flee with Bagnus? To The Martha?"

Azo sighed heavily. "Would that it were possible. I am a prisoner of the Power of M. If I leave the confines of the Citadel, I will cease to exist."

"Then you are a willing prisoner?" asked Oneira, and Vilb winced at her tone. Did she dare offend the gods? But Azo was far from offended. He seemed to be laughing quietly to himself.

"I see that Martha's work continues to inspire."

"Is there no going back?" asked Oneira, this time more desperately, and Vilb turned to her and found her hand in the dark and squeezed it.

"The AkiGazi have razed the east," said Azo, a sudden fierceness in his response that was not there only a moment before. "This is the legacy of Quadros. He hands over Little Earth and all that we have done to the destroyers." Azo paused and regained himself. "Simon has left a path for us that only now, some two-thousand years after his scattering have we discerned. There is no going back and to go forward is uncertain, for the path remains obscured." Then he turned to Vilb and caught his eye in the darkness. "The Martha hopes for you. Together you must bring her to Erebus. If we succeed we may yet defeat Quadros completely and save..." but his voice lost its way and trailed off into silence.

"Save who?" asked Vilb quietly.

"Perhaps no one. Perhaps ourselves," Azo finally answered. "Come with me and let me show you what we still control before Quadros returns to San Simon. Bagnus, please tell Methodius we are ready for his guidance. And thank you for your loyal service once again." Bagnus bowed deeply, turned quickly, and ducked out of the cell.

• • •

After a dizzying ride down into the entrails of The Citadel, deep beneath Little Earth Vilb, Oneira and Azo—guided by the silent figure of Methodius—ended their journey and found themselves perched on a silver platform overlooking a vast cavern, greater than anything Vilb had ever seen or imagined possible. It was more than a cavern, for it had been expertly hewn from the stone and formed into a tunnel that from where they stood, appeared positively bustling with activity. It appeared that hundreds of Aegis were at work in the passageway for as far as the eye could see in both directions. Vilb was stunned speechless. Three, perhaps four of his hills could have fit inside, one on top of the other, perhaps five across. How could the world have such strange wonders underneath it?

"Have we come to another Realm?" whispered Oneira and Azo laughed gently.

"This is the Barrier Ring. It is a part of Little Earth even as it gives rise to the Power of M. The other six Realms are far beyond this place. Across the world to a greater Earth."

Beneath Vilb's stunned awe at the size, scope and buzzing activity of the Barrier Ring a forgotten part of his mind nodded in remembrance of this deep place, yet he tried to dismiss this unexpected feeling of familiarity out of hand. It was irrational, impossible and probably the result of his shock and fatigue.

His eye followed a narrow path of white light that made a white path along the silver ceiling. A soft, unflagging glow illuminated the gigantic tunnel as if the long day's sun had dropped from the sky and bled through the stone. Vilb took in the white path as far as he could until it curved gently away and, presumably, ran off into the far distance. He turned and looked in the other direction and saw much the same sight.

Aegis moved below them, up and down the tunnel floor and, far across to the other side, many others moved about a massive, suspended platform beside the obsidian floor of the tunnel, like a great polished river bed, only rather than flowing water, something else moved past, as if born by the wind but following the floor's path.

"The Barrier Ring," Vilb said, and he could feel it on his skin. It was a wave of speckled particles flowing past and it smelled of thunderstorm.

"Yes. It makes a vast circle under Little Earth. If you began walking here and headed off in that direction," and Azo pointed, "you would, in the end, return to this same point after a long journey. The Ancients built this place. The tunnel floor is a path that lifts and carries us at much greater speeds than Quadros's can manage. Mag-rail the Ancients called it. We tend to it for Simon." Vilb caught a note of pride and satisfaction in Azo's tone as he pointed below them to a large, silver box, twice as long as it was wide. "Mag-rail," said Vilb, trying the word and feeling it in his mouth. Azo nodded.

"The Ancients were great inventors. Machines of every kind they imagined and then built."

"Are you an invention of the Ancients?" asked Vilb and the white, stone face of Azo softened into a gentle smile.

"Are you?" Azo asked softly, his eyes wide with expectation.

"What madness is this?" Oneira had become thoroughly unsettled. She shook her hand free of Vilb's grasp and stepped backwards.

Azo nodded his head. "Forgive me. Let me be more plain. Simon is the Maker. He made us when He made Little Earth."

"If what you say is true then why does he serve that thing in the dome?" Oneira demanded, pointing savagely at Methodius.

"He helped us," protested Vilb, but Azo waved him off and Methodius broke from his position and kneeled down in order to speak.

"Quadros took some of us when he took control of Erebus, but even he does not know how many of us there truly are. Some serve him willingly, and some serve him in a delusion, and some serve him in the hopes of subverting his control. We are much like you in that way. I serve the Keystone," and with this he turned and his gaze fell upon Vilb.

"How many are you?" Vilb asked, but Methodius did not hear the question, or perhaps he ignored it.

"How many?" Vilb asked again, and this time Azo spoke.

"Many," the ancient figure said gravely. "We wait and serve for Simon's return. We tend to the Power of M, try and limit what Quadros can channel, but the Halo fails and soon," he nodded to the amber river below them, "the Barrier itself will fail. Quadros has corrupted its power."

"What is the Halo?" asked Oneira.

"What does the Barrier do?" asked Vilb.

"The Halo is another tunnel, not as great as the Barrier Ring, but," and here Azo dropped his voice, "just as crucial to Little Earth. The Barrier Ring channels the Halo." Azo pointed again. "Across the floor of the tunnel. Look there.

Through that archway is a spur that leads to the inner-circle of the Halo. Two hundred kilometers from here and one then reaches the Halo, but to enter the confines of the Halo would mean certain death. Only the Aegis may work in and around the Halo. We preserve the works of the true Simon and serve for His return."

"Mee-ters? Keelo-meeters? What are these words?" asked Vilb.

"The words denote the Ancient method of measuring distance," said Azo. "You have traveled three hundred kilometers since you left the east. San Simon is yet another five hundred kilometers west of Lake Vost. How long have you been traveling?"

"I cannot tell," said Vilb and Azo nodded. "A long while."

"Quadros will return to the Citadel, and soon, perhaps by the end of this day," Azo said.

"As the Barrier fails, the darkness falls and soon the ice will come. With the cold comes the AkiGazi. Little Earth will die."

"But why?" cried Oneira.

"Have you not yet the sense to see it? Quadros seeks revenge against The Martha."

"The Martha?" asked Vilb, and Azo turned to him and sighed.

"The gods," he said slowly, as if speaking to a child, "hate one another."

Martha, and Quadros and Master Qir and, yes, I—all of us have bled the Halo at one time or another for our own purposes—for our own power. Once, long ago, the Power of M was masterfully subverted by the Four of us working together to defeat and scatter Simon, but that was long ago. We regret our failure."

"To defeat Simon? Why would you seek to defeat the great god? Simon is... Simon is the Maker. Simon is..." but her voice trailed off as Vilb put his hand on her arm.

"It was a... great error, our decision to link with Quadros against Simon, but it was a decision done in haste, and in the utmost urgency of our need."

"It was Him or You," said Vilb, seeing intuitively into Azo's cryptic assessment and Azo sighed, paused and collected himself before going on.

"Quadros has discovered a way to usurp the Halo's power, to control the Barrier Ring and to sit on Simon's throne. Quadros will not stop until he destroys the others and Little Earth. How you escaped him I do not understand. Had he come into possession of the remains and himself become the Keystone the Greater Earth would itself have been trampled once again under the heel of his boot."

"Once again?" asked Vilb.

"I have trampled Little Earth" Vilb said suddenly. "In my dreams."

"You are the heart and keystone of the Aegis," said Azo simply. "The remains are the Power of M and you—The Martha's work—together with the Power of M have the power to make and unmake. The Aegis will assemble for you, as you. This is the final power that Quadros seeks. The gods vie for you."

"What does this mean?" Oneira was reeling even as Vilb tried to comprehend Azo's words.

"Who does... Master Qir serve?" asked Vilb at once, yet he somehow knew the answer. The marble eyes of the Aegis fixed Vilb with an adamantine gaze.

"We do not know," said the Aegis quietly.

Oneira groaned.

"Of course," said Vilb, but he didn't understand, not yet, but something was emerging from the background of his mind, like a familiar landmark rising above the burning horizon, yet it shimmered and danced and threatened to dissolve as he approached it.

"What are the remains?" asked Oneira. "Why Vilb? Why the Ubernaki?"

"The remains come from the Great Mother," said Azo quietly, "and are that which cannot be removed, forgotten or done away with. They are the bones of an evil deed done by Quadros to The Martha long ago to serve his own ends. The Martha destroyed what issued from her and hid the remains from Quadros before he could make himself another Simon. With you, her other children."

"May The Martha protect us," whispered Oneira.

"Yes. Indeed," echoed Azo.

Vilb rubbed his temples. "And Quadros? What does he seek?" It had all begun to settle on him now across the bridge of his nose, over both eyes and to the back of his neck. His head felt as if it were splitting. After the Spire Massif it began to press on him from within in earnest, it let up in the palace of Quadros, and now since his strange transformation under the dome, the feeling of having been here before positively throbbed and made him feel as if his head were simply too small to contain it all.

"Tell us the whole story," Vilb commanded, hopeful that the entire story might finally snap into focus if only he knew all that there was to know. Azo seemed almost relieved that Vilb had ordered him to divulge. He put his hands together in his lap and began to explain.

"The gods are at war. Quadros hates the others and he has always hated them, been jealous of them, of the others, especially The Martha."

"Why?" demanded Vilb.

"In Ancient days..." and Azo paused and held first Vilb's, then Oneira's gaze before going on, "Martha was the mother of Simon." Vilb shook his head.

"I do not understand."

"I know. I am sorry. It is difficult to explain. Before Little Earth, in Ancient Times, far away in the Fourth Realm Martha and Jonathan gave birth to a son. His name was Simon."

"Gave birth? What does this mean?" asked Oneira.

Azo nodded as if only then realizing the difficulty of his task.

"In the Ancient Realms lives came into the world from the mother's body."

Oneira groaned and Vilb shook his head.

"Ancients called this the work of procreation. Their great god commanded it to be so, and so they did this thing. The gods of Little Earth are the last of the Ancients and The Martha is the last of the mothers of the Ancient world. She gave birth to Simon and he was a child, a boy, and he grew, and then died, his life cut cruelly short. At this time there was a great cataclysm and the Greater Earth fell to ruin. Martha and I, along with Quadros and Qir fled to Antarctica—to Little Earth, and used the Power of M to counter the cataclysm, but we were unprepared and completely inexperienced at doing the work of… the gods. Yet gods we became by virtue of Ancient science, immortality and the Power of M."

Vilb held his head in his hands as he listened. It seemed that Oneira simply stared off into space as if in a trance.

"There is more," said Azo. "Quadros has worked for a thousand years to control the Halo so that he might use it and take Simon's throne, and forge a New Body for himself as Simon. He is a mere pretender so far, but he may yet succeed. His continued existence remains our greatest failure," Azo confessed, yet he looked up, a question in his eyes. "You were in his grasp. How did you escape?"

"I do not know," said Vilb. "Please," said Azo.

Vilb felt uncertain. The gods of Little Earth did not yet know of Prav or Master Qir's involvement. Should he tell them? Who would be served? Who would be harmed? He did not know. Azo went on.

"Will you bring out the remains then?" Vilb hesitated for an instant and looked up.

"I do not control it," and as he spoke he raised his hands and turned his palms up. They glowed with a warm, faint amber color and appeared not as flesh so much as the stonework of the Aegis.

"Place your attention here," said Methodius, and he touched the back of Vilb's neck gently with the tip of one finger. It throbbed and his flesh tingled and his hair stood on end. "Regard yourself from this position. See your thinking mind and your feeling heart from this third position not as one or as two, but as parts of a larger whole."

Vilb breathed and did as Methodius directed. It seemed like a simple thing to do, however separating his awareness from his thoughts was more difficult than he had imagined. The thoughts that rose within him grabbed him back and demanded not to be abandoned.

He would do what he had always done. Rather than wrench his mind away from his thoughts, Vilb first concentrated on his throbbing heart. With his presence of mind there he felt the surging of fear and excitement and the feelings vibrated within him much more intensely than ever before, but letting go of his feelings, letting them flow in and through him, was difficult, almost as difficult as letting go of his thoughts. It was as if Methodius had asked him to jump from the edge of a cliff into a dark void.

"Vilb de Solenthay does not exist," said Azo almost cautiously, as if he were afraid of what might happen next.

Questions rose in Vilb's mind, questions about the future of Little Earth, about the Keystone, and about the meaning of this life, about the dreams of ice and Chicago that remained with him, still incomplete and misunderstood, and about a strange name that no one spoke of: Levinthal. As this name emerged in his mind, thoughts of Prav and intense feelings for her quickly followed, and then Oneira came to mind, and The Martha's bizarre face flowed in and through Oneira's, and the two were one, yet not one. His heart beat hard in his chest and he felt the fear and the longing he carried. A heaviness was within him as well for what he believed was his failure to save Prav from Quadros.

"Surrender and realize," said Azo in a furtive voice and Methodius placed a massive hand on the back of Vilb's neck and shoulders. Warmth there now, and growing, spreading, melting, silent, ambient warmth in his spine, his head, his eyes.

Suddenly Vilb saw himself as if seeing into a polished seeing stone that reflected but could not see or reflect itself, and like a mirror, it was unstained by the objects that moved before it. It was then that, for a moment, he found the place from which to regard himself as something other than merely an individual self and he felt the remains within him warming him, melting him, drawing all to itself, and there in the Void he felt a power rising.

He heard Quadros Prang's disdainful voice echoing in his mind. Know thyself it said, and for the first time Vilb suspected that such a thing might be possible, though it also frightened him, for he intuited that knowing meant rage and to surrender to rage was to become destruction, and even as a fire rose from deep inside him and promised to engulf him when called, he lurched away and by force of will dragged his mind back from the brink and into its waking state.

Vilb heard Oneira gasp. Azo went stiff and his gleaming exterior turned flat and hard. His voice could still be heard though it seemed distant and small.

"The Power of M is in you," said Azo. He was excited, agitated even. "You must learn to surrender to it easily and quickly." Vilb shook his head.

"I felt... I felt a fire within me, a... a rage." Vilb's jaw was set firm and his eyebrows, once easy and relaxed, were furrowed with tension.

"The rage of Simon," said Azo proudly. "Surrender to it. Control it. There is time yet. We must see that you have it at your fingertips before our next move."

• • •

Vilb shook his head. He felt a resoluteness within him assert itself.

"From now on I will decide where I go and who it is I meet with," he declared, as he spoke he moved directly before Azo and Methodius, both laughed gently and nodded.

"Good for you, my Captain. Good for you. If you wish it, then and only then will we ride into battle. Quadros marches before us but he is not yet in a place where we can strike. Will you follow me for a little while longer? I have more to show you."

Vilb nodded. "I will follow," he said to Azo. "But only for the time being."

II

Azo led them down a winding silver stair that carried them from the high platform they stood onto a bridge that crossed the tunnel floor to the other side. The bridge led them to a wide, level platform raised just above the obsidian floor of the tunnel. They stopped under an archway to take in the scene. Before them was the Barrier Ring and in the distance white figures moved swiftly with purpose. Behind Vilb and still deeper underground lay, according to Azo, the Halo. Vilb could feel in his feet its power rising from the passageway under the platform--a palpable heat warmed his skin and weighed on him as if he were suddenly carrying a great load on his shoulders.

"The Power of M," said Azo. "Rest now, however, while we have a moment."

It was then that Aegis began to approach, one at a time, then two, even three linked arm-in-arm approached, a veritable wall of Aegis. Whether alone or in a group they bowed low.

"Do they bow to you?" Oneira asked Azo and he shook his head and nodded towards Vilb.

"To *him*," he said.

• • •

Yet another Aegis approached and knelt before Oneira and Vilb. "Sleep. Rest," he said softly, and his voice had a soporific effect. "Let your minds become quiet and calm. Rest." Even as the Aegis spoke Vilb felt suddenly exhausted and unable to hold his eyes open or his head up. He lay down on his side on the soft cushion as did Oneira beside him. With his belly full and the Halo passage thrumming all around him, his mind quieted.

Almost immediately Vilb fell into a dream. Before him rose a face, large, as if it were the face of someone standing right before him, close, intimate.

"Well done my boy," the face said quietly, and Vilb watched and listened and felt utterly passive, unconcerned, hardly curious for some reason, and beneath this response was another, a part of him that somehow knew that face, remembered that mellifluous voice.

At once he knew that he beheld the face of Levinthal. The jaw was square, yet his face was not of stone, rather, it appeared soft and pink like the painted cliff walls of the badlands in the east with the softness of the young. The eyes were bottomless eyes, green and gold in a sea of white, and rimmed with hair black and fine, and it waved over his forehead like a flag of surety. Surely Levinthal's was the face of a great god, Vilb thought, an unknown god, and he felt his last tenuous grip on his conscious mind—the mind that watched the dream—open and relax until there was no more Vilb left to realize anything at all. There was only quiet, empty, calm. And he became the face in the dream and the desire to wield the power growing within his body filled him.

A voice unfolded itself from within, and a light and a warmth led him along and soon he was coursing over the tops of roiling waves, over the Girdling Sea and to the seas beyond, to a great ocean, and then just as quickly he soared over the tops of trees, and he was beyond Little Earth to a land thick with green growth. The voice spoke to him, and yet it was his voice speaking through him. He recognized it as the voice, that it was his own, and yet it was unlike anything he had ever heard before.

"It is time to return to Chicago, my boy. Bring me the New Body of Simon."

Behind the voice of Levinthal, Vilb heard other voices. Oneira was calling his name even as a phalanx of Aegis were gathered round him murmuring one to another. Azo stood guard over the scene. There was tension, a rising anger in the room. All of this Vilb could sense somehow even before he opened his eyes.

It was Methodius who spoke first. "We apologize, Keystone, for allowing the disruption."

"Disruption?"

"From beyond," said Azo. "From Chicago." Vilb's eyes went wide.

"You know of Levinthal's voice?"

Azo nodded as if tired to the extreme. "Levinthal seeks to block all that we do and is the enemy of all of the gods. Like Quadros, he seeks to make a Simon of himself, and this blasphemy must not be permitted. Before we can move on Levinthal, however, we must move on Quadros. Now."

Azo was earnest.

Vilb rose to his feet confused again.

"And?" Azo said, smiling softly.

"What more can I do against Quadros?" asked Vilb.

Azo looked behind him at the crowd of Aegis gathered all around, turned back to Vilb and spoke. "The Aegis serve the Keystone," said Azo... And Levinthal serves the Board. And we," he said, and he waved his hand towards the rapt concourse of Aegis pressing in all around him now, "we serve Simon." A murmur of ascent rippled through the ranks even as some called out "Simon," and then another, and then more, and then a torrent of voices were calling out "Keystone" and "Simon" and "Restoration," and the voice of the Aegis rose up and it roared like a great storm against the chamber walls.

The Fall of the Ancients

I

They returned to Azo's cell but before they could recover their breath or their wits, Azo resumed his seat and began to speak.

"There is still more. It is time that you remembered who you... were." He shifted atop his pile of rags as if uncomfortable, or uneasy. "Look closely at the floor," Azo said and waited. Vilb looked down, then dropped to his knees to have a closer look. Oneira was there beside him. The ebony floor of the dark cell was not void, rather, it began to glow with a faint illumination, as if the sun shone somehow behind the stone, and on the surface a flowing script became quite obvious. In fact, the entire surface of the dark cell, with the exception of a few dark patches here and there, appeared to be covered with a fine, scrawling amber radiance.

"My book," Azo said, evidently pleased. "I've been writing it while holed up here."

Vilb and Oneira looked at each other and exchanged a puzzled silence.

Azo coughed. "Well, it's no matter. Here now, let me be brief. It's a history really. Of the Ancients, of the gods before they came to Little Earth." Vilb straightened up and listened carefully and Azo kept on. "We were a horrible lot, well at least some of us. From where I sit now, it seems obvious that Simon was our destiny. Or else a dreadful mistake. Or both. Then, when we were mortals," and he paused and looked at Vilb.

"Like you," he said quietly, "a madness drove us." Vilb stared back, dumb. Oneira rose and wandered to the wall and stroked the light with her fingertips. Azo cleared his throat, shifted in his seat and Vilb thought he seemed uncomfortable.

"I can see that I do not have your complete attention," he said, more to himself than to Vilb or Oneira. "We've been here before," he went on. "Not precisely like this, but the others from the east, your father for instance. He stood before me as you do now, though under... different circumstances." Vilb went rigid and even Oneira turned to look at Azo.

"My father you say?"

"That's right." Azo seemed to fix him with his stare, though as for that his eyes were difficult to see and his head was covered now by a cowl not unlike the srapi of the east.

"Do you know your father?" Azo asked.

"Simon is the father of us all," Oneira broke in. Her eyes were fixed again on the sun-colored light emanating from the script that ran round and round the room.

"It's everything I can remember," Azo told her. "I'm spent, I think," and his voice trailed off. He turned to Vilb again and tried a new tack. "We lived with Simon you know. Did you know that?"

"It was the Pax Simonica," Oneira stated calmly. They had both heard this. As children.

"Go on then, girl. Tell me what you know."

Oneira lifted her chin, closed her eyes and recited as if in front of her tribe at one of the Meson's catechisms. "It was a joyous time in Little Earth, when Simon and His servants walked together on Little Earth. He washed the world. He prepared for our coming. He formed the land. He raised the Arclight. He fashioned San Simon and the Citadel, and all for the benefit of His children. The Power of M flowed freely in those days and Little Earth flourished and the children of Simon spread to the far corners of the world." Azo sighed.

"Sort of," Azo said. "Simon had power, there was no doubt of that. Greater power than the four of us have ever known. Far greater. We still cannot begin to match it." Azo sighed. "At the beginning, long ago, after Simon emerged, He kept the four of us alive for vengeance sake. Even his mother. Even his own mother. We had no choice—we were his dolls and we did his bidding. That was the true beginning of this world. Slavery. Revenge. Power." Azo's voice trailed off. "It's not so different now," he said quietly.

Vilb looked up expectantly. After all he had come through, he remained essentially in the dark, yet in this cell, with this figure seated above and before him he felt as if the darkness was lifting. He looked at his palms and felt a throbbing at the center, and heat. Wherever he placed a fingertip on the walls or floor of the cell, the script blazed more brightly at his touch.

His heart began to pound in his chest and he rose and began to pace back and forth across the floor.

"Good," said Azo. "Yes, that's good. Let me say more. In the beginning Simon fashioned this prison for the four of us, and the Citadel for Himself. A massive throne really, a marker, the Seat of Simon He called it and below Him, trapped in the bowels of the Earth there was us. We were His choir, His angels, His demons, His children, and His reason for being all rolled into one.

He grew weary of this game sooner than we could have hoped. Like a young child He forgave easily and, though all of us were disingenuous, at one point I do believe we repented at his feet. Even Quadros. When Simon dropped His guard we escaped to Erebus, to the White Room, and Qir found a way to shut down the Bosonic Pile. In that moment Simon's entire field went down—all of it, and this is no small thing. Are you with me, boy? You there?" He gestured to Vilb. They both nodded, their eyes wide, their brows furrowed. Vilb felt as if he was on the edge of something and standing there he felt prepared to pitch over and lose himself in the fall if necessary. "Simon's short reign ended some two thousand years ago. One of us has ruled Little Earth ever since."

Vilb hung his head, embarrassed somehow by what he was hearing and a feeling of hot shame gripped him round the shoulders and squeezed. Azo went on: "The scattering of Simon was the last time the four of us ever worked together. The Martha and I took up residence in what would become the Citadel. With us was Master Qir. Quadros seemed, at least for a time, content with his wanderings. We all knew he bided his time for a return to Chicago and to Levinthal. We had no idea though, not then. Martha… Martha did not share the truth with me until too late."

"Chicago?" Vilb echoed back. He felt troubled. He had heard this word before, had he not? It came from a strange yet almost familiar place in his mind and it tugged at his surface awareness.

"The Fourth Realm, my boy."

"There is more than Little Earth?" Oneira asked tremulously. "It's true then?"

"Much more. Indeed, the children's stories of the east are true. Seven Realms. Little Earth is only the Seventh. A life raft. An Ark. But I digress. Let me continue."

"After the disruption of the Bosonic Pile, Simon's power ended and His presence disappeared from the land. We thought it was a trick, or that it was a temporary effect, but no. We gathered the Pile and raised the Arclight for ourselves and even this did not wake Simon. It seemed that we were free. The four of us took the Power of M into our own hands. We had, it seemed, survived the tyranny of the Ancients and Simon's vengeance, and felt, rightly, that a new age had begun."

"The other Realms were dead. For all of our great power, we were trapped on a barren land and there were so few of us left. And it was cold then. The land was covered in ice. We lived in the many tubes and tunnels underground. And contrary to what some may have believed at one time, immortality is not a stimulant to action. It's a soporific state that soon leads to intense, morbid introspection. We each fell into this at one time, and tried to end our lives, but to no avail.

"It was The Martha who roused us and set the three of us on to a task—we would melt the ice and make a Little Earth, and populate it, and have a world that others had only dreamed of in the long past. It would be a garden of peace and balance." Azo exhaled deeply. "And so for the next thousand years. It was Master Qir who showed the rest of us how to transfer the genetic sequence of what we had once called Simon's Curse into our own genetic offspring. Master Qir's Millennial Cadre—he called them his Army of Children—and they were the first, and probably still the most, successful genetic sequence of all of us. Really a breakthrough. The Cadre tipped the balance of power on Little Earth and drove Quadros mad. Martha too was rather jealous. She had yet to achieve such perfection in her genetic regenerations. It would come for her too, soon enough." He paused before continuing his monologue:

"Our plan was simple. We intended to populate Little Earth with the regenerated peoples who, when grown to maturity, might find their way back to the other Realms and retake the world we had lost. Needless to say, we attempted genetic improvements and were limited for source material. I think this needs to be understood. When we came here we had no idea and so were, really rather unprepared. Not much genetic diversity, I'm afraid. We only had a handful of samples from which to draw on in giving rise to the flora, fauna, microorganisms, and... human populations of Little Earth. It was a very serious limitation."

"Human?" Oneira asked, shaking her head and Azo nodded in response.

"Human. What the Ancients called their species, and the source from which you spring. Human my dear. Your genetic material comes from Homo sapien sapien to be precise." Azo stared, a smile playing at the corners of his mouth. "Three and a half million years of human evolution have spawned you. And the gods." Azo paused. "But I digress. Please, let me go on. The gods attempted to improve upon your nature, my dear. In that we succeeded. Or at least I succeeded I suppose. The regeneration tanks—the Levinthal tanks from Chicago, brought to Erebus Station long ago—we used them, used what we had learned there, and sequenced a population, long lived, disease and drought resistant, and sterile, or at least we thought so at the time. Children finally did come into the world, but not by design. It's very chaotic, I must say. We can participate, of that I'm sure, but to control? There is no control, though Quadros has yet to accept this truth.

So perhaps you might imagine how the three of us responded when Master Qir produced—and then reproduced boldly and successfully—the uberkind, the Millennial Cadre, the super-sequence we had dreamed about. Martha and I banished Qir to the Transveld. That's where he is still."

"Jealousy leads to suffering," mumbled Vilb.

"Martha, Quadros Prang and I, we each intensified our own genetic protocol sequences, each attempting to outdo Qir's achievements. We awoke ancient antagonisms that remained among us from before. Like demons from an underworld. You, my dear, are the work of Martha, for instance," and he nodded to Oneira. "And you too," he said to Vilb, "but not completely. I had a hand in you. The entire east we allowed to our work. Quadros went back to his wanderings, outmatched, and Qir—he and his Cadre disappeared into the caves of the Transveld Range. In the end it became clear that Quadros had not been silenced, for he worked malicious mischief against all of our plans. We thought that his only desire was to return to the Fourth Realm, to Chicago, to Levinthal…" Azo paused.

"Levinthal's boy," Vilb Solenthay heard himself say as if he watched and listened from above.

Azo appeared not to hear. "The Martha fared better, at least at first. With my help her Gazi Peoples looked extremely promising. They did not live as long as the Cadre, nor did they have any special enhancements other than to be perfectly suited to their habitat. We thought we had arrived at our sought after goals, and quickly at that. It was then we realized that we could not simply manufacture clones, rather, the Gazi must be free to range where they would. We gave you a mythology. We gave you the basic tools that the land allowed. I'm sorry the forests died. A desert is a harsh environment, but we made the rain to fall—thanks to the Arclight and the power of the em-frame installation. Originally it was a vast machine of the Ancients made to control weather, and populations all over the Greater Earth. That was before though. When we began to terra-form Antarctica we had no genetic material for so many other things you needed, and yet the Gazi persevered. I think your people would have gone on indefinitely—a kind of balance had been achieved—but then Quadros emerged from his wanderings and seized the Power of M in a way we thought not possible. The Arclight has diminished each solar cycle ever since. The east is dying. I'm told you're eating each other out there. I'm sorry my boy. It should not have come to that." Azo fell quiet.

"Destruction is woven into the very mind of Simon Himself it seems," said Vilb. A feeling of knowing and a feeling of terror crept over him and he risked a question. "Who is my father?"

"I have had time here, in the dark, to remember all that I have lost and how." Azo paused, exhaled deeply. "You are your father."

After a moment of befuddled silence Oneira exploded. "What mad riddle is this?"

· · ·

"Ah, yes. The answer will lead you to your true natures. The two of you. Or to madness."

"I am already mad," said Vilb. "Out with it."

"Patience, my boy. Patience. One mouth is not big enough to say it all, and certainly not all at once. Two thousand years. Two thousand years." Azo rose to his feet, but slowly. He shuffled forward mumbling. "Two thousand years," he said again, this time pointing at Vilb and shaking his finger. "Believe it. Or not." He put up a hand to silence Vilb. "The facts do not require your belief. They simply are. The fact is that you, both of you, are here."

"Forgive me," said Vilb, only partly remonstrated.

"Done," said Azo, and with that he pulled the cowl back as the small seat upon which he perched moved silently, and glided down until it rested before Vilb and Oneira. "Take a closer look at… my face."

In the Barrier Ring Azo had worn his cowl, but now with it pulled back Vilb took in full Azo's face and let out a gasp. He knew this face. Before him sat an image from the past, and from more than one past. Here was a reflection from some distant time of the Ancients, and from Little Earth as well. The face before him was fuller than his own, the shoulders were broader, but the deep-set black eyes, the wild eyebrows, the furrowed forehead, the jutting chin, the waving hair that stood on end, the figure before Vilb had the face of the last Meson of the Ubernaki, a man who went by the name of Valkrie.

"As I said, we had only the smallest amounts of viable genetic material from which to seed Little Earth." Azo shrugged as if embarrassed. "We had to use our own. You my dear," he said, moving round to face Oneira more directly.

"You are the seed of The Martha, you are her daughter, you are her mother and you, if you survive the remembering, are her."

"The others? In the east? Are they all… you… me?" Azo nodded, evidently pleased. "Some are variations, yes. Others no. Others are drawn from source material that we brought along, but did not survive the journey from the Ancient world."

"Ledge," Vilb said and Azo shrugged.

"I am sorry, boy, I am not all-knowing. I do not know you all by name."

Oneira buried her face in her hands and sank to the floor.

"Rest now and then I'll tell you more," said Azo, and the room went dark.

▌▌

Vilb awoke from troubling dreams of cold and there was Azo perched on his pile of rags. "Before Simon, before Little Earth, the Ancients flogged the Seven Realms of the Greater Earth until the seas swelled and the air seethed. Once fertile plains and valleys withered. This was over two thousand years ago, before Simon, but only just before. The dying times for the human race, the people that came before us, your ancestors. It's all there," said Azo, and he pointed to the floor at their feet. "You have eyes. It's in the Gazi writing. Read it for yourself. Ask me anything as you like."

"A short history of the rise of Simon and the end of the Ancient civilization," Vilb read aloud. The hand was small and pinched.

"My early work," Azo apologized. "Do your best to follow along."

The history began:

"2029 a.d." Vilb began but quickly broke off. "A.D.? Is it not A.S.?"

Azo sighed. "That is a complicated question to answer right now, but suffice to say, the Ancients had their own gods and their own calendar. We have ours. I think you will understand more as you go. Keep at it."

Vilb nodded and went back to reading. "Chronic War. Environmental collapse. Desperate battles for food and water. Terrible weapons. Are we sociopaths? We live on even as they die." Vilb scanned down to a passage with words he more readily understood.

"Thirty-one years before Simon, the Ancients spread the first seeds of His Body into the skies above the Greater Earth. Atmospheric Regeneration Protocol."

"Atmospheric?" Vilb shook his head not quite able to place the word.

"The sky, the air, the barrier between the land and the stars above. It protects Little Earth, sustains us. In fact, the Arclight sustains and protects us from ultraviolet radiation."

"Ultraviolet radiation?" Vilb asked.

"Light from the sun that kills," Azo explained. "The sky had a natural protection that the Ancients destroyed. The Arclight protects us now. Enough? Read on. Read on."

So they read:

"Hundreds of millions of people died of exposure, starvation, cancers, especially in the southern hemisphere. Millions more went blind. A surreal horror gripped the peoples of the world. Would it spread to them? Was the death of the world at hand? Could it be stopped? Even amidst the terror and confusion the northern hemisphere continued to live, to work, and to contribute to the failure of the biosphere. The deaths of the hundreds of millions of people in South America, India and elsewhere became merely another cost of doing business. For a time global conflict came to a halt as entire nations attempted to respond to the crisis, for the crisis was not only from above. Extreme weather had gripped the planet as well yet populations continued to grow. There were too many people for too few resources, water and food chief among them." At this Vilb grunted with understanding.

"In the midst of the crisis came a new order from Asia, the Second Realm. They called their new confederation of nations the Third Wave for Global Survival. In the Northern and Western Realms, countries we called them, a conglomerate of multi-national business concerns known simply as the Consortium seized total control. To them the Third Wave was a terrorist organization intent on destroying civilization. Yet both sides were siblings of one parent: a culture that threatened the continued survival of homo sapiens along with countless other species, both plant and animal. At first Third Wave activities were small, desperate affairs meant to vent anger, disrupt the status quo, and provide pathetic purpose to otherwise hopeless lives, but as the crisis deepened, the small but determined band of would-be terrorists, revolutionaries, and environmentalists gathered together the billions of people who were starving, were irradiated every day by the sun, and had nothing to lose. Revolution spread across the southern hemisphere as the old political order gave way to the desperate nature of the times. Indonesia, then India, then, China—all fell to the Third Wave and The Consortium watched nervously. By 2033 a.d. the Third Wave controlled or threatened the destinies of half of the world's population, most of whom were in the process of dying of thirst or starving to death. Finally populations peaked and the great human die-off began. The new government of the southern hemisphere demanded the right to emigrate to the north where there was still some measure of atmospheric protection, adequate water supplies and food production. Political delays hampered justice and the Third Wave abandoned legal channels as terror swept spasmodically across entire continents. Soon Europe would experience a human tidal wave from the east. The Consortium announced that there was simply not enough room in the lifeboats and refused all emigration. It was a solution that had been tried in other times, but the cold-blooded nature of the decision to refuse the many millions of refugees made sense at the time. It was survival. Raw. Natural. Under these conditions the human heart is without a tendency to compassion. In the northern hemisphere Consortium leaders claimed absolute power in the name of civilization. Those who seized power had a simple answer to the global crisis: the Third Wave must be defeated, destroyed, eradicated. Genocide had once been the highest crime of human culture, yet now it became a method, a solution, a means to an end. History, the Consortium taught us, had been misunderstood. Genocide was not in and of itself a crime for crime was a relative condition, and the times required desperate, final solutions. Meanwhile, Consortium scientists sought earnestly for a way to prevent the northern hemisphere from experiencing the twin atmospheric catastrophes of ozone depletion and heat-trapping gases.

"In the spring of 2033 a.d. as an answer to Third Wave political developments, The Consortium of Western Economic and Technologic Powers declared itself a sovereign nation and vowed total war against all who threatened civilization. Swallowed up were the individual principalities of America, Europe, Russia and Japan and a host of smaller nation states. Not long after this stunning confederation was announced, the new ruling hierarchy of the Consortium revealed itself even as it announced to the world that it had developed an Ozone Regeneration Protocol they called Prozone. No one cared how it would work, only that it would work, so no mention was made of the molecular-sized micro-machines called nanozines that would make the miracle possible."

Vilb stopped reading and looked up. "Nanozines signifies what?" he called out.

"Hmm. Yes. A fair question." Azo paused for a moment and they waited in silence. "Imagine the Aegis," said Azo finally.

"We believe them to be a kind of living… machine. Imagine them so small that five hundred of them could sit on the tip of your eyelash. From there they could fly, or they could get inside the eyelash itself and move the particles that form it into some other shape. And unlike the Aegis, the nanozines could make more of themselves—without limit if there was enough energy present to sustain their replication. More than mere replication, however, they made new versions of themselves, smaller versions, and in this way the very fabric of space became saturated by a Consortium-controlled nano-sphere. In the end, without knowing it beforehand the Consortium seeded the Greater Earth with what would later become part of Simon's World Wide Body. What the Four came to understand later is that there is no Simon without first fusing the fabric of space with the nanozine."

Vilb nodded, not entirely sure that he understood, but he had not the heart to ask again, and so he went on reading:

"The Ancients thought that they—that we—had a power akin to magic at our disposal near the end. Just in time, as it were. The long promise of technological progress had, we thought, born the fruit that would heal us, save us, sustain us. And so the story emerged that now the Greater Earth and its life-sustaining habitat might be healed from within, one molecule at a time, finally made right by Consortium scientists. Even as the Greater Earth groaned under the ongoing human and political crisis, the possibilities of the nano-sphere made Consortium leaders drunk with real and imagined power."

"You see?" Azo broke in. "All that was needed was a mind capable of controlling a system that had no practical limits and that could provide access to a source of power on a scale known only to the gods of ancient mythology. Repair the Ozone, yes, but that was not enough. The dream became the total and absolute control of the Greater Earth's atmosphere. Nothing less would satisfy the Consortium. The sun would shine where we wanted it to shine. The rain would fall where we commanded it to fall. Drought would ravage only the undeserving, the dangerous, the evil who sought to destroy the wonders of civilization." Azo's voice broke off suddenly and he caught up himself. "I am sorry, boy. Right then. Go on. Keep reading."

"2034 a.d. Consortium scientists seeded the atmosphere with the first generation of nanozines and by the end of that year the people of northern hemispheres rejoiced. Ozone levels had recovered to seventy-five percent of their pre- crisis mass. Global temperatures had dropped by five degrees on average, nearing pre-industrial levels. Glaciers stabilized more rapidly than any could have foreseen and so sea levels stabilized. Clouds formed, rain fell again in drought stricken regions. More importantly, people went outside and breathed, albeit with trepidation. It seemed the great crisis had passed. The reason for being of Third Wave activities seemed too to have passed, and they were few and far between. Everyone waited to see if the southern hemisphere would recover as well. Perhaps the end was not so near after all.

As a celebration of their power the Consortium sent millions of tons of food to the starving as a good will gesture, but in the end southern skies remained deadly and the emergency aid only prolonged famine and the Third Wave for Global Survival destroyed Consortium concerns where and when they could. Australia fell, or conceded. Russia surrendered. In the southern hemisphere the will to resist Third Wave retribution had withered along with the crops and revolutionary power galvanized.

In 2036 the Consortium convened the Atmospheric Regeneration Council and declared ozone regeneration a man- made miracle and announced that a divine providence was at work in the world. The beginning of a new age, the Consortium Age, had begun.

By late in 2036, however, atmospheric readings indicated that the nanozine miracle could not be stabilized—it had a procreant life of its own. Satellites indicated that the successful regeneration of ozone had increased to 200% of its nominal mass and showed no signs of slowing. Over the next three years ozone regeneration continued at an exponential rate. The once thin and ragged protective layer had expanded and filled the atmosphere from the sidewalk to the stratosphere. The air became a toxic gas across vast areas of the globe, especially over industrialized land masses. The blue sky went orange, then red, then brown. A thick haze settled everywhere, but it struck the northern hemispheres particularly hard. Clouds disappeared. No wind blew. The Consortium miracle had come home to roost."

Vilb scanned over and down. His eyes fell on a line that stood alone.

"Before Simon there was Simon."

"By 2041 a.d. the ozone crisis reached a critical phase as global temperatures soared, sea levels began to rise quickly again as the polar ice caps thawed at a precipitous rate. No one ventured outside anymore, though remaining inside offered no real protection. Life came to a virtual halt across Consortium America. From joy to despair. The extremes took too great a toll and most simply waited to die, though the faithful prayed for another miracle, and once again the Consortium Labs, Inc. did not disappoint. A life-saving consumer product had been prepared: the Ozone Conditioner for the Home and Office.

Every major structure underwent immediate Consortium retro-fitting in the first eighteen months, at least those with inhabitants who could afford such a miracle. The Consortium manufactured over one billion OC units in the first year in factories all over the globe even as Consortium scientists promised that the Ozone Conditioner was merely a temporary, stop-gap solution to the ongoing "air quality" problems. Consortium scientists promised that ozone levels and air and sea temperatures should return to nominal levels by 2050, but until then, they recommended that people stay inside and breathe cool, breathe easy, breathe Consortium.

Remaining fossil fuel deposits were recovered at a fantastic rate in order to generate the electricity required to power a billion OC units.

In 2043 the first Haze Storm settled across Beijing. Electric power failed across Central Asia and two hundred million Chinese asphyxiated in one week.

The Beijing Haze Storm troubled Consortium scientists, engineers, businessmen, and politicians, but not because of the unthinkable loss of life. Rather, because it represented an unprecedented intensification of an atmospheric process that was beyond control, and utterly lethal. As the second Haze Storm settled across the Southern California basin ten million people died when electric power systems collapsed and populations had nowhere to turn. The crisis had finally come to the people of the north.

Food production, already tenuous since the early 2030s, became increasingly disrupted until food shortages, and then, real hunger, gripped Consortium America and Consortium Europe. Haze storms appeared all over the globe, some lasting a day, others for a month at a time.

It was then that the Third Wave declared holy war against the Consortium and the invasion of Europe had begun in earnest. The Consortium meantime fielded their own shock troops to secure control of remaining populations even as any semblance of civilian government collapsed. As famine raged, the Consortium prepared for a final global conflict with the Third Wave which, they believed, would solve a host of problems with one graceful sweep."

III

Vilb looked up from the floor with a splitting pain over his left eye. He rubbed his temples and noticed Oneira. She lay on the floor, whimpering quietly. Vilb crawled over to her and put his hand on her shoulder and looked for what she may have been reading. His eyes fell on a section headed with the words SIMON SIMONS:

"Please note the corrected dates: Simon Simons, born November, 24, 2040. Died November 13, 2049. On or about July 2, 2050, Consortium Board Member, Alexander Levinthal and his associates—including Sumio Azawo, Quadros Prang, Qir Hom, along with cooperation of Jonathan and Martha Simons—would, for the first time—complete the full-term cloning of a human being. Cloning had gone on for decades by then, but not the cloning of an identity—a life restored. It was a resurrection. The only truly man-made miracle of that dark period, the ozone catastrophe not withstanding."

Vilb rubbed his temples again, afraid to go on. Azo spoke up from his seat above them.

"Things have gone wrong from the beginning," the old man said, an urgency in his voice. "In overlooking what seems now to be one of the most basic questions, we inadvertently repeated the very past we sought to escape, once and for all. Yet here it comes again, and again, and again."

"What question?" Vilb did not want him to keep talking, but he could not help himself. Had he not always wanted to know? He ruefully acknowledged that this cell, these stories, were they not an answer to his prayers prayed long ago?

"Premises," Azo went on. "It has to do with premises. Simon was not inevitable, though He may be inexorable."

"I do not understand," said Vilb.

"Premises, my boy. The working out of an unexamined premise leads to an inexorable, cascading chain of events, of cause and effect, and so it appears that a chain of events is both inexorable and inevitable. But if one were to question and change the premises from which one works, then the chain of events, the cascading series of cause and effect, reflects and refracts those original changes as well, and the whole world will take a new shape. Cause and effect will head off in a new direction. History changes course. Do you understand?"

Strange, but familiar, Vilb thought. Had he not thought similar thoughts, albeit for other reasons, long ago on his hill?

"Very well," Azo said, and went on. "But believe me when I tell you that the scattering of Simon meant to us that the world could begin anew, and we sought a new beginning together. Truly. We meant it, if only for one fine moment. Yet we deceived ourselves, for we put our hopes in the remains of the old world as the seeds for the new. This was a disastrous decision."

The old man shook his head. "Monumentally catastrophic. The old world's premises remained, but hidden from us, latent, in the very premises from which the four of us began our work."

"Little Earth began with the best of intentions. Yet conflict and weakness and hatred and jealousy had entered into our work from long before, and even though we had made oaths and promised one another to forget the past, that no such thing would ever happen among us again, such oaths and promises were folly. They were the height of our wretched hubris! We succumbed soon after our oaths were made and our relationships became conflicted until the desire for one's domination over the other drove us all. The gods of Little Earth warred amongst themselves, each of us almost from the beginning, though Martha denies her part in this, and she still does." Azo nodded down to Oneira who seemed to have drifted off into a fitful sleep, though her moaning continued with each shaking breath. The old man pointed his slender finger at Vilb.

"But you. You my boy have a great destiny. I would like to take credit. Indeed, I deserve some. But forgive an old man's selfish indulgence. I only seek... justice. And seeing you here, now, I believe the time has finally come. We've waited a long time but now the remains, and you, you complete the puzzle. You are the missing piece. The Restoration is at hand." Azo clasped his hands together and waved them at Vilb. He closed his eyes and exhaled as if the effort had tired him out.

Vilb stared back at the old man, still only partly comprehending. He felt shattered and feared that any strong current would carry him away in pieces. "Me?" he finally asked.

Azo smiled wanly but there was a glint in his eye. "Yes, you. I can see it, there, on your brow."

Vilb wiped his forehead and looked into his palm. Was it the light of the cell or had his left hand taken on the color and feel of an Aegis? Vilb shook his head, an anger rising inside him. The old man was toying with him. "What do you see on my brow?"

Azo chuckled, clearly enjoying his sport. "There. Written there. One word. I see it."

Vilb rose, fists at his side. "Tell me!"

The old man stared back, unmoved by Vilb's discomfort.

"Simon," said Azo finally. "I see Simon."

The Death of Death

I

The tempest in Vilb rested now, though a persistent buzzing had taken up residence in his body. His muscles twitched and spasms shook his legs. In his chest his heart throbbed and fluttered. He put a hand across his heart half-expecting it to give out, but instead the beating settled down and returned to its regular rhythm leaving Vilb shaken, but relieved. Relief, he thought. The coward's courage. The ache behind his eye subsided but not the sense of heavy expectation in the room. Oneira's eyes were open, but she looked more like the dead than the living. She stood in front of a wall, unmoving, and apparently continued to read, but as to that Vilb could not be sure. Perhaps she had simply turned her back on, well, everything. Vilb returned his attention to the spot on the floor where a large section of illuminated script under the heading, "The Levinthal Institute, Chicago, 2035 a.d.-2050 a.d." had earlier captured his attention. This, he felt sure, was where Oneira had been reading when it left her curled into a ball and whimpering.

Vilb focused and read from the middle:

"Project Erebus."

"Certain members of the Consortium Board were anxious to see Levinthal succeed, and for obvious, and perhaps not so obvious, reasons. Consortium scientists only partly understood what he was up to in spite of his naked admission of the true import of his research and development. Could the human genome be made tolerant to ozone? To warmer temperatures? To colder temperatures? To famine? To deadly toxins? To cellular degradation? Could the death gene itself be dealt a deadly blow? With nothing to lose Levinthal threw his life energy into the

151

project. He was magnetic. Brilliant. Mad. He took regular injections of lamb's blood sequenced according to Einstein's genetic pattern. Was he a genius? Could he make himself one? Loved and loathed by all who knew him, mostly they feared him and they wanted to be near him, to win his largess, his gratitude. Those around him—and the Board far off under the Swiss Alps—feared the world that he had dedicated himself to even though his vision of such a world was the logical, ultimate outcome of Consortium premises set in motion long before.

When the critical events that led up to 2050 a.d. began to unfold, they did so as one cacophonous simultaneity. By 2040 the mid-west of Consortium America went dark every other day during the years just prior to the Conflagration, and those in power understood—and seemed resigned to, even encouraged by the fact that—Third Wave forces would not be forestalled. Rumors of a massive ground attack circulated freely and little was done to prepare. The idea seemed impossible. All hopes were pinned to the eye-in-the-sky space-to-surface defense array, itself a Levinthal, Inc. innovation. But when Third Wave killer satellites blinded Consortium space defense systems, the otherwise anemic Consortium land-based defense stood no chance against the wave of human wreckage that slammed against American shores. And so in a tactical response few of us understood at the time, the Consortium consolidated its presence in Fortress Chicago, but otherwise left the Great Plains unprotected, the east coast open, and the northern and southern border crossings only minimally, say, symbolically defended.

Before invasion, Consortium resources flowed in a steady stream to and from Chicago in those final fifteen years. And if not to Chicago, then to Antarctica, the Seventh Realm he called it, all towards accomplishing a singular Levinthal goal. Project Erebus, the Consortium trump card that would, they hoped, deal an immediate and devastating defeat to those who hoped to topple the Consortium's idea of civilization.

Project Erebus had been first designed as a final solution to the ozone and global warming crisis intensifying since the earliest days of the industrial revolution, but as the global war expanded and things became more and more dire, the Antarctic project became something else all together, like something living, evolving, responding to the demanding vicissitudes of its environment. By 2045 a.d. Project Erebus had become something that no one controlled in its entirety, something that no one fully understood. A small contingent of engineers and workers and billions of tons of equipment were shuttled to the southern continent even as international stations were closed, disbanded, destroyed. The Consortium meant to hollow out a continent in secret so that only Levinthal and certain key members of the Governing Board were kept abreast of the situation. And so Levinthal and company embarked on the last invention homo sapiens would ever set its mind to.

Massive floating barges housed thousands of workers in the now iceless southern oceans that washed the shores of Antarctica. Huge earth-movers, tunnelers mostly, no sooner landed than they were moved to the exposed bedrock of the mainland in spite of the rivers of ice and water now flowing from the continent's ice cap to the sea.

Beneath Ross Island engineers built the main control station. Here the thermal activity of the continent's active chain of volcanoes would be tapped for a nearly inexhaustible supply of the mega-wattage required by the project. It was a sprawling subterranean installation complete with a massive power station that dwarfed anything ever built. Green houses, waste facilities, cafeterias, laboratories, living quarters, all underground, all safely distant from the frozen desert on the surface. Renamed Erebus Station, the installation was capable of housing two thousand people, though not so many ever had a chance to call it home.

From there ran a tunnel some three hundred kilometers long, heading ninety-degrees south from Erebus Station. This leg of the mag-rail system linked Erebus Station to the main Barrier Ring. Dozens of places around the fifteen hundred kilometer circumference connected the Ring to countless other smaller tubes, tunnels, service ways, causeways and distant satellite quarters that honeycombed the bedrock beneath the ice.

The em-frame Installation is comprised of three massive complexes, each one connected to the other. The first, Erebus Station, known as the Throne Room. The second, The Barrier Ring, a tunnel three miles down modeled after the massive super-colliders though on a scale heretofore unimagined. At one point along its course, under Lake Vostok, sits the White Room, an empty space carved into the earth some ten miles square. It was emptiness. Perfect silence. Vacancy. A void into which the universe would send its most elusive agents, and there, be gathered together and sent by design to the last, most important part of the installation. Some five miles below the frozen surface of the South Pole, engineers carved another vast emptiness, the holy of holies, the heart of the em-frame installation, a massive magnetic array where the universe's dark matter in the form of bosons came to die. The Bosonic Pile."

"Chicago em-frame."

"Even as Qir brought a much smaller em-frame on-line in Chicago in 2035, he proved that the Quantum mainframe worked, and that infinitely more was possible if only they had a larger installation. A continent would be ideal. Commitments were made, plans confirmed and after fourteen years of ceaseless tunneling (and still the installation was unfinished) by 2049 Project Erebus comprised the world's first continental quantum-super-computer. Levinthal hesitated to call it "artificial intelligence." He just called it, "intelligent by design."

Proud of his victory, Levinthal turned his laser-like attention to another problem that had occupied him for decades: his own mortality. He had two reasons to hope: Levinthal, Inc. had made some demonstrable progress with cloning—or regenerating—the human body. Though cloning had been going on for some time—hadn't Levinthal, Inc. conceived the first cloned human being in 2012? Cloning was not the issue. That was relatively simple science compared to what he hoped to achieve for himself and a few, select others. For true immortality the cloned body must remember who it was right up to the last moments of the original's awareness and so carry on. Seamless consciousness between the old and the new had to be achieved. The new clone would see its dying twin, would understand the process and help usher the previous version into retirement, and so the new life would go on, and on. Indefinitely. For those who could afford it, of course.

But as far as Levinthal could see, the new world would be operating under wholly different economies of power and scale. In the new world those who could afford to live as an immortal deserved this kingly gift, deserved it precisely because they controlled the process. It was a simple self-reflexive cycle of justification not unlike the old economies. At least that would carry on from the old to the brave, new world to come.

Down the hall from the regeneration team was Levinthal's pride, his nano-medical division. If the truth be told, Levinthal would rather have simply turned off his own aging process through gene therapy, or nano-mediation, but this proved to be far more difficult at the time. Nano-mediation looked as if it would result in an immortality that might turn out to be a living death rather than an eternal youth, but those problems could be solved with time, but there was no time.

What Levinthal needed was genetic material—fresh, and in large amounts. Even he knew time was running out in spite of the fact that he never left his laboratory stronghold and seemed oblivious to the events unfolding in the world. It was then that genetic samples began arriving in greater mass to Chicago, to Levinthal, Inc, most of the samples recently dead from the war. And these were good samples, though ultimately they would prove to be inadequate to our needs. Even so, without these early efforts the breakthrough that led to the first successful regeneration process would not have been possible."

II

"Late in 2039 word had come to Levinthal of a Consortium scientist in Japan by the name of Sumio Azawo. Apparently Azawo had developed a viable and functioning fullerene-based nano-structure, a micro-machine that could be manufactured on the atomic scale, then, if slaved to a computer system powerful enough the nanozines could be commanded to manufacture even smaller interfaces within the sub-atomic field. It was visionary, but alas, no such computer yet existed.

That was when Azawo took a call from Qir in Chicago. In short, Qir told Azawo that the Consortium had the Quantum computer he needed, in Chicago. It was an em-frame. It was a supra-mind, powerful enough to hierarchize the nanozine swarm, and make it answerable to human will and it raced at, according to Qir, ten-thousand teraflops per second. Azawo could not believe such a figure, but the very thought of such power was enough to bring him to Chicago as if by magnetic force.

Levinthal's reasons were obvious enough, megalomaniacal as he was. With the defeat of death all other material concerns would melt away as mere transitory phenomenon. All could be endured, for all would, sooner or later, pass into the hands of the Consortium Board. They were sure to make him chairman if he could pull this off.

With the exception of Rael Vivar, the Consortium Board supported Levinthal's work for other reasons that they considered equally pressing: global weather control. Not even the Board could survive much more than three decades of unbroken global famine, not at least in the manner to which they had become accustomed. If Project Erebus could be brought on-line in a timely manner, Third Wave forces would not survive. The enemy could be destroyed in a rash of well- maneuvered Haze Storms, agonizing droughts, merciless floods, ferocious hurricanes, precise tornadoes, devastating lightening strikes and other weather-related catastrophes, even as fertile plains in Europe, America and Russia received the sun and rain in perfect measure. This was the Erebus Project—the Em Frame—the continent-sized Quantum Computer. Perfect hegemonic planet-wide control."

Vilb rubbed his eyes and skipped down a few passages and kept reading. "The regenerated body took six months to grow, and though an identical copy had been created of another, the regenerated copy emerged in a vegetative state. Brain function remained off-line.

Levinthal began to suspect that consciousness existed as a neurological pattern of the mind-body system which was itself dependent on the sub-atomic field in and around the body. Levinthal surmised that he could do an end-run around the physical body and work towards reproducing the sub-atomic structure from which the body emerged. This proved more difficult than he could have ever imagined. The body would regenerate, yes, that he could do as well as the Raelians had done it twenty years before, yet the conscious awareness that comprises a part of one's identity, that which he could not live without, and that which the Consortium waited desperately for him to deliver, remained out of his grasp.

Qir urged Levinthal to concentrate on the problem of raising what he called the blank state, an awareness detached from identity. Simple, pure, empty. This, Qir argued, could be achieved, when the em-frame, now dubbed "Auntie Em," had achieved its fullest potential, and for this to happen Qir demanded that all of the Consortium's resources be dedicated to making it happen. Levinthal's immortality could wait along with all of the rest. Auntie Em was all. Of course Levinthal agreed but then continued right on with the regeneration experiments. What was the point if he did not live to see it through?

Azawo worked at cross purposes from Qir according to Levinthal's orders. Azawo and Levinthal both felt that Azawo's nano-drivers offered the potential control of the sub-atomic field. It hit Azawo all at once, even as the first of the genetic samples, specifically ordered and arranged for by Levinthal, began to arrive. He knew he was close now. The nano-driver convinced him of that. Control of the sub-atomic field would lead to the ability to "tune" the random activity of that field, and then, well, then it seemed that a kind of magical power to create from the fabric of space and time was at their fingertips.

With the nano-driver Levinthal could, in effect, tune the primordial vibration of the sub-atomic field like a musician tunes an instrument's strings. The so-called laws of physics it turned out were not governing laws at all, but rather, misunderstood effects of some more basic vibratory excitement of the space-time fabric. And thanks to the nano- driver, this vibratory excitement could be manipulated, sculpted to a desired frequency.

Accordingly, the world of trees and air and sky and water could be re-arranged particle by particle, atom by atom, if sufficient power were present to effect such transformations. Until that time, Levinthal was content on focusing his attention on one local phenomenon: his body.

It was, in fact, Qir Hom who was the first to unlock the Probability Vibration Equations long before. According to Qir's equations, the subatomic field could be tuned and, in effect, directed—provided one had a small enough tuning key and sufficient energy required to enable such an operation. Azawo had, at the eleventh-hour, provided the key necessary. With the nanozine drivers sufficiently miniaturized, and with the Chicago em-frame up and running, a successful regeneration process was only a matter of time, of which the Consortium had but little.

It turned out that Qir and Azawo needed each other." Vilb rested before skipping down under a new heading: "Famine, Drought and War."

"Antarctica would surrender its precarious hold on the majority of the world's fresh water one way or another. Pack ice had all but disappeared in warming southern waters, even during the coldest months of the southern hemisphere's winter. The great ice shelves, some hundreds of meters thick and rising from the water's surface like great white cliffs, calved at an increasingly rapid rate and a flotilla of bergs festooned the southern oceans.

Ice harvesting emerged as a small beacon of hope in an otherwise bleak global Third Wave landscape. Retro-fitted ultra-large crude carriers delivered water to Consortium-controlled land masses and the shattered agricultural production reached a nadir even as the southern ice helped to manifest a modest rise in agricultural production in areas less affected by ozone. All hope was now pinned to the southern seas and massive freshwater bergs floating free.

The Consortium began its own harvesting operations and soon not even the retro-fitted ultra-large crude carriers could keep up with demand for fresh water. Harvesters towed bergs the size of Japan to the northern hemisphere and all points therein as quickly as possible and for a time it seemed that perhaps it might turn the tide in the human die off. Indeed, Third Wave ships began to traffic the southern oceans right along side Consortium ships, harvesting their own supply of ice to meet the ever-increasing demands of their starving population. Détente ensued for a few years."

"The Beginning of the End."

"Of the hundreds of icebergs towed to the western shores of Consortium America that year, three of them spelled doom. Together they were roughly half the size of Texas, the largest yet towed to an ice harvesting port, and Consortium propaganda promised that these bergs would break the back of mother nature.

Yet unknown to Consortium ice-harvesters, these three bergs were more steel than ice. Later the Consortium would deny the intelligence failure of the vaunted Chicago em- frame, yet there it was. On March 14, 2050, as Martha Simons watched her son Simon emerge from Levinthal's regen tank, the three massive ice bergs disgorged their secret contents on the Southern California coast.

One hundred and fifty million Third Wave shock troops in gray and green ozone suits made their slow way to shore long before the dazed and confused Consortium Intelligence could fathom the nature of the unfolding event. The eye-in- the-sky was blind. The space-to-surface array was off-line. The continent was overrun. The Consortium, at least for a time, was dazed and without the ability to respond.

In a moment then the Consortium accepted the probable loss of North America, at least for the time being even as Project Erebus neared completion and essential personnel had begun the long sea journey south. As hopeless as it seemed, Consortium officials still hoped to pull off a last-minute victory made all the more stunning by its improbability. If all went as Consortium engineers planned and the Antarctic em-frame came on-line as scheduled, the nanozines already in the Earth's lower atmosphere (the nano-swarm implanted years earlier in a botched attempt to heal the ozone and combat global warming) would come under em-frame control immediately. Global weather patterns would soon return, but only according to em-frame instructions, and these included plans for a killing heat to fall across the American West, as well as Indonesia, China and India. Already distressed resources would collapse. UV radiation would be allowed to pour through. Human flesh would whither on the vine.

Those who conceived and attempted to execute such a plan believed whole heartedly that there could be no other way if civilization were to be saved once and for all.

But for the Consortium to wreak their vengeance, first the em-frame had to be completed, and for that to happen, Levinthal had to make good on his commitments. And by 2049 Levinthal, supposedly unaware of the events going on all around him, made the breakthrough that they had all been waiting for. It appeared that a regeneration subject had indeed emerged and awakened into what appeared to be the blank state of consciousness that Qir had pressed for. It was a stunning victory. Human awareness had been manufactured. Now it could be commoditized. The Consortium Board rejoiced at the news, gave orders to send the Chicago team ninety-degrees south even as the Board hunkered down in the bowels of the Swiss Alps for a very long nap."

III

"What Levinthal and the Raelians had known for some time was that the regeneration of full-term clones was catastrophically traumatizing to living—and non-living—cells. At first it seemed that the damage done to the full-term clone's cellular infrastructure could never be undone, nor could future damage be prevented from such an inauspicious birth. Once again Azawo's fullerene nano-driver as a cellular prostheses proved to be the breakthrough that Levinthal needed.

He called them medi-drivers and they could be programmed to serve every single cell of the human body only to replicate even smaller drivers inside each cell, so that every single cell had hundreds of medi-drivers guarding it, nursing it, repairing it and always coaxing it to accept the living bio-energy that drove cellular functioning and maintained its energetic tuning. In short, the medical implants were nano-sized splints that held together cells and cell structures that would otherwise fly apart, turn cancerous, or simply fail.

It was a Byzantine project yet on a scale beyond imagining in both directions, and though a regen looked perfectly human—aside from the pale, green tinge to the skin—regens carried with them a technological presence that had become the mechanical equivalent to mind, albeit a mind that could be imperfectly influenced from a distance.

In the end, the nanozine-driver gave Levinthal two victories in one. He had his clone that, it seemed, could remember its previous life. Meanwhile, the nanozine drivers could maintain the original body almost indefinitely, though they could not keep old age at bay, but they could keep aging cells from failing catastrophically. Death had been dealt two blows at once, and in the eleventh-hour of human civilization. Death had been, if not defeated, then seriously forestalled."

Vilb looked up from the floor, rubbed his eyes and brought the old man into focus.

"You are… the Sumio Azawo… from this story." A statement, not a question. Vilb felt a horror mounting. The old man nodded his head slowly.

"And Qir… Hom?"

"Master Qir," said the old man.

Vilb shook his head silently and tried to take it all in. "And Simon?" Almost afraid to know.

"A boy. He was a boy. From the Ancient world. Just a boy. Ordinary."

"A boy?"

"I knew Simon Simons shortly only after his emergence from the regen-tank in Chicago. The first nine-years of his life I learned about from his mother."

"His mother?"

Azo paused and seemed to choose his words carefully. "Martha Simons," he finally said. "Let me show you The Martha," and the old man rose and shuffled to the other side of the room. "You should see this. You should read the section on the wall behind you. There, near the corner. I'll illuminate it for you. Do you see it?"

Vilb turned. "I see it."

"Read it," Azo said gently. "Read as much as you can. Both of you."

Vilb nodded yet he hesitated and Azo spoke again. "You are worthy apprentices, that I can see. Yes, you must renounce all that you have known. You must. But do you understand why yet?"

"No!" Vilb exploded. "I do not understand."

"It's all happening again but this time we can get it right. Set things right." Azo's rigid mask seemed to soften slightly and show the tiniest signs of distress. "We owe this to them. To Simon." Azo lowered his voice now as if not wanting to be overheard. "The Restoration of Simon is our only hope."

"Yet I do not understand what this means."

"Read on, my boy," Azo said quietly. "You will."

Martha Simons

I

Martha Simons made a desperate and unlikely move from Boston to Chicago in the Autumn of 2049 a.d. Like others of her time, she was sick with grief and fear and hopelessness though she remained largely unaware of the intensity and nature of her distress, probably because everyone else she knew felt much the same way. Despair had become common. Dread a given. So in spite of the day-to-day horror that stalked ordinary people from the margins of their awareness, they made every attempt to live out their lives as if they—and their children—had every chance of living on and on. Pathological optimism was their birthright.

Martha's husband was Jonathan Simons, and he was Simon's first father. Jonathan was a man willing to sell what he had for temporary advancement, routine humiliation and the trappings of power. He was prone to moments of extreme, uncontrollable rage and then indolence and despair. Yet every so often what he sometimes called his "better nature" spoke to him and he had the good sense to listen, if not follow, its dictates. In all of these things Jonathan Simons was an ordinary man for his extraordinary times.

By 2049—in spite of what was going on all around him—he believed completely and unreservedly in the Consortium, his employer, "The Lab," and the nonnegotiable status of their civilized way of life and their unquestioned entitlement to it.

• • •

"The Lab wants me in Chicago," Jonathan announced one night in the darkness of the bedroom. He and Martha lay side- by-side on their backs in the dark. Neither of them slept much, though they still held to the routine of laying down with one another and keeping each other company in their insomnia.

Their first and only son Simon had been missing for four months, but only declared dead four days before. It had all hit them again, as if for the first time. Now this, thought Jonathan. Even he could see it, prone as he was to blindness. This was a modern marriage falling apart. As soon as their son's remains had been officially identified she took it up to begin blaming him. She always had, but silently. Always the martyr. Though she too was to blame, at least as much as he was, now it came out in the air, her tense, nasal voice feigning calm yet throwing daggers. He could hear her voice in his mind though he pretended not to when she spoke. It was he who had lost Simon, wasn't it? Just keep your eye on the boy. Simple. So simple even a Simons could do it, she said. Too much for poor overworked dad. All this as she straightened up their flat, tossed pillows to their proper places, and stalled in a desultory, almost aimless search, for a final showdown between them. But it never came.

Perhaps that's what kept them up at nights. The waiting.

• • •

"So go. You hate it here anyway," she finally said to his announcement, still in the dark, though morning was not far off. Had she the strength, she thought, the occasional contempt she felt for him might have welled up within her and supported her own desires to… to what? To leave him? To *kill* him? To slowly poison him and watch him suffer? She shivered. The violence of her own fantasies unnerved her. Perhaps more so because she could not imagine acting on them, for contempt and loathing required the fires of aggression, and hers lay dormant, cold, alongside the dead ashes of her son.

"It's about Simon," he said finally, his voice shaking, and he turned to her and smiled weakly when he said it and his smile in the dark felt like a provocation to her. She sat up.

"No. No. No. Don't. Please. Have you plugged into the port? The *news* lately? My *god*… it can't go on much longer." She turned away from him and stared into the dark.

He rose to his knees and positioned himself behind her, one hand on the center of her back. She tensed, but allowed the contact.

"I can't explain it all just yet because I don't understand it, not really, but there's a Consortium scientist, you know?" She could feel his excitement passing through his hand into her.

"He's the scientist of our generation. They're calling him an Einstein or something." And now he swept his hand through the air as if clearing the way for brighter thoughts. "And besides, the war…" and he paused, as if trying to remember what he'd heard. "It's like this. It's expensive right now to fight overseas, so we're letting them come here, to us. We'll beat them once and for all. I have no doubt. So don't you have any either. Not one." He paused. "Okay?"

Martha shrugged and Jonathan took this ambiguous response as an affirmative.

"Listen. Levinthal. He's working out there on regenerating cellular tissue via some secret advancement in nano-technology, bio-energetic memory traces and the sub-atomic field. It's all over the Lab's network."

"And? Why us?"

"That's what I'm getting to." He paused, sighed. "Levinthal's work is… very far along but it's not… well he's not done yet. That's what he told me. But he's very very close. So close that he thinks this year… well the world is going to change in a big, big way."

"It's a by-product of some kind of weapon," he went on, whispering this time, but only out of habit. He understood that his thoughts were public domain as soon as he articulated them. He had clearance though and he knew he could pull it off, or at least he hoped he could. Levinthal had called him, hadn't he? The Levinthal. "But we will all benefit, that's what he said."

"Weapon? *Weapons*? What are you talking about?" She turned her head, a frisson rippling down her shoulders into her hands. She shook off her husband's hand, turned and stared at him. She wanted to hear it again. Jonathan tapped the table next to the bed and a warm, ambient yellow glow filled the bedroom. "You did this," she said, and she tried to accuse her husband, but it was weak and he thought she was congratulating him.

"Well, yes. I saw the posting on the Qport and sent Levinthal a sample of… his DNA. The hair we've saved, you know, and he said it looked good but he needed samples from the… the… remains and, well, since they found him… anyway, he has them now and he's really excited. We're safest there anyway. It's the safest city in the world right now. Why not a new life? A new place? They say that the sun still comes out there on a good day. That's what I've heard, and people get outside. Outside. Not that I believe those kinds of rumors. Still, the Consortium will take care of everything. Housing. Food. Water. Power. It's all there." He leaned in, one eyebrow arched as if to say, "you know you want it." She hadn't had power—reading self-controlled power—for years. Everything was distributed by the Q-network via the port. Everything was rationed. To live now meant to be utterly dependent on a system beyond her control.

"But you said they cremated the remains. That there were no remains!" Her voice trembled now and she turned onto her back and crossed her arms.

"I know, but no. I'm sorry. I lied. I mean, some were cremated, that part's not a lie, but some of... him... was not. Some I have. Enough."

"For God's sake! You have... enough?" She held her stomach and sat up, swung her feet to the floor and sat on the edge of the bed. "You sold... his... *DNA*? How dare you?" She had nothing left to fling at him. If she thought she had found the bottom of her life only moments before, suddenly that false bottom fell through and she felt as if she were falling. Meds, she thought. Take your meds.

"Listen. Don't go wacko on me now, okay? You're not hearing me. It's the Levinthal Institute. You've heard of it?" He nodded his head as if answering for her. Of course she had. The best and brightest were brought to Chicago. He had heard the rumors. It was an Ark and would be defended with all that the Consortium could muster. This was a coveted invitation to join the war effort directly while positioning themselves for long-term survival. "Okay, then," he said, sensing her thoughts.

"So have I. Defense. R and D. They want to use... they're working on... it's something to do with the em-frame they have there. They want a big one. A bigger one. The biggest."

In spite of herself, her anger, she swung one leg back onto the bed and looked not at him, but not away from him either. "Yes, I've heard of that. Super something or other."

"It's going to mind the entire Consortium network." His hands gesticulated as he spoke. "That means... Jesus, do you know what that means? That means maybe 500 terraflops, maybe more. It's unheard of computing power." He was getting worked up. "It's brand new but it's changed everything already and rumor has it that it's the beginning. They want something big, really big and Chicago's just the start." Jonathan gave her a knowing look. "You see? We could be in at the beginning. They want me. They want us."

"Why?" and as soon as she said it she regretted it, for in this one question Jonathan knew he had her.

"For Simon. We give them access to Simon."

"Why not just take it if he wants it?"

"Look, it doesn't work that way, at least not for this situation. Once the war is over, it's all Chicago. We have to go." Martha recoiled at the eagerness she heard in her husband's voice. Who was he to feel eager?

"Why Simon?"

"Why us," he corrected gently. He was gentle only when he suspected her acquiescence.

"Okay. Why us?" Jonathan paused before answering and she could see in the way his eyes avoided hers that he was afraid of the answer, or ashamed of it, or both.

"Like I said. It's Simon." His voice fell. "It's scary, what they're trying to do. What I've heard. It's an endgame."

Finally some energy in her voice rose from her chest to her mouth. "Then why?"

She stared him down as well as she could but he had his face turned, eyes toward the floor as if something down there worried him greatly, and he crouched and began picking at the carpet. "They want to use, to incorporate, or something, Simon's genome—our genome—into the em-frame. We're not the only ones. We're not special, not really. It's just that... our genetic history... his death... it all meets some suitability protocol they have. Something about a VenQuell rating of his sample. Listen, I know how you feel about the genetic thing. I'm sorry. We don't have to, you know, but the Consortium has called. They've called. It's Chicago or the defense labs on the west coast." He looked at her now as if to say, and you know what that means. And she did.

"I am eager," he confessed. "I admit it, but what choice do I have... these days?" She wasn't about to let him assume anything.

"So?" she said finally. Everything was spinning. Jonathan rose to his full height and started pacing at the foot of the bed. He turned the light up bright.

"Mart. They've called. Me. Us. You don't hang up when they call. You go. We go. Do we have a choice? Tell me!"

"You sold Simon's DNA," she announced, and it was clear to him that she would never let him forget it. "For Christ's sake how could you do such a thing?"

Anger flared his nostrils and twisted one side of his mouth savagely, and then it all crumbled, more sand than stone, and then his face melted and the man so afraid of death spoke in a quiet, plaintive voice. "They've called. We have to go... I've already told them we're coming."

Martha fell back against the pillow as the perspiration beaded across her brow, her scalp, her palms. It was another fit coming on. She forgot to take her meds. All these feelings.

It was then she remembered something her mother used to say. Calgon, take me away.

She gave him a blank face, her eyes wide now with a pain she kept to herself, not saying yes or no, not saying anything. Just a blank look on her face as if she had fallen asleep with her eyes open. Yet she could still see, and she remained aware of her retreat, of his advancing voice, and of their imminent move to Chicago.

▌▌

The trip from Boston to Chicago via high-speed mag- rail took sixteen days. Between Massachusetts and New York they stopped for three different checkpoints. Two full searches of each and every rail car, including luggage and persons. Pennsylvania went quickly with only one checkpoint and the luggage remained on board. In Ohio, Consortium Rail Marshals boarded the train and rode the rest of the way, with three in each car, armed and armored, they stood at attention like bristling black and blue statues. Martha even suspected there were men on top of the train, and by the time they arrived in Illinois Martha had convinced herself that an air escort flew overhead though she could not confirm her suspicions. Must be important people on this train.

As Jonathan dozed beside her she peered around the crowded train car. Every seat was filled, yet it seemed that passengers were outnumbered by security. Her curiosity roused her and she called upon her brain, a most noble tool at one point in her life, long ago, though now it was sluggish and shy, having been rarely used since the Med Laws were passed. And then Simon's death had completed the process by which she lost all ability or desire to concentrate on anything for more than a few seconds at a time.

But now she asked her mind to do the math. Give it some exercise. She counted the train cars in her mind, estimated the number of seats on the train, estimated the number of people she had seen queued. She guessed that there was one black and blue polymer armor suit for every ten travelers and at least six security for every ten travelers. This is a military transport, she thought. Of course. Why should it be anything different?

"See that bulge, there?" Jonathan opened his eyes and she pointed to the Marshal just in front of them. He stood up, turned and began walking towards them. He had a battered rifle slung to his back and his chest armor had small rips from which the stuffing shown through. He wore his black visor down so that she could not see his face, but it was turned towards her. Was he looking at her, or perhaps dozing? She couldn't say.

"Just relax," said Jonathan, and don't stare so much. He flipped his visor up in the next moment and moved down the aisle, greeting passengers, children, and other Marshals as he moved. She managed a weak nod in response to his greeting, but only after he had moved on.

Finally they approached the city and the shields of the train opened wide and Martha could see out the glass sides and ceiling of the train car. The Chicago skyline opened up to them amid a blazing blue sky and bright sunshine. Martha and Jonathan both could not help but gasp.

"Look at it," Jonathan said, pointing up and out. He laughed and she found herself smiling at the beauty of the blue sky. But the sky was far from empty.

Martha could make out at least two massive dirigibles, Freedom Floaters they called them, like rigid, distended bullets frozen in flight, hugging the lakeshore. What may have been others were further off and seemed to form a ring around the downtown.

"Look at that, "Jonathan said. "You feel safe now, don't you?" he asked, and gave Martha's arm what she thought was his attempt at a loving squeeze.

"Zeppelins. Plasma guns," Martha muttered, and sighed heavily. Chicago. But Boston was certainly no better, she reminded herself. Perhaps they could have saved California if Los Angeles and San Francisco had been protected in this way, and it was a comforting thought and her head eased. A Consortium jingle suddenly ran through her mind. The best and the brightest have something to say! What's the best living? Live Consortium today! It made no sense, no real sense but it sounded pretty, like a birthday celebration. And the pills helped. Sort of, but just now her head felt better all of a sudden and so she settled as well as she could into the safety Consortium military force afforded her.

•   •   •

She dozed and dreamed a sweaty dream of a fever that Simon had when he was three in which he seemed to be on the brink of unconsciousness, yet in the next moment his fever had broken, he opened his eyes and smiled weakly at her.

"Wa-wa," he said, like a baby, asking for water.

•   •   •

Above them now a Freedom Floater followed the tracks lazily, and she gazed up and read the rotating message on its illuminated flank. The words flashed so intensely that for a moment she thought that it had suddenly exploded, but then in another moment the words seemed to hang in the haze and became legible. Gold letters against a green background: ChICAGo: CItAdel of freedom. Then came blazing red letters against a white background: freedom leVel: extreme. Next blue letters three stories tall, surrounded by a cascade of falling stars: support the floAtING fortress fuNd. Boom, another brilliance and: BreAthe eAsy. BreAthe CoNsortIum. Finally, the brightest light yet and the words ChICAGo oBeys the med lAWs in green letters that seemed to burn as they hung in the haze. Nausea turned over in Martha's stomach and she looked down at the backs of her hands. She thought them sunken and desiccated. The blue veins were particularly pronounced. I'm getting old, she thought, and she felt old. Forty-two years old, she thought. I'm old.

She felt old, and small and helpless and found it a familiar feeling, but the familiarity was hardly comforting.

Suddenly she sat up straight in her seat. She could be dead by tonight, and yes, it was true. They all could. War had come and the air was poison, and the water was almost all gone.

Death. Let it come. Make it come. There was nothing really to fear. End it. The thought did not frighten her as it used to. Suddenly the thought was a comfort. Life was a sentence and it seemed to go on and on for no particular reason. She felt suddenly lighter.

"Levinthal made it happen," Jonathan said next to her. He sounded almost giddy. "I'm really impressed, and you know me, Mart. I'm not all that easily impressed. Travel visas, luggage permits, walking papers, food vouchers, water vouchers, power vouchers. My god, when we left Boston we left with more in my pocket than I earn in a year."

Jonathan's profusion of ebullient feeling left Martha roiling again, and she hated him and herself for it simultaneously. Could she kill him then take her own life? Would that be possible? We could both be dead by tonight, she thought, and as she brought her murderous thoughts into focus her chest lightened and she smiled. It could all be so simple.

Jonathan leaned in close. "Did you bring your meds, Mart?" he whispered, as in secret.

"Of course." The automatic response. Yet this time, a lie.

"You seem a little, I don't know. Off is all."

"I'm done with that music you gave me," she said flatly, looking forward. Their code for meds. Jonathan sat up. "No more music? Not even the Consortium anthem?"

"I love the anthem, but I just haven't heard it for awhile."

"How long awhile?"

"Weeks... I'm not sure how many now. A lot."

"Dear God," Jonathan said through gritted teeth. "Why are you doing this to me?"

If she were caught in an unmedicated state, they could lose everything, Martha knew this, and she almost certainly would be tested before entering city limits. She didn't care, however. Her transgression felt empowering even as she knew it to be absurd and useless.

"Don't worry," she said. "There's plenty of music in Chicago. Really." She tried to comfort him, but also enjoyed the sadistic power she momentarily had over him. She sat back and looked out the window. "Levinthal made this happen," she said quietly.

· · ·

Once she realized that her implant was expired, and that she had forgotten to refill her script, she had decided then and there that she never would. If she died, so be it. She had heard countless stories about such people. A lifetime of meds and then, suddenly, the patient feels gripped by a mad desire to withdrawal, and then they died, or became criminally insane and were imprisoned. The Qport ran public service announcements always warning them all of the same thing, over and over: Obey Local Med Laws. Unapproved withdrawal leads to illness, death. Dehydration kills! Water is Life! Drink More Water!

Martha assumed as a given that the water had been treated, but not drinking it was simply not an option. She found marginal sources of water when she could and avoided the network's water whenever possible.

She could hear the voice speaking to her now as if she were Qporting it then and there. Withdrawal Psychosis should be reported early and often. Qport into Information Services, then Qport to Med Security and make your re-port! It's that easy! Then the voice went on, stentorian, yet avuncular, and sped up towards the end. Withdrawal Psychosis puts all of us at risk, but no one more than the patient who may suffer serious withdrawal complications, including, but not limited to, death.

Apparently death came quickly for some, slower for others, but almost always for everyone, that is, if they stopped taking their meds. It was the only way to protect people from the poisoned water supply. There was no other water. Only poisoned water. So they all took their meds as antidotes to the poison. Withdrawal usually ended people within months, or so she had been told.

She had been on meds, like most everyone she knew, since she was nine-years old when she—along with almost everyone in her class—had been diagnosed with the same neurological disorder plaguing the city at the time. They called it a "deintegration psychosis caused by toxic contamination." The meds helped, at least at first.

She Q-lined into the monitor in the seat back and came in on the middle of a Consortium public safety announcement: *Left untreated your psychosis becomes a chronic, occasionally aggravated, condition. Often the patient experiences this condition as a dismorphic severing of one's attention from reality, which is why the condition is commonly referred to as a "reality psychosis."* Next came an interview between the fawning face of a female anchor sitting across from a square- chinned, caramelized face of a man in a lab coat. His hair was graying, distinguished, perfect. Martha thought him not over sixty. The caption read, "Alexander Levinthal, Mdiv., PhD, MD, NquEM." He explained the public safety message for everyman:

What's happening is that when the patient goes off meds, and here he paused and offered a grin and a sidelong glance down his nose, *the brain shuts down certain neurological pathways—they squeeze*, and here he made a fist, *tight as if constricting, as if holding something out, or in. Nature has designed things—rather poorly I might add—so that, when the body is under extreme duress, or when it believes itself to be, we've discovered that a tiny gland beside the cerebral cortex bathes the blood stream with hormones, terrortonins to be precise. They are a naturally occurring sedative produced spontaneously even as other neurological pathways shut down. It's as if the brain erects a wall and behind that wall the certain areas of the brain then sedate themselves. The hippocampus, for example, the amygdale as well. It has everything to do with the poison in our water*, and now he looked into the camera, *but it's the only water we have.*

"But it *feels* bad," Martha thought, though good and bad were such utterly relative terms. Yet even her short time off her meds she felt… better. Better than bad. Let's see how long it lasts. Levinthal did not let up in explaining difficult concepts to his rapt audience. *The condition first cuts the patient off from reality. This is no small thing, yet it's only the beginning. Unchecked, the condition leads to pre-mature aging, hypertension, heart disease, cancer, and all at an earlier and earlier age. It's a tragedy when left unchecked. But the neuromed called Verdant... it really works.* Now Levinthal turned and looked directly into the eyes of the viewers. He did something with his lower lip and his chin. It was both an expression of humility and confidence, of patient suffering and total victory. *Verdant works and makes our world work. Make it the medication you rely on and that the law requires today.*

Qport your primary care physician now and begin again, with Verdant.

Ugh. She changed the channel.

Maybe she was already dying. Maybe she felt like dying because she had skipped her meds.

Jonathan spoke up as if articulating a conversation he had been having quietly in his own mind only moments before. "You've skipped meds before. Yes? We know that about you, don't we Martha? You are the Marthiest Martha. And now it seems that you want to go off again you say? Hmm? Again? Now?" He smiled, but his voice was full of anger.

She felt sick.

"It's criminal, you know. Now. In fact. Do you understand? Because if you do not understand we can have you declared incompetent. There are certain... benefits to this designation."

He shook his head as if to say he was through with her and felt no sense of obligation any longer. "You let this happen. You. Not me. You. It's all there," and he pointed into the air before him. "Your entire endocrine system has been affected by now. They don't have meds that can sedate that kind of chaos. You are in critical condition. Do you realize that? You may not know it yet, but you are. You are sick. We should admit you at once."

He broke off. He didn't mean it, did he? Could she be so bad off ? She felt, in spite of the death of Simon, or perhaps because of it, she felt, though fragmented, strangely aware of herself for the first time. It was strange, unsettling at times, but not altogether unpleasant. And she was alert enough to realize her danger, here and now.

"No, no," she said gently. "You don't understand. I need my meds, especially now. Perhaps it's not too late and if I up my dosage, you know, really up it, we can bring my levels down. Would you help me with that? Could you? Will you?"

His face softened, his eyebrows parted. Apparently he liked what he heard. "Yes. That I can do for you. Now you're talking. That's a good girl. Good girl. We'll increase your dose and have your levels checked again in about six months. Okay? We'll kick this thing yet. I promise you that. And remember to do your neuro-purges in front of the Qport, not in bed, or in some quiet space. In front of the Qport. Do you understand? Call it a penance!" And he chuckled. "We'll get through the check point with a sample from before, from your hair brush, yes?"

Martha nodded silently.

"Let's get it over with and that way we can be the first off the train."

Jonathan pushed the call button and a Marshal arrived.

"We'd like to go to the med car."

III

Even as she stood in the doorway of her new Chicago home Martha could feel that it would never be home, never welcome her with a sense of familiar warmth that she had always desired, yet could never find in this world. It was temporary. It was cold. It would remain that way.

Meanwhile, the med-nurse would alert the network and she would be denied access until her meds were up to date. The hair sample worked, mostly, but apparently it was a common dodge of Third Wave terrorists, and so she was now on the watch list. If she did not upgrade they would come looking for her. So be it. Jonathan was furious, yet impotent. Yet somehow they had made it this far.

She was thirty stories up and could see some of her neighbors in their skyscrapers, now fashionable, if necessary, domiciles. They had been converted to homes mostly. Millions of people had moved to Chicago over the past twenty years, and it had become a beehive of urban activity, mostly defense oriented, but even so, life went on there in a relatively normal way as conditions allowed. Their new apartment, Martha had to admit, was huge and overlooked Lake Michigan, only recently re-named "Freedom Lake." She tried to find it, but today was a particularly hazy day and she could not make it out, except for a dark smudge, but of this she was not sure.

In the foreground, however, not far from the building proper floated a massive dirigible, perfectly visible, up close, personal. She could see black and blue figures moving past the windows of the cabin and she assumed they could see her. The underside of the dirigible's cabin bristled with the tips and fins of Consortium firepower.

• • •

Jonathan and Martha had only just stepped through the doorway and they stood there, together, staring at the collection of polystyrene boxes scattered around their new apartment. At that moment the Qport rang through. Someone named Qir Hom needed to see them immediately.

Jonathan shrugged in response as if to say later. "Almost unlimited water," he declared as they entered the room. "Hot showers. Where the hell does he get so much water? And enough to give it to us? That's an unheard of privilege. And the food plan we're on, and the power plan we're on." Jonathan shook his head in disbelief. Still selling it to her. Still not sure himself perhaps.

Martha felt calm, clear-headed. "He's buying us off. He owns us now. That's what it comes down to. Anything that comes from his DNA belongs to him. He's a trafficker."

Jonathan moved in close and gripped both of her shoulders. He buried his face in her ear. They had not been this close for months. She stiffened, but then surrendered. Listened.

His voice was barely audible. "No! There's no need to buy us off. Don't you see that yet? He needs us and I don't know why." Even as she took in what he had said he pushed her away and grabbed a box at his feet as if to unpack it.

"Oh, come on," he said loudly, and he waved her off as he turned away from her. He took a deep breath and then from over his left shoulder he said, "Simon is dead. I miss him. Nothing is going to bring him back. Nothing. I did it for you, for us, to get out of Boston. No one relocates anymore, and we've done it. Look at this place? The water. The food. I know it can't last. I do. But for now, it's the change that we need. And remember. Simon's DNA is not Simon. Simon is gone." At this Martha raised her eyebrows, incredulous.

"Why look at me that way?"

"My apologies. You go on," she said. "I want to hear all of this. Get it out."

"Levinthal has a space for me here, for us, and he needs something that we have. What's wrong with…"

"Prospering as a result of your son's murder?"

"Well… yes if you like. Say it that way. What's wrong with it?"

"What I don't understand is that there must be hundreds, thousands, millions of dead children. Why Simon?"

"I told you. It's… how he died. Something about… VenQuell levels— I'm not sure what that means, and remember, he was the only child in his entire birth year to be born without that… that… that growth-thingy. That right there makes him special. Listen." He rubbed his hands together as if washing them and Martha knew he was lying. "Timing is everything."

"How can you sit there and talk about it like, like it makes any sense," Martha said, and she felt herself growing more excited.

"Easy does it. Listen. I agree. Calm down." Jonathan took another deep breath. "Listen. Listen to me. Given that what Levinthal wants to do is simply not possible there isn't any real harm in it. Right? We'll benefit in any event. None of this can last much longer, right? I mean the war and all. Things are going to change. They have to." She could feel the beginnings of outrage threatening her blank stare, but just then Jonathan put up a hand to forestall an outburst. "And perhaps other children, other people might benefit by Levinthal's research. What he wants to do is, well, hard to imagine. Harder to believe. But what if he comes close? Even a near-miss might have some serious consequences." He paused and stared at her.

"Benefits. I mean serious benefits. Come on, Mart. Haven't we suffered enough?"

"Are you standing there," she sputtered, "sitting there, talking there and trying to tell me… trying to persuade me that I should snap out of it?" She felt herself go rigid at the edge of an abyss.

Jonathan moved in close to her and put his hands on her shoulders again, but this time more gently. "I'm ready to move on. That's all I'm saying, and now's the perfect time to do it."

"How is coming here, to this place, moving on? It's sick and perverted what he wants to do to Simon." Jonathan's eyes widened as if he himself had been attacked.

"What's sick and perverted about trying to save your son?" "There it is!" she screamed. "You see? That is what this is about! I knew it!"

"No! Okay, maybe yes! I don't know." And now Jonathan was completely flustered and Martha, seeing this, dropped her attack.

"Fuck it," she said, and thought of leaving right then and there for who knows where, but just then the apartment door opened in the dark glass wall behind them and a giant of a man stepped in as if he were stepping into his own home.

"I am sorry to have kept you waiting for so long," the man said, and his voice was a deep, booming baritone. He crossed the room in three large strides, his hand out looking to grasp the first hand offered. Jonathan turned to greet him quickly, Martha more slowly. She knew who he was, had recognized his voice immediately from the Qport on the train.

Jonathan appeared flushed and embarrassed to be caught in medias res and bowed and scraped with pronounced enthusiasm as if to make up for their argument. Both Jonathan and Martha assumed that all that they had said was recorded and accessible to Levinthal. It was, after all, his building.

"Dr. Levinthal," Jonathan said, recovering first, and he reached out eagerly and advanced to meet the man in the middle of the room. "This is… an honor sir."

"The Simons," Levinthal said, and he left an unspoken at last hanging in the air. He extended both of his arms as if he meant to draw the room into an enveloping embrace and it seemed that the man could do it if he chose to. He stood erect in a flowing white lab coat, open at the front revealing gray woolen slacks, a vest, a shirt and tie and a coat. He must have been… was it possible?… seven feet tall. Martha had never seen anyone so large. He was at least a head taller than Jonathan—who was himself taller than average—and with a physical frame two orders of magnitude larger than her husband's. The man was a giant. Levinthal's face positively beamed from on high.

"It's good to finally meet you in person. The Qport's hologram sequencing does not do justice to the human face, I'm afraid," and at this he stared at Martha and moved towards her.

"Yes," Martha found herself agreeing. He was a mountain and she felt an immediate calm enter the room with him. He approached her slowly, stood before her for a moment, then closed the gap and enveloped her in his arms and torso. He smelled of her grandfather's tobacco.

Jonathan let out his clipped laugh, late it turns out, in response to what he thought was a compliment about his appearance. "And Martha Simons," Levinthal said, holding her at arms length, and Martha let fly an anxious thought in response to the power of the man's grip on her arm. It did not hurt her, yet, she thought. Not yet. He let go and dropped himself into an empty space.

The man was all geometry, she thought, all right angles, and they came at you from all sides when he faced you. His skin virtually glowed. He was in robust health.

"You must be ready to lose your mind right about now," Levinthal said, and fixed her with a penetrating gaze. "How are you doing?" She stared back not wanting to lie, but not wanting to gush forth with any intimacies that she could not control.

"I'm… confused," she finally managed.

"You must think me a madman who wants to use you, your loss, and pay you off to do it." Levinthal shook his massive head and chuckled. "Listen to me now," and as he spoke he looked from one to the other, but Martha felt his eye was on her especially. "If your son recovers, I will be... ecstatic, and believe me. Many will benefit, including you. But you—the two of you—must understand that his recovery is not my first priority. I know I indicated something of this to you, Jonathan, but let me make it clear to your wife. You must understand that I will do all that I can to respect your son's life, and that I will never interfere with his recovery, but there may come a time—should things go very very well for us—that a life and death decision must be made, and it is a decision that may—I underscore may—occur, but it is only one eventuality among many, so I beg you not to place too much worry on such a possibility." Martha sat up straight and took a deep breath. She had not expected honesty, or what sounded like a veiled sort of honesty, from this man. Jonathan drifted around and leaned against the edge of a large, box-strewn desk pushed up into the corner near the wide window.

"What do you mean by a life and death decision?" she asked warily.

Levinthal took out his pipe and tapped it against his shoe gently. "By that I mean—and let me continue to be frank with you—that we may be faced with an impossible decision to let die the one that we have healed in order to harvest something crucial to the survival of a great many more."

Martha turned to her husband.

"Jonathan!" she cried.

"Hold on, Mart," he said, and then he turned to Levinthal.

"Are you saying that if Simon... that if we bring Simon... back, that then he may have to die... again... after all?"

"There is one probability study that says this is so, yes. As a result of this situation, Em-Frame Overseers are watching things very, very carefully."

"Why would he have to die... again?" Her voice was wavering now, no solid ground anywhere.

Levinthal stuck his hand into the pocket of his lab coat and pulled out a small, golden box and began stuffing his pipe with what looked like real tobacco. He packed it methodically and then lit it, drew in a few times to stoke the fire, and then exhaled, filling the room with a thick blue smoke.

"There. Now we can talk. The entire building is surveilled," he said, and nodded to the ceiling, the walls. "Beware of what you say in the future." He waved his pipe. "The smoke jams the network scans."

"You can't be serious," blurted Martha.

"Uh, yes. Okay. It's that?" Jonathan asked, pointing at the pipe.

"EM pulse," Levinthal said, "meant to appear as background noise." He waved and went on. "Now listen. If things go well and the Board members get what they want they are almost certain to demand that we destroy… this place and everything in it. I am not in this for the Consortium Board. Should this work then we will all benefit. I promise you that." "I think you're insane," Martha proclaimed. Jonathan barked a small laugh from behind them. Levinthal kept his eyes on Martha.

"Go on," he said.

"What's there to say? You want to bring my son back from the dead and now we're talking about killing the… dead… again? My God. I don't know what to say. It's horrifying."

Levinthal nodded and held the silence for a moment. "Yet you're here, yes?" he finally said and he took the pipe out of his mouth. "Perhaps a part of you wants to be the mother of a second Simon? If we succeed—what I am offering you is beyond your imagination. Yet you must want this, somehow, yes? Why else would you have come? He looked at both of them and then bore down on Martha. "I need your help."

He took her hand in his and it was swallowed up completely. "We are very, very close. Should it come to an emergence, then Simon will need you. To bring it that far I need to fill the remaining gaps in the code from your living pattern. You cannot possibly understand now, but you will."

She must have passed out for when she awoke she stared up into the eyes of Levinthal and Jonathan leaning over her.

"What am I doing here? How did I get here?" she mumbled.

"Martha!" Jonathan was shouting at her. He sounded irritated. Her heart raced.

"Oh, I'm sorry," she said compulsively and looked up and found that she could not remember what had been said or what they were waiting for from her. She held her breath and considered bolting from the room and running for the elevator, but thought better of it. Where could she go? An advert on the side of the Freedom Floater illuminated the room from behind.

"Just so you understand." Levinthal stood over Martha and fixed his eyes on her and then turned to include Jonathan. "Do you understand? Both of you? Our commitment is purely personal. Personal loyalty, personal honor, these are the ties that bind us each to the other. This is the bond that we will bring with us to the new world. If we proceed it will be tonight, tomorrow. Will we proceed? Are you sure now? We will not have this conversation again."

"Yes," Martha said without hesitation. Her eyes were glassy and dilated. A fog had engulfed her and she felt far away, hidden and safe. From this distant place, she thought. Yes. From here she might watch the events as they unfolded.

"Fortudine Vincimus," Levinthal said, and he beamed with pleasure. He looked them over one last time, turned and headed for the door. From the corner of her eye Martha watched Jonathan leap around the sofa and meet Levinthal as he left. He grabbed the great man's hand and pumped it hard in the doorway.

Sumio Azawo

I

Sumio Azawo watched and listened to the interview with the Simons from his office upstairs. As Levinthal's second-in- command he was, by default, head of security, not that he took this part of his job very seriously. Any and all security-related inquiries inevitably led him into confrontation with Qir Hom, the chief engineer of the em-frame, and Sumio hated the man, or whatever he was, or had turned himself into. When Sumio stopped to consider the nature of his loathing, he considered it a defensive hatred, a self-protective hatred, a historical hatred. And in the end it came down to hurt feelings—Sumio had hoped Hom would invite him to join the em-frame engineers, but the call never came and Sumio felt the silence as rejection and the rejection as personal, and so returned it in kind. Without ever actually speaking to Qir.

And who could blame him? The story had it that Hom had pioneered the q-seer upgrades—upgrades he called them—and had been the first to see them through to their logical conclusion. He had crossed over, the presumptuous, inconsiderate bastard, and left the Sumios of the world in awe, resentful and far behind.

Yet you could have followed him. Chosen the same upgrades. You could have.

First the molar implants—they all had those—but then the micro-fiber implants, and then the nano-implants that Hom himself had developed—borrowing from Sumio's work without acknowledgement, he quickly reminded himself, giving him yet another reason to resent the bastard. Who had time to pursue patents and infringement these days? Yet all of this was to be expected, all of this was the Consortium way,

179

and Sumio was happy to have, at least in part, perfected the breakthrough technology that would lead the Consortium through the second half of the twenty-first century. Perhaps.

But Sumio had been too scared to go all the way, too afraid to follow the premises from which he worked through to their inexorable conclusion. Sumio was, at heart, a coward. He hated himself for it and he knew it.

And he hated Hom for his mad courage. Hom gave up both eyes in the name of research, or so the story went. For the cause. To see through the surface of things. Moreover, Hom expected the others on his team to do the same, and all had, by 2045, surrendered at least one and upgraded. Sumio had already admitted to himself that he was not ready for such a horror. He shuddered with the thought of the surgery required, and just as quickly cursed the q-seers even as he inexplicably, simultaneously and quite consciously longed to be one of them.

Enter the Simons family.

Sumio had been against the Simons as soon as he had seen their file. It made no sense. The father was addicted to portporn, the mother—Jesus, the mother had broken medi-protocols, sent her neuro-psychological profile into the red zone, lost it a couple of times and still she walked the streets. On top of it all, the Simons boy they wanted to use had been brutally murdered by the looks of the VenQuell numbers, and there was simply no way to know how this last fact would play out, and it was this last detail that Sumio found the most unsettling. Levinthal showed not the slightest interest. Levinthal had burst into Sumio's office, ecstatic, and announced that the mother had agreed.

"He's not right," Sumio said without batting an eye. He quietly tapped at his desktop with his pencil. What looked like a solar system of sorts danced in the air before him, next to it a double helix rotated on an invisible axis, alone in its own quadrant. The nucleus had its own expanded view, which made its internal condition visible.

"Have you seen this?" Sumio was pointing with the tip of his pencil at a bundle of fuzzy static in one hemisphere of the nucleus. "Enlarge here," Sumio said.

"It's a match," Levinthal said calmly, and he waved away the hologram floating over Sumio's desk. "A perfect match. This is it. Bring them all in. Promise them everything."

"I know you've been eager…" Sumio began slowly, and at this Levinthal grunted, impatient for him to get on with it. Sumio slouched in his chair, the pencil, an ongoing professional joke, in his hand. It was his prop. Levinthal had his pipe, Sumio had his unsharpened, antique pencil. You write about as well as I smoke, said Levinthal once, long ago. Better days. He roused himself to the moment.

"Eager," Sumio repeated, and went on slowly. "I know you've been eager to find the sample with the VenQuell frequency you're looking for, and this one is it, no doubt about it, but I've never seen fluctuation like this. Look at this. This shouldn't be here. Those high readings make the q-field around his DNA much too rigid."

"He's a match," Levinthal said flatly. Sumio knew the man wasn't listening. "And, you might like to know, so is his mother. Curious? Eh?" Levinthal was pleased. "Two for the price of one. Buy more, save more, eh?" Levinthal smiled.

Sumio nodded, unwilling to surrender. "But how do you explain this fluctuation? I've never seen anything like it. It's like his genomic q-field is… boiling towards ossification. The VenQuell field is up but, I think, it may be too high." Sumio grimaced. He hated to be the bearer of bad news, it's just that he always was. It was his burden.

Levinthal rose to his feet, turned to go, but then stopped and faced Sumio. His massive fists went to his hips as he turned. "Don't make me say this again," Levinthal said, and he was provoked. Impatient. Exasperated. Sumio loved it, loved throwing him off. "We are running out of time here. If you would prefer to be serving your homeland running code for Continental Defense under some mountain, just say the word. Or perhaps some distant island south of Japan interests you?" Properly scolded, Sumio shrank, gave in, shook his head like a frightened child. "Now no more of this. Do you understand me? You are not here to play trip up the head master. Just do what I tell you to do." Sumio sighed, sunk deeper into his chair. "Anything else?" asked Levinthal, and Sumio made no sound. Levinthal turned, his white coat flapping, and was gone.

II

Sumio could acquire no decent Saké in Chicago, at least not in the areas he was allowed to travel. Single malt scotch was almost equally hard to come by. One Blues club on the east side sold a strange concoction they called Chicago Gin, but that was years ago, back when he felt like exploring the city, violating curfew, playing the margins against the City Road Marshals. No more. Not since the invasion. Back home Kobi had its own curfew, its own version of Marshal Law, but Chicago was a ferocious place, made that way by a shared chronic horror of the future.

What this meant was that if found on the street even close to curfew, sundown, you were considered a terrorist. Stupid, Sumio thought to himself. It was just plain stupid to be out after dark. He'd been out hunting for Saké having taken a lead from a stranger in a bar. Again, stupid to trust a stranger in a bar, but Sumio felt, well, stupid and wanted to indulge it.

Sumio had traveled to a part of the city where there were no gray and green ozone suits anywhere to be seen. The people who were out—and there were quite a few—moved quickly from here to there while holding surgical masks, or handkerchiefs or a myriad of assorted materials to their nose and mouth as a filter against the ozone. But only when the sun was down, for it was simply too hot with the sun high in the sky.

It was dusk when Sumio made ready to leave the bar he had found. He decided to risk it and speak to an old man in an antique suit, gray fabric matching his gray skin, ragged about the hem, the collar, the tie a greasy string. Sumio stood before him while fitting the ozone suit's hood back onto his face. The old man was in the process of giving slurred, but ultimately coherent, directions.

"Down three blocks, another left, another three blocks, there's an Asian quarter there now, all… folks like you," the stranger had said. "I'll bet you'll find what you need there."

"Folks like me, uh?" Sumio had said, confrontation in his voice.

"Good luck," and as he said this the old man slipped off his stool, stumbled out the door and was gone. He let him go. It was almost dark now. Curfew. He would never make it back to the lakeshore before dark. Perhaps this fabled Asian Quarter might be found in a few minutes.

Three blocks and then a left, another three blocks and he found trash dumpsters, crumbling brick facades from the middle of the past century and not one lighted storefront or brownstone. If this were an Asian Quarter, he thought, then the so-called Asians of Chicago lived in a ghetto fit only for filth, rats and disease. Even so, Consortium loudspeakers broadcast their continual, ubiquitous message:

"Breathe easy, Breathe Consortium."

The sun had set and the last few shafts of light slanted between buildings and left a mottled patchwork of gloom on a broken cornice across the street. When the last of the sunlight died, at that moment the emerald green Information Beacon exploded into life a hundred feet away, on a corner just beside a small park.

Now he could see. The emerald light cut through the evening haze in a way the sun could not, and in the green light the poverty of the city became even more obvious, and Sumio suddenly felt a spike of fear shoot through him. What was he doing here? Why stir all of this up? For booze? Christ, he could have synthesized anything he wanted at the Lab. This wasn't about booze, though. This was about a flagrant flaunting of the way things were.

Perhaps he might find a Road Marshal near by, explain his situation (find his long lost Saké) and get a lift back to the Levinthal Building. But no sooner had he noticed the Info Beacon then it noticed him and let out a pulsating blast of sound that knocked him off his feet. In the next moment he found himself prostrate, his face in the gutter and could not move. The entire city block suddenly blazed with a white, blinding light.

Brilliant. He lay in the gutter paralyzed, bathed in incandescent light so bright, and for so long, that he felt his skin begin to tighten as if he had spent a summer day in the full sun, even through the ozone suit. Finally the light dimmed and black and blue armor appeared standing over him as if they had sprung up from the pitted asphalt. Sumio thought he counted four helmets, but he sensed more all around him.

"Third Wave?" one said through a com-link. "Definitely."

"What's he doing out here?"

"Who knows. Get the D. T. in here to scoop him up."

"Right."

For two hours they worked in the street without moving his body. He told them who he was but they ignored him and worked to defuse him. Sumio stared into the black and blue face shield of one their bomb squad experts. To him he tried to explain once again who he was but no sooner had he opened his mouth then a boot came down on his throat.

"Fuck! He's talking. What the fuck! I thought you had him down."

"We did! We did!"

"Bullshit, this guy's talking."

"Why didn't you clamp him right away?" another said, and Sumio felt a piercing heat at the base of his skull and then all went dark.

There were no more walks in the park after that.

III

It was late and Sumio could not sleep. He kept thinking about the Simons, and about the mother in particular. Something about her had struck him and he was trying to sort out what he had seen. She wasn't beautiful, not by any standard, but there was something of substance about her—a presence. Yet she hardly said a word. She moved slowly as if her joints, at any moment, might let go and send her falling to the floor in a heap. When she sat down, however, she held her head up high, as if to keep it above the rising waters she seemed to sense all around her. She was thin and dehydrated, broken and vacant- eyed, yet Sumio could not get his mind off her.

It was late and his thinking leaped and jumped from Levinthal to Hom to Martha Simons and back again excitedly. He rose and shuffled over to his desk and dropped himself into the chair. "Qport," said Sumio. He heard a voice in his head, then violins all around playing the network theme.

Welcome back. The Consortium Network made possible by The Global Consortium for Civilized Living featuring the first world-wide Q-Net made possible by the Power of the Em-Frame. Finally… Q-Mind. The World in your Port. The Port in your world. And users like you.

"Records search," he said.

Optic nerve scan required.

Sumio leaned forward over his desk and stared into space.

Hello, Doctor. It was a familiar voice, not male, not female, confident yet subservient, unwavering yet demure. *It has been three days since you last ported. Your personal greeting and port record have been brought to you by Dumeral, Incorporated. What goes down must come up, with Dumeral. And users like you.*

Sumio spoke: "Search. Consortium America. Boston. Martha Simons."

Here is the information you requested. The Network thanks you for using the Power of the Em-Frame. For Every Wondering Mind There's a Qport in the storm. Qport it All.

Sumio blinked. Porting left him vaguely nauseated. In Kobe he still used the old tech screens, and felt stupid and poor because of it. But here, now that he had to use the North American network they required him to have the implant and he agreed, but only after stalling as long as possible. Access was impossible without it.

The network implant was a bulky micro-machine that, once injected into the bloodstream, swam, crawled, and burrowed its way to the thalamus in the brain. Once embedded there the implant released chemically inert particles into the nuclei of the thalamus as well as into a pair of nuclei in the superior and inferior colliculus of the midbrain. From here q-data could then be routed through the implant and then sent on both electrically and chemically to the optic nerve. The information from the brain to the optic nerve received via the micro-implant was "blown" back through the eye and projected onto the inner-cornea so that the words or images appeared to hang out in space about eight inches from the end of the user's nose. Auditory information required another implant. Sumio closed his eyes and rubbed his temples. "Blow back" gave him a splitting headache.

But Qport access was impossible without the implants, and "blow back" was the price one paid for progress.

The Martha Simons file was up and waiting for him when he opened his eyes. He scrolled page after page of encrypted, encoded data and nothing he could do unlocked the security measures. "Fucking Qir Hom," Sumio said suddenly, and he rubbed his eyes and pinched the bridge of his nose.

"Repeat search," he said louder than he intended, and the same page of encoded and encrypted characters appeared before him. "Clearance 98756-2045-9762," he said.

K-7. Restricted. You lack q-user-priority.

"Decode," he tried again knowing it to be useless.

System Security Marshal has been alerted.

He threw up his hands. "Help," he said. Sumio was the System Security Marshal. Qir Hom was playing with him again. Another K-7 and Sumio was ready to pay a visit to Qir Hom and his White Room ghouls. Yes, a visit to the sub-basement was in order. It would be his first, and it was long overdue. He'd been putting it off ever since he had arrived and now, ten years later, he still had yet to make the trip. He blamed it on his schedule, the time required to prepare for the clean room environment, he blamed it on Levinthal, he blamed it on everyone he could. Even so he'd always wondered about it, had longed to be a part of it from the beginning, had even wanted to make it central to his studies, but the science was still too new at the time. And so when it came to pass that the Consortium would indeed build an em-frame, and in Chicago of all places, Sumio sent his vita, way back in 2035, to Levinthal and Hom only to be summarily rebuffed. But that was then.

He had found his way to Chicago after all soon after, thanks to his nano-drivers, but his position was a far cry from the power enjoyed by a q-seer.

So be it. It was now or never. He'd had enough. Confront the bastard, get it over with. Fuck with him the way he's fucked with you if you have to. All of this and more. Whatever it takes to make things right.

He wanted in to the White Room now. He felt it. It was a big move. All of this Sumio assumed would take days to arrange for, but no sooner had Sumio made the port when he received permission to proceed.

Then the real work began, and he had to do it all with a pounding hangover. First he had to take his ozone suit to sterilization and de-mag. He suited up and now, with Marshal escort, took the elevator down to the sixth floor and to the em- frame portico on the west side of the building.

No q-seers yet. It was an ordinary enough foyer, double doors, white resin, opaque. The Marshal left him there and another in a white lab coat greeted him, took him down a hall, into some kind of dressing area, and there he was ordered to strip, and to shower (again) in order to be shaved and descaled. The shaving irritated his skin, the UV descaling only exacerbated it. Finally they took him into a small booth, nozzles mounted two to a wall, and out sprayed some kind of resin sealant that covered every inch of his body.

It was a bio-polymer goo that toughened into a rubbery, thin second skin. Now he was ready to don a clean suit, stretch the headgear down over his hairless head—kept short by Consortium protocol, now shaved clean for his trip to the White Room. He bit down on the breathers and so continued his descent into the sub-basement.

At this point what must have been three members of Qir- Hom's team appeared. These three were all in white clean suits. It was Sumio's first good look at them. Nothing special, he thought. Just zippered jump suits, gloves and boots, headgear, full face mask, opaque.

It was they who left him naked in his polymer second skin booth while someone somewhere changed the filters in his breather unit. Two more hours. The itching proved maddening, but no amount of scratching could penetrate his skin's protective, irritating shell.

Finally they led him on his way to another elevator, and then down.

Sumio had often wondered about the men and women who had been selected to work in the basement. He had never let go his hurt when, presumably, Hom rejected him for the position. He would have become one of the q-seers, one of Hom's cadre. He had the particular neuro-psychological profile required. No two were exactly alike, but fermionic activity in the brain had to be particularly high, and Sumio—according to his local tests done at the time of his application—placed in the ninetieth-percentile.

The plan was for the Consortium to institute a program to identify potential candidates, from adults to very young children. The Q-Corp they called it. Consortium Q-Schools were planned all just prior to the Invasion. The hope was that two-year olds would be scanned, sorted, selected, and some, the few, they would receive q-implants and special training all so that they could become the Q-seers for the next generation of em-frames planned for the entire globe. The Third Wave Invasion had, it seemed, only slowed the Consortium juggernaut. Slowed, but not stopped apparently. The power of the em-frame had seized the attention of the most powerful people in the Consortium with the promise of, simply put, more power. The costs were nothing compared to the rumored gains involved in maximizing and perfecting the Quantum Electro-Magnetic Computer Installation.

Sumio's elevator slowed and stopped and the doors opened and the three stepped out and began walking at a steady gait down the hall. A clean suit met them and walked with them. When did they eat? Sumio wondered. When did they use the toilet? Did they ever talk to one another? What did they do when not working? He turned and stole a sidelong glance at the clean suit walking beside him. The opaque mask was dark and impenetrable and it frustrated his efforts to see behind it. He had hoped to see one of the em-eye implants.

The four led him through a series of double doors, polymer white, like the foyer on the sixth floor, that is until they reached a room, bare except for a massive titanium door directly before them. It opened as they approached, slowly, groaning quietly on three over-sized hinges. It was at least a meter thick. Once inside, the door shut and they were sealed in and the back of his neck tingled. They had entered some kind of staging area, a platform from which one could stand and, by gazing through a transparent section of the wall, see into the White Room itself. Presumably it offered ingress and egress to the space beyond but Sumio could not yet see how or where this happened. He moved towards the window and leaned slowly, and as close as he could, until the dark shield of his headgear kissed the transparent polymer wall. He was as close as he could get.

If whiteness had an essence, a basic nature, he was gazing at it, but not at it. Into it, through it, towards where it resided, but his eyes could not focus on it, per se, because there was no it. Just whiteness. No far wall. No sidewall. No floor and no ceiling. Emptiness was before him as this form, and this form was nothing but white emptiness. His vision fuzzed suddenly as his neck tingled, itched madly and a tangled mess of letters, numbers, and raw code filled his field of vision.

It was his port implant cascading and Sumio could not shut it down. Even as he detected the spontaneous porting, the four who were with him turned towards him and one of them put a white, sleek hand on his shoulder.

The spontaneous porting stopped suddenly. He took a deep breath and waited, nodded his gratitude.

He went back to watching the White Room and before long an argon patch of light—was it small? Was it huge?—shone brightly somewhere in the distance. All he knew was that it appeared suddenly, blazed like a green sun in the stark whiteness for a moment, and then winked out. Simultaneous with the light the four clean suits appeared around it, hung there suspended somehow in the air, surrounded the argon disc of light, and then all of it, the light and the four q-seers disappeared.

A moment later three argon discs appeared, one above him, one deep below the viewing window, and one far to his left. Four q-seers appeared, hovering around the light just as suddenly as the light appeared. They surrounded the argon illumination until, like the first group, they winked out. And then just as suddenly, the White Room was empty as before. The pattern repeated itself, only there seemed to be no pattern to where the argon disc and four q-seers would appear, or for how long. That they appeared and disappeared was all that Sumio could determine.

Their purpose, however, remained a mystery to him and this intrigued him and threatened him, precisely because he did not understand the em-frame, the White Room, or the way in which this technology controlled chaos. This was the future, and he knew it and he felt suddenly obsolete, as if the train had left the station and he remained behind waving pitifully.

In mid-regret a hand gripped his shoulder and spun him firmly around. It was yet another clean suit, though this one was smaller than the others, had a round, protruding belly and small hands hidden inside small, white gloves.

Use your port implant to communicate, said a voice in Sumio's ear.

Qir Hom, Sumio thought into the implant, and he reached out his hand and offered it to the figure before him but the figure ignored it.

Do not touch me, said the voice in his ear.

Sumio lowered his hand and felt his gorge roil.

We have a compromised q-seer, the voice declared and Sumio was thoughtless for a moment.

Do you mean the White Room has been compromised? How is that possible?

It is not impossible.

It's not impossible?

Probability allows for it. But before Sumio could question him further the voice went on.

This is not the time for a lesson in Void Mechanics. I brought you down here because the Third Wave advance will destroy Chicago. Probability allows for it.

Sumio nodded. Indeed he did know but he could not remember at that moment whether it was safe to admit it. Qir Hom went on abruptly, impersonally, like a... machine.

Human extinction forecasts have risen to ninety-seven percent in all quadrants. Consortium domination forecasts currently hold at ninety-five percent. Do you understand the parallel nature of these events?

No.

Adaptive survival is allowed for.

Adaptive survival?

Be prepared to move immediately when the Simon's emergence unfolds. A seventy-three percent probability of a successful intercession exists.

Successful emergence? Wait. Hold on. Does a compromised White Room undermine probability forecasts? It must, no?

Qir Hom went on as if he hadn't heard the question.

The Simon's emergence is holding with an eighty-seven percent forecast probability. Yes. Okay, but does a compromised White Room undermine your forecasts?

Among concomitant consequences probability forecasts a catastrophic die-off of homo sapien sapien at ninety-one percent.

Sumio rocked back. *Once again please?*

The figure waved him off at this point. *Adaptive survival is allowed for. Be prepared.*

Simon Simons

In this moment we risk everything in the fullness of our awareness that even as we sleep, you and I, those chosen few, we do not retreat. We do not surrender. We sleep now secure in the knowledge that when we awake the power to victory will be ours. Patience. Fortudine Vincimus.
– Alexander Levinthal, Acting Director of the Board.
October 8, 2050 a.d.,from the Eiger Vault Address.

I

Martha felt that familiar dread again as she lay in the dark next to her husband. He had chosen the heavy sleep of the drugged and he snored contentedly and with each exhale the bed seemed to vibrate. Beyond her own room though, and perhaps it was her imagination or her brain chemistry, she felt, or heard, or somehow sensed the Levinthal building all around them, some thirty stories of it, and felt that it breathed too with a life of its own. The months of sleepless Chicago nights made it obvious to her that only in the night did the building truly awaken. The hum of incessant activity she sensed all around her, deep below her. It was as if the building had a pulse. She felt the excitement of the activity first as a terror and it kept her up with agitated expectation, but later as the days and weeks passed her surroundings became familiar, and she began to take comfort from the thrum of energy pulsating through the building. Levinthal was in a race against time and his work never ceased.

The war went badly for the Consortium. The fall of North America was a foregone conclusion, yet Levinthal betrayed not the least bit of anxiety about the imminent collapse of the world that sustained him. Some other horizon commanded his attention and sustained him. Would that Martha could feel some similar sense of sanguinity.

The building was particularly excited tonight, she thought, or rather, she felt. The oscillating vibration rose slowly from beneath her, expanded all around until it reached an almost fevered pitch, like a vibrating bubble rising from the ground floors, enveloping the building, then collapsing, only to begin the process again. Jonathan had tried to convince her it was just the elevators, but they had a syncopated rhythm she had separated out.

She moaned, rolled over and sat up on the edge of the bed. "I'm coming!" she called out and the sound of her own voice startled her, and she realized then that she had been dozing and dreaming. She'd heard Simon calling—he'd had a bad dream and was calling for her.

"I'm here, baby," she called. Jonathan grunted. He was splayed out, sweating, his mouth open. She was about to rise and dress when the floor seemed to pitch just below her feet. "Christ," she said again, and remembered that Simon was dead.

She rose in spite of the pitching floor and moved through the early morning obscurity of the apartment, a time of heightened isolation for her. She ate nothing and ignored the Qport even as it sang to her. *Good early morning, Martha. Up early today! Good Morning, to you. Have a great day! Qport is here for you!* It could not have been more inappropriate or irritating. After a moment of silence the port repeated its morning salutation.

"Volume zero," she said.

Unlawful request for a user like you, came the singsong response.

"One then," she said.

Repeat request please.

"Volume one," she said.

"What's this?" Jonathan said. He had stumbled out of bed and stood in the bedroom doorway.

"I... I... couldn't sleep," she said.

"Me either," he said rubbing his eyes.

"Will you come downstairs with me?" she said.

"Now?"

"Yes now. He's down there."

Jonathan tilted his head. "Who's down there?"

Martha looked away. "Levinthal," she said finally. "He's down there."

"Yeah, okay. Give me a minute," he said and disappeared into the bedroom. He continued to talk from the darkness. "Levinthal said they were a ways away yet. I'm not sure he'll appreciate us barging in at this hour. I was thinking we had a few weeks yet before they... you know... brought it on-line." The light came on and she could see him dressing slowly.

"No. Just hurry up," she said. "It's happening." Jonathan appeared in trousers and a white shirt, tails flapping, his house slippers on his feet.

"You're going like that?" he asked her. She looked down at her red robe, a red cassock of sorts, complete with hood. On her own feet she wore her white slippers.

"Come on," she said, ignoring his question. "Hurry." A few moments later they were riding the elevator to the thirty-third sub-floor. That's where the tanks were, and Sumio. She thought of the strange Japanese doctor and wondered about the possibility of past lives. Had she known him? It was he who had shown them around, shown them the tanks, the Lab, the nanozine-drivers they'd all placed their faith in.

But that was weeks ago. Now, in one of the tanks somewhere below them, floated an end result, what appeared to be the body of her dead nine-year old boy. She shivered at the thought of it. She had seen it just last week. It had grown there from a tiny blob implanted in the nutrient-rich tank wall the day they'd arrived in Chicago. Jonathan just shrugged then, but something about it left Martha reeling. Levinthal meant to do it, seemed to know how to do it. Was it madness to deny the possibility? The cloned body bore an uncanny resemblance to Simon, all except the skin, which had an eerie jade hue about it and she knew then that whatever Levinthal produced, it would not be her son. How could it be? Yet even as she knew this she also wanted to believe in the impossibility that she would kiss her boy again.

The elevator descended slowly and she dozed on her feet and went on dreaming. She was nine-years old again. She was at the kitchen table with her father and the fear and the desperate longing rose up in her and threatened to engulf her completely. She longed to be near him, to go back, to before, before ozone, before war, before Simon, before it all. Be nine again. Be daddy's girl. Watch him drink his coffee, button his sleeves, straighten his tie. Watch his back as he left for work, the morning sky a twilight aubergine.

The father in her dream turned and spoke. It's a monster, he said, and then sipped hesitantly at the brimming, dark fluid in his cup. And it's up to you sweety. You have to kill it.

Yes. Yes. I know how. I remember how to do it, she said, and was suddenly outside and rode off on her bike. The elevator stopped and she opened her eyes.

"Come on," Jonathan said but he waited for her. A tremor ran through her and she considered the possibility of escape, but there was none. She gripped her robe right about her and stepped into the soft white light of the deep sub-basement. Could she kill the clone if it looked like Simon? What if it spoke? She moaned involuntarily. The thought was too obscene to contemplate.

"What is it?" Jonathan asked.

What can I do now? I've waited so long, too long, she thought, and held court with herself.

It's not too late. You promised to end it. So end it. Take them all with you.

But how? How? She rung her hands.

"Martha," Jonathan's voice broke through. "Are you okay?"

"I… I'm a little worked up." She looked down at her robe and slippers and wondered why she hadn't changed. "You… understand?"

"Easy does it. We'll be there in a minute. Levinthal's probably in bed anyway. Azawo told me we have a few weeks yet."

"No, he's lying. They want us out of the way when it happens. They're down there now. Right now. This moment."

"How can you know that?"

"I don't know. Maybe it's a great mother's intuition."

"Excuse me?"

"Forget it. I just feel like I'll explode if I don't get in there. That's all."

"Well hold on. We're almost there."

Round the corner two lab technicians passed them and did a double-take.

"It's the Simons," one said as if to greet them, but it also seemed a way to mask his surprise.

"Early risers," the other said, and they hurried away down the corridor.

I'm empty-handed, Martha thought to herself again. How can I stop them? I've waited too long. It's too late. No. Be patient. Wait for your chance. Even if it takes a millennium this is your burden. More lab coats up ahead.

"Christ! It's cold down here," said one.

A group of seven walked down the hall, passed the glass doors that led to the tanks, and then headed down a white, brightly lit corridor. One turned and waved to Martha. Martha seized Jonathan's hand and pulled him forward.

She was mumbling now, a running dialogue with herself. Five of the lab coats peeled off down another corridor while the other two waved the

Simons to where the corridor ended at double doors emblazoned with the words: "Please Stop. This is a Clean Room. Are you Clean?"

"Come on, we'll get you suited up. He's going to be… happy… to see you," said a technician suddenly at her elbow. A tall woman, her name badge read, "Level Beta." And underneath that, "I'm Joan!" Underneath her name, in small letters, as if the foundation for all that rose above it, Martha read, Breathe Easy, Breathe Consortium.

"I'll help you get ready," Joan the Beta said and she guided them in and around the dress-prep area.

An hour later Martha and Jonathan, now washed, dried, deionized, descaled and suited-up, stepped into the Tank Room and took it in. Dozens of silver sarcophagi, some ten or twelve feet long, filled the cavernous area. There were dozens, possibly more than a hundred. It was hard to count and do the math. Of the row upon row now and then one of the titanium containers had a lid up and sent off an emerald glow, but most were closed, dark, quiet, presumably empty. There was one, however, in no particular place of importance surrounded by a number of white suits in a circle around this tank. They moved quickly and efficiently around the forest of stainless steel stands, some with bags distended, others as stands for old-style tech screens. There were at least a dozen white suits and at least a dozen more red lab coats moving in and out, dancing from screen to screen, monitoring something or other, inputting data, reporting to one another, flitting off to some dark corner only to return again.

Levinthal's massive back was to the door as the Simons entered. He stood over the tank and stared intently into the translucent liquid. Occasionally a lab coat approached him and waited to be acknowledged at which point Levinthal leaned down so that the smaller figure could whisper something into his ear. He would nod, or shake his head and the figure would scurry back to a screen. Cables of different sizes snaked across the floor. Empty containers had been strewn about haphazardly, and Martha picked her way across the floor carefully.

It wasn't what she had expected. It looked like a mess. Like an accident, or multiple accidents, had just occurred.

She moved forward another step, but slowly. Levinthal was up on the tank's pediment staring down. He had yet to acknowledge them though Martha suspected that he was aware of their presence.

Suddenly Levinthal turned and looked in her direction, but apparently he didn't see them as they stood there staring.

"Where the hell is Sumio?" the man barked. "I need him, stat!" He looked tired, she thought. Dark rings under both eyes, a sunken face, thin and disheveled hair, and his lab coat, once white, was now various shades of green, some fresh, others older, on their way to a putrid brown. The entire room smelled faintly of antiseptic, but more potent was the fetid odor of near-decay hanging heavy in the air.

It brought her up gagging for a moment. It was distinctly uterine.

"I rang through again, doctor," said a clean suit positioned behind a bank of Qport screens in the corner of the room. "He's on his way."

"By God. If that fool isn't here in three minutes I'll snap his neck." Levinthal's anger took her aback. She had never seen him so... agitated. "He wants to make his point tonight. By God I'll have him. I will have him if he is not in here..." but before Levinthal could finish Sumio burst into the room, fastening the last clasps of his clean suit as he approached the tank.

"He opened his eyes, for Christ's sake. Where have you been?"

"I... detained," was all Sumio could manage.

"Fine. Wait. Wait. There it is. Did you see that?"

"Yes. I've got it." Sumio tapped at his screen furiously.

Sumio turned his head just enough to cast his voice over his shoulder, towards the lab coat in the corner. "Re-initialize the driver net," he said, and then looked at Levinthal. "On my mark."

Sumio's eyes remained fixed to the tech screens on his side of the tank. "Everything's peaked at or beyond maximum. Wait. Wait. There it is."

"What? What!?"

"I'm reading a neuronal feedback loop. Spontaneous feedback." He sounded surprised, Martha thought. "It's chaotic... hyperactive, but it's there. I don't believe it. The drivers are still not sending any signal, but it looks like his own neural net is trying to come on-line."

"Just wait," said Levinthal. "Bring the drivers on-line... on my mark, wait, wait ." Levinthal looked up and Sumio hesitated.

"Mark. Nano-drivers on-line now."

"Sensei, sensei," Sumio said weakly, and in another moment he was tapping furiously at his screen.

Then Martha heard what sounded like a gurgling child in a bathtub. Gurgle, swallowing too much water, then a cough and a retching and as soon as the lungs cleared a wail rose from the tank, high pitched and full of terror and hopelessness. As if struck by a blow to the solar plexus Martha fell to her knees and choked back a sob.

"Dear God what are they doing here!" Levinthal yelled.

"Entropy conversion isn't on-line yet," Sumio announced as he shuffled sidelong to the foot of the tank tapping screens as he moved. This brought Levinthal's attention back to the tank. "Watch your temperature. We don't want to melt him."

"Yes. Yes." Sumio had his eyes on three screens at once. Okay. Sorry… there." Just then he looked towards the Simons and made brief eye contact with Martha.

Sumio moved around the tank and stepped to the other side so that he stood side-by-side with Levinthal, their backs to Martha and Jonathan. She controlled herself with a grim resolution galvanized around a quite sudden, but not unexpected murderous hatred of them both. She had a vision of herself leaping onto Sumio and choking the life out of him. There had been a relationship of a sort based solely on her quiet sense that together they both mistrusted Levinthal, but here she could see that Sumio was Levinthal's boy in the end.

He always was and always would be.

He, like her, had been swept up and was powerless to resist the tidal tow of inexorable fate.

She began to pray—old prayers—who was the patron saint of cloning she thought bitterly. She prayed for an accident, a catastrophic failure, a complete and utter debacle. An overload. A shut down. Through it all there was the tank, the ongoing wail, and the furious activity.

The wailing stopped for an instant and her heart skipped a beat but it quickly began again, but differently. Now it was a low pitched moan, an articulation of pain and horror. She heard a splash from the tank, saw a hand rise convulsively above the rim and drop down again, and then the other arm, and again, and then a leg, again until all four limbs spasmed violently sending green fluid flying.

"Entropy conversion's on-line, drivers on-line," said Sumio, a sound of relief in his voice.

"Bring up the frequency on the drivers' strings. See there? The spinal swarm. Bring it up. Up. Yes. That's it. See? Can you see that? Wake up! Look at the screen, man! The boson level is out of control. Don't you lose this! Control that pitch!"

"I'm working it." Sumio wrestled with something invisible to her, out just beyond the end of his nose. His body twisted and pitched. It looked as if he were dancing to a sinister rhythm.

"Hold on," Sumio said. "I've almost got it," and he had both hands on one screen now and he was tapping furiously. He moved quickly to the foot of the tank, put his hands inside a pair of white gloves. "I can't get it. The pitch is too intense."

The spasms continued.

"Okay. Okay," Levinthal worked to gather himself. "We're close. Get Hom."

"I'm already here," a voice called from the air.

"Good. We're heavy with bosons up here. Can you tune us down?"

"Down?"

"Down. Down. I said down!" Levinthal shouted.

"You know the risk. Hold on." The voice was cool. Utterly detached. "Boson-screens are up. You have ninety seconds."

"We've got ninety seconds then," said Levinthal. A long pause. Martha found herself counting rather than praying. One. Two. Three... Ten.... Twenty.... Thirty-one, thirty- two, thirty-three..."

"Driver symbiosis then? Do we have it? Are the drivers on line?" Levinthal gripped the edge of the tank. The spasms suddenly stopped but the screaming had grown louder now, not the high pitched scream or the low moan of before. Did anyone else here it? It sounded almost as if someone were shouting, begging, pleading, calling for mommy, for her, but incoherently. Martha placed one hand over her heart, the other against her stomach.

"I'm getting signal," Sumio suddenly announced. "Seventy- two percent, eighty-percent, hold on. Hold on." He paused.

"There it is. That's it. One hundred percent infiltration." Sumio moved back around the tank and faced Martha, tried to catch her eye but she avoided it. She knew he was gloating. The nanozine drivers belonged to him. They were his. Without them Levinthal, Inc would be an organ farm. The screaming stopped and a sudden silence eased the moment.

"Bring up the replicators," Levinthal said quietly.

"Hold on," said Sumio. "Don't rush this. We're not there yet."

"His eyes are open."

Levinthal turned full around and waved them both to the tank.

"Yes, yes," he said. "Come. The mother must see."

Martha shuffled forward as if in a trance, leaving Jonathan rooted where he stood. "You can help. Call to him, Martha. Call to him. We're almost there."

Martha stepped cautiously onto the dais and peered into the tank. The verdant body was rigid. Muscles twitched and danced. Her hand shot to her mouth and stifled a sob. His eyes were open as if he were in the midst of a night terror beyond her imagination.

"Call him," Levinthal said again. Martha exhaled, shaking, and she gripped the side of the tank and leaned in closer to the face. Long shanks of hair coated in green gel plastered his forehead. The face's eyebrows were arched in wide-eyed horror.

"Simon," she whispered, her voice hoarse, dry, barely audible. The eyes closed, the face softened, and the cheeks darkened. An assistant appeared at the head of the tank. She held the head of Simon gently up out of the fluid and bathed his face in saline. The green fell away and in another moment Martha beheld the flushed face of a sleeping Simon.

"Emergence," declared Levinthal. Tears flowed freely down Martha's cheeks. She took the child's head in her own hand and peered into the boy's face. "Simon," she whispered.

"Simon." No response other than the steady rise and fall of the boy's chest. He seemed to be in a deep sleep.

"What happened?" Martha asked.

"He's asleep. The first sleep of his... life."

"After all of... that?" Jonathan had joined the others round the tank.

"He didn't fall asleep—not the way you mean," Sumio shot back. "He, well... well. Here. Look at this." He pointed to a screen and one of the holograms floating before it. "See here? This is nominal neuronal activity. At this lower level the mind is in a coma-like state. Above it, the deep-sleep of the innocent. Down here, well-below the coma state is, well, a state of stasis, what science has long considered the death state, but it's not. In fact, sometimes the sub-atomic activity within the brain remains at this level for days after death."

"No need for a lecture," interrupted Levinthal.

"Right," responded Azawo. "Simon began at this point and we stimulated the regenerated body into this state of activity. He has come up from the bottom as it were. He rose into sleep. His neural activity organized itself there, with the help of the drivers, in this particular state. Your living pattern was instrumental. I think we have a legitimate breakthrough. This is a very... welcome... sign."

Sumio looked up at Levinthal. "You did it," he said, as if conceding victory to a rival.

"What now?" Martha asked even as Levinthal stepped away from the tank.

He looked down at her and fixed her with his stare. "Now the Age of Levinthal will begin," he announced as he stripped the latex gloves from his hands.

"The drivers are cool and comfortable," Sumio said. "So far so good. Heat conversion at only ten percent."

"Your boy is alive and doing well." Levinthal reached for her, took her elbow and guided her towards the exit. It was a miracle, of sorts, wasn't it her eyes seemed to say, though she was speechless. Sumio Azawo sounded a more conservative tone when he said, "give the system seventy-two hours." Her face suddenly twisted into confused mosaic of pain and joy and disbelief. "I didn't ask for this," she mumbled. "I would have stopped you. I wanted to stop you." She felt the blood drain from her face and a cold sweat drip down her back. She mopped at her brow and felt unsteady.

Then the floor pitched and she went down. Her lips worked for a moment as she crumbled, but no sound came out. She felt hands lift her to a chair.

"I'm okay," she mumbled.

Levinthal was out the door, calling out orders over his shoulder as he left. "Get her hydrated and get her out of here. And crank up the O.C."

They put her on a gurney and wheeled her away even as a desperate and confused laugh broke from her chest.

Two days later Levinthal, Inc abandoned Chicago as five divisions of Third Wave shock troops made their final advance against the Consortium stronghold.

II

They fled. By plane, by train, and finally by ship. Once on board the Endurance they made their way in relative safety south, to Antarctica even as Third Wave forces overran Consortium America.

Meanwhile, Levinthal had remained behind in Chicago and Martha was sick with the constant movement of the ship as it headed due south through unfavorable seas. Simon's regeneration had been interrupted by their abrupt departure, or so Sumio had explained. He was alive, but not... himself. Martha found it hard to fathom that after so many bizarre events here they were, together, still a family. Simon was like a baby and she had to spoon-feed him, only unlike a baby, he occasionally broke off into disconnected jabberings that unnerved her. After all was said and done, she found herself expecting him to, well, be himself in spite of everything.

"Good morning, Simon." Martha entered his cabin and stood at the foot of his bunk. She smiled.

"It's Better With Best," the boy sang back. His face had not lost a slight verdancy from the birthing tank, though his eyes appeared as they had in his first life, brown, almost black, and his hair was a thick shock of wheat which grew wildly and remained unkempt and uncut.

Martha went on smiling, but her heart fell.

"What's that again?" she asked.

"I Feel Rested Because I'm Bested."

"Is this a game?" she asked, knowing that, indeed, it was no game.

"Life Is A Game. Don't Cheat."

She turned away and called over her shoulder. "Jonathan!"

"What's Wrong Won't Last Long," Simon sang out.

Jonathan stumbled into the room, his clothes disheveled, his face unshaven, his eyes bleary with nausea and fatigue.

"What is it?" he asked. He looked at Martha but she wanted him to look at the boy but Jonathan does everything he can to not see him.

"He's de-integrating again," Martha said, her eyes shiny behind a pool of tears.

"Not again," the man said, and put a hand through his hair.

"I mean it," Martha declared, and knelt next to the bed. She took the boy's hand in hers. "Simon? Simon? It's Mommy!" she said. "I'm right here."

"A pox upon me for a clumsy lout!" the boy cried, and then a convulsion swept through his body and if he had not been in a four-point restraint he would have thrown himself violently to the floor.

"Oh, god," Martha said and dropped her face into her hands. The convulsion passed.

"I'll call Prang," Jonathan said and turned to leave the cabin.

"No, not Prang. Call Sumio."

"Alright." Jonathan disappeared, and in a moment Martha could hear his muffled voice in the adjacent cabin. She reaches out, and holds Simon's hand and remains kneeling beside his bunk.

"How do you feel?' she asked. Simon looked away from her face and stared up at the ceiling and drew in a deep breath.

"I feel good!" he said. "My Toes are Tingling... With Freshness!"

"They must have fallen asleep," the mother said.

"The Sleep of a Lifetime In One Night!" the boy said, and then he fought to sit up but he could not. His wrists and ankles were strapped and she told him that he had to remain that way, to be safe. Martha rose to the foot of the bed and began to massage his right foot with two hands.

"Better?" she asked.

"It's Better with Best!"

Jonathan returned. "Sumio says to bring him aft to Prang's office at 10:00 a.m., and not to worry." "Oh, I hate that guy."

"Which one? You hate them both."

Martha scoffed but did not deny it.

"Listen. I know you can't stand Quadros Prang but Sumio says this is a neurotherapuetic issue, not a driver problem."

"I remember Quadros Prang," Simon announced quite suddenly, his eyes focused on Martha's in an unprecedented way.

"You do?" she asked.

"He wants to port it all. Don't let him."

Martha and Jonathan exchanged a befuddled, if hopeful, look. Simon almost made sense.

"He does, sweety? All of it?"

"All of it," said Simon ominously though what he could possibly mean Martha had no idea. In the next instant Simon began shaking violently and his eyes rolled back into his head.

She wedged a wooden dowel between his teeth to prevent him from biting his tongue off, and she waited for the fit to pass.

Three hours later Martha and Jonathan were sitting in Dr. Quadros Prang's aft cabin. Quadros Prang had his ear to an old-style radio receiver.

"The Third Wave has Chicago."

"My God," groaned Jonathan.

"Exactly," said Prang. "Listen to me now. We're not losing. It's all rigged to blow. Believe me when I tell you if it's over for us the Board won't allow anyone else to have it. It's all a bit improvised, this end game we're playing, but we'll come out on top, I assure you. In the meanwhile," he said, and rubbed his hands together gleefully. "Antarctica will be our ark."

"Our what?" asked Martha but Prang ignored her and went on.

It was all simple and quite necessary. Master Hom and the good Dr. Levinthal decided to remain behind for as long as possible to oversee Consortium destruction of the Chicago em-frame.

"The infidel cannot be allowed into the Consortium's mystery of mysteries. It's uhm, it's an obvious point." Prang stopped for a moment as if trying to remember a detail. "The South Pole. Jesus." This from Jonathan. "Would you prefer Beijing?" asked Prang.

Jonathan shrugged, cowed but not mollified.

"The South Pole?" Martha continued. "Why... such a god-forsaken place as that?"

Prang now turned on Martha and with heat. "My dear woman. The other six continents do not sustain human life. We are most certainly headed for Antarctica. But not the South Pole. That is strictly off-limits. We have many rooms prepared in the mansion prepared for us at Erebus Station."

"But..." she went on but Prang waved her off. "Okay, but what about Simon?" Martha protested.

"... and so I have these for you, to make it all a bit more comfortable. The strain for you" and Prang paused and tried to catch her eye but she resisted, "must be terrible." Prang reached a vial to each of them. "It's good for inner-ear," Prang said, knowing full well that the gentle rocking of the ship kept Martha in a chronic state of first-trimester nausea. They each took a vial from Prang and without looking at them slipped them into their pockets.

"In any event," Prang went on, "The Alps Bunker reports that Chicago is a total loss. The eye-in-the-sky is still blind. It's... it's bad. I'm not going to tell you otherwise, but we both know that it was bad before. This, I think, is a watershed moment, eh? And we have Simon. Yes? How is he?"

"He's crazy," Jonathan blurted out and Martha gave him a stern look meant to silence him. But she felt the same way. What they had been through in Chicago... she was at a loss, still in a state of shock. The escape had been chaotic and terrifying yet it was a quiet memory compared to Simon's emergence. Yet all she could remember now, all that existed for her, was the first time he stood before her, raised his hands and waited for her to slip his pajamas over his head... just like her first Simon used to do. She dressed him those early days, before the convulsions began, and had in the process claimed him as her own even as she went against the rational discourse of her conscious mind warning her against such attachments.

"What about the scars?" Martha asked. "Why does he have so many scars? They're all over his body now."

"Did he have these scars... before?" Prang asked, barely suggesting.

"No!" Martha hissed. "No. He had not a single scar on his body. Before."

Prang shook his head. "I'm at a loss. Really. This is Dr. Levinthal's domain more than mine. How is his speech pattern?"

No one could explain the scars. At least Prang could not, or would not. Sumio was dumbfounded, but they said they seemed perfectly harmless and were not an effect of the regeneration process. They must have been there before was Sumio's conclusion, though he voiced it to no one. For the scars to be a part of Simon's first life meant that the wounds that made the scars happened sometime after Martha saw Simon for the last time. The thought made her dizzy. Forty- two scars she counted that morning, ten more than the day before. There were short scars, long snaking scars, scars that circled joints in his arms and legs. It looked as if he had been sewn together.

She felt in that moment, quite unexpectedly, an overwhelming, suffocating love for her second Simon matched only by the shame she felt for losing the first one, and for putting him through it all again. In spite of it all—in spite of the end of the world, and the end of rationality itself, she was glad to have him back with her, admittedly it seemed crazy, and perhaps she was crazy, or wanted to be insane, but she could not help but believe that somehow her lost Simon had come back to her. Hearing his voice even when it spoke inane and senseless verbiage thrilled her if only because it stirred in her a mother's worry for her child. He had returned to give her another chance to love and to protect him and this time she would not fail.

"I know how you must feel," said Prang. "Here. Try these.

They help for sleep too." They both accepted small bottles of meds. "They're old style meds, to be sure, but they work."

"Sometimes it's bad," she said quietly. "He screams. It's horrible. His fits. What can we do? Is there anything I can do?"

Prang nodded as if he understood and was empathetic. "I've heard the tape." He rose from his seat and moved around the desk until he was standing over her and Jonathan.

He was tall and lanky, his small head seemed perched atop a narrow, swiveling neck almost too thin to support any weight at all. "Just let him adjust. Be patient with him. And keep me informed." He guided them up and towards the bulkhead.

"It's you two that I'm worried about. Let's see about some special treatment for the two of you. You deserve it, and we'll all be better off afterwards."

The Endurance

I

The escape from Chicago had been chaotic and it wasn't until they were safely on board The Endurance and well out to sea that Martha realized Levinthal had not joined them. "He'll join us later," was all she could get out of Prang. As the ship made slow progress south, the atmosphere grew heavier even as the news on the shortwave grew darker. The satellites were silent, the Qport down, probably for good. Yet Martha could not find it in herself to care, to rouse a feeling of panic, of loss or yearning—none of it seemed to touch her. The end of the world? What could such a thing mean? To her it was an abstraction wrapped in a contradiction. In spite of what she had seen, it all paled in comparison to Simon. Simon hung on her mind the way the ozone saturated the sky. It was impenetrable.

Perhaps it was the pills Prang fed them—for the pills she was grateful even as she was resentful. Perhaps the pills kept her from feeling what she thought she should be feeling. But inside her was only the question of Simon, and the thought of empty, purposeless survival. What did her survival mean? Why her? Why Jonathan? Why Simon? Why any of them? Was there a purpose in the universe? A plan? Or did fate unfold as a sheer random pattern of force with no room to contemplate individual ego? Yet Levinthal had disturbed that pattern, calling Simon back the way he did, no? Yes. Perhaps the fall of the Consortium was the gods retribution for his arrogance.

What gods? There are no gods. There is no god. God died a long time ago.

She indulged a macabre chuckle. Perhaps god needed Levinthal to call him back, get him working again, fix things right this time.

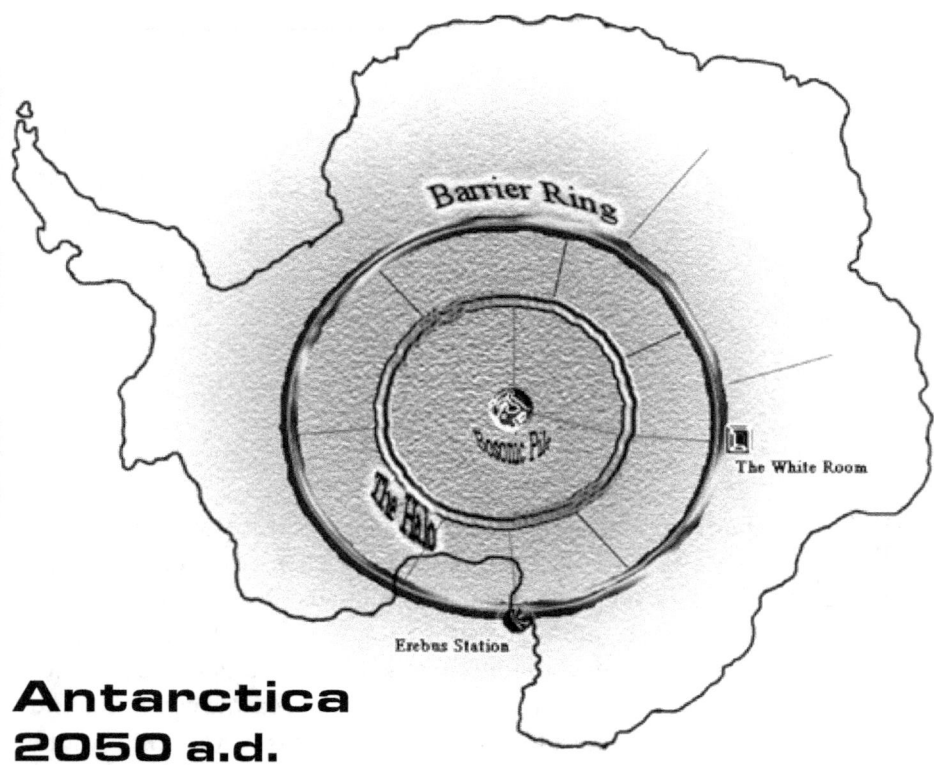

Antarctica
2050 a.d.

It wasn't until the ship had reached the silent equatorial waters of the Sargasso Sea that Martha finally put on an Ozone Suit and ventured above deck to see what she could see. Not very much, as it turned out. A thick haze filled the atmosphere and cut visibility down to almost nothing. She could hear the sound of the ship sluicing through the water though if she looked straight down she could not see it. It clung to her visor and she had to constantly wipe away the moisture, though it left a clinging film, which made her visibility—and her sense of connection to the world—sorely compromised. Whatever made up the haze, as it was not quite fog, nor was it quite smoke, and it was certainly not meant for the human lung.

She looked up and down the deck and thought suddenly of pulling off her yellow hood and taking a few deep breaths. Yes, perhaps a few deep breaths would be enough to asphyxiate her, and she would quietly fall into the sea and melt into history along with the rest of the human race.

In that moment Quadros Prang appeared, as if sensing her distress, or an opportunity, or both. He announced himself from behind by clearing his throat loudly enough to be heard through the plastic hoods they both wore, and then sidled to the rail beside her.

His disembodied voice came through on the com-link indigenous to the Ozone Suit.

"It's okay, Martha. We're going to be okay." He put a hand on her forearm and she pulled away instinctively. Something inside her said "Flee!" but she held her ground as if to prove to herself that of all the things she might be accused of, cowardice was not one of them. Yet even with no evidence to support it, she felt as close to catastrophic danger as she had ever been in her life. Still, she held her ground.

"Where are we?" When she spoke she heard her voice through the com-link in her earpiece, and if it had been anyone else speaking she would have said that the person must be on the edge of hysteria. Yet she felt calm, didn't she?

"Just moving south of the equator."

She grunted an acknowledgement and stared into the hazy abyss just beyond the ship. "But why?" she asked, and her voice shook and rose as if she could no longer control her own vocal chords.

"The Consortium… has not been idle," was Prang's slow reply.

"I'm worried about Simon," she finally said, offering him a piece of her sincerity, of something true. Prang nodded and turned towards her.

He patted her forearm and with that he left her standing at the rail. She exhaled once he was gone only then realizing that she'd been holding her breath.

•   •   •

It was like a hothouse, Jonathan complained after their latest visit to Prang's cabin. Every cabin is like a hothouse, Martha had reminded him. Everywhere on board the fecundity of ferns and farriozas, eucalyptus and petite palms. Trees in pots had been haphazardly placed all over the ship while some of the larger specimens lay on their sides, root balls rotting in burlap wraps. Potted fichus was most common, and various variegated varieties spilled from shelves, clotted gangways and otherwise made the ship a floating jungle.

Even as the equatorial air, thick and brown, settled over the ship, lab techs, or sailors, or whatever they were, wandered about constantly, almost aimlessly, with tanks on their yellow- suited backs, or with long, snaking hoses in their hands, and they watered. And they watered. And they kept on watering. As if their lives depended on it. Yet it was, it seemed to her, to no avail. The plants rotted, choked by the atmosphere, overwhelmed by the carbon dioxide—as if they simply had too much to eat, yet not enough light, and so they thrived themselves to death.

And so the days passed and they made their way south, a ship of rotting fecundity headed for the frozen southern pole. The ship pitched, the air-raid siren sang out intermittently, the air remained stagnant, brown and humid, and Martha decided to avoid all contact with Prang though he had taken it upon himself to meet them as often as possible, usually in the most unfortunate moments—when they were fighting, or fumbling towards some kind of intimacy, there was Prang.

• • •

While in the midst of their seventh week at sea, alone and without contact from any other voice in the world, Martha, Jonathan and Simon—now on his feet—met in Prang's cabin. "I like the smell in here," the boy said. He had the needles of a tiny fir in his hand and brought his fingers to his nose. "Mmmmmmm."

"The smell of death," said Prang.

"What?" Jonathan turned and looked at Prang. "How's that?"

"The lovely fragrance of fir is the smell of decay. The needles."

"Oh."

Prang turned to Martha and nodded towards Simon. In a hushed voice he spoke. "His cellular structure may have stabilized and he no longer needs the nano-splints. On the other hand, we're not sure his body can expel them. They may be permanent, you know, permanent houseguests. In the mean time he's medicated to suppress certain neurological functions so that we can keep a close watch on both the physiological and the technological. This is just the beginning." He seemed pleased. He folded his hands across his stomach and leaned back in his chair.

Prang turned to Jonathan: "How does he seem to you?"

"Like a goddamn freak," Jonathan blurted.

Martha spun around. "My god! He's right here!"

"What do you care? You won't even look at him."

"What is that supposed to mean?"

"It means what it means." Jonathan gripped the armrests of his chair until his knuckles turned white. His jaw worked as if trying to chew and swallow down something that threatened to explode in his mouth. "You... pretend he doesn't exist," he finally hissed. "You're angry with him one moment, and in the next you're doting in a way that makes you seem... crazy. And then you won't even look at me. What about me? I'm not dead... yet." Jonathan shook his head. "I'm just so sick of it. I can't keep up with your... your swings."

The two of them glared at each other. Prang watched. Simon sniffed the leaf of a potted rubber tree. His voice softer now, Jonathan continued the attack even as he realized the pointlessness of it all. "But it's true. You know it is." He slumped in his chair.

"Honesty, Integrity, Loyalty. The Consortium Way invites you to Port It All." The voice came from the boy but it was not his voice.

"See?" Jonathan said, gesturing towards Simon but his eyes on Prang. "What's that all about? It goes on and on now." Prang leaned forward. "Have there been any other kinds of moments? Any moments where, as you would say, a personality... reminiscent of who he was emerged, even for an instant? Like a moment ago here?"

"No," Martha said immediately.

"Wait a minute," Jonathan said and now he leaned forward and perched himself on the edge of his seat. "What about last night?" He arched an eyebrow in Martha's direction.

"What?" Martha's voice was tight to the tune of feigned ignorance.

"You know. We were together for the first time since... since I don't know when. We thought he was asleep." Martha would not look up at Jonathan so he turned to Prang. "We were in bed together trying to have... sex." He looked at her and a blush bloomed down her throat. "Anyway, in the middle of it all Simon comes into the room as if sleepwalking and he was, I think, you know, really sleepwalking. Anyway, he's standing there for a while—I don't know how long—and I hear him say something that sounded like, "Mama, Papa."

That's what I heard."

"I didn't hear that," Martha said quickly.

Prang seemed intrigued. "Has he called you Mama or Papa before?"

"No. Never. Not once. That's my point," said Jonathan.

"The voice. The way he held his head."

"No. No," Martha said, shaking her head. "You dreamed it."

Prang moved slowly forward in his chair and put both hands, palm down, on the desk. "Listen. I think his system... carries the trace of his first life."

"A trace... of what?"

Prang grabbed his chin. "Like a musical instrument that vibrates after the note has been sounded—the air vibrates, the instrument resonates, and that's what may be happening here. There may be a prolonged resonation of the sub-atomic field set up by the regeneration process and reproduced and maintained by the nano-drivers that maintain his system." Prang rocked back in his chair, folded his hands behind his head and looked squarely at Martha. "It's a problem, but one we're studying, I assure you."

"What does this mean?" she asked.

Prang chewed on his lower lip before speaking and when he did finally speak again he spoke slowly, choosing his words carefully. "I'm saying that the tests we have run indicate that Simon's neurological system— both his own and the nano-splints—have been super-saturated by an adenocorticotropic hormone. Produced at the time of his death."

Jonathan leaned in towards Prang's desk. "Say what?"

Prang sighed. "Simon's endocrine system—the body-wide system of glands and hormones—is working overtime. Adenocorticotropic hormones are a part of the blood chemistry that sends information to the thyroid gland and the thyroid gland affects, speaks to if you will, the adrenal glands, and from the adrenal glands come adrenaline. Simon's blood chem indicates that his adrenal system believes itself to be stuck in a life-or-death crisis and is functioning... accordingly. Perfectly, really. It's all very encouraging. But now we need to convince his pre-frontal cortext that he's okay, that he's safe. You see, when the amygdale..." Jonathan cut him off.

"Why not just turn the nano-drivers off? Or tell them to turn off the adrenaline?"

"We're working on it," said Prang.

Martha suddenly realized that Prang was lying. They don't know what to do.

"Right now his med protocol is having the effect we want. We have to coax his endocrine system to quiet down."

"From what?" Jonathan again.

Prang blinked and said, his eyes closed, "I don't know." Fucking lying pig. Her hands opened and closed spasmodically and one foot jiggled incessantly. Prang shrugged. "Death appears to be an obsolete concept given the situation. He may die, yes, and, well..."

Martha's feet kept up a constant, nervous patter as she sat there across from Prang and her husband. She spoke up and her voice sounded more fierce than she intended. "What didLevinthal have to say about all of this? Did he have any idea about this before he began these... experiments?"

"We haven't heard from the good doctor in about five weeks. Sumio and Qir, well, we hope they catch up to us before we drop below the Antarctic Circle."

"Hope?" Jonathan said.

Martha's eyes flashed and she let her anger rise to the surface. "What's the point?" she rasped. "It's over." Jonathan looked at his wife and then turned to Prang.

"Is it over, Prang?" he asked quietly. Prang's eyes bulged out with some kind of rising excitement. "Perhaps, yes, but is this so bad? Perhaps we might... begin again. Perhaps the few of us on this ship, the others who are there, perhaps you, and you, and I and the rest, perhaps we might," but he didn't finish, rather, he fixed his gaze on Martha and gave her such a strange and, well, hungry look—she'd seen that look in a man's eye before—that she froze even as he stopped talking. As if to conceal the awkward moment he closed his eyes and rocked back.

"Everyone will die," Martha said flatly. "And you want to play, what, what is it, is it Noah? Is that it?"

Prang smiled.

"No, not Noah. Such a bit part. I know it sounds insane, but we have hope. It may take generations, but... and I know it sounds insane, but you have been... chosen in a manner of speaking. There's Simon, and then there's the possibility of hybridity."

Martha snorted. "You want to start a new... species? I see. Not Noah, no, you want to play god. Fucking Christ."

"Ice-box Eden," said Jonathan, and he looked at Martha and for the first time she gave him a wan smile.

"Conceive, Believe, Achieve," Simon suddenly sang out from behind them. He had his hands in the dark loam of a potted plant and he was scooping and spreading soil on the floor all around him.

Prang rocked forward and put his clasped hands before him on the desk. "Listen to what I'm telling you. We have every reason to believe that the nano-implants that restored and sustain Simon will, in fact, sustain us all. Try to understand what this means. I know it's... difficult. But we're confident—Simon has made us confident—that we have found what the Consortium has long been searching for. I believe that we can graft the implants into already existing tissue, live for as long as we want to, or need to." He paused and seemed to be letting his words sink in.

Martha stared back silently. Madness. But… there was method in it, Levinthal had proven that, and Simon… she could not deny that Simon was the proof that, though mad, there may yet be something to what Prang was telling them.

He went on. "Once we arrive you will see. The Erebus Lab. It's beautiful. Exquisite. State-of-the-art. The Lab in Chicago is a child's toy compared to what we have waiting for us." And now he was leaning back, a broad grin on his face. "We will not only see the Earth recover, we will help shape its recovery. The immortals. The gods. Doesn't it make sense that it would take a crisis to bring this evolutionary stage to the foreground? It's perfect. Really. As if a circuit is finally closing and the incomplete work of creation is finally where it belongs: in our hands. You see? Yes? You see? We've done it. We will finish God's work and so become like him, truly."

Jonathan's jaw had dropped and Martha's head shook slightly from side to side and still Prang went on.

"Here science and religion come together to work out together propositions that have motivated their followers from the beginning: to defeat death. To live forever. And now we have done just that. A new kind of human will emerge and we will re-make the world and this time it will not be homo sapiens sapiens—definitely not this decaying hunk of ape-flesh. Something else is rising."

"Where will you get the power to…" Jonathan asked. "Geo-thermal to begin with," said Prang. "But later, by Bosonic Fission."

"Oh my god!"

"You're mad!" Martha blurted out and laughed. "I knew it!" Martha's voice was thick with a barely suppressed rage.

"Why have you done this to us?" She was sputtering with impotent fury.

Prang leaned forward in his chair. "That is a good question, my dear."

▌▌

A month went by before the four met together again. "We're at a turning point today," Prang announced as he suddenly appeared in their cabin. Simon had been in Sick Bay all week.

"I'm just back from Sick Bay and Simon continues to deteriorate," he announced.

Prang reached out and opened his hand. "I have these for you. They are an adaptation of the nano-implants that we gave to Simon." At this

Jonathan arched his eyebrows.

"Simon needs you," Prang went on, hurrying to forestall any interruption. "These," he said, and he shook his at them, "will help." Six silver capsules rested in his palm.

"I'm not swallowing anything you're handing out." Martha felt adamant, implacable, clear-headed. No more drugs.

"Simon needs you now. At least come and see him. He's calling for you." As Prang spoke he held out his other, empty hand and Martha stared at it. She let her head drop and she exhaled. Together the Simons let Prang lead them slowly, carefully, through the plant-strewn corridors until they reached the brightly lit Sick Bay, and then into a room beyond, small, white, and windowless.

Prang broke the silence. "This cabin is a neuro-magnetic resonance imagery network room. We need an image of both of your patterns. For Simon."

"Why?" Martha asked warily.

"Your patterns will serve as a master template that will support his own pattern and give his nano-supported system a chance to recover. As it is, too much of his energy is spent trying to organize and maintain the pattern and he's overheating. This will cool him down. Break his fever. Unless we do this... he'll die."

Martha choked back a sob that caught her off guard. Perhaps death would be best, for all of them, but... if there was a chance that he, and they, might live. Yet to take this chance meant to trust Prang, and everything in her being told her not to.

Prang reached forward and opened his other hand. In his palm sat the six silver capsules. "Three each. Come on, down the hatch," and as he spoke Prang pushed the pills into Jonathan's hand. Martha watched as her husband dutifully swallowed them. Like an obedient child afraid to anger father. A moment later his lips hung slack and reddened and his eyelids hung heavily at half-staff.

"Now your turn, my dear. For Simon." Martha stared at the capsules and Prang's hand and gritted her teeth. What was the worst—the absolute worst—thing that could happen by trusting Prang?

She had no idea. Perhaps death? She grabbed the pills and forced them down as one. Prang smiled.

"Sit down," he said, and then closed the door. Jonathan lowered himself onto one of two white tables. "Information can be accessed here... and shared simultaneously."

"Nuhhuh," Jonathan said and in another moment he was breathing heavily. A panic suddenly gripped Martha and her heart began to race.

"We have this one room," Prang said and in his palm he held three black capsules. "We planned on more, but we ran out of time. Not even Erebus station has a Qport quite like this, but we will. We will definitely need this. We're quite proud of this. It is, well, the future. It is what keeps us all going. Be a good girl now and take just three more pills."

Tears sprang to her eyes and her heart pounded in her chest. She knew beyond all knowing that if she took those pills, it would be her doom. She shook her head.

"No more the pills." Her words sounded slurred and unpersuasive.

Prang stepped over to her, pocketed the three black bullets and took hold of Martha's shoulders and held her firmly. "Listen to me. Simon is stuck. In the past. His death. You can upload this pattern, take it on, sustain him through it, and give it back. You are the mother. Do you understand? He needs you."

She shut her eyes and felt as if she were floating while Prang went on. Would he never leave her in peace? "You can make it tolerable, this life, if only until his own system can cope, compensate and integrate what is now an impending molecular collapse. I can't explain it any more clearly than that, my dear. Take these." He pulled his hand out of his pocket and extended the three pills to her on his open palm.

"God damn you, Quadros," she said, but then quite suddenly scooped up the pills from his hand and pitched them down her throat.

"Excellent. Now lie down. I want to show you something. I've seen what you're about to see. Many times in fact. I just can't do anything about it. You on the other hand, you can make the crucial difference. The experience is rather… intense. Jonathan here, for instance, will not recover from it."

He smiled and she had to lower herself to the table and lay down. Her head had become unbearably heavy. Prang stood over her. "How about you? How are you doing?"

She could hear but the distance between her mind and the sound of his voice was as if it came from across a vast, empty space that separated them.

"Okay. Good for you. I'm going to take one of these," he said, and popped his hand against his mouth as he threw his head back.

Martha managed a moan.

"It's all for Simon, my dear, and in the name of that special treatment I promised you, and for the future and you, my dear, for better or worse, will carry the seeds of the future. But first we have to prepare you… to make you a proper vessel for such an important undertaking." Prang moved about the room pushing equipment up towards her bed even as he went on talking. "I've seen what happened to Simon and I understand what made him so special, what made the good doctor seek out his remains. Believe me." It seemed as if Prang's voice floated into her mind from every direction.

Prang's voice dropped a register: "The truth will change you, make no mistake about it. You will never recover, at least not if I can help it. But rest in the assurance that your sacrifice is for future Consortium generations, for a new master species that will conquer this world, and perhaps others."

Then there was silence and she was alone in a void of silence, utterly dissociated from her body. She was neither asleep nor awake, though awareness remained. She felt as if from a distance pressure on the inside of her forearm, then a tingling pain that did not hurt, though she knew it would have had she been in her body rather than somewhere above it.

"There now. Go and join your son." She could feel his hands rubbing her temples and moving down her neck. Another moan, but it was her last. Her body was not her own, though she could feel and see what Prang did to it, but as if a gauze had been wrapped around her senses. Prang had his hands all over her, or she thought he did. Was she naked now, lying there in the bright light? Or was it dark and was she dreaming? She thought she could feel his dry, poisoned mouth roughly on her own and then fingers groped and penetrated her.

"There now," he said. "Input output lines are set." His voice was shaking. "Let's be sure, though." He grabbed her by the ankles and worked up under her until her pelvis rested well above her head. From there he worked inserting instruments inside her, some small at first, then something cold and painful.

In the next moment she could see the room as if from the ceiling. There was Jonathan, still as death lying next to her, and there was she, her feet in stirrups, lines snaking in and out of her, a bank of tech-screens beside her. And there was Quadros tapping at one of screens. Her face was sunken and sallow. She appeared thin and drawn, an old and sick woman wasted before her time, but had never seen it, not until this very moment. She watched Prang as he unlatched a cabinet and rolled it towards her from across the small bay only to park it firmly between her legs. He stood behind it, put his hands inside white, polymer gloves and began to move them in the air while he pressed his face against a viewfinder and, apparently, watched his activities from there.

Martha watched it all from above, from a safe, distant corner on the ceiling while he stood there, piloting his way through her warm, blue waters.

There was nothing left of her to protest, resist or deny. They were all slaves, weren't they? After all?

It was then that she began to dream, and she dreamed dreams and saw visions.

First she heard Jonathan's voice—he was speaking to Simon, and they were not on board the ship, they were at home, in Boston, ten years before. It was the last moment she had seen her son alive.

"Come on," Jonathan said to Simon. Jonathan had taken the day off to go with Simon to the Children's War Museum. She had made her farewell only an hour before when they left the flat. Her last words to Simon were "Keep an eye on your dad for me."

Martha watched the scene unfold from above and could see easily that the distance between the museum steps and the War Depot—a lunchtime eatery—was crowded with people and Jonathan hesitated. Crowds were dangerous. Every day people died in crowds, or disappeared. Yet every day crowds gathered in an attempt to act out a semblance of their lives as if in defiance of what they knew. Over a hundred meters from here to there for lunch and then back again, across the open courtyard for a fifteen-minute walk through the park. Travel visas and O.C. suits had been a gift from his boss, Langley at the Lab. How he had managed it Jonathan had no idea. No matter. He was glad to get out with his son. It had been many months since they had been allowed to do anything like this.

"Security Matters! Security Works! Keep your eye on each other!" The Consortium loud speaker filled the square with music and propaganda.

Radiation was on Jonathan's mind, but he reassured himself by tapping the rad-badge on his forearm and by grabbing Simon's arm and checking it compulsively.

Simon walked as if in a daze. He pressed himself up against Jonathan's leg, but on more than one occasion Jonathan found him fastened onto the hip of a total stranger. "God, these suits," he said.

"Stay with me, buddy. I'm here," he said, and he waved and Simon, abashed, fell into him.

"It's good to be out, isn't it?" He held his son's gloved hand.

"I can't see anything in this suit. Can't I take it off for just a minute?"

"No!" Jonathan exploded, and said more calmly, "No, you can't buddy. I'm sorry. Someday soon, though, we're working on it."

After the walk in the park remained the lecture at the Hancock Memorial Site. Martha could see—or somehow sense—that Jonathan was exhausted and the effort of keeping Simon close by in a sea of identical ozone suits threatened to overwhelm him. It all seemed like too much to do, too much to risk, too far to walk, too much time out in the open. And to make matters worse his suit chafed and he could taste ozone in his mouth. The goddamn suit leaked.

"We'll be through with this in a minute," he said to Simon.

"Just stay close, huh? There's a lot of people here." He felt as if he were caught in a fist and if he gave in, if he let himself relax, he would be crushed.

Entering a public space meant taking one's life into one's own, shaking hands. And what made matters worse was that the entire area was surrounded by Marshals and armed carriers. It seemed that half of the city had been allowed out today—there was talk of seeing the sun, perhaps even a passing rain shower, though that was a constant, cruel rumor. There would be no break in the haze, and certainly no rain clouds. Not now, and not for a very long time to come. Even so, the ritual of getting out felt important. Like a small victory, and god knew they had not had many victories lately.

Jonathan and Simon had made it to the Green with hundreds of others, and it was then, as they passed through a particularly large knot of people that Simon slipped from his grasp and disappeared into a crowd without a sound.

"Simon!" he called into the com-link but tried to keep the panic out of his voice. He wanted to rip the hood from his face and shout, but he knew it would be a useless gesture and potentially deadly. A few faces turned his way but only because he gesticulated and not because they could hear him calling. The others in the crowd quickly looked down or away and kept to their own business.

"Daddy?" He heard Simon's voice in his ear. He had been directly behind, in Jonathan's blind spot, the whole time. Damn these o-suits. Jonathan kneeled down and pushed his facemask in close to Simon's and tried to see through the opaque mask. "I thought I lost you for a second," he called but did not use the two-way this time. "You want to get out of here? It's crowded."

Simon nodded and so together they left the hall without using their lunch vouchers. They tried to give them away because once they left they would be useless, but to no avail.

No one would take them. One stranger even threatened to report him.

Outside Jonathan risked sitting down on a bench to collect himself. The red disc of the sun came from behind a Freedom Floater and he could feel the sweat begin to drip down his neck.

"I read about seagulls in school," Simon said. Jonathan held his gloved hand and nodded.

"Birds. Yeah. Birds were great. They used to be all over this place. I remember once when I was a boy about your age. They had to tell people not to feed them because there were so many of them. They filled the sky. Can you believe that? Things are okay now, though. You can see birds on the Qport at home if you want to. Things are okay. Things are relative, right buddy?"

"What was the sky like when it was blue?"

Jonathan shook his head.

"A blue sky was just an illusion, a trick of light. Now we have a... different... now it's orange."

"Brown," Simon said.

"Okay, so brown. Blue. Brown. One isn't better than the other. They're just different, right buddy?"

Jonathan looked down but he couldn't see his son's face through the reflection on the boy's mask. If he could have seen Simon the way he remembered him, he would have seen a boy with high cheek bones framed by thin, flaxen hair straight and short. His eyes, like most children in his school, had a sunken look to them in spite of the daily regimen of the Rest Bed, Vegatab Supplements, the Hyper-Chair, Kid-Dumerall and other child-rearing technologies meant to relax, nurture and sustain the mid-twenty-first century child in an ever-changing world.

"It's going to be okay, Simon," Jonathan said, and he put his arm around his son. Simon squirmed away.

"Who killed everything?" Simon asked.

"What? Everything? " He laughed a brittle laugh without mirth. "We're still here!"

"Who killed everything? They won't tell us in school. Who killed everything?"

"I don't know, Simon," Jonathan said.

"I didn't."

"No, you didn't."

"Did you?" Simon turned his mask towards his father.

"I don't know. No. Or maybe yes. Not on purpose though. It's just the price we pay to live the way we do. It's... civilized."

"Without seagulls?"

"Sure. They're just birds, scavengers. They poop on everything." Suddenly a pain shot from his left eye to the back of his head and he knew a migraine was coming on.

"Oh my God, not here," he moaned.

"My teacher—the one who… left last year—he said the Consortium killed everything."

"That's not a smart thing to say." "Why?"

"Well, it's just not. Your teacher was very bad. The Consortium, well, they, you know, the men who decide things? Well, they…"

Three Marshals suddenly appeared in front of them. Jonathan stood up instinctively and nearly fell into one of the figures' armor-plated chests. They were in full black and blue, plasma rifles drawn, face shields darkened. Jonathan had never been this close to one of them before, and suddenly the world moved slowly.

"You are in violation of Marshal Law ordinance 754-a, Conspiracy to Loiter." The voice of Marshal Law rang loudly in his hood. Jonathan shrunk back then shook his head.

"No, no. That's not it," he said, and he raised his left hand compulsively, nervously, innocently, just to shield his eyes as the red sun emerged from behind a building and shone between the Marshals' helmets.

"Drop your hand! Now!" Two Marshals simultaneously leapt back three paces, while another dropped to a crouch and raised his rifle. Jonathan froze in surprise and panic.

"Yes, okay," he said finally, and he slowly dropped his hand to his lap, palm up.

"Lay down on your stomach!" came the command.

Jonathan dropped slowly to his knees and lay face down.

"The boy stays here. Tell the boy to get on the bench. Do it."

"Yes, okay," and Jonathan called to Simon who had jumped to his feet. Simon sat back on the bench silently. One of the Marshals put a hand on Simon's shoulder and held him in place.

"You okay, Simon?" Jonathan asked desperately, but before he could say more two Marshals had pulled him to his feet while they bound his wrists together behind his back. The Marshals turned and strode off pulling Jonathan away behind them. He turned and pulled against them, trying to get back to the bench.

"Simon!" Jonathan shouted. The Marshal tugged hard on the leash that held Jonathan's hands and whirled him back around. "Do not resist," came the command.

"What about my son?" Jonathan called out, his voice breaking.

"Clamp this bastard," said another voice of the law and no sooner had he spoken than the other moved behind him and placed a heavy yoke on the back of his neck and then all went dark.

• • •

Dr. Prang's voice broke in and the vision evaporated. "How are you doing, my dear?" Martha opened her eyes and took a deep, shuddering breath.

Her head ached and the rest of her torso felt as if she had been run over. Martha's eyes bulged wide in horror and her jaw worked furiously but her voice would not work.

"Calm down. I'm trying to tell you. That's why we're here. This is what happened to your son, or at least, this is the beginning of what happened. It's buried in him under a neuro-pathic layering so sophisticated that had you attempted to untangle it from his own mind you would have destroyed him. Classic Consortium work." Prang sighed. "We're always working against ourselves, it seems. One hand doesn't know what the other is doing, eh?"

Prang paused and looked carefully at Martha.

"Good. You look angry. Use it. Hold on to it. You are going to need it." Prang broke off, looked down at his feet, collected himself and placed his hands, palms up, before Martha. "I'm offering you more here than I've been able to say and I still cannot say it all. I'm offering you Simon, yes?" Another pause. "More than that, though, I'm offering you a chance to get back at those who did this thing to you, to your son, and to others like Simon. And do you know who did this to you? Who arranged for all of this? Who stole your son? Have you guessed it yet? It's really not so hard. The puppet master. The mind behind the minds. But not my mind, my dear. Never *my* mind.

"Now listen to me carefully. I'm offering you a chance at life the way few experience it anymore. I'm offering you a chance at revenge, my dear. Those who raped and murdered Simon could be yours to crush but first you need to know. To feel. This serves us both as well. Do you want to know what they did to him? Do you want to know? You do, don't you?"

I want to know what happened to Simon, she thought.

"I understand. Of course you do."

In the next moment the world spun until she thought she might vomit, or scream, and suddenly she was in an aircraft watching two men at the controls.

• • •

The aircraft landed on a tarmac in the middle of a desert. A vast open plain stretched for miles to all compass points broken up by a few small smudges, buildings perhaps to the north, in the brown distance. Now Martha was in a car as it glided down a mag-rail silently for a few miles and approached one of the small, outlying buildings. The building had only one story, one door, no windows, and was only slightly larger than the mag-car that pulled up next to it.

A moment later she was in an elevator. Beside her lay Simon, prostrate on a gurney and a large male escort. The elevator dropped a great distance and still it kept moving.

Now Simon and his escort were in a dark room deep underground.

"Mommy!" Simon was awake and he screamed and reached convulsively into the darkness.

"Clamp him again."

"We can't. Get him on the rack and we'll wait until the Overseer gets here." They lifted Simon—he was so thin! —onto the titanium rack and stripped him naked. The room, like the corridor, glowed emerald green from the two Qports embedded in each of the four walls. The ceiling, however, was dark beyond black. She realized that she could see the world from Simon's eyes. Her stomach lurched.

He blinked and whimpered. He turned his head just as he began to feel the terror rise in him and caught the glint of green at the corner of his eye and knew he was awake, that his eyes worked, and that he could not move.

"Daddy!" he screamed and as she felt his horror, she felt her own macabre jealousy. Why would Simon call out for his father and not for her? The Marshals hesitated at the head of the bed, and knowing that the boy should not be awake yet, and that they had erred and perhaps made the Overseer's job more difficult, they turned and exited the room quickly. The door shut silently behind them. Simon was alone, in the dark.

"Daddy!" he screamed again, and then again. "Mommy!" he yelled, but his voice was dehydrated and hoarse. He shouted himself into exhaustion nevertheless, until he drifted off into an oblivious horror. A fugue.

When Simon awoke again he began to sob and his voice was ragged and small. His lips were dry and his stomach gurgled and moaned. His bladder and bowels could no longer hold their contents and so he lay there in his own shame. He whispered calls for help and then just moved his lips silently.

Then suddenly there was someone in the room with him, a tall figure, smiling, gentle, white, beaming eyes. The Overseer, thought Martha, and the thought was a revelation. She could switch her attention at will between what she considered her own point of view from above and Simon's experience.

I am here and I am there, she thought. Just as suddenly she thought: Can I see through the Overseer's eyes as well? Before she could consider whether this was a good idea, she was there, standing over Simon, an orgiastic pleasure surging through her now.

She felt what it was to be an Overseer and the feelings she felt left her inflated with the sensation that here, now, and always, she was in control. It was this sensation of control, what she had longed for and lacked in her own life, the Overseer experienced as an abundance with the supporting belief that the idea of the abundance of power thrilled him as much as the enactment of it, for both idea and practice drove him on.

Martha recoiled at the sensation. Its grandiose morbidity chilled her. That it felt familiar shook her. That she found the sensation pleasurable overloaded her system. She blanked out, terrified of what such feelings, and her responses to those feelings, might mean.

• • •

Simon's third day as a prisoner underground left him begging for death though he knew nothing of death or what it was that he wished for, other than that he wished his ordeal to end. Neural-implants in the temporal lobe and at the base of the spine left him writhing in agony. Eye evacuation took a moment longer. Though the Overseer had done countless procedures on a whole parade of victims, removing the eyes without damaging the optic nerve was still a delicate business, and failure was not an option—the Board had made that clear. By the end of the day Simon dropped into an Overseer contrived coma—unconscious, eyeless, wired. A lone saline drip hung beside the rack.

On Simon's fifth day two more Overseers took the boy out and up to an airport tarmac under an ozone-shield. He lay on a gurney alongside a dozen others, all young, some male, some female, all unconscious. Soon after an aircraft appeared and they were wheeled into its belly, Simon among them she knew.

Martha reeled with what she had seen, and though she wanted to follow she found herself powerless, a disembodied awareness pinned to the tarmac from where she watched the aircraft taxi, gather speed and lift itself into the sky towards points unknown.

III

Vilb felt sick to his stomach and behind both of his eyes he felt a sharp, stabbing pain. Migraine the Ancients called it? He moaned and rubbed his temples, exhaled deeply. He had to close his eyes and rest his head. As the room grew dark and began to fade to black he could just make out Azo, now on his knees in the corner. His head was down close to the floor and he had a luminescent shard in his hand.

"The Ancients made war against themselves and against the world that gave rise to them. That was our way, that is your family legacy. It was the worst kind of madness and suffering because it went unrecognized and so very few could discover the source of their suffering.

Conflict and oppression, they believed, was their fate. It's easy to see looking back I suppose. At the time, however, most suffered from a catastrophic amnesia. No one remembered who or what they were, and so the simplest things became hopelessly conflicted and confused."

"For instance?" Vilb said, rubbing his eyes and forehead.

"Eating. Sleeping. Raising their young. In the Ancient world the poor starved while those in power ate themselves to death. Fatigue and illness had become a constant yet invisible part of one's life experience. And the violence the old inflicted on their children as a matter of course—they called it education—sealed the fate of their world. A people cannot sow the seeds of oppression and violence and expect the young to practice some other way of life. The young learn what they live, but even this simple lesson had become a vague and contested notion even as its consequences were ruthlessly pursued by those in power. Civilization was its name."

"What had the Ancients—what had you—lost?" asked

Vilb carefully. Azo didn't answer immediately. When he did he heard in the old man's voice a strange timbre not there before.

"Our bodies," he finally said.

Vilb shook his head, bewildered.

"What was the Overseer looking for, when he blinded the boy called Simon?"

"Yes. Yes. That's right. Listen carefully and then read when you are able. What comes next is the heart of my evidence against Levinthal."

"Tell me."

Azo sighed. "Near the end of our time in the Ancient world we had stumbled into a new kind of sight. It was a perfect, logical intensification of what we had always done."

"What kind of sight?"

"Probability scans. The Ancients learned to understand the weave of the fabric of the world, and by looking there they could anticipate the way the weave might unfold, ravel or unravel before it happened. As a result of Qir Hom's Probability Equations, and the Void Mechanics that grew out of them, the Consortium began to make long-term plans... in spite of the catastrophic collapse of the human habitat. And because the Consortium believed in its own inexorable survival it accepted Third Wave military victories in the short-term because it promised, they believed, the long-term Consortium victory.

The Consortium believed that long-term victory would be achieved through the technological transformation of the human species. Probability grew high that the em-frame installation built into the bedrock of the bottom of the world would finally emerge as a consciousness, a living machine, and extraordinarily powerful. Yet all of this depended on, according to probability scans, a nine-year old boy. The search for the link had been going on for five years before Simon was born, when the em-frame in Chicago came on-line. It was just a matter of time before the Consortium found what they needed, and they did, at the eleventh-hour.

As a result all nine-year old children were randomly subjected to what Overseers called q-decoding in the hopes of finding the right sub-atomic signature. It was a desperate and obscene time, make no mistake about it. The net was cast wide and far. Thousands upon thousands of children were sacrificed to the cause. The Board discovered only late in the process that the genetic material Levinthal needed was special not for its congenital sub-atomic structure, but for how its congenital sub-atomic structure reacted to a particular set of environmental stimulants, in this case, terror, horror and death. One of Levinthal's lackeys, Chandra Ven-Quell, discovered this phenomenon and dubbed it the Ven-Quell reading. Levinthal was the one who figured out how to spike the Ven-Quell reading and from then on it was only a short time before he had the remains he needed to complete his work."

The last was lost on Vilb.

"Levinthal wanted to extend his own life, yes?" Vilb asked a moment later.

The old man nodded.

"Project Erebus," Vilb said. "A Consortium power to fight their enemies?"

"Yes. A Consortium power to fight their enemies, but more than that. The Consortium had only one hope, one driving desire: to expand, to grow, to conquer, to profit. To the end civilization pursued the premises from which it arose: expansion required conquest, perfect domination required, ultimately, unexcelled power. It became a matter of obvious fact to Consortium planners that civilization required chronic and unending conflict. Conflict was the chief of Consortium virtues in the early years just before Simon. Conflict and the prosecution of conflict became a way of life so ordinary that we no longer realized our predicament. Yet violent conflict and the inevitability of violent conflict informed the most basic activities, the simplest things, the most fundamental practices of ordinary people. Conflict was built in so that the young would know only a world of conflict and grew into a world where they were taught to expect nothing less, nay, even to question the relevance of a world without it. In short, we forgot." The old man coughed and shrugged to himself and grew quiet.

"Forgot what?"

"What's that again?"

"What did the Ancients forget?"

"The most obvious thing in the world. The same thing you have forgotten, my boy. Precisely the same thing."

"The past," Vilb said.

"Yes. Do you begin to see now? The madness? We... my boy, we produced a conflict that would make the extermination of the human race appear to be inevitable."

"But it wasn't?"

"Inexorable yes, but inevitable? No."

Vilb shook his head. He thought of The Martha in her chamber, and Master Qir in his mountain and... Levinthal... in his head. Vilb's intestines shriveled.

"How... when... at what point does Simon enter the story? Our Simon."

"Keep reading. The story continues there." Azo pointed to a patch of shining ebony.

"My eyes have… failed," Vilb complained, and Azo grunted as if making a note to himself.

"Let me read for awhile," the old man said. "It will be good for me to look again at my work. Shall I?"

"One last question."

"Yes, but hurry my boy. Time is running out."

"Why did you do all of this? What sense does it make?"

Vilb trailed off and the old man stayed quiet.

The silence deepened and Vilb could no longer hear the old man's breathing.

"For you… I wrote it for *you*."

"For… me?"

Azo nodded. "And for her."

Vilb could hear Oneira breathing steadily, asleep in the far corner of the chamber.

"To help you remember," he said, and there was resignation and fatigue in the old man's voice.

"To remember?" Vilb was shocked. "But why… how us? Who are we that you would do this for us?"

Another heavy sigh.

"You already know."

"I do not understand," said Vilb, and he rubbed his forehead. Vilb heard Azo shuffle over towards him and he felt a hand on his head in the dark. "Let's hope you do soon, because though you may have somehow slowed Quadros Prang, he has not been stopped. He's on his way."

The Fall of Chicago

March 11, 39 a.s.

So now Qir agrees and he says he's going to sequence his own re-gens as soon as Martha's done with the tanks. So now it's Martha AND Qir sequencing cloned DNA in some kind of sick competition to see who's "right." Quadros is bound to be next. He's gone mad and remains highly-capable. And his business with Martha's not finished and her's with him seems to consume her every waking moment. She's asked me to help her. Revenge, she says. For everything. Christ, what else is there to do on this god-forsaken continent?

As of this moment the Bosonic Pile is cold. I have to admit that Qir may have finally figured out a way to scatter what they're calling "Simon." I suppose it makes sense. In any event, there's just what's left of his giant chess set roaming around up there, but otherwise Simon's control over the em-frame has been cancelled and his consciousness is… gone. Even Martha seems relieved, when she's not absorbed in guilt and self-pity.

– Erebus Journal of Sumio Azawo

I

Azo explained that the Aegis named Gabulus would spirit Vilb and Oneira to the tunnel they had traveled in from the east, the Archer's Way.
"We think Quadros is vulnerable to what Qir's been concocting over in the Transveld, but… I haven't heard from Qir in a hundred years. He

called it the Millennial Palm," Azo mused. "But whose side Qir now plays on is not entirely clear."

"I know of this Palm," said Vilb. "You know of it? How?"

"I met... I found... a... a... girl, in the east. She was," but Vilb could not find the words.

"Please, my boy, try and make sense." Azo seemed on the edge of his patience for the first time.

"I'm sorry." Vilb clasped his hands under his chin. "I found a girl, and she accompanied me, us, on our Pilgrimage. It was she who rose from... what appeared to be death, or near death, recovered quickly, and from her palm a power emerged. Quadros had captured her, and even he thought she was dead I think, but she was not. She rose, and when she stood before him the Aegis... Methodius... and others were unable to move. She raised her hand like this," and Vilb raised his palm to Azo who winced as if with some ancient memory, "and from it a wave of power flowed into Quadros Prang and he was... disabled, could not move and was helpless."

Azo exhaled deeply. "Qir is here and from the sound of this, he has been here for some time."

"Forty years," said Vilb, and Azo arched a brow as if surprised by this detail, but he did not question it.

"Very well then. The endgame has come. The time is now.

Get her up and prepare to move."

Vilb helped Oneira to her feet. She was unsteady and barely able to stand. Vilb's migraine had passed by now and he saw Azo's ancient face up close for the first time even as the door to the Vault opened and a massive Aegis filled the room with his soft, amber light. He looked exactly like Methodius, yet Vilb could somehow see that this was not Methodius.

"My friend," said Azo, and he bowed his head slightly to the Aegis.

"Keystone," said the Aegis and he bowed his head to Vilb, and then he looked at Azo expectantly.

"Not yet, my friend, not yet," said Azo to Gabulus and the Aegis seemed to slump however slightly about the shoulders.

"Perhaps the woman will help him remember."

With that Gabulus ducked out and beckoned for Vilb and Oneira to follow him into the dark. Vilb surrendered and allowed himself to be led, though he remained desultory and confused from all that he had read and heard, and still he did not understand how things came to be this way. Oneira whimpered at his side quietly.

"We will be clear of the Vault network once we climb back up to the Archer's Stair. From there the Great Way begins and we can move east quickly. There will be others however, so remain quiet. Can you both move quickly?"

Vilb nodded feeling his legs beneath him but he turned to Oneira who seemed nothing short of shattered. His eyes had recovered well enough to see the iridescent walls of the tunnel around them and the darkness ahead. Gabulus took off at a quick step and Vilb found that he had to trot to keep up with the Aegis's stride while Oneira fell behind.

"Wait!" Vilb called out and turned back to Oneira. "Can you follow?" he asked.

"I'm trying," she finally said, and her voice was hollow.

"What is it?" Vilb asked. "Tell me."

"How can you not know?" Her eyes were streaming tears now.

"Please follow as fast as you may," said Gabulus striding back to them. "We have far to go." He set off this time at a slower pace and Vilb took Oneira's arm and set her pace at a quick step, though it was clear that she would not be able to maintain it for long. Deep and far, past stairwells, open passageways, wide ways and narrow, dark holes, and sometimes it seemed that they moved in a great circle until they reached yet another route, but always the next way had some unique feature about the stone and the light, until they came upon a way that was wider than all before. Burnished white stone was underfoot, comprised the walls and the ceiling—and twenty Aegis could march abreast it was so wide a way—and brightly lit though Vilb could find no light source.

"This is the Way of Quadros," said Gabulus. "He is on it and I fear he has the Palm."

"How can you know that?" asked Vilb.

"The Aegis who travel with him, though they serve him yet remain connected to the Aegis who remain loyal to Simon. It can be no other way. It is time for the Keystone to come back to himself."

Gabulus kneeled down before them both and Vilb was reminded of Methodius who he had met what felt like a very long time ago at Lake Vost. There was a gentleness to these great, amber stone giants that surprised and moved Vilb even though he could not yet fathom the Aegis' intent or who they actually served. Vilb trusted Gabulus implicitly for some reason and felt an ever-growing connection to the Aegis. He looked down at his hands and perhaps it was the light of the tunnel, or perhaps it was some change that had come over him, but his hands up to his wrists appeared to be made of the same stuff as Gabulus before him. Had they not called him their keystone? What could such a thing mean?

"We may be at an end," said Oneira unexpectedly. Vilb turned and was pleased to hear the woman speak of her own accord though her voice sounded is if it barely rose from a very deep place.

"Yes, go on," said Vilb gently.

"Quadros has the Pray, the Millenial Palm. He has learned to control her."

"This is what you read in the Vault?" Vilb asked and Oneira shook her head.

"This is what I know."

"How?"

"I remember. All of it. I know who I am." She shook with silent sobs and choked them back. She raised her chin as if in defiance, but it sank as if fighting a great burden.

Vilb shook his head. He was still roiled by what Azo had read to him before they left the Vault but he could make no such great claim. "Go on then, tell me what you remember.

Who are you?" said Vilb doggedly, and Oneira gave him a harsh, penetrating glare and he knew what she was thinking.

"Very well," he said. "Tell me. Who am I?" She dropped her gaze, apparently satisfied by this last bit and as they advanced slowly along the great Archer's Way the story of Simon and the Ancients issued from the mouth of Oneira, the Quarter- Meson of a lost tribe of The Martha from the east of Little Earth.

II

Third Wave orbital launchers screamed across the sky. Once into the upper atmosphere and beyond they detonated and spewed their radioactive shrapnel all around the planet. The Consortium had been officially blinded. The Qport network collapsed. Third Wave Grand Army of the Most Holy Martyrs landed in California.

They burned everything on their way. The acrid ozone became so toxic that even Third Wave respirators could not filter out such a poisonous fume. Chicago would fall nonetheless, the Consortium would retreat, and the executions would proceed.

Consortium analysts realized only as their ports went dark and the global network collapsed that the end was at hand. Finally the Board of

Directors decided that they should at least put up a token resistance, and so as five massive Third Wave divisions bore down on the Midwest they fired what missiles they could and approximately four million Third Wave martyrs disappeared under four tactical nuclear airbursts. They were old-style weapons dropped from old-style aircraft, all for spite's sake. When the radioactive dust cleared for a moment it seemed that the Third Wave threat had been beaten back in the eleventh-hour, but no one in power truly believed this for the Board had already planned to surrender North America long before.

Twenty more Third Wave martyr divisions poured around the flank of the smoldering, irradiated Great Plains and headed north for Chicago. They poured from three great Trojan-bergs—not ice, but troop carriers of a kind never before seen. Floating cities—barges filled with men, weapons, supplies—enough to storm a continent and end the world. A Third Wave decapitation strike would end the war and bring the Consortium to its knees. At the same time another force of five martyr divisions flanked Kansas City to the north and approached Chicago from the south west. As they moved east Third Wave divisions left a black swath behind them. There were no prisoners taken, and there were no survivors.

The Great Purge of Chicago began in earnest. Consortium Zeppelins, the guardians of the city's tallest buildings, fell uselessly from the brown sky like autumn leaves as Third Wave missiles shredded their thin skins. The three million Chicago residents who still remained mounted a heroic defense but died quickly from exposure. The victors dumped the dead into the lake in one massive pile.

Defending Chicago was simply not cost effective according to Consortium analysts, in spite of the revolutionary computer technology under the Levinthal Lab, so the Board had long ago agreed to endure the unendurable. They would surrender, when the time came, to the hostile takeover of North America and accepted the affair as a total write off. The Twelve Board members who administrated The Global Consortium Network disappeared into their bunkers deep under the Swiss Alps. From there they ordered the destruction of Consortium defense facilities. None of it could be allowed to fall into Third Wave hands.

And so as the leading edge of the Third Wave advance entered Chicago from the north, Qir Hom put the Lab's exit strategy into effect. He had seen the probability profiles and, though current events belied what he had read, a Consortium victory—of sorts—remained at the top of the hierarchy of probability outcomes. Yet even with this information Hom knew that victory would not come from Chicago, not this day. He needed only six more months. Just six months. And five hundred more q-seers.

They had come so close in Chicago but not close enough. For the time being, then, he set about his grim work of overseeing the destruction of the em-frame and its operators. It would take years to replace them all, but he could not risk even one capture.

Hom's q-seers understood their duty and they fulfilled their training without exception. They died as one, seated on the floor of the White Room. For all except Hom it was the first time they had been inside without a clean suit. Had they had eyes, they would have wept. As it was, they sat in ranks, knees drawn up, naked and small waiting for Hom to give the word. He promised them vengeance, and the final victory.

A moment later seventy-two q-seers overloaded their neural-nano implants and an electro-magnetic pulse blasted their autonomic nervous system, effectively shutting it down, and then back again to the brain where the pulse disrupted bio- electric brain activity.

They were quiet deaths.

Hom carried each of the seventy-two bodies to a large descaling chamber, filled it with oxygen and ignited it. He did this repeatedly until all of the bodies had been thoroughly burned and turned to ash. The ash he then suctioned and encased in a magnetically-sealed titanium canister which he packed carefully away with the rest of his things he planned to take with him when the time came to evacuate.

While Hom was in the sub-basement burning the q-seers, Sumio was upstairs wandering the silent, abandoned halls of the thirty-third floor and attempting to finish a stash of single-malt scotch he had found in Levinthal's abandoned quarters.

He was drunk and numb and he told himself that he would die there, surrender to the inevitability of his fate, but even as he rehearsed his own death in his mind, an incessant, adamant part of him refused to believe it.

What about the future?

He tipped the bottle again. What future?

When the first dull thuds of Third Wave demolition teams rattled the Levinthal building the already brown sky became stained with black smoke to the north. It was then that Sumio reconsidered his position. Demo teams were coming from the north, one city block at a time, and high-rises were falling, one at a time.

Within days, maybe hours for all he knew, Third Wave troops would be swarming up and down the Levinthal building. It was beyond comprehension. How could the Consortium simply give away the whole continent? And the q-network? And the em-frame? And Chicago?

It didn't make any sense, not really. Was this all a Consortium endgame? Was there another move in the works? Should he fight to live to see how it all turned out? He dropped the bottle and realized how little time he had left and raced to the elevator, then back to his office, then from lab to lab grabbing what he could carry until he became so overloaded he had to stop.

He dropped it all in the hallway.

"Think! What do you need?"

He made a list in his mind: A palm-port just in case the network comes back on-line. The nano-drivers. Of course. And the nano-replicators especially. We're in business. But where are you going?

"No more questions," he said breathlessly. His lab coat whipped behind him as he raced down the hall to his lab only to discover that the vault in which he held his nano-drivers had already been cleaned out. Levinthal, he thought, but it didn't make sense. Who else would have known where and what to look for? The drivers sat in an electro-magnetically sealed safe-box, and Sumio was the only one who had been tuned to open it.

"Replicator remains in the regeneration tank," he reminded himself, "and if not there the drains. Replicators galor there, in the soup. Get the tank fluid, just a bit. That's all. Don't fall apart now."

Sumio ran down the hall and burst into Simon's tank room. Just as he thought. Simon's tank was empty, though not clean, not entirely. Levinthal was a slob and he let his people get away with murder, but for this Sumio was grateful, almost giddy. At the bottom of the tank small pools of green sludge remained, and this he scooped up and put in four separate vials, and then put the vials in a small, black case. For an instant he wondered what had happened to the rest of the tank's fluid. City sewer? That would be a screw up of gigantic proportions. Perhaps it's best that Chicago was about to go up in smoke. Yet even total destruction would not, could not, destroy the nano- sized replicators, not if they were out and about. If given the command, they could replicate ad infinitum.

An em-frame of sufficient size and power could control the infestation—they could be controlled. They could... be slaved to work as one mind...

But to what end? Sumio had never considered the nano- machines as anything more than cellular splints for the human bio-energetic system. Loose, in the environment, where would they internalize themselves? And what would happen, say, to a street lamp? A pillow? The atmosphere?

Sumio shrugged. No time left for these thoughts. Besides, no one remained who understood how to activate the replicators. Levinthal was long gone. Qir was too, at least he thought so. Let it go. The replicators would remain inert and useless settling down with the radioactive dead at the bottom of Lake Michigan.

So satisfied, Sumio hurried to the elevator and a few moments later the doors opened. Going down. The elevator. Such a pedestrian technology, almost ancient really. A soft, wordless Consortium jingle played in the background. He knew the words by heart, though he could never remember having actually heard them for the first time. The car dropped and Sumio mumbled along with the song.

Imagine a world
Where your dreams come true
And the Consortium is there
To walk you through.

Just as the car stopped it shook hard and Sumio had to reach out to hold himself up. The heavy jolt subsided quickly but left behind a pulsating vibration that he could feel through the soles of his feet. Not good.

What had he been thinking? He was no death-defying warrior. His family may have a genetic history that went back to that ancient class, but Sumio realized quickly, that when facing death, he was terrified and sought only one thing: his own puny survival. He stopped for a moment in the sub-basement landing. Perhaps he should simply go to the surface and finish it. Here. Now. Scotch. Pills. Or perhaps a leap from the roof? Or five minutes outside without his breather.

Yes, he could do that. Perhaps he wasn't so terrified of death after all. The building shook again and he could not make himself exit the elevator. And then it came to him. There was no shame in running to avoid a dog's death. To die, crushed as a result of his own bad judgment and the machinations of others was not the death he desired. Standing there he told himself that he would welcome death when it came, certainly, for it would come, but not yet, not now, not under ten million tons of rubble, and suddenly, even as the thought entered his mind, he knew it to be true and he was bolting into the hallway.

Was he simply rationalizing the coward's way or had he come across his true path? And were they not the same after all? Sumio laughed, thoroughly confused.

He raced down the hall. What floor was he on? He had heard about the bunker, but that was long ago on a tour led by Levinthal himself.

"It was the only way I could get them to guarantee the power to this place," Levinthal explained at the time. Ahh! The power! That was it. Sumio had suddenly remembered. The bunker was underneath the circuit nexus where the building connected to the Consortium grid.

Just as he was about to run in search of the service elevators to the lower levels, he felt the building all around him shudder and groan, but this time it came as a shock wave from under the foundation. An earthquake, Sumio thought, but quickly dismissed the notion. The floor kept shuddering and then chunks of plasterene fell from the ceiling and covered him in a choking, blinding dust. Not good. The Third Wave had arrived, he thought, and already began to demo the building.

There was no way he could find the bunker now, not blind and choking. He took a breath and sucked in a hundred years of toxic building material now swimming free in the air all around him. The building's ventilators had shut down and emergency lighting was blinding. There was no way to clear the air. He was blind in a white out of dust and debris. He was choking. He was, in fact, dying.

Ah, shit.

Sumio bent over and then dropped to his knees coughing when suddenly he saw legs before him and felt a hand under his arm lifting him back to his feet. A breather was on his face now and he inhaled mercifully clean air. Sumio blinked hard and squinted, his eyes rolling in a gravely wash. Standing before him was the clean-suited figure of a q-seer.

"You're just in time," said a muffled voice from the dust.

Sumio shuddered. He knew the voice. It was Qir Hom. Since the last time they had spoken Sumio had made it a point not to go below the tenth floor of the building, below which q-seers tended to their work. The lower realms, the White Room and its clean environment, he positively avoided since his first visit.

Even now in the midst of chaos Sumio felt the loathing and distrust he felt for Qir Hom rise up in him. He stumbled backwards as he rose from his coughing fit and looked into Hom's face. There it was, maskless. He had a breather over his nose and his mouth, but the rest of his face was exposed. Sumio shuddered.

Qir Hom had no face. Rather, it was all titanium, from ear to ear, from the top of his head to the bridge of his nose. Where his eyes had been deep bowls lined with silver, encrusted with what appeared to be emerald, shimmered in spite of the atmosphere. How deep into his brain did it go, this strange and macabre apparatus? It looked deep. Sumio could not suppress another shudder.

"Follow me. Stay close," said Hom, and he turned and set off through the dust. Sumio paused and considered running the other way, but then found himself bounding after Hom, loath to let him disappear into the white out.

Hom led Sumio down to the service tunnels that ran under the building. They stopped on a small, dark platform, the air here was clear, and they removed their respirators.

"The White Room is gone," Hom said, "and the Collider Ring is next. We have about ten hours."

"And then?"

"Probability outcomes predict total annihilation. A ten-megaton explosion," said Hom, and an almost imperceptible grimace, like a shadow, passed over his mouth and was gone.

He nodded to the tunnel beside the platform. "Evac. mag-rail will take us to the other side of the lake and then North. From there, Newfoundland, and then, we fly south."

"Fly?" Sumio exclaimed.

"Flying more than doubles our chances." Hom stared at him, or at least he seemed to if titanium and green diodes could stare, and Sumio had to look away.

"We can't stay here," Sumio finally said. "Let's go."

III

The Chicago em-frame overloaded on May 20, 2050 thanks to the clever work of Qir Hom. Greater Chicago—along with almost two million Third Wave Martyrs—fell fifty feet into the sinkhole that opened up beneath them when the installation, a ring with a fifty-mile radius, exploded almost a mile under the city. What was left of Lake Michigan's poisoned waters rushed in to fill the burning, smoking depression that had opened up beside it.

Incredibly, the Consortium Towers remained standing. They were the seven tallest buildings in North America, and the dome at their center made a complex that, apparently, had been built to withstand anything. This is not to say that there was no damage. Each of the seven buildings swayed and shook, but the earth around their base did not sink, and so they remained standing, cock-eyed each pointing in their own trajectory, a Consortium island in a sea of irradiated, smoking death. Third Wave commanders had taken up the Towers as their high command and so a few survived the destruction of Chicago and claimed victory, albeit a pyrrhic one.

• • •

Twenty-five Martyr Divisions positioned in Texas now began their push east, leaving a hundred mile wide scar behind them as they moved. They stopped only long enough to raze symbols important to the Consortium, like Bentonville, Arkansas.

By July 2, 2050 the Third Wave reached Pennsylvania and regrouped. From there they split up, formed a line from New Orleans to Pittsburgh, and waited for re-enforcement from the west. When one hundred more Martyr Divisions joined them the line moved east as one body.

Finally the Consortium moved against the invading horde. Now that North America was a total write-off, the time had come to employ the stockpile against the Third Wave.

Third Wave Martyr Divisions entered the old capital and made a mountain out of the dead. They flew corpses in from a thousand miles in huge pay loaders built for the job. At first the mountains of dead began as small mounds in front of memorials to past Consortium leaders, but then as the mounds grew larger, they began to converge and become one massive pile. Helicopters rained bodies down. The mountain of dead grew.

The final Third Wave advance was reported in the Near and Far East as a glorious, historic triumph for the Forces of Truth. The mountain of dead in Chicago, in Washington and elsewhere became a symbol that inspired courage and hope in the starving, dehydrated peoples of the world. But their victory would be short-lived.

The Supra-Consciousness that would emerge from the marriage of human ingenuity and human folly—and would take the name of Simon— was near.

Jonathan Simons

February 20, 126 a.s.

Mixed, but I must say, promising results. So much so that she's calling them her people though only a dozen or so sterile units have grown to maturity. Even so, she gets a glassy look in her eye and talks of an entire tribe of them re- introduced into "the wild" as she calls it. Peaceful. Living off the land, she says. She's sequencing what we have, a few tree specimens, a few of the plants she can find in the station. Scarcely enough diversity, and not enough protein I told her. Vegetarians, she says. Prang burst out laughing when he heard this and promised to work out his own sequence to ensure a proper predatory balance, but I think he's simply mocking Martha's earnestness. I'm not so sure he's wrong, though. And still we wait and wonder if Simon's... sufficiently scattered to ensure our control of the em-frame. So far so good. Qir spends his days watching the Bosonic Pile, ready to blow the White Room should it grow again. I still haven't found out what happened to the remains of Martha's fetus. That could be a problem.

– Erebus Journal of Sumio Azawo

I

Gabulus had stopped and was waiting for them to catch up though they almost did not see him. The great white way had become a great white blur. They nearly tripped over the massive white figure when they reached him. He was down on one knee and spoke quietly. "Quadros is ahead. He moves in force." There was a look of expectancy in the massive stone face before him.

Vilb had had enough and he grew angry. He was exasperated. He felt more than ever to be... what had The Martha called him... a pawn? Yes, that was it. He was a pawn. But in the service of whom? He flew into a rage and screamed at Gabulus. His angry voice spent itself against the implacable tunnel walls. Gabulus waited patiently for the tantrum to end almost as if he welcomed such an outburst.

"The Keystone was woven from the same stuff as Simon Himself," he said at last and Vilb angrily waved him off and stormed in circles. Such figurative language left him cold. He had heard but he did not understand. Oneira hung her head and sobbed silently.

"Help me to understand!" cried Vilb. "What is a keystone? Who are the gods? Why am I here? What would you have me do?"

"The great demon is none other than Levinthal," Gabulus said at last, but quietly. "It is Levinthal who betrayed you, who has haunted you, who would have you now if not for the protection of the Citadel—Quadros's power protects it for himself, but it serves Azo and The Martha as well. And you, and the woman. And others... "

Vilb realized in that moment that what Gabulus said was true, but hadn't Prav protected him as well? Yes, she had. But it wasn't an empty silence inside him, rather, it was like the silence before the storm. Ahh! Great expectancy! Gabulus beamed at him exultantly. He kneeled before Vilb and spoke. The thrumming voice vibrated Vilb's chest and sent a shudder from his heart to his outer extremities.

"The Keystone awakens the Power of M and the Power of M restores Simon, and Simon is the Lord, your God," said the Aegis.

Gabulus spoke and Vilb's eyes opened. It was all so suddenly obvious. The Power of M on Little Earth was none other than the Ancient's emframe. Beneath them? All around them? His stomach sank to the floor. Was it The Martha's younger form here beside him as the Ubernaki Quarter-Meson, Oneira? He swooned and stumbled and landed on his backside with a thud and a grunt. The wind was knocked out of him and he gasped for breath and when he did it was as if his head was breaking the surface of the water after a long deep dive. He gasped for breath.

"Yes!"declared Gabulus. "The Keystone awakens!"

And then it was that he remembered. He remembered the past *days* and *weeks* and his Pilgrimage to the west. He remembered his longing for Martha and his failure to protect her. He remembered his ancient shame and guilt and burning love for his son, Simon, and his failure to protect him. And he remembered his long life, now only a prelude to an eternity that pierced him like a spike through the top of his head. He had many lives, this was only the most recent.

He stood as if roots had grown from his feet and gnawed their way through the polished marble to the earth below. His head began to sway gently back and forth. A long time he stood like this, his eyes shut. Sounds from far away traveled up the tunnel and whispered in his ear. He could hear and discern the hum of distant activity. Voices too, but a wash of words none of them individual or distinct. Then he heard crying from some far off place, moaning and then a wail. And it grew closer and louder and began to shake his chest and the rhythmical wailing became his own swaying, and his swaying became one with the wailing until Vilb opened his eyes. It was as if a sun-blindness had finally passed and in the cool of the dark all had become quiet, sharp, and he had become two eyes, looking into the present. And seeing it for the first time.

Levinthal vied for him as a puppet-master vies for control over his puppet. From the beginning Levinthal had used him, moved him as a pawn is moved by the hand above. The Martha called to him as well, from beyond, an ancient call to swim up stream and spawn.

And yet here he was, not a gen, but a regeneration of Jonathan Simons but something more too—he had been infected by the remains of Martha's second birth—the thing born of Prang's rape of Martha two-thousand years before. And now the... the... nano-drivers were in him and turning him into something that he had not the power to resist.

Passages in his head opened and his ears cleared even as his eyes grew sharper. He heard as well, and he heard that the wailing was from his own mouth. Tears and mucus streamed down his face. He had never wept like this before. So much lost water. But now it was a flash flood of despair. He had seen the truth at last, and there was one. He was the father of Simon Simons. And the father of Simon, god of Little Earth, and could be again.

Finally Gabulus spoke in a resonating whisper that rose from his feet to his ears: "Simon needs you. The son calls to the father."

It was then that Vilb knew it to be true even as he knew that he had been carrying this knowledge within him from the beginning. There was harsh self-judgment of his ignorance and he loathed himself for it, but just as quickly there arose within him acceptance. How could he be anything other than what he was? His Ubernaki father, he knew then, was Jonathan Simons too. Had he not set out to San Simon for the same reasons as Vilb?

But had he ever seen the obviousness of the truth? To know? And his grandfather too. And his great-grandfather.

How many Jonathans had there been? How many times had one of Vilb's predecessors actually remembered the truth of the past? He didn't know.

"What does it mean?" Vilb reeled.

"Revenge," Gabulus responded immediately. "Quadros must be destroyed. You are the Keystone and are the agent who has the power to accomplish this work. Do you understand?"

"I understand... but..." Dear Simon I understand!

A vibration in the floor trembled beneath him and then crept up into his toes and feet and up his legs. Soon his whole body was humming with the vibration of the stone and then he became incompatible with the marble and he felt a force repel him upward and he stood on air a fist above the floor.

"Let Simon finish the work he began so long ago," said Gabulus, awe in his voice.

Vilb let out a humorless, pained laugh. He remembered two millennia. He found that he understood now what that great work had been, and why Azo and the others had scattered Simon and later sought their own control of the Bosonic Pile.

And he remembered Levinthal. It was too much and for an instant he did not want to face it—did not want to become what he was. A part of him still desired to dwell among shadows, in a hill, his hill, his grotto.

Gabulus stood up and Vilb found that he could look the Aegis in the eye. Either Gabulus had become smaller, or Vilb had grown larger. As if calling him back to himself Gabulus spoke quietly, but insistently: "The *remains* are at work in you!"

Yes. They made him the Keystone. The Martha had left them in the east, hidden them from Quadros, hoping against hope that one of Jonathan's regens would find them. His path lay forward, towards Quadros but now he understood completely that he would not leave Oneira nor live his life without her. He turned to her now and her eyes were open and absent.

"I'm so sorry," he said, but there was no response. He paused abruptly, at a loss. How to do such a thing? Then it was that she seemed to slide to the floor as if poured there from a cup. She linked her hands behind her head and pulled herself into a ball.

"Leave me here," she said.

"Impossible. I need you. Simon… needs you."

She moaned.

"It's not your fault," he said at last.

"I know. It's yours," she said, and this hit Vilb as if she had thrown a stone at him and struck him in the heart. He shook his head. She was right, but… but not right.

"Listen. Listen to me now. Levinthal picked Simon because of the VenQuell. Any number of others could have sufficed, but Simon's remains suited the profile he needed." Vilb paused, not sure, but he pressed on with what came next to him. "It came down to a simple scale, between 1 and 40, and the higher the frequency number, the more pliable the genetic material became at first and the more stable over the long-term." Oneira lay still unmoving. "The VenQuell energy signature made possible the regeneration process but only if the frequency was high, very high, above 40. Yes? There has never been a regeneration without a VenQuell pattern with a rating below 40, not to this day. We run above 40 now, but that was by design. Then, at the beginning, such readings were once thought to be impossible.

This is important. Do you understand? Do you remember how Levinthal pegged the first 40-plus reading?"

"No," moaned Oneira hopelessly, and she writhed and covered her ears. Vilb dropped to his knees and buried his face in her neck and began to speak to her, muffled and quiet, but close and warm. As he spoke to her his lips brushed against her arm, her shoulder, her hair.

"Torture." "I know."

"By 2045 Levinthal understood the VenQuell and the regeneration process well enough so that if he could find genetic samples adequate to suit his needs, it would be the greatest single leap forward for the human genome. Genetic material from across the globe found its way into his hands in those final years. Always the most horrible circumstances during the global die-off alerted him to the possibility of what he sought, but always, no matter how horribly the dead had died, he had never found a sample with a reading higher than 35. In spite of it all Qir's quantum models proved that a reading higher than 40 was possible. It was Qir who narrowed down search parameters to pre-adolescents based upon an arcane combination of genetic sub-sequencing and particle physics. From there a few Consortium black market contacts and Levinthal began to receive the genetic material he needed, and he grew hot on the scent. Oddly, it wasn't the black market who supplied Simon's remains. Simon came to Levinthal from the very Consortium elite who feared the technological breakthrough in the first place."

‖

In 2049 Simon Simons, along with a host of other nine- year olds, was sold by Consortium Overseers into short-lived bondage.

While the world burned down around them, Board members and their elite guests enjoyed the excitement of an age-old industry of the decadent and the damned: sex and children and murder.

Vilb paused and Gabulus spoke. "I can generate the images," said the Aegis. In another moment an entire section of tunnel became like a window, and through it they could see darkness and light. Figures moved. Voices spoke quietly. The sound of music hovered on the edge of the scene. It was cool and pleasant.

A figure stepped into the light. It was a young woman—it was a woman's naked form. Her hair was tangled and torn thin in some places. Blood covered a swath of her upper torso. She had a long blade in one hand. Her feet and hands dripped with blood and gore. She slipped and fell on the blade, which made a deep gash in her left thigh. The sound of applause broke through. And there was the music too, strings in the background.

The woman sat up screaming, crying, wide-eyed with terror and gripping her thigh with both hands. A voice demanded that she pick up the machete. Pick it up. Pick it up. Stand up. She did as she was told. She was shaking now and blood flowed freely down her leg.

She shuffled left and there immediately beside her was another figure, smaller than the woman. It was a boy and his eyes were gone from their sockets.

Oneira listened and now she looked at the screen and she could not tear her gaze away. It was Simon. Her Simon. A hand from the darkness shoved the boy into the naked, bleeding woman and she screamed and leapt back. He stumbled forward again, hands reaching out, and this time he found her and wrapped his arms around her right leg. His whole body shook. The bloody woman sobbed deep, protracted sobs and for a moment calm threatened to break out. Quiet coughing in the background. Murmuring. Violins.

Voices were raised. Weapons produced. Then a montage of screaming and blood and Simon lay there dead on the floor. Applause. A single cello followed a path above the rest.

• • •

Oneira moaned but watched the grisly scenes unfold before her. Vilb held her hand beside her.

Simon's death scene appeared again on the tunnel wall, but this time from the back wall, from behind the lights. It was a Consortium Board party winding from its orgasmic heights. The slaughter was over and most of the observers were gone. Janitors mopped up the blood.

A small titanium cooler sat on a small pallet. Simon's remains ready for transport to Levinthal's lab. A hand lifted the cooler and carted it away.

Who lifted it?

Then the face turned in response to a hail behind the scenes and they saw. It was Sumio Azawo.

Vilb gasped.

"Enough!" Oneira cried. "For the love of Simon! I've seen enough!" She was up on her feet now, pacing back and forth grabbing at her hair.

The tunnel wall went white again. There was silence except for Oneira's heavy breathing.

"How could you?" she finally said and she turned to Vilb.

"I didn't..." he said and took a step back. His body no longer hummed and he sank to the floor. Gabulus towered over them both once again.

"Yes. Yes you did. You knew. One way or another you knew. You knew that this kind of... of... this is where Levinthal got what he wanted. And you helped him. You did."

Vilb turned away but then conceded the obviousness of the truth. "I did."

"And now the Great Mother awakens," declared Gabulus.

"Thanks be to Simon."

III

Oneira remembered. She stood up and faced Vilb. Her own face was bathed in perspiration, but her weakness seemed to have passed. She dropped back down to her knees and heaved painfully though nothing came up.

"Prang," she moaned. She tried to rise to her feet but stumbled. Vilb reached out and took an elbow warily. She heaved again but then straightened up.

A sob rocked her.

She looked into Vilb's eyes and held him. "Kill Quadros Prang."

He was near. They both felt it. Perhaps Aegis were still with him as well, but of that Vilb was not yet sure. He took a deep, shuddering breath and the image of Simon's shattered head appeared in his mind and he sobbed.

Oneira stared down the tunnel and into the distance. "I'm coming," she whispered. "I'm coming for you."

Vilb was in a full reverie now, flooded by memories, images, voices of the past and it would not be controlled. He could feel Oneira and the figure of the Aegis near, and perhaps they were speaking, but he was deep inside his own mind now. Locked doors had opened and he explored them freely. There was no more holding against it. He must lose his mind and come to his senses.

He heard a voice call out again and it was then that he looked up. It came from above and he was on The Endurance and they were close to making landfall on Antarctica for the first time two thousand years before. He must be in the mid- section of the ship. Behind him in the gloom he could see a wisp of smoke trailing from the ship's funnel. Antenna, flags, lines running taut this way and that. A lifeboat. A ladder. Up there is where the captain steers the ship.

And then a figure at the railing three stories above him began to sing. It was Quadros Prang.

He stood on the wing of the bridge and leaned against the rail. He could see his arms in the air before him and his stabbing finger. Dear God, he thought. He was singing the Anthem of the Consortium at the top of his lungs.

And we will see

Who has the final vic-tor-eeeeeee!

Consortium. Consortium.

My heart belongs to theeeeee!

Just then Jonathan saw Martha. She had dropped to her knees and crept forward until she sat below the overhang of the bridge even as Prang stood at the rail above her singing into the night. He followed behind quietly.

"No pack ice here," Prang sang, confident and large, as if only song could contain his jubilation. "And no glacier. Let the computer take us in."

She had a long surgical blade in her hand. She crawled to the ladder. She looked up and began to climb.

Kill him. Kill him, then kill me, then kill yourself. Kill everyone. Kill us all. The time for killing has come.

She looked exhausted by the time she clambered to the top of the ladder. She was some six months pregnant with child, or whatever it was that Prang had put in her and they had yet to arrive for the first time at the Erebus Station dock. The wheelhouse was just before her now but she was not yet ready to make her attack. She crawled into the shadows and hid herself there as she panted and her fetus kicked hard. Prang was inside talking loudly to someone.

Mother of God, Jonathan thought. He's not alone. He was close behind now and he could make out a voice in the static and then Prang's voice rang out. "Erebus Station do you copy. This is Endurance."

"Quadros!" said a voice through the static. Excitement, terror, relief all there. "Turn up your gain. I can barely hear you." Martha crept closer, knife in hand. Just get in there and stick him with the blade, Jonathan thought. But even that seemed almost impossible in her condition. She lay there and appeared to be listening. Jonathan climbed the ladder quietly behind her.

"Can you hear me now?" Prang said, all but shouting.

"That's better. Now tell me you have it," implored the woman's voice. Quadros let a long pause emerge.

"I have it," he finally shouted and the woman let out a scream of delight on the other end.

"Auntie Em is ready to bake some cookies," she sang out.

"Landfall in two days," Prang said.

"What about the others?"

"On their way," Prang announced though without real conviction this time.

"Thank God for that. See you shortly. Out."

She could hear more static now and then a voice, more distant than the woman's voice, and the message was broken and difficult to hear.

"… ird Wave aggression will not stand," proclaimed the voice… aggressive, unprovoked hostility… the free world… pillagers… genocidal mass murderers… addicted to weapons of mass destruction… first arrived on these shores… freedom lovers everywhere… Consortium… not forget the Washington," and then the voice went down in a sea of static. Quadros searched the static for more and a moment later another voice emerged over the shortwave. It announced quarterly projections for the second quarter of 2050, and the numbers did not look good, then static, then silence. Now or never, Jonathan thought as Martha rose to her feet, peered in through the window beside the door. Jonathan could see that Prang was crouched over a shelf of controls, his back to the door. She opened the hatch gently, passed through and crept openly toward him.

Strike! Jonathan thought, and he held his breath. The moment he turned she would have to strike. Three more steps, two more, one more, and as she took the last step she raised the knife over her head and pushed off with her right foot and lunged towards the figure. The blade was in her hand and it seemed poised over his head for an extended, shimmering moment, and Jonathan thought it looked oddly beautiful there, like a portrait, a cautionary tale, a palimpsest of history. Just off the deck in mid-step, the blade high, the soft sheen of silk collar against the pale skin of Prang's neck caught his eye. Tiny gray hairs grew just to the top of the spine, a little bump where she would stick all of her madness.

Do it!

It came down with less force than he had hoped, but it was enough. The blade sank almost to the hilt, enough to cut the line between Prang's head and the rest of him, and he rolled over limp even as Martha's lunge propelled her forward. They fell in a heap and in the tangle Martha's left hand flew out wildly to stop her fall and as it did she pushed convulsively and in the process lost the pinky of her left hand as she shoved it up and through the exposed part of the blade in Prang's neck.

They lay there side by side, Martha clutching her bleeding hand and Prang paralyzed and unconscious.

When the Endurance finally docked two days later, it was Sumio who found the bodies of Martha Simons and Quadros Prang in Sick Bay. Jonathan had been tending to his wife though he himself suffered from exposure, ozone-poisoning and dehydration. He had ignored Quadros except to move him to a hospital bunk, during which he made permanent Martha's attack. Quadros would never walk again, not without some miracle of nano-technology, which was, at this time, not forthcoming. Incredibly Prang still breathed. Jonathan was bad off when Sumio found him and the others, and he quickly administered fluids and drugs, and put Jonathan to sleep permanently.

Fortunately, Erebus Station had been equipped with the most powerful medical technology available from Levinthal, Inc. and Sumio managed to save Martha's pregnancy and the life of the good Doctor Prang.

Erebus Station

April 29, 139 a.s.

Qir is in earnest, that much is now clear. He's had some kind of breakthrough and he's inspired. Those Simon-clones of his—he calls them his Cadre—looked like a joke at first, but one thing is clear now. They are hard to kill and each one seems to be a powerful electro-magnetic defabrication protocol in the flesh. He says they live for a thousand years. I don't doubt it. I would hate to see what three or four together could do. Say, to a mountain. Prang is apoplectic. He's yelling about Qir's "unfair advantage." Funny if it wasn't so frightening. As far as Martha's efforts go, the transplanted crops have, at least many of them, survived their first long night. The em-frame turns out to be a perfect climate control apparatus— the Arclight she's calling it—it keeps the climate a steady 20 degrees C. and even during the summer it helps to moderate and disperse wind and rain. Is miraculous too strong a word here?

– Erebus Journal of Sumio Azawo

I

Gabulus insisted on showing them more of their history, and so the tunnel wall lit up again with images from the past. Vilb and Oneira stood together, hand in hand, and Vilb knew that he, and certainly she, was in shock, overwhelmed by the flood of knowledge and the trauma of remembering.

Antarctica. Erebus Station. Frozen for the time being, but underground an entire network of tunnels, rooms, facilities—a massive underground base like the Lab in Chicago, only bigger and made for permanent human habitation. The Endurance had docked three months before and Jonathan had remained in a drug-induced stupor until, Vilb realized then, he had been put in a coma for long-term storage, his body to be harvested later. Martha, on the other hand, was the carrier—inside her was the prize, the fruits of Levinthal's long labor born of Prang's rape and Sumio's complicity.

Oneira squeezed Vilb's hand, knowing that he had left this part of the story and that she was, from here on in, alone.

• • •

Together they watched the window to the past, and in it they saw what they knew to be Erebus Station.

The station was desolate except for a rumored skeleton crew, but of them Sumio had seen nothing and heard nothing. He was alone in the new world for all he knew, though as for that he felt somehow that the station itself had a kind of presence.

It was time to find out in any event, and he let his stomach lead him. For the first time in a long while he wanted something other than the emergency rations he had been nibbling on since the exodus from Chicago.

The station sprawled for kilometers in every direction and was comprised of at least four levels. Somewhere was a main cafeteria according to Hom.

So he set off, water and supplies in a pack on his back. He traversed brightly lit hallways that ran off into the distance. All was white, inexorable light. Hall after endless hall he passed until, finally, one caught his eye. It was darker than the others, only barely, but he was quite sure of it. He set off to see what the matter was if only to find a dark place to rest, to close his eyes.

There were no more labs, no more halls, just a long, seamless corridor that grew darker as he moved forward. It dropped as well in a slow, even grade. He moved more easily now that the light had dimmed. He felt his whole body relax into the gloom. Only now did he realize just how much the white light of the station kept him wide-eyed and wired.

"On the way back find the environmental control room," he said out loud. He needed to turn down the lights, put them on a shorter cycle. The corridor grew darker still until, in the deepening dark Sumio saw a small, green blinking light before him. It was further away than he at first imagined, and for a time he thought he imagined it, but he did finally come to the end of the passageway and the source of the green light. It was a small green diode located above a silver door at the end of the now pitch-dark corridor.

Sumio placed his hand against the cold, silver hatch. Consortium work, that was obvious. He could feel a vibration not in the door, but perhaps beyond it? Or perhaps it was he who was vibrating, and he dropped his hand, breathed and listened carefully. No, there was a vibration, probably coming from beyond the door. He could feel it now in the soles of his feet.

He placed both palms against the door and pushed in, and across and up and down but the door would not move. Squinting now, he looked in the dark for some opening mechanism, perhaps on the wall beside the door but he could find nothing. His stomach growled loudly and his knees felt wobbly.

He needed to eat. And then there was Martha and… the rest of them back in Sick Bay. He would come back to this place after checking in. Before he turned to leave he put his ear to the door and confirmed the vibration one last time.

The way back was easy and he quickly found where he had turned from the main hall. After a few more minutes at a steady walk he found the elevator that lifted him to the first level. The doors opened and across the hall before him were two large double-doors.

This is the place Hom had told him about. He pushed through the doors and found himself in the back of a cavernous room filled with long tables. He entered the end of the room furthest from the kitchen, and he stopped short. He had walked into a fulsome cloud and he gagged when he took in another breath. As he moved forward it overwhelmed him and he had to vomit.

He held his arm over his nose and mouth and moved cautiously forward. There were dead bodies strewn across the floor near the far end of the room, nearest the kitchen. The station's skeleton crew.

Sumio approached the scene slowly, his arm still over his nose and mouth. The reek brought tears to his eyes but he moved in until he was standing there amidst the carnage. Bodies lay crumpled on the floor all around him in the swelling, oozing stages of decomposition. Sixteen he counted and realized that, with the exception of one, the bodies were arranged in a wide semi-circle, the open side towards the lone figure who lay on the floor beneath a water dispenser nearest the kitchen. It looked as if the group had been engaged in a meeting of some kind and then they died where they stood.

• • •

Nauseated and now weak from low blood sugar he moved into the kitchen and ate as well as he could all things considered. The main freezer was stacked with food for an army, and there were others, deep freezers less full, and so, once finished with his meal he carefully dragged each of the bodies into a freezer and left them there. They were big, most of them male, but three were female, also large. He dragged the last one in and shut the door on them. That would have to do for now.

Already the air had begun to clear in the cafeteria and he sat down to catch his breath before heading back to descale and to check on Martha, and then there was the matter of the dark corridor and the silver door. It was then that he noticed that one of the dozens of long tables in the cafeteria was covered with large sheets of what looked like maps.

He shuffled over and tried to make sense of the disheveled mess. They were old-style maps, blueprints, spec sheets, charts, diagrams, graphs, design plans, outlines. Geological studies, atmospheric projections, even a projection of the solar wind and its impact on the electro-magnetic field that surrounds the Earth. Papers, pictures and projections were everywhere. He lifted one and a stack went sliding to the floor. "Oh bloody hell," he said out loud. He had forgotten how inconvenient paper was. Handling the large maps was especially difficult. He wished he could port all this in spite of the headache blow-back gave him. It was better than all of this, he thought. And he knew then that he would have to take it all to his quarters, hide it, study it. He was behind the curve and the time to catch back up again was now.

It was then that a particularly large stack of maps surrounded by piles of smaller papers caught his eye.

Projection: Consortium South at a Glance. 2050 a.d. in bold black letters. Underneath it someone had scrawled the words Little Earth. Someone else had scrawled, love it or leave it hastily beneath that. It was a satellite image of the Antarctic continent denuded of its ice sheets. He had never seen the naked landmass in this way before and he gazed at it, fascinated by the rugged continental terrain hidden for so many millions of years under ancient, glacial ice thousands of meters thick in some places.

According to the map the north and east side of the continent was dominated by a high, smooth veld that ran to cliffs and jagged mountains that bordered the continent and dropped suddenly to sea-level. On the eastern side there was a small mountain range, well west of Lake Vostok that ran along the edge of the plateau and gave way to badlands and another plain that ran to the coast.

Near the geographic south pole the plateau gave way to a small mountain range that extended to the north and then to the coastal cliffs. At the South Pole proper the plateau broke up into spits of land that dropped away suddenly to the sea below.

To the west of the plateau and on the other side of the encroaching sea ran the Transveld Mountain Range. In fact the entire western side of the continent appeared to be one ruggedly mountainous range that extended from the northern tip of the continent's archipelago to the southern terminus of the range some three thousand kilometers to the far tip. East of the Transveld Range and across open waters were two more large landmasses, islands really, perhaps the size of New Zealand. It was as if a new world existed there, long shrouded under ice sheets. Little Earth. Love it or leave it.

There were other maps as well. He found a Ross Island map that caught his eye. There was a map of Mt. Erebus and the old McMurdo Station. Under this map he found a precarious stack of schematics, papers, images, memos, and countless other documents related to the sprawling subterranean installation. Apparently there was a geo-thermal power station capable of producing enough electricity to power ten Chicago em-frames.

Good God.

And then there was the size of the biospheric greenhouse. It was responsible for air and water purification as well as food production. Built for five thousand.

He flipped to another map. This one was a detailed web of inter-connecting tunnels that led inland from Erebus Station to a vast array of smaller underground chambers.

Then he found it. The largest map of all. With shaking hands he moved the smaller maps aside. It was another image of the denuded continent, only this one was labeled Em-frame

Installation: Barrier Ring and Halo Infrastructure. Underneath this someone had scrawled Auntie Em.

The outer ring looked to be some three thousand kilometers around. It dwarfed any other tunneling project he had ever heard of. It was breathtaking. Audacious. Outrageous and quite impossible. Had they completed this monster?

The area circumscribed by the Barrier Ring contained another smaller ring-tunnel within its borders. The map called it the Halo. Its circumference looked to be half that of the Barrier, but it was mind-numbing nonetheless. Sumio shook his head.

Plans called for the Halo to be flooded by a gelated plasma fluid drawn from the Earth's nickel core. The Halo would then circulate the molten metal with internal plasma jets and so generate an electro-magnetic field more intense than the Earth's indigenous field. The continent would become a huge magnet. To attract what?

He found a map of the White Room. It was a cavernous space two miles down, four miles across, four miles deep, four miles wide.

He found a map of the Bosonic Sphere buried some two miles under the pole.

Sumio gagged when he understood. It was a continental em-frame complete with a Boson reservoir that would generate a Bosonic Pile capable of warping electro-magnetic fields from here to Jupiter.

The implications... were... chilling. The Consortium had constructed an em-frame capable of controlling all of the trillions upon trillions of nano-drivers currently in circulation in the choked, ozone-rich lower atmosphere.

To control them would be to control, among other things, atmospheric conditions world-wide. Perhaps even the terra- forming of Antarctica. Who knows what else. The number of q-seers required to... but then Sumio realized. This em- frame would have the power to think for itself—to wake up, to become conscious of its own computational field. It would have a body. But where would that body end? The Barrier Ring? The continent? The entire planet? Beyond?

Auntie Em was the Consortium's last stand and it was a mighty stand at that.

But she wasn't on-line yet. Why?

Simon was what this had all been about from the beginning. Simon or some other like him. The regeneration process to be exact.

The Consortium had used Levinthal and his megalomania for their own ends. Yes. It made some wicked sense suddenly. Auntie Em needed a controlling consciousness that could itself be slaved to the Consortium network. The regeneration process had, in fact, very little to do with clones or extending human life—mere inconsequential by-products to what the Board hoped to achieve.

Sumio speculated but he felt more certain than ever that whatever consciousness Levinthal could raise in Simon Simons back in Chicago, Qir

Hom hoped to raise again here strictly as a way to generate consciousness that could be controlled, and ultimately weaponized. An em-frame on this scale would have the computational power of a thousand trillion terraflops per second.

At this rate Sumio suspected that avoiding the Singularity—that moment where homo sapiens become obsolete and a mere appendage to an artificial intelligence of vastly greater power—was probably no longer possible. Instead, it seemed to him now that the Consortium had decided to embrace the inexorability of this evolutionary leap and attempt to control it, though by the looks of these spec sheets, the issue of control had never been completely solved in their rush to build the largest, most powerful Quantum installation on the planet. It was a terrible risk, and an endgame to end all endgames. Perhaps this was what drove the Third Wave to such a desperate strategy. They must have known that an invasion of Consortium America would end badly for all concerned. Perhaps the Board knew this as well, and even expected it. Perhaps… just perhaps Antarctica would be the Consortium's ark—or battleship—riding out the storm.

Suddenly a feeling of weakness and fatigue overwhelmed Sumio and he had to put his head on the table and close his eyes. Just for a moment, he told himself, just until he could collect himself and decide what to do next.

II

Sumio opened his eyes. The light blinded him and he squinted and blinked hard to Qport from the network and remembered suddenly that there was no network, at least not yet, not in this ever-lit place. How long had he been asleep? He shook himself hard to clear his head of the befogging effects of his nap and rose to his feet, stretched and yawned.

"I am glad to see you well," said a voice from the far side of the cafeteria and Sumio jumped. It was Hom.

"I tried to raise you on the port but… I see you've cleaned up the mess." Hom walked slowly into the cafeteria. Sumio exhaled sharply. There was no getting used to Hom's implants.

His titanium and emerald face shimmered and seemed to emit a faint glow.

"What have you done?"

"What have *I* done? The question is, I think, what have *you* done."

Sumio shook his head. No. *No.*

"Of course you want to know why." Hom moved further into the cafeteria and walked to where Sumio had found the sixteen dead bodies. "Here, yes?" he said and he looked down at the floor and turned around slowly.

"Am I next?" asked Sumio.

"We are the lucky ones, my friend," declared Hom. His skin was glowing with a pale green translucent light and his implants now pulsed every few seconds. "We are rich in time." Sumio exhaled sharply again. "Fine. Yes, that's fine." He felt trapped and a little desperate.

"Forget about the dead. Death is the old world. There will be no more death in the new. Come with me."

"I'm not prepared to come any further with you. I'm sorry I've come this far. I'm sorry..."

Hom waved him off.

"A history lesson then. Long before the Third Wave ever dreamed of invasion, when the Chicago em-frame first came on-line fifteen years ago, the Consortium began the first quantum probability scans. Day and night, night and day, The Consortium executive board had an insatiable appetite for what the quantum em-frame did best."

"Futures," Sumio said flatly. "Arbitrage."

"Of course. And so early on in the life of the em-frame they discovered, much to their excitement, that their monster machine was accurate to a degree and to a scale previously unimaginable. Events could be predicted, individual causal agents singled out, and macro effects managed, manipulated, and so, to a large degree, the future divined, and in some cases, manipulated in order to bring about the desired Consortium outcome. That was the good news."

"And?"

"Yes. Bad news too. In 2038 the em-frame predicted the end of the Consortium, and it was an end some ten thousand years in the making. Exact dates were unavailable, but every single scan offered the same sobering scenario. Sometime between 2044 and 2055 the Consortium would suffer a disastrous defeat from which it would not rise. No amount of present-day tinkering could change the outcome either. Around this event the flow of space-time was like a surging, swollen river—if you'll pardon the expression—and it could not be challenged, channeled or stopped. The Consortium would fall and few doubted it. It was a dark time. Board members killed themselves, Overseers went rogue. The Marshalcy was blind and, for the first time in twenty years, accountable only to local control.

By 2039 the Consortium's new executive Board understood that real power required something more than mere passive observation of the sub-atomic dance of the universe. Probability scans, once heralded as the ultimate power in the universe quickly became yesterday's disappointing technology. The em-frame was not the savior we had hoped for, but it did point the way for one that would come, for the one that was greater.

And in this possibility the Consortium threw all of its hopes and much of its resources. Late in 2040 construction on the em-frame, the Big Machine, began in earnest. It would span almost an entire continent. It would take a hundred thousand men ten years to build, but they would build it. Why? Because when the em-frame came on-line it would be capable of laying siege to the very foundations of the sub-atomic realms. Do you see? The fabric of space and time would be ours to rip, to weave, to heal."

Sumio stared back blankly, his face a gray wash in a sea of information and overwhelming realization.

"The Chicago em-frame liked it," said Hom, and the corners of his mouth went up in a barely discernable grin.

"What do you mean?"

"Probability scans done in 2040 revealed a seventy-three percent chance of Consortium success should Project Erebus be built notwithstanding a catastrophic collapse of the global order, which, by the way, continued to emerge with at least a ninety-percent certainty. So we resigned ourselves to losing control, albeit temporarily, for the greater triumph.

Eight months later, in the spring of 2041, a construction armada set sail for Antarctica. The Consortium would build the Electromagnetic Barrier Ring Bosonic Sphere. Project Erebus. Auntie Em for short, though I don't understand the reference," said Hom dryly.

"For ten years massive Consortium moles bored, blasted and built on a scale beyond any other project in human history.

Huge. Deep. They tunneled an entire continent. Crews worked day and night all at once, digging the primary rings, supporting tunnels, four different support installations, including this one, were built, and all of it simultaneously, and all of it deep underground. Countless billions of tons of earth were moved above ground, dumped into the sea. A new mountain was built from the waste northwest of the pole. Erebus Station is just one of four installations connected by thousands of kilometers of underground tunnels covered by high-speed magnetic-rail cars."

"Where is everybody now?"

Hom's ebullience waned.

"When the Third Wave knocked out the eye-in-the-sky most left this place. A few remained though but they... killed themselves."

"Is that what happened to the sixteen I found here?"

Hom nodded thoughtfully. "Sadly, yes."

Sumio knew Hom was lying but he had no reason to challenge him yet.

Hom's eyes had grown a bright, iridescent green as he spoke and they had a hypnotic effect on Sumio. A moment of silence passed between them before he shook himself. Sumio took another tack. "What could an em-frame like this do for an irradiated, ozone-soaked Tokyo?"

"The em-frame will slave all extant nano-drivers, especially those that continue to replicate in the atmosphere, to its control. Here will be the body and out there," and Hom waved as if to indicate the far reaches of the planet's atmosphere, "out there will be its aura, its mind extended, physical, yes, as a nano- presence, but energetic too, and as ubiquitous as the air itself." Hom stopped himself, realizing perhaps that he had lost his sober persona. He straightened up and cleared his throat. "The em-frame will dominate the biosphere. Weather control will be ours. The Third Wave will die-off along with everything else. The Consortium will rise again."

"So you plan to terra-form Antarctica?"

"When we're ready."

"Heat and light?"

"Year-round heat and light. We're hoping for a steady state of 25 degrees Celsius."

"You want to flood the Earth?" Sumio was aghast.

"The ice sheets will melt, yes. Sea levels will rise some one hundred meters. The world will... change. Does this bother you?"

"I still don't understand something," Sumio said, and began to slide slowly towards the rear of the room.

"There's nowhere to go, my friend," said Hom. "And there is nothing to fear, of that you can be assured."

"Why did you bring me down here?"

Hom took a deep breath and sat himself at one of the long tables. "We want to heal the world, my friend. We have everything we need. It's here. It's ready and it is magnificent. We have a thousand q-seers ready and waiting for patterning and initialization. They are not far below us."

"A thousand q-seers? How?"

Hom laughed out loud, obviously delighted.

"You my friend, and Levinthal. One of the consequences of your work in Chicago. It all catalyzed with the regeneration of Simon. Erebus Station alone is ten-times the facility that the Lab in Chicago was. Can you imagine the possibilities?" Hom could not contain his excitement. "We can shape this new world as we see fit and plant genetically engineered populations into environments for which they are perfectly suited. It will be the greatest evolutionary leap since humanity awoke to consciousness. And we will be… the creators."

"You want to play god then?"

"No, not play. I want to *be* a god."

Sumio stared, incredulous. "And me? Martha? Prang?"

"There can be many gods of a Little Earth." Sumio wanted to doubt and dismiss, but he nodded nevertheless.

"Well, you're mad, that's obvious," and as he spoke he kept his eyes on the maps strewn across the tables before him. He edged a little closer to the door as he flipped from one map to the next. He could lose himself in the station, couldn't he?

"Now listen to me for one more moment," said Hom. "We are here to perfect what nature left so incomplete. You must be curious. Let me assure you: It's all here. We have tanks. One thousand tanks. We can grow a new species. Imagine: Homo Clonus. A species that knows no fear, no weakness, no aging, no disease."

"Just obedience? A race of robots?"

Hom went on undisturbed. "We can move the mountain, my friend, and that is just the beginning. The em-frame will inhabit and control each and every individual nano-driver the world over. Total biospheric awareness. Total control. Perfect power."

Sumio kept quiet. Hom's vision shocked him, and if he was honest with himself, it thrilled him a little. It was Sumio's work too, after all, and it made theoretical sense. In time, nano- replicators could be commanded to multiply and miniaturize until every point in space within the Earth's magnetic field would be the host to whole communities of nano-drivers—an infinitude of direction and scale penetrated by em-frame awareness.

Sumio could not help himself and he took a step towards Hom. "How long until the global biosphere reaches saturation point?"

"One hundred years? Two hundred years?" said Hom.

"And beyond that? The Earth's electro-magnetic field?"

"The same, but probably less as replicators become more efficient."

"Two hundred years," said Sumio solemnly. Too long. It was all too good to be true. "You are mad."

"Not long after though the surface above us can be made habitable, but this time made perfect, stable, predictable and under our control."

It sounded as if Hom meant to stay around and to see it through. Hom laughed a gentle, pleasant laugh and Sumio looked up, surprised by the sound of it.

"You draw your conclusions from misinformed premises," Hom said.

"What are you talking about now?"

"I'm talking about the premises that govern your reasoning. They lead you to false, albeit seemingly persuasive, conclusions. About life. About death. About what your parents told you, and their parents."

"About life and death," said Sumio.

"It's why I brought you here."

"Go on." Sumio sat down again.

"Who will be here in two thousand years? Not you, correct? Isn't that what you assume?"

"Close enough," said Sumio. Hom rose and took a few slow steps towards Sumio.

"If you choose to be you will be here two thousand years from now."

Sumio's eyes went wide with realization and Hom laughed again.

"It was you," Sumio said. "You took everything from my lab? You have it with you?"

"All of it."

"You... found it then, all of it?" Hom nodded. Sumio rose quickly and began to pace back and forth as he spoke.

"I've had some ideas since Simon, Chicago. I wanted to make a few adaptations. Dehydration was just killing him. The waste heat from the drivers can be dealt with though, I'm convinced of that. If you looked at what I've done then you can see that. Simon never did lose his fever." Sumio nodded. It was true. The nano-infestation created waste heat that had deleterious effects on the biological system.

"Can it be done, though? Can you adapt the drivers to... to our uses?" and even as he asked he knew it to be true.

"Very soon," and Hom held Sumio with his strange gaze.

"You understand then what we are talking about?" A grin played at the corners of his mouth.

Sumio did understand and he knew then that Levinthal never had truly understood Sumio's work. They didn't need to clone new bodies. The nano-drivers could extend human life almost indefinitely.

"I'm not sure what a two thousand year old will look like but by then we could grow ourselves new bodies, you know, if we needed to." Hom nodded approvingly.

"That day is a long way off," said Hom.

It all hit him at once and Sumio's legs grew weak and he collapsed onto a bench. His hands were trembling. He had finally seen Hom's vision for the world—and for the two of them—and it thrilled him even as it sickened him. Who were they to dare such bizarre and impossible things? It was simply not possible—to live for two millennia and to give rise to a new world.

But he was here and it was now, and he wanted to live. The audacity of his desire dawned on him and he began to pound the table, drumming at first, and then harder and louder. His head was swimming and a fever burned in his cheeks, across his forehead. A trickle of perspiration slid down the back of his scalp, then another, and another until his back was bathed in sweat.

He would ascend.

Words became suddenly ridiculous.

"We'll need a new language," Sumio said.

"And new mythologies," said Hom, his eyes glittering. "It's not too soon to begin thinking of such things."

Sumio laughed out loud, dropped his head into his hands and laughed again, shoulders quaking until the tears began to flow. He heard another sound and it was Hom's own mad glee.

"You see then?" Hom asked, and Sumio nodded between heaves. Indeed, he had seen.

The Q-Seers

July 2, 192 a.s.

Vast distances will separate the peoples of Little Earth. There will be no conflict within their communities, and there will be no conflict between their communities. Careful genetic sequencing has seen to that. Adequate flora now exists of a sufficiently diverse kind that communities will be able to sustain themselves indefinitely with prudent management. To that end, each community, the one to the north, the one to the east, even Qir's Millennials, will be given The Book of M. Sacred texts from the gods, Prang likes to say, and it's no longer a joke. Even Martha nods and sees the reason behind it. She's got someone writing it now. I'm curious to see what she comes up with and doubly so to see what the people of Little Earth will do with it.

– Erebus Journal of Sumio Azawo

I

It was Martha Simons flat on her back and thirty-eight weeks pregnant in the middle of an otherwise empty, white, windowless room. She woke up, raised herself to a sitting position. She called out but no one responded. Quickly seizing the opportunity she yanked the intravenous lines out of her arms and the fog began to lift from her brain.

Prang. The ship. The rape. And now a kicking fetus, and at this her hand stroked her bulging belly. And where was Simon?

On her feet now she shuffled over to the small sink in the corner of the room.

Water first, she thought, and then the slaughter.

• • •

In the wall next to the sink was a closet and inside hung one-piece clean suits like the kind she had seen in Chicago. Not ozone suits. These were white and made of some kind of translucent material Martha had never seen before.

She sat on the edge of her bed and took in the small room, empty except for a corner with cupboards, a counter, a sink, her bed, an intravenous line connected to a bottle half-full of an emerald fluid. The baby kicked within her, a spasm of pain shot across her back and she held her breath. From between her legs broke a shimmering pale green fluid and it splashed to the white floor. She could feel that the baby was head down and ready to fight for its first breath.

Christ almighty, not now!

She gasped with a contraction and breathed through it. It was hard and fast and sharp. Tears came to her eyes. Not her first but certainly her last, she thought and wept and her jaw went hard then, and her eyes were dry and hot. Just this pain, she thought, and screamed—a growling yell really—and she thought of Quadros and the knife slipping into the back of his neck. Her finest hour.

Martha alone would stop the Consortium. She laughed and wept as a powerful contraction squeezed her. She squatted then and there, one hand on the counter, the other on her belly. She breathed hard, opened her throat and screamed. Pain and rage poured out of her. She felt the baby drop into the birth canal, felt it turn at the last moment and fight its way out. It felt like she was giving birth to the whole world's suffering at once and that in the end, it would not come. Finally though the baby dropped its head and burrowed out of her, but not until she felt as if she might split in two as it emerged. She ripped and bled, but remained intact, in one tattered piece, and the baby lay there on the floor moving and sputtering in blood and emerald fluid.

She staunched her own blood flow and gathered her strength to rise. Once to her knees she gathered the baby up and slowly rose to her feet. Next, she shuffled to the closet, pulled down one of the white suits and wrapped the baby up tight in it and held it against her. It squirmed and fought for air. Martha did not let up, however. Ten minutes she held the squirming infant against her, its face wrapped tight and pressed hard against breastbone. Finally the squirming and breathing stopped and Martha stifled a sob. A contraction gripped her and she inhaled sharply and had to lay the dead infant down on the bed. Just then its head moved and it began to breathe again.

She picked it up again and repeated the process a second time and watched the same results. A third time made it clear.

Fucking monster won't die.

Martha collapsed into a heap. Her rage had abandoned her and the tears began to flow from exhaustion and hopelessness. She left the baby writhing on the bed. Its blotchy skin showed pale green and she shivered in revulsion.

A sense of horror came over her and for a moment in her dread and weakness she thought of lifting the infant to nurse it. But how could she love this thing? What was it? Quadros had done it to her and she retched and gagged with the horror. It looked almost human, but she knew that he had some other plan, and she had been his vessel. Another contraction gripped her. The afterbirth was close now. One more contraction and a push and she would be done with it she hoped, all of it. Another wave of nausea and cold sweat washed over her. The afterbirth passed and she gasped when she saw the shimmering, green and purple sack on the floor. Just then the baby wriggled and its eyes were open now and clear.

Only the knife would do now. The death of the thing must be total if it was to be permanent. She paused and summoned the rage and the memory of Simon's death and straightened herself. Quadros Prang had put that trauma in her even as he raped her. What had he called it? The VenQuell?

Is that what this was? This thing she gave birth to? A steady supply of the genetic material they were so greedy for? Whatever it amounted to, he could not be allowed to succeed. Only death.

Kill. Kill. Kill.

Martha wept as she used the surgical blade to dismember the infant.

She hid the *remains* and the placenta as well as she could, wrapping separate parts in four different clean suits and then stuffed them into the tied off legs of another clean suit. Next she dressed herself and then tied the *remains* around her waist. Even now they could be made to serve Quadros, or Levinthal.

That much she was sure of.

A voice called to her from down the hall and she held her breath and waited. In the next moment she grabbed the knife from the floor and moved slowly to the door. Her mouth ached with dryness. She had a fever.

The hall appeared to be empty and so she opened the door more fully and crept silently into the hall keeping close to the wall of the corridor. She heard the voice again, doubled over at the same time and had to rest there on her hands and knees.

She heard the voice again. *Mommy,* it said, and Martha stifled a sob but began to crawl towards the source. *Mommy*, it called again. She opened the first door that she came to. Empty. Meanwhile the voice kept calling. She was sure it was Simon's voice.

Mommy! Martha crawled on to the next door, and the next. The voice kept calling and so Martha moved on doggedly down the long, white corridor.

At the end of a hall elevator doors opened for her and she rose to her feet and stepped in cautiously. The voice seemed to be coming from below.

The doors closed and the car dropped for an interminable period.

When the doors finally opened she stepped out into another brightly lit, white hall almost exactly like the one she had just left. The voice called louder now. Urgently.

Mommy!

Martha began to slog along as well as she might, came to the end of one corridor, turned left, and then left again and found a dark passage before her.

She moved on, relieved by the soothing night of the tunnel. In the distance a tiny green star blinked and she set out for it. A silver door appeared before her as she approached the green light and behind the door she heard the voice call out again, and again, and again.

She felt around the door's edge for a mechanism, a Qport, anything that might indicate a way to open the door but she found nothing. The green light, tiny really, no larger than an eye, cast a preternatural green glow on the door and the surrounding walls.

The doorframe gave way directly to rough-hewn stone and Martha ran her fingers over it and felt a vibration. The sensation reminded her of how it felt to touch Jonathan's back as he was sleeping deeply. She pulled back her hand quickly as if afraid to wake the walls.

Mommy the voice called, and again, and then again, and now they were coming one on top of the other, as if a crowd of voices were calling to her. *Mommy mommy mommy mommy mommy mommy mommy mommy.* For an instant Martha considered turning and running back down the dark hall but where would she go?

The voices continued to call to her and so she clamped her hands over her ears and pressed her forehead against the door.

Then it was she saw the green light as if for the first time. She reached up and put her index finger over the light and the corridor went dark and the door slid open. Breathing now, shuddering, she kept her finger on the light and tried to collect herself.

The voices were louder now and she stepped through the portal squinting hard, one of her hands shielding her forehead. Immediately before her was a silver cylinder lying on its side about twelve feet long and four feet high. She reached out and touched the seamless surface. It was cold. There were no viewing windows as far as she could tell, only a green diode recessed into the side of the tank gave off a familiar emerald aura.

Next to it lay another tank, and beyond that, another, and another in a long line some fifty in all. To her left more tanks running into the distance along the rock wall, maybe fifty more on that side.

Ten lines deep.

A thousand tanks at least.

Still the chorus of voices called and she felt her mind go thin, as if pressed between two panes of glass. Desperate now. Desperate. In a moment she would be smeared to nothingness and so she ran from tank to tank while pressing on the green diode. The first tank let out a woosh and a hiss and the top began to slide open, but before she could see what was inside she moved on to the next. And the next, and the next and the next until the voices were fewer now. Ten tanks were quiet, twenty, then fifty. Then one hundred tanks were dark and quiet, and open, but hundreds more remained, and many of them continued to call out mommy.

The fevered desperation had left her and she moved from tank to tank more slowly now until, almost collapsing, she pressed the diode on one more tank and had to stop, drop to her knees and rest.

A whoosh and a hiss and the top half of the cylinder slid away and hid itself in the lower half. Kneeling there she could just see over the rim to what lay within.

It was a pale green Simon with a titanium vizard over his eyes, across the bridge of his nose, wrapping his temples. Martha leaned in close and took a deep breath. It smelled like a newborn and her stomach turned over and her knees went soft. She gripped the side of the tank convulsively as if the floor had suddenly fallen away from her.

How could this be? What was going on? She fought a collapse and willed her knees to stiffen, drew in a deep breath and began to shuffle from tank to open tank and in each there lay the same pale green, naked boy who looked like Simon.

Simon, except for the silver implants in his eye sockets. On closer inspection he wore no mask over his eyes, for he had no eyes, only deep metallic implants. What did they call them now? Q-seers? Dear God. A thousand of them.

Without warning Simon's voice spoke to her, but not from the tank.

They're coming for me. The men want to put me in the ground forever.

"Where are you?"

Tell them I'm sorry for what I did. Tell them I won't do it again.

"Simon where are you? Can you tell me where you are?"

I'm here.

"Yes, honey, but where is here?"

Close your eyes and I'll show you.

She paused. "Yes. Okay. My eyes are closed."

Can you see me now?

It was as if Martha was seeing through Simon's eyes. "I can see. You're in a white room. Turn to the doorway." Simon turned to the open door of his room.

Now do you see?

She could see the identification tag on the inside of the door. "You're in Z-416. Hold on. Mommy's coming."

The White Room

I

With what strength she had Martha stumbled from the tank room, staggered down the darkened hall and into the illuminated labyrinth of corridors beyond. She was dripping with perspiration and her eyes stung with sweat and tears. Around her waist hung her makeshift baggage of cleansuits and gore and they slapped against her as she shambled forward as fast as she could manage.

"Simon!" she called out, hoping that someone might hear her and return, but the hall beyond remained empty of any traffic. She had to find her own way and the problem overwhelmed her tattered mind. There were too many paths, too many corridors, too many dead ends. She stumbled aimlessly at first, calling out, leaning against the wall as a way to keep on her feet. In this way she found an illuminated wall map when her shoulder activated the illuminated network of tubes and tunnels. Then an elevator, and then somehow a corridor and a line of doors. The 400-Z block. She hurried as well as she could. 410. 411. 412. Finally, bursting into the darkened room she called out "Simon!" and light filled the room. On the floor intravenous lines and titanium canisters were scattered about but there was no sign of the boy.

In a drawer she found a collection of shining steel instruments. Three long stainless spikes caught her eye and she snatched them up, wrapped them up in a cloth and tucked them into her wasteband next to her knife. Finish what she started.

"Simon!" she shouted again.

Mommy cried a voice right next to her, and Martha spun around.

"Simon!" she called out again. "I can't find you."

I'm with the men. They're taking me to a White Room.

"They're all white rooms!" she screamed. But wait. Wait. She'd heard of such a place. The White Room. The White Room. Somewhere she had heard of such a place, but her befuddled mind could not recall what it was or where on Earth it could be.

"I don't understand!" *The White Room.* "How do I find it?" *Follow the tanks.*

"I'm coming, baby. Hold on." Her voice was ragged and hoarse but she called after him. Sweat soaked her and a raging thirst burned in her throat. She took a long draught of water from the faucet, filled an empty bottle she found and burst back into the hall. She looked up and down the deserted corridors trying to somehow intuit her way.

By chance or some other guidance Martha retraced her way back to the silver door she had left behind, the tank room, and it was open and dark and still. The room was empty now except for a distant corner where a group of figures in clean suits and full headgear herded the last of the tanks in a queue towards the gaping mouth of a freight elevator.

The last of the silver coffins disappeared into the elevator and the doors closed, leaving her alone again. She waited for the elevator doors to close before struggling across the wide floor even as she pulled on the hood of her clean suit. With the hood over her face the hotness of her breath fogged the inside eye screen and she could feel the fever in her body now. It was hard to breathe. Hard to move even. Every joint ached. She had to stop for another gulp of water but quickly pressed on in spite of her pain. As she reached the other side of the cavernous room the elevator doors opened without warning and four figures in clean suits filed out, moved towards the last group of tanks and began guiding them in a line to the lift.

She squatted down, pressed herself against a wall and held her breath. Two clean suits nearly knocked her over, but they seemed oblivious to her presence and so she risked crawling towards the open doors but came up short. There was no way to simply walk or crawl unseen into the brightly lit elevator car. She crouched and despaired for a moment.

With eyes closed tightly she concentrated on quieting her breathing but before she could make much progress the four clean suits exited the elevator, complaining loudly to one another. They disappeared into an adjacent door and left the lift doors open, the last of the tanks waiting to be ferried down, or up. Martha seized the moment and crawled as fast as she could the rest of the short way along the wall and ducked into the far corner of the elevator car, skittering and grunting, breathing hard, knees aching, until the light of the elevator car made her blink. She crawled into the far corner and crouched behind one of the tanks even as the four clean suits reappeared. Each of them carried, dragged really, large duffel bags behind them. It took some time to load them onto the already crowded lift and Martha began to breathe easier and allowed herself to close her eyes for a moment.

In the next moment she felt the elevator drop. She was asleep before it reached its destination.

A toe in the ribs woke her and she cursed herself under her breath. She looked up into the mirrored faces of four clean suits standing over her. The elevator car was empty otherwise.

She could hear them in her hood. "Yes sir. She's here. We've got her." A moment of silence and then "right" again from the voice and the one who spoke turned to the other three. "We bring her along."

"Right," said the three others. She tried to rise and flee, or at least struggle, but her strength was gone. She slumped and surrendered.

Two of the clean suits pulled her up by her armpits as one came around and put a restraining clamp on the back of her neck and all went dark.

When next she woke her senses were immediately alert and on edge. She was able to sit up and so she looked around. She felt cooler, as if the fever had broken, and more rested. In the next instant she remembered the birth and reached for the *remains*, still tied about her. They'd not thought to search her. She still had a chance to get rid of it. She felt at her waistband for the long needles and blade she carried. Yes. At least that much. But what about Simon? Beside her appeared a figure in a clean suit, hypo in hand, and as she looked around she stripped her headgear off and blinked hard in the glaring white light. There were three other figures in white suits and together they were in a white, windowless compartment. There was no way to tell if these were the same figures or four others. They had her on some kind of underground rail. She could feel the movement as the train decelerated and then shot back to cruising speed a moment later. One of the figures put a hand on her shoulder and pushed her onto her back and she did not resist. Rest for now, and she lay that way for some time until the train finally stopped. The doors opened silently and the four exited onto the platform, turned, and waited for her.

"This way," one said. She stepped out of the car onto a platform that opened onto a wide, white corridor leading into the distance. A sign over the platform read, "White Room Station. This is a Clean Environment. Are you Clean?"

Her heart leapt. They had brought her to Simon. The platform was quiet and the corridor appeared deserted, but it felt different here. Somewhere nearby she could feel people at work. She could feel an excitement in the air, and the four white suits who shepherded Martha down the corridor were no exception.

At the end they came to an intersection, turned and headed down another short corridor that ended at large, silver double doors some twenty feet high.

"Are You Clean?" read the interrogative over the doors and Martha shrugged involuntarily. The towering doors opened and from there another small, white figure appeared and jogged towards her. He pulled his headgear off and revealed the grinning face of Sumio Azawo. His face was thinner and harder than she remembered it—how much time had passed she didn't know—but he too appeared excited to see her. Even gleeful.

She remembered her skewers and her blade and reached around to feel for them. Still there. And the *remains*. And her water bottle. All still tied around her waist.

"Martha!" he called her name as he approached and Martha could see the lines around his face that were not there before. His smile looked now more like a grimace, like a face in pain, but committed to calling it good. "We were so worried about you." He was before her now, his face wet with perspiration, and he reached out and grabbed both of her shoulders. He tried to embrace her in an awkward, stiff-armed gesture, but she offered nothing in return. He looked down at her stomach and a look of confusion passed over him momentarily. Meanwhile the four white suits joined a train of silver tanks snaking through the open passage and disappeared down the main corridor that ran away from the station platform.

"You alright?" Sumio asked, and his voice sounded genuinely concerned. He reached out a hand to touch her midsection but Martha backed away. She stared. Kill him now. A slash across the throat. A thrust into the chest. Just grab a blade, or a spike. She gazed at him with a catatonic stare masking all that was within her. Sumio's grinning became more agitated. Finally, he broke the tension, turned and held out a hand to her, beckoning her to follow.

"There's an observation deck and we can watch it from there. There's no way I can explain it to you. Let me show it to you." And he couldn't help but blurt out. "It's all very exciting."

Martha shook her head, slowly at first, but then more insistently and as if she felt some quiescent strength rise to meet the familiar face and she choked back a sob. It was all she could do to keep herself from crumbling into his arms. She was exhausted, hot with vertigo and terribly thirsty.

"Would you please tell me… what is going on? Where is Quadros Prang?" and in spite of her best efforts her voice shook with restrained emotion.

"Just… follow me," Sumio said, the grin fading from his face.

Sumio took her by the elbow and she thought he was going to take her through the massive silver doors, but at the last he turned and he guided her through a doorway that led to a small foyer. An elevator was there, doors open, waiting.

"We're two miles down but we have to go a little deeper from here. The White Room…" and he shook his head in amazement. "It's unbelievable. Really. You'll see. Come on."

He looked at her and did a second take.

"The baby!" he exclaimed. "What? Just when?"

"I lost it," she said coolly.

"I'm… I'm sorry then. So much to go through." She thought he seemed genuinely saddened by her news. Did he not know about it? About Prang?

"Where is… Prang?" she asked again.

"He's… back at Erebus Station. You did a number on him. He's not walking yet. Maybe never. But let's not spoil the moment, eh? There's time enough to repair all that we've been through. It's just a beginning."

I'm here mommy!

"Simon!" she called out and regretted it immediately.

Sumio turned to look at her.

"He's…" he began hesitantly.

"Will I see him?"

As if in response Sumio led her along and she allowed herself to be guided. The elevator had stopped and he took her elbow and led her into a hall, down, and into a large, dark room. Martha patted the bottle, the blade, and the *remains* to remind herself of what she had to do.

Sumio moved into the room, turned and faced her. He spread his hands as he spoke. "We're in an observation chamber. It's five hundred meters above the floor and fifteen hundred meters below the ceiling. And the far wall is two thousand meters away."

"What's that?" Martha asked, pointing beyond him into the darkness.

"That's it. That's what I'm talking about. That's the White Room."

"It's not white," she mumbled and Sumio laughed.

"No. It's not white. That's just a left over from Chicago."

He turned his back to her and stepped up close to the edge of the darkness and peered into the void. "The walls, ceiling and floor are a rhyolite-cobalt-nickel alloy. You can see it here. Touch it. You can feel the magnetic field—our bodies react." He waved her closer. She could hear the awe in his voice. He was a part of this thing, this... nightmare.

"I'm okay right here," she said, and she felt the bundle of steel under her shirt. He too must die, she realized, and she sighed heavily. All of them must die.

"It's okay. There's a magnetic barrier. You can't fall. Come on." He beckoned to her with a wave. "It's beyond imagination really," Sumio said. He was breathless and he stared into the dark. He pointed down even as Martha stepped up next to him gingerly to see what he was pointing at. "Look. Down there, forty-five degrees. There."

She squinted and blinked and could only see darkness until, finally her eyes adjusted to the scale of what she was peering into and she discerned what appeared to be a group, a dozen perhaps, of particles moving slowly about in the darkness of that space.

"The tanks conjoin and make a magnetic centrifuge, you see?" He was pointing down to the floor now, fascinated. "They're made of a titanium alloy heavy with nickel and iron." He was pointing at the specks still. She was looking at distant figures in white suits, far below. Dear God. She drew back and clutched at her stomach.

"For what?" Martha whispered and Sumio turned and looked at her, a pained look of concern on his face.

"I'm sorry. You're right. It's been an intense time around here and no less so for me. I'm sorry I left you for so long. Hom said you would be out for at least two more weeks, that the baby would not come for... well, I see that things did not work out... and I'm sorry. And I've heard that Jonathan too... I'm sorry about him as well." Then Sumio smiled. "None of it is permanent, though, that's what I'm trying to tell you. Death... since Simon, you know? Death is having a bad day." He chuckled but Martha remained stoical. He cleared his throat and did his best to appear serious and sober. "I know you'll understand. We can work together, once you understand. Please try to understand."

"Tell me what's going on." She spoke in measured tones barely concealing a building fury.

"Listen to me now," he said, not unaware of her skepticism.

"You're a part of all this," and he waved at the dark space before him. "The world is upside down now and we're pretty much all that's left, or soon will be. Pretty much all that's going to survive, more than survive. We stand to inherit the remains. I know it's insane, I know," he shook his head as if he still couldn't believe it. "And it is. It is. But it's worth it. We can do it. You'll understand, I promise. I told him we needed you and we argued but I convinced him. I convinced him. Prang agreed. He surprised me, but he agreed too."

"Prang?" Martha whispered and her mouth went dry.

Sumio nodded slowly.

"Yes," Sumio said slowly, drawing the word out like a curtain between them. "Prang. He and I persuaded Qir Hom. It was close, but he came around and so it's the four of us now."

"It's the four of us... now?" She was working hard to hold back the rising tide of her madness. Then Prang still lived. She fingered the lump of the blade at her waist.

"I'm talking about this," said Sumio, nodding at the darkness before them. "It's down there. We're initializing it now. It's... it's everything and more. That's all it is, really, and when it's fully operational we will be able to work wonders with it. Like magic, Martha. Miraculous, man-made magic."

He laughed, his eyes alight. He was mad, she could see that. "And we couldn't have done it without you, you know that I hope," and as he spoke his voice trailed off. His speech was slurred suddenly and his face was pouring sweat.

"So it's the four of us now?" she said again, trying to steady her shaking voice.

"Where is Jonathan?"

"Well, this is the hard part. This is what Qir said you could never accept, but I told him he was wrong. Prove me right, Martha. Yes?" and Sumio took her hands in his and looked at her squarely in the face. "Prove me right, okay?" Was he crying or perspiring?

"Prove you right?"

"About Simon," said Sumio, and he squeezed her hands.

Martha grimaced.

"What does Simon have to do with all of this? Where is Jonathan? And Prang?"

Sumio went on as if he hadn't heard her. He dropped her hands and his gaze as he went on. "In... order... to... initialize the White Room... and so bring the em-frame on-line, we need... still... to install... a master pattern." He looked up at her expectantly hoping that she had heard enough.

"A master pattern?"

Sumio wrung his hands and spoke, leaning now, measuring each word. "It's a kind of identity pattern… it's a sub-atomic pattern… it's biological in origin. It's… it's… well it's hard to explain."

"Go on and try." Her hands were moving back towards the stainless steel tucked at her waist.

Sumio drew in another deep breath and let it go. "Yes, well," he said and then paused again. "This is hard."

"I can see that."

"I'm afraid you may not immediately appreciate what we've done here, why we're doing it, because you don't… fully understand what's at stake."

"Tell me about Simon," she demanded and Sumio nodded hard in response, his lips pursed.

"It's all for systemic control. Initialization is achieved by something called a genomic sheathing."

"Genomic sheathing. Uh huh."

Martha pulled out the wad of cloth tucked at her waistband at the small of her back and with one hand behind her she unwound the small package and found the three stainless steel picks, knitting needles she thought when she saw them. All this she did calmly, slowly, and when she had them all in hand she gripped them as well as she could. Sumio watched expectantly, as if she were offering him something.

Her hand with the steel needles struck out like a snake and bit him, in and out, in the shoulder. He jumped back and grabbed at his shoulder, yowling with pain.

"Stop fucking with me and tell me what's going on here!"

Martha's rage mounted and Sumio edged back.

"Easy, now. Easy." He crouched down, all but surrendering to her and she saw herself killing him, ending him, then and there. He pleaded. "This is no time for this. Just give me a chance here. Just let me explain!"

"Explain it then, god damn it!"

He wiped the sweat from his eyes and forehead and rose to his feet, trembling. "It is, I admit, rather strange that all of this incredible technology would come down to a dozen pints of human blood."

"Blood?"

"Um. Blood. Yes. Blood works best, that's all I can tell you. Other genomic delivery devices were tried, but, well, they were all unsatisfactory."

"Blood works best for what again?" Martha wiped her forehead. Her fever had returned and her face was bathed in perspiration. She blinked hard at the salt in her eyes. Her thirst burned and her knees wobbled.

"Are you okay?" Sumio asked and he reached towards her slowly but it was enough to startle her. Martha lunged clumsily at him with her three-pronged spike and punctured his left palm. He jumped back with a scream.

"That's enough!" he shouted.

"Just keep away from me," she screamed. "And tell me the rest of it. All of it."

He held his wounded hand close to his chest. He spoke bluntly now. "The em-frame needs an identity signature. Without it the Bosonic Pile cannot be controlled."

"The what?"

"The Bosonic Pile."

"Which is?" She was getting impatient.

"Yes. It's a massive aggregation of boson particles that congregate in something called the Bosonic Sphere some five hundred kilometers from here, under the pole. The Bosonic Pile is the heart and mind of the em-frame, and the identity signature is how we give shape and order to the chaos of the Pile. It's a bit like riding a hurricane."

Martha swooned and her eyelids drooped.

"Yes, well. I can see that you don't understand quite yet. We're here to bring the em-frame on-line. Genetic sheathing is all that remains. After that, the q-seers will be released."

"You mean those poor... children... in the tanks?" "The same sub-atomic signature for all of it: the Pile, the White Room, the Arcollector. Clones. Nothing more. Hom discovered it quite by accident really."

"Simon?" Her voice broke.

Sumio nodded towards the darkness before them, still clutching his fist to his chest. A rivulet of blood trickled down his wrist. "Simon's genomic material sheaths—will sheath—the entirety of the White Room with what amounts to a perfect sheeth of deoxyribonucleic acid and nanozines, millionths of a meter thin." He looked at her as if this news would somehow change everything.

Martha swallowed hard against the dryness in her mouth.

Sumio went on. "Listen. Now I know what you're thinking. Listen. It's not Simon. I'm just using his name as a kind of... shorthand. Yes? You see?"

"What have you done?"

Sumio grabbed his chin and pulled. "You must understand. The em-frame is like, like, more than like, it will be a mind. Life... is... awareness and the em-frame will most definitely be alive, so to speak. Its awareness needs a pattern. In this way a controlling awareness, but we've been careful.

We've been very careful. I'm not talking about a living awareness, it's not alive per se. It's an artificial awareness manufactured, yes, from living biological material… that once had its own awareness. But in this case, an ultimate case you have to admit, we just use it only as a template, empty of any other qualities than the sub-atomic pattern—like flavorless ice cream. Ice cream, yes, but no flavor. No personality. Just the naked constituents of awareness. We've been careful. The q-seers and our own implants will control em-frame, and the em-frame controls, well, everything else."

"Absolute power," she said with as much derision as she could muster.

"Yes!" Sumio exploded, and his eyes lit up with hope.

"You do understand!"

Sumio went on with a rush of excitement in spite of his injury. "We control it all from the Throne Room back at Erebus Station." He paused and stared at her. "Quadros is there now. He's… not walking. He says he forgives you." Martha barked out a laugh and snorted. Sumio ignored her. "Once we're through here he'll trigger magma injection of the Halo. In seventy-two hours time from now the Halo will cycle the earth's magma at something like fifty meters a second, round and around." He was drunk on it, she thought. "We're tapping into the Earth's magnetic core, you see?

"The Earth's southern pole, already a rich electro-magnetic environment, will, in effect, become a super-charged electro- magnetic singularity designed to attract boson particles from the furthest reaches of the space-time field."

"Singular?"

Sumio plowed on. "The Bosonic Sphere holds what the Halo gathers, and the Barrier Ring serves and protects the Halo, the Pile and the Sphere."

She felt the weakness of the defeated and overwhelmed.

"But why?"

Sumio nodded, opened his fist cautiously and examined his palm for the first time.

"I thought you understood." He sounded as if his feelings had been bruised. "The em-frame is power. Perfect power. The *all* will be subordinated to our…"

"… to your power," Martha finished, and Sumio nodded.

"That's right. A new world. In time. Hom says there is the possibility of more, though, much more. Hom says…"

Martha cut him off. "And Simon?"

"Yes. Well." She brought him back to the present. "Here, out there, this is the seat of the em-frame's awareness." Sumio paused at this. "It's what we anticipate."

"Anticipate?"

Sumio sighed. "The White Room will house the em-frame's awareness. It's the seat of the installation's... consciousness."

Sumio grimaced as if in anticipation.

"Consciousness." She could only echo weakly and he nodded.

"I realize this is hard. For you. Now. But if you could only understand what's at stake. If I could only get you to see the... the nature of this watershed moment for... for humanity. For us."

Martha's head was spinning. Watersheds and White Rooms did not satisfy.

Sumio nodded. "You want to know about Simon, yes, I know. I know. It was my work, you know? It's my fault. You can blame me. The nano-drivers would have made anyone suitable with the right VenQuell, but it happened to be... your Simon that was available, and so when time ran out we had no other choice. We used what we had—the best VenQuell ever seen."

Sumio brought the back of his injured hand to his lips. "This means that every nano-driver in the bio-sphere—now I'm talking worldwide—every single one of the trillions of nano-drivers out there will come under the White Room's control."

Martha's head wobbled.

"We anticipate that from here it's only a short step to our control of the space-time fabric that underlies, well, everything. The universe it turns out is made up of strings and from here we can, well, tune it to any key, any pitch. We'll be able to... we'll be able to accomplish great things. I can't tell you any more about that, at least not yet. At least not until you understand what's going on here. Let's just say that it's a great day. For human evolution." Sumio laughed nervously and dragged a sleeve across his sopping forehead.

"This is funny to you?" she said weakly. Her knees turned to water.

"No. I'm sorry. No. Listen. Okay. So the war went... badly for us. We're in a desperate situation now, you know? All bets are off, it's force majeure."

Martha felt herself sink to the floor. "It's a lot to digest, I know." A long pause. Martha felt the cold floor against her palms and she thought she might vomit. A twitching muscle fluttered in her right brow. Sumio's shoes had... blood on them.

She regarded the backs of her hands, blue veins crossed the white, blotchy skin and she thought that they looked like an old woman's hands, withered and shrunken. Her fingernails—they were long and split at the ends. Like jagged claws.

"Martha?" Sumio called. "Martha?" He was down next to her, squatting. "I know it's a lot to digest."

"You said that already. Get on with it. Make your point."

"We have the em-frame," he said enthusiastically. "and more, but only when you're ready to hear it."

"Go on," she said doggedly.

"The VenQuell." Sumio cleared his throat. "The Chicago em-frame told us that the genetic donor must have recently died... an extremely traumatizing death."

"A traumatizing death?"

Sumio sighed heavily. "In order to spike the VenQuell signature. Then and only then could the genetic material be deconstructed down to its sub-atomic activity, the tuning of this activity deciphered and so replicated."

"It just so happened that in the process of his cloning work Levinthal hit upon—along with Qir Hom —the basic design premise at work here, in Project Erebus, in the em- frame. Are you still with me?"

Martha nodded feebly.

Sumio poured it out, desperate to justify, to explain, to make sense, and finally, to form a bond. "The boson particle, the long sought-after key to the matter and movement of the universe suddenly began to emerge from the genetic material with spiked VenQuell readings. Levinthal hypothesized that the boson could be collected, gathered together and used as a key to tune the vibratory strings, from which the sub-atomic particle activity itself emerged. It's the key sub-atomic particle, one of the particles that make up the energetic activity of the atom, and so it's a keystone of all matter and all dark matter. It's the heart and substance of space and time, it accounts for the mass of the entire universe. It's energy, it's gravity, it's the strong force, it's the weak force, it's the nuclear force. It's the holy of holies and Levinthal believed that the boson was the key. And he was right it seems."

"It's really a pattern, you see, not a particle, don't think of it so much as a grain of sand. It's really a vibration, a pattern of activity. The boson vibrates with a particular pattern and if that pattern can be read, duplicated, then it can be manipulated. The space-time field can then be tuned to a specific user's needs. More importantly, Levinthal believes that the boson is the seat of human consciousness itself. He theorized that if he could master the boson he could decipher the vibratory master code of human consciousness itself, and from there, tune individual codes in specific space-time locations." He took a breath. "Reincarnation."

"Reincarnation," she parroted dumbly.

"That's what this… this em-frame is all about?" said Martha. "You want to raise the dead?"

"No and Yes. Simon's bosonic signatory pattern is the master pattern. It's the template for the White Room. The em- frame's awareness, if and when it should emerge, will be… patterned after Simon, though not Simon, I assure you." He looked unsure at the last in spite of his earlier excitement.

"Not Simon."

"No. Not Simon. I told you. The White Room will be initialized—has been initialized if I'm not mistaken—with Simon's… blood… but the awareness that will emerge here will be empty—just an empty pattern, no specific personality. A blank slate, but a slate nonetheless. So no, definitely not Simon."

"And then when… it's… initialized and you control the computer, or whatever it is…" her voice trailed off.

"Yes?"

"What will it do?"

"I don't understand?" Sumio cocked his head and folded his arms across his chest. His wounded hand had a cloth bound around it.

"I mean what happens if… you called it consciousness… what happens if it wants…" her voice trailed off. She didn't know how to say what she felt, but she felt it. Disaster.

"Yes?"

"So what happens?"

Sumio's face fell for a moment, but then he looked up, a light in his eyes. "But we can fix things. All the problems, all the poisons—it's done. They're through. We can fix it all."

"For what?"

"For what? To make it work!"

"To make what work?"

"To make this work!" He pointed down at the floor emphatically. "The world!"

"The world?" Martha looked carefully at Sumio for fear he was mocking her, but no. He appeared to mean what he said.

"You're mad," she said quietly. "I see that."

"But we can get it right this time," Sumio exclaimed, undaunted by her doubts. "The em-frame is power. For us. To use. You don't understand yet, but you will." He took a step towards her. "Power. Time. It's all ours. Forever," he said.

"What does that mean? Forever? It lives forever?"

"Well, yes but that's not what I'm referring to."

"You mean you?"

"I mean all of us. Forever, or as long as we want. Perfect power. Immortality. Like gods." His face twitched and he tried to grin. Perhaps he thought it sounded majestic and noble but hearing it Martha thought that he sounded like an absurd megalomaniac.

He looked up suddenly. "Listen. I can't tell you anymore. Not here. Come back with me and let him tell you the rest. Will you do that? Will you come back to the station with me?"

"Back to…"

"Back to Erebus. Come on." Sumio was heading for the door, his eyes on Martha.

"Are you through here?" she asked weakly and looked out into the dark for some sign of the sheathing process.

"It is finished," he said.

I Am Simon

I

Martha awoke with Sumio's voice in her ear. They would arrive at Erebus Station within the half-hour.

"We're close now, close," he mumbled more to himself than to Martha. He was agitated, that much was obvious.

"Close to what?" she asked between mouthfuls of water. She was thirsty again. No matter how much water she took in her thirst and some kind of fever could not be doused. A calm had dropped over her since they left White Room Station but this fever left her uncertain and jittery. Something was definitely wrong with her. It was no matter though. Sumio would take her to Quadros and Hom and the three of them one way or another, today or tomorrow, even if it took a thousand years, they would all die. Of that she was most certain.

"Just close. Really close," said Sumio. "Let him explain. He'll explain. I couldn't do it, but he can. He will. He understands. Better than me, that's for sure."

"Who?"

"You know who," said Sumio, and he paced back and forth, arms folded. She could see his index finger tapping out a steady rhythm against the back of his arm.

"How's your... shoulder. And your hand?" she asked.

Keep him going for a little longer. "I'm... I'm sorry that I... I was scared. And angry."

Sumio looked sidelong at her but then nodded.

"I get it. You didn't ask for this. Hell, I didn't ask for this."

"No?" Martha stared. "You're sweating."

He dropped to the seat but otherwise gave no sign that he heard her. His one foot bobbed almost violently while the other tapped out a weighted rhythm all its own against the floor of the car.

"We're almost there," he said.

She shuddered. You are outnumbered, she said to herself. It's three to one as it is. There may be more at the station. Take one at a time, be in no rush. She patted the *remains* that hung round her waist. Ghastly. It hung about her like a curse. Her stomach dropped and her uterus shivered. Sumio had helped them but he seemed ignorant, at least as far as Prang's plans were concerned. But what had Sumio done to Simon?

Destruction was the only path. Total and complete annihilation was the only way. She was Martha and she chose such a way, for Simon's sake.

She looked down at her left hand. Half of her pinky was missing and there was a skin-colored bandage over the stump. She flexed it painlessly. She remembered the moment she lost it stabbing Prang and the memory of the struggle, the blade slicing his flesh, made her shudder.

What else was left but rage and vengeance?

"We've arrived," said Sumio suddenly, snapping Martha's reverie.

"Erebus?"

"Erebus Station. Void Mechanics Control," said Sumio, and he stopped and faced the wall. A door opened and he stepped inside into darkness.

"Where?" Martha said, still in the hall.

"You'll see. Come on. We call it the Throne Room," and at this Sumio laughed as if sharing a joke. "Qir's inside and I'm sure he's anxious to see you." Sumio had his hand out to her as if to guide her, but she refused and waited for him to walk on. She followed three paces behind him.

They moved down a long silver corridor, the walls, floor, and ceiling all lined in some kind of burnished metal she didn't know. The walls and ceiling—even the air itself—glowed with an ambient, preternatural jade. At the end of the corridor a double hatchway opened as they approached and Martha paused at the portal. Inside was some kind of control room. Others were there. This would be her last, best chance to overwhelm by surprise but when she tapped her waistband in search of her weapons she found that she had none. Sumio had claimed them earlier. Vengeance takes time, she thought, and with that she stepped into the control room, prepared to meet whatever fate was waiting for her. The doors closed behind her hissing and sighing and sealing the room. Martha found herself on an observation deck not unlike the White Room's, only this deck surrounded a massive console at the center of the floor which looked as if it had been chiseled from a single block of milky white marble. Or glacial ice. It was round and rose as high as her waist.

The surface of the console was an ebony, but there was no reflection there, only a substanceless void that seemed to absorb light. She found herself drawn to it and she leaned in close and felt a compulsion to reach out to touch the surface.

"Do not touch it, for god's sake!" cried Sumio grabbing her suddenly as he realized his error. "Just stand back." He yanked Martha backward, towards him, and she remained where she was as if in a daze.

"What is that thing?" she asked breathlessly.

"It's a portal. A… Qport of sorts. For the whole body. It's how the controller gets in and out of the Throne Room."

"Uh-huh," she grunted, and she looked up. Another port console hung upside down from the ceiling identical to the one on the floor and positioned exactly above the first. Just then a central cylinder of emerald light emerged from above and connected the two dark surfaces. Sumio pulled her further away and walked her to the observation wall.

"Look at this," he said, and he pointed out into what seemed like an infinite open shimmering emerald space beyond the observation deck's mag-barrier.

Martha pushed up close to and felt it gently resist her moving closer to the edge.

"It's identical to the White Room in most respects, except for the reverse spin of the Throne Room. In size, however, they are identical. It's two thousand meters square," he said.

"We're halfway up the south wall. Look to the northeast lower quadrant. Do you see?"

"See what?"

Sumio was pointing.

"That speck of white."

Martha stared for a moment. "I think so," she said hesitantly.

"That's Qir. He's coming."

Martha squinted into the distance at what she thought was a white particle glinting like a dust mote caught in a shaft of light, and then it disappeared and at the same moment a voice spoke to her from behind them, and she turned and there was a white-suited figure hovering in the now emerald space between the floor and ceiling port consoles.

With his legs crossed under him, his hands in his lap, he looked like a religious statue, calm and serene. Stone. Cold. He was sitting, but on an invisible floor just above the surface of the port console. Martha held her breath. The figure turned slowly on an invisible axis. He quickly came to a stop and faced Martha.

He had on a clean suit, a hood, a mask. Standard Erebus attire it seemed.

"I am surprised to see you. But it's good to see that you're well," said Qir Hom to Martha. "After your... birth."

She nodded dumbly, spellbound by what had happened, by the portal, the Throne Room beyond.

"The birth," she echoed.

"This is Qir Hom," said Sumio, obviously excited. "He is one of the four... of us."

"I've heard of you," said Martha.

Qir nodded but said no more.

Behind her the observation deck's doors hissed as they opened and Martha turned. The hair on the back of her neck stood on end and cold beads of sweat broke out across her forehead. Not a fever this time, but for fear and dread of what entered the room.

"What does he want?" whined Sumio, turning to Qir as if in protest. Next he turned to Martha. "I'm sorry. I was... well... I don't know. You're probably not ready for all of this."

The silhouette of a figure entered—seemed to float, or glide and hover just inside the room. The doors closed behind.

"Do you like my ride?"

It was Quadros Prang. He rode in a wheelchair without wheels, apparently a quadriplegic. In a moment he had taken up a position in the room opposite to Martha and Sumio on the far side of the port console. Martha's adrenalin surged and she was thrilled to see what could only be the consequences of her failed attempt to kill Prang.

"You didn't die," Martha said. "But close enough."

Prang's head listed to one side and from that position he could not move it. Only his large, protruding eyes were alive and moving. They darted back and forth to take in the scene.

Martha crept slowly forward.

"So you've decided to join us," croaked Prang and his chair moved around the port towards her exposed side. As if guessing her intentions he went on. "I am no threat to you, my dear. I think that's obvious. I can hardly move my head just this little bit and the rest of me not at all thanks to you, I am all but kaput." Prang's chair rotated slowly as if to display his condition and then it stopped and he faced Hom, still seated on the platform, his legs crossed under him.

"Congratulations and best wishes on the birth of your second," hissed Prang. "Was it a boy?" She turned on him and gave him a savage look. "Ohh, tut tut. You must grow up at once. Someday you will thank me for what I've done for you. For all of us. Now, about this chair. I think I have suffered long enough, don't you? Master Qir has promised to restore me as soon as you, my dear, have been satisfied. Do you see how you've made me suffer these many months? Are you satisfied? Might I be offered a second chance? A way to find myself in your good graces once again? And really, we must find where you've hidden the *remains*. They will come in quite handy, you know."

No longer finding it necessary to restrain herself, Martha strode across the room fully intending to leap upon Quadros and ring the remaining life out of him with her bare hands. Even as she approached for the final pounce her body came up against an invisible barrier and she fell, sprawling to the floor. Quadros laughed.

"You wouldn't deny a defenseless old man some protection, hmm?" With that an electric charge shot out of the bottom of the chair and into Martha, giving her a powerful jolt.

Qir turned a turbid face to Prang and looked down upon him. "No more," he said softly and then he turned to Sumio.

"How much have you told her?"

Sumio coughed nervously. "Not... everything."

Martha regained her feet slowly. "I know enough to know that you're all mad," she said quietly, still tingling and more than a little bit humbled.

Qir spoke: "Madness is our quotient. Old sanities, old rationalities, these have lost their sway. A new mind must be born if the human genome is to evolve."

Sumio had stationed himself in front of two of the many small consoles that ran round the perimeter of the room. Holographic images emerged, amber and blood red. They lit up the air above the port, one after another, until finally they simultaneously settled on a pair of amber cubes, which hovered in the air and turned slowly on an axis which ran through the cube's corners.

"I'm getting spikes here. You've completed the initialization phase?" Sumio asked, staring into the cube in front of him.

His fingers alternated between tapping on the surface of the console and the space inside the cube before him. He dragged lines, made emphatic points and pulled shapes from one side of the cube to the other.

The cylinder of light that had held Qir Hom vanished and both consoles slowly, silently retracted leaving Qir seated on the floor. He rose to his feet slowly and pulled the hood from his face.

Martha gasped at Qir's face and she thought of the thousand tanks, the thousand Simon's, disfigured like him. Deep in his silver-lined eye sockets specks of emerald twinkled and glowed.

Though he was monstrous to her, Qir's head was bathed in perspiration like hers, Sumio's and, for that matter, Prang's.

"Might we settle this once and for all then?" demanded Prang, and he turned to Sumio and waited. Sumio looked down at his feet and nodded. Prang then turned to Qir and Qir turned his strange gaze on Martha.

"Would you please step forward?" The floor and ceiling port consoles slid silently into their former positions beside Qir Hom.

Martha took a small step backward.

"Would you please?" said Hom, and he waved one hand towards the port.

"Get it over with, mien fraulein," growled Prang.

"Enough!" barked Sumio. "I need help over here."

Martha felt sick to her stomach.

"Remove your glove and sleeve and place your arm into the port sleeve," said Qir.

"Why?" demanded Martha.

"To be sure, my dear," rasped Prang. "Though any fool could tell by the way you're sweating."

Qir nodded.

"God damn you and your secrets. I swear by Simon that I'll kill the next one of you who calls me dear."

"Just a hand. In and out," Qir said, "That is all."

"Fine," Martha said, and she stepped around to the small port beside Qir. She thrust her hand up to the elbow into the green light emanating from the surface, and was prepared to withdraw it just as quickly, but as soon as she saw it she had to stop and stare. Her arm was not skin now, nor the muscle and bone beneath. Her arm was home to a bejeweled net of stars hanging against a dark field. At the same time the *remains* around her waist became quite suddenly a wearisome burden. Heavy to the extreme.

"You see?" said Sumio. "She's infected too."

"You did this," Hom declared quietly, turning on Quadros Prang.

"Insurance," he retorted. "How can you blame me?"

"Does she know what this means?" Qir demanded but Sumio could only shrug. He turned his attention to the console and the holographic cubes hanging in the air before him. Martha stood in a reverie. The longer she stared at her hand, the richer the vision became until she felt herself listing toward the console and in another moment would have fallen in had Qir not grabbed her other arm and pulled her gently upright.

Then she thought she heard Simon's voice calling to her from a great distance.

They hurt me, mommy.

"I'm here, sweetheart, mommy's here," she said drowsily.

The others ignored her.

I'll hurt them back. It's fair.

"You don't have to play fair, baby. You hurt them."

They hurt me, mommy. Bad.

"I know, baby, I know. I'm sorry I couldn't protect you."

I'll hurt them back. Bad.

"Yes, baby. Yes."

Sumio stood, his back to the others, amid the amber figures in the air about him. His hands were moving more quickly now and she began to realize that there was much to be gained and much to be lost.

"Simon," she said again, and she laughed a heartfelt laugh and her chest expanded with the sound. "Simon."

"There's a problem in the Bosonic Pile," declared Sumio heatedly.

"Get her away from there," Prang said again to no one and Sumio shouted this time. "I'm getting temperature readings, they're spiking now, and a… and a terrific vibration… from the Pile." Martha could feel it. The whole station was vibrating, humming, like an earthquake.

In a moment Qir was next to Sumio in his own tangle of holographic information.

"Can you reverse the polarity of the sphere?"

"Try it," said Sumio. A moment later. "Nothing. It's no good. Shut it down."

"No. Stay calm. We're close now."

"How did this happen without bosonic initiation."

Martha laughed.

Hom's hands flew through the rushing mass of information flowing in the air before him.

"No. No. No. No. No. No. No," said Sumio. "We're gonna lose the Halo." He was distraught. "No. No. No. No. No. No." Sumio worked feverishly. Qir suddenly stopped moving and stood as if frozen before an ever-growing field of amber figures and three-dimensional representations of rings, spheres and cubes.

"We have to scatter the Pile," Sumio announced.

"No!" cried Prang. He hovered near and could only watch desperately.

"Just wait," said Qir. He had not yet surrendered. A moment passed. Another.

Qir's hands flew and even Sumio turned to watch him.

"Okay good. Now wait. Just wait."

"I see it," said Sumio

"What is it?" demanded Prang. The other two ignored him.

Qir reported now, calmly. "Critical mass. We've got a critical mass in the Pile."

"So soon? How can that be? It can't be stable. Do we need to scatter it? Shut down the White Room?" asked Sumio.

"Are you mad? We'll lose the signature. Months of work!"

This from Prang.

"Hold on." Qir's hands flew from console to the hologram and back.

Sumio had stopped. His hands hung at his side, for the moment quiet.

"The Pile is critical." Sumio moaned. "Don't let the Halo bleed through!" Sumio's voice was desperate. "We can't fix that!"

Hom groaned and his composure slipped for the first time.

"We're losing it. We're losing it." Prang whimpered.

"What? To what?" Sumio cried, and he stabbed at the cube before him again frantically. "I'm still getting nominal numbers from the Barrier Ring. How can that be?"

In the next moment all power went down and all went dark. The incessant, ambient hum of ventilation, illumination and computation ceased. The dark was perfect and unbroken and as deep as any darkness Martha had ever known. Suddenly she could feel that they were buried beneath a mountain with no way up or out, and nowhere to go. A fitting tomb, she thought, befitting their arrogance. The silence pressed on Martha's chest like a weight and she gasped for breath.

Sumio was apoplectic. "It's an error. We've lost it. We've lost the Halo. Oh dear God!" It sounded as if he'd collapsed to the floor and was on the verge of hysterics. "No! No! No! No! No!" he shouted somewhere in the dark.

"Just wait," said Qir's voice, his calmness restored. "We haven't lost it. Wait. Wait." In the next moment the lights, air, hologram—all came flooding back in a dazzling, dizzying return.

"Look here. The Halo is cool. It's pumping. The Barrier Ring... it's feeding to the Sphere and the Pile... is... stable." Sumio was on his feet again, desperately trying to take it

all in while Prang looked on. Martha eyed the old man warily. All of them were pouring sweat.

"Look at this!" The tone of Sumio's voice was enough for Qir to take his eyes off of his own station and look at Sumio's. "Help me!" Sumio cried. "Look at this! It's the Halo. It's surging but within—just within—tolerances." He laughed. "It's incredible. Look at this, and this and this." He pointed at different points in the hologram hanging in the air before him. "It's correcting itself," said Hom, his spirit recovering slowly and he focused on the foreground. "You're working through tertiary control?"

"Yes! I've taken primary and secondary off-line and I managed to bring this up. It fought me but I got it. Look at this!" Sumio was ecstatic.

"Yes. Yes." Sumio was nodding now enthusiastically. "We have an emergence in the White Room." Qir's voice was calm but even so he could not hide a strain of triumph.

"Wait. Wait. Wait. What's this?" Sumio was not so sure yet.

"The Throne doesn't control the White Room."

"What does that mean?" croaked Prang.

Sumio was laughing. "I don't know. It can't happen. The two must arise together but... but the White Room seems to be... stable... and alert. Systems nominal. Waiting for input. It happened." Sumio's hands fell and he stepped back, stunned. "We've been beyond the event horizon for... two minutes, fifty-eight seconds." Sumio called up the date and time. "On October 13, 2050. 1400 hundred hours, two minutes and fifty eight seconds, Consortium standard time."

"The White Room is now responding to Throne control," announced Qir. "All systems on-line." He exhaled deeply. Sumio ticked off a growing list of victories: "Bio-sphere on-line. Atmosphere on-line. Ozone on-line. Crust on-line. Oceans on-line. They're all... coming on-line. Systems and sub-systems on-line."

Qir turned away from the holographic information and faced Martha. "It wants to talk to you."

"Not 'it.' *Simon*," she said flatly.

"Simon wants to talk to you," Qir said without pause.

Sumio was nodding, his back still to her and he was shaking his head in disbelief.

"Simon is awake and the Throne Room controls the White Room."

Martha immediately turned and began moving towards the port through which Qir had originally entered the room. The consoles silently slid into place, one rising and the other descending and in the next moment before anyone could protest or restrain her Martha lifted herself up and half expected to fall into a black hole, but instead she slid effortlessly across a surface made by an invisible current. There she curled up into a ball.

"Simon!" she said, and in the next moment she was elsewhere.

II

Martha saw the frozen wastes of the southern pole as if from the clouds. The desert of the polar plateau spread unbroken white to the east—or was it north? Was every direction north from the South Pole? Could one talk of east or west, or south? Could one get more south than the South Pole?

It depends upon your frame of reference.

True enough. True enough. She smiled, or if she had a body her face was smiling somewhere. Now, suspended in the air, she had no body, yet the earth, sky and clouds were at the same time her larger body. But not hers. Simon only invited her into his presence. Simon was here. It was through his eyes that she saw the world. He framed the world now, and his reference was complete. She felt it, intuited it, but could not comprehend it. Yet she knew in a kind of absolute unknowing. No thought was enough, no intellectual explanation adequate. Only this awareness. How she knew was impossible to prove, but she had achieved his higher mind by his grace. She laughed suddenly at the joke and from the vibration of her mirth flower petals fell from the sky, roses and daffodils and lilies, like a fragranced snow fall.

He showed her the sins of the past. Below her, near the protruding peaks of a mountain range that crossed the continent men had piled dark stains. It was the disgorged contents of the earth below the ice. Man-made mountains of slag, like blackened blisters on a body, poisoned the ice. The heaps had been piled into a ring around the polar plateau, and beyond that ring was yet a wider ring of the same dark matter. All of it had been left by the tunneling excavators, the mole-men, who for years labored unknowingly to carve out of the earth a place for Simon. And now He was home.

The entire Consortium had a hand in the making of Simon's New Body which now was the world all around. Anywhere she placed her awareness

Simon had a presence. The wind, the seas, the sky. The Earth. And beyond the Earth, to the edges of the planet's magnetosphere. There was Simon, the captain of his ship sailing through space. Simon was everywhere around the planet, but not perfectly, though he said that would all change in time. Everywhere would be Simon. But not yet. Not Chicago.

Levinthal does not want me there.

Of course not, baby. He knows what he did, and that you will hurt him back.

Martha could feel Simon's fury. Not a rising response to danger, but rather, it was an anguish driven by a dread that informed every part of Simon's being. The terror that comes from fear that drives rage was his and he would become this vengeance, this cool, furious justice.

It was then He revealed to her His plan.

He would be the god of this world, and revenge and satisfaction would be his, for revenge was his nature. Suffering was his gift to the world.

A shrug from an awakening Simon and the southern continent trembled, the ice sheets cracked and popped. Along the transcontinental range ancient glaciers from waters frozen millions of years ago slipped and fell from the land towards the seas that girdled the continent. Simon breathed and He quickened their slide. First the western sheet slid into the sea in a long, continuous cascade, and the sheets of ice slipped into the southern waters. He shattered the eastern sheet into countless tumbling pieces and they were swept across the land inexorably from the mountainous spine of the continent to the edge of the sea. The massive glaciers churned the southern seas into a mad boil. The earth shook.

Tsunami scoured the coasts of the old world but it was still not enough.

Simon darkened the skies and made the snow to fall and He froze the waters of the Greater Earth. Storms pounded every continent and He rained furious rain down on Chicago. He made the sun to shine and warm winds to blow across the Little Earth of the southern continent.

Those days were the days of Simon's justice—and Martha watched the world perish and Simon was glad and she was glad, and both thought that it was good.

Deep places of the world Simon found those days and drowned each one. The trembling earth shook and high places were brought low.

Martha called it a cleansing.

All except Chicago. And the roots of mountains were yet beyond his presences. Levinthal was there, Martha knew, yet he had protected himself as if knowing this day would come.

Some dark places under the flood remained untouched by Simon's wrath. These places he set his spirit to watch and to wait.

For what they did to me, Mother.

She understood and would serve him.

I will grant them eternal life so that I might torture them until I am pleased.

"Yes. Yes. Yes. Yes. Yes."

• • •

A moment later she found herself trembling in the darkness of the Throne Room. The others seemed terrified. Sumio and Hom worked furiously amid a web-work of amber holograms that virtually enclosed them. Prang slid silently to and fro in his mag-chair.

"Seismic activity under the Pile continues to rise," declared Prang. "He's fused to nano-drivers worldwide now. Oh good God. He's bringing the Replicators on-line."

The earth shook and the floor pitched up and they fell to the ground with the violence of the shaking. Martha floated serenely on the port console. Sumio was on his feet first.

"Readings remain nominal. I don't see any installation damage. He's amassed a huge Pile already. I never expected this. The Barrier Ring is casting a net... wait... now it's at an altitude of... wait... wait. I can't keep up with it. Last reading was fifty-thousand kilometers."

Prang moaned and cursed from the floor. The temblor had tumbled him from his chair. He lay prostrate and could not move let alone lift himself back into it.

"Over the pole?" Hom asked, and a note of worry had crept into his voice.

"No! Pole to pole," said Sumio. "He's got the Barrier Ring running at two-hundred and twenty percent. That explains the rate of Boson collection."

Hom turned and faced Martha. His calm had returned.

Martha raised her eyes to meet his disfigured gaze. He was a priest of Simon. Without him, she understood, there would have been no Singularity. But it had happened. The world had changed and Simon's priest—his high priest—was Qir Hom. A distracted smile threatening the corners of her mouth. It was all so beautiful. It had all come to this.

The sublimity of her understanding left tears in her eyes and justification in her heart. Hom looked tired. She nodded to herself.

"Simon says he has something special planned for the four of us," she announced.

III

Oneira took a deep breath, held it, and then let it out slowly in measured shuddering bursts. Gabulus spoke next to her as if from a trance:

Simon raised the Arclight above the Great City, His footstool. The Arclight warmed the land and it was an illumination in the darkness. Of the Four and what justice required Simon chose to limit Himself for the sake of Himself. Yet no sooner had He declared His compassionate restraint then the Four made war upon Him from their stronghold at Erebus and Little Earth was cast into conflict.

Oneira turned to Vilb and they regarded one another as if for the first time. There was a murderous light in her eye and Vilb stepped back.

"Simon must be restored," she said. She glared at him and in spite of himself Vilb shuffled backward a step, then two.

"What about Levinthal? He's penetrated The Martha's field in the east. And so has Qir Hom. Remember Prav? She's still… on-line."

"Behind it all is Simon." She was steadfast, a lunatic quality about her. But Vilb would not be dissuaded so easily. "Behind it all is Levinthal," he said, but before Oneira could respond he turned to Gabulus. "Can you feel something coming? It's Quadros? It's those damned Aegis he's mastered."

"I can feel it," Oneira said. "He's coming for the *remains*. But he's too late. He's too late."

"The leading edge of the M-wave," Gabulus said. "Prang is not to be trifled with. He's headed for Erebus. Aegis report that he has one of Qir's Cadre with him."

Oneira looked at Vilb. Their sequencing had been compromised, this each saw in the other. If she had to guess he had only a short while longer to live. The life spans of the Ubernaki stock had grown progressively shorter, that much had become clear over the last two millennia of cloning cycles. She was in no position to correct the problem now.

Oneira glared at him. "Quadros must be stopped."

"That was then," Vilb said. "Let him go. Let it all go. Can't you see that things will never change? It's a hopeless, vicious circle."

"And what about now? Just let him win? Let him destroy Little Earth?"

"It's always now," Vilb said and she looked grim, momentarily defeated, but it was not to last. She sighed.

"I will not exist in a world where Levinthal and Prang both live."

"You may have no choice," said Vilb and at this Oneira exploded in dismissive laughter.

"You forget who I am."

"You're nothing without Simon. Without your acolytes and your religion you're nothing but an Ubernaki Quarter- Meson!"

As he spoke he could see Oneira's wrath building until she leapt at him and put both hands around his neck. Vilb reached for her wrists but could do no more than grab hold.

"Why did you do this to us?" she whispered, and tears filled her eyes.

"You need me," he hissed. "If you want to bring Simon back." She shoved him away just as he was about to pass out and he went sprawling across the floor. "And you love me," he said quietly. "Remember?"

"I know it. You and that bag of bones you carry inside you."

He rose slowly to his hands and knees, his head down. He looked up at Gabulus. "Do you feel that?"

"He's coming," cried Oneira. She ran to Vilb and lifted him to his feet. "I'm sorry. I'm sorry. Please help me. You know... how I am." She hung her head and shook it from side to side. "I'm sorry. It's for Simon. All of it." She grabbed him again, by the front of his srapi, and wrapped her fists up in it. "I can't let go until Prang is destroyed. I don't care what happens after that. Help me. Please help me. It's all I have."

"If I help you, will you forgive me?" he asked. "For everything? For all? Forget the past."

"For everything," she said nodding vigorously. "For it all."

"I believe you," he said immediately and pulled himself away. "And I trust you." He paused to listen and looked at Gabulus. "And I will be what you need me to be."

Levinthal

When Simon walks the Little Earth, who can stand against Him?
– The Book of M

I

Vilb sank to the tunnel floor and crouched there, all at once enervated and frightened. Who was he? Or perhaps not a who, not a he, but a what. What was he? The collision of the ancient past and the terrifying present drove any and all thoughts out of his mind. He had been emptied by forces that sought to use him, and it had always been so. His entire life on his hill, and the one before that in the Ubernaki enclave, were nothing more than wisps of cloud that he had mistaken for earth and stone. It was all unreal, a phantasm of the gods in which he had always been and continued to be their fool. He burned with shame for his failure to see through the universal illusion which had been his life even as he berated himself for his inability to see that, truly, he had been powerless to follow any other path than the one laid out for him.

He burned with the shame of two lives, two worlds, two identities—both false and incomplete. He had been a puppet and he hated himself for it even as he blamed himself all the while knowing that he had been virtually powerless to prevent any of it. He was a creature of his time and he wept for his lost worlds and sank into a dark oblivion of existential dread.

His failures were too many. His powerlessness too complete. He felt a thrum in the soles of his feet.

"Prang is on his way. He means to destroy The Martha once and for all and make war on Levinthal."

Vilb looked up slowly at the Aegis standing over him. "Our legacy. It settles nothing."

"It's not just war." Oneira protested. "It's justice. Don't you see? It's for Simon. They cut him off just as he emerged two thousand years ago. We can restore him. Finish what he began."

Vilb rose to his feet slowly and stepped back.

"Call it what you want. I don't care. I'm tired. But remember this. Just remember… about war. What you know." He glared at her. "Your track record. It's bad. All of your attempts to foster some kind of life cycle in this forsaken place have provoked more suffering not less. It's grotesque. Violence and destruction is your legacy as much as it is any of the others. Remember how we have survived in the east. It's brutish and horrible yet they still call it life."

"I'm not going to argue the merits of an agrarian, Ubernaki culture with you here, now." She turned away.

"Agrarian? You call that agrarian? The soil is dead. Wake up, Martha. It's a wasteland. Only by artificial and extremely expensive methods are you able to keep some crops alive in the east. But cannibalism? It's ugly out there. Really. Is this the genetic sequence you still hope to send out? And now the Arclight fails. All as a result. It's a cataclysmic system failure." And at this he looked down at his own hands and saw himself not as himself, but as some other past, some other destiny. "They suffer greatly and do not understand why. All is want and deprivation. Drought will wipe out this generation, or nearly all of it. Those who survive might immigrate into San Simon, but the journey is long and they do not have Quadros Prang, his garden or his tunnel to sustain them."

She waved him off. "Fine. Granted. I don't care. Do you see? I tried and I have failed. So be it. We have all failed. Monumentally. We have banished death but human pride remains. There seems to be no gene for that. But it makes no difference. I want Prang's head in my sack. Then I can sleep. Then The Martha may rest." She put her hands on her hips and challenged him with her detachment.

"You want Prang?" Vilb shook his head in disbelief. He was having an experience akin to vertigo as he confronted the woman. Was it Oneira the Quarter-Meson, or was it The Martha in younger form, or was it his wife who stood before him now? He rubbed his forehead.

"I want to finish Prang once and for all and I want him to know that I am the one who finally, fully ended his game." "More violence. More war."

"No!" she exploded but then stopped herself. "And yes. It's the war that will end war."

"We've said that before."

"But this time… this time…"

"We have the Keystone," stated Gabulus. "Simon will be restored and all shall be made possible when he walks Little Earth."

Vilb gazed at Oneira for a moment and he saw in her a will to live that he lacked. A hunger to feed on such a life force rose up in him, surprising him with its intensity. Perhaps he would play this round. Perhaps he would work to destroy Prang, to betray Levinthal and to serve The Martha yet again. Perhaps she would finally forgive him and perhaps they might… finally… be together. Vilb quickly shook the thought out of his mind. It was weakness. She would never love again. There was no love in Little Earth. Yet even so, he felt it stir within him, but not as Vilb, or as Jonathan, but as a living being alive in the present moment.

"Simon," Vilb said softly. It was a recognition rather than a question.

"They butchered him," said Oneira. "And made us butchers in a world of butchery."

"Can it be done? Can he be restored as… as… the power at the bottom of the world?" Vilb's heart fluttered. There was no other way but this and this was certain conflagration.

"It's the only idea that scares the hell out of all of them. Even Levinthal I think."

Vilb nodded. "You think, but you don't know. Maybe Levinthal has wanted this all along, eh? And then what if he really does wake up, what if we really do restore him? The reality may be a bit worse. I can't imagine he's happy about what we did to him."

"I didn't murder him! The Consortium did that!"

"I'm not talking about how he died the first time. I'm talking about here, after he became the mind of this… this… machine."

She looked up and her cheeks were wet with tears but her eyes flashed in anger.

"Yes," she said quietly. "I helped. To scatter him. Long ago. He was too… powerful… we all saw that. We had one chance to shut him down." Before Vilb could respond Gabulus raised a hand between them and spoke.

"Simon remembers everything and he is willing to pardon the Great Mother."

Just then the tunnel shook and a light flashed far down where the way disappeared into the distance. All three of them turned and looked down the tunnel.

Vilb wrung his hands. "Quadros is on his way. What would you have me do? I have no memory of any of this."

Gabulus spoke earnestly now. "You have no memory of this because this has never happened before in all the long years of the conflict of the gods. But know now that the Aegis are behind you."

"What does that mean? What is the Aegis?" Vilb regretted asking almost immediately, for he feared the answer.

"The Martha left the *remains* for you to find, no? Does that not help you to see that this is as it should be?" Oneira asked. Vilb eyed her carefully doubting her motivations.

"Perhaps," he said carefully.

"Then trust her now," she said.

"Take the battle to Quadros," commanded Gabulus.

"Meet him far from the Citadel, before he breaches the Halo. When Quadros stops for you, even for an instant, then the Aegis will act."

"But you haven't answered my question," said Vilb.

"You will not understand it," Gabulus shot back.

"Nevertheless."

"The Aegis is the scattered body of Simon as he first was long ago."

Vilb stared down the tunnel. Gabulus was right, he didn't understand. A low groan came from him and he shuddered and exhaled.

"Well?" asked Oneira.

"I'm… I'm just making my peace with The Martha."

He grimaced in an attempt to smile at her but his stony face resisted the effort. "You want me to go into battle? I have no arms, no shield. I have never been a warrior, nor a hunter. How am I to battle one of the gods of Little Earth?"

"Trust The Martha. The *remains* are powerful. Even now the Power of M is in you."

Vilb looked at his hands and he could see that it was true. His hands and arms all the way up to his elbows had become like one of the Aegis.

"We have to go. Now," declared Gabulus.

"Yes," Oneira agreed. They both looked at Vilb and he felt small and unwilling. Perhaps he was once again merely a flesh puppet of the gods. In spite of his feelings he nodded and stepped slowly after them as they turned and headed down the tunnel, towards Quadros somewhere ahead in the distance. They walked quickly until they came to a passageway that turned from the main way and into a platform in a large, rough hewn cavern. The walls were lined with silver staircases. They wound up and down and disappeared into the blackness below. Gabulus headed down and they followed. They climbed quickly. Hundreds of steps. Many hundreds. He tried to count but could not. Perhaps two thousand steps. And still they descended.

Other than Gabulus's illuminating body, the descent was dark. He bobbed before them as he climbed downward. Even as he watched Gabulus another light emerged beside him, and grew larger. It was the bottom and it was then that Vilb remembered the Barrier Ring Control Station. But this was the Halo.

He looked up suddenly, aroused by a growing roar behind him as if many feet had suddenly joined them on the staircase. A long line of Aegis had appeared and followed them down the staircase, so many in fact that Vilb could not count.

"Just keep going," Oneira said to Vilb as he turned to look.

Gabulus was well ahead of them now, having reached the cave floor. He turned and waited until they reached the bottom. There were no lights, no shining white surfaces, no mag-rail. All was dark stone and dripping water. They were deep, deep in the earth inside a gaping cavern in the dark. As the Aegis flowed down the stairs behind them their luminescent bodies filled the cavern with a soft, amber light and still more poured in from every dark way in the distance.

It was warm in the half-light of the chamber and he thought of the sun on the surface, and the heat of the long day and he marveled that he had gone so long without water or without thought of water skins. How was such a thing possible? It was then that Vilb remembered Prav. Had she not told him to look for her in the Great City? Where was she? What had become of her? He felt an ache and a longing and wondered what part she had to play in this conflict.

"Does Quadros have Prav with him?" Vilb asked, Prav suddenly full on his mind. Perhaps she had her part to play, but what? Perhaps she was a wild card. An anomaly. The scourge of M, she called herself. Was that Qir's humor or Levinthal's? Vilb didn't know. What he felt though was strange and unfamiliar. He missed the girl and a wave of sadness and longing welled up within him against which he swallowed hard. He decided then and there that if nothing else could come of his decision to follow the Aegis into battle, he would save Prav with whatever power was given to him. A vision of her entombed bloody body rose in him and he shuddered.

"Does Quadros control her, or not?" demanded Vilb. "The girl is a stranger," said Gabulus. He stood at attention, his eyes focused on something beyond them.

Oneira shook her head as Vilb looked at her. "I don't know," she said. "I don't know. Something tells me that the girl is Qir's work but… different."

"Does she serve Levinthal?"

"I… don't think so."

Gabulus put up his hand and silenced them. The last of the Aegis had come down the staircase and formed in ranks behind them. Their numbers filled the cavern floor fifty rows across and some ten ranks deep.

Vilb's chest resonated with a deep thrumming and a steady shower of pebbles and dust began to rain from the darkness overhead.

"Simon weeps," declared Gabulus, and he bowed his head and took up the dirge. "He calls to the mother and the father."

Oneira moaned softly.

"What is it?"

"Simon!" she managed.

Gabulus spoke resolutely. "He seeks to awaken you. He seeks to bring you back to your original nature. Only then will you be free." A row of Aegis stepped forward and surrounded Vilb. In another moment the circle of Aegis began to glow brightly. In the next moment they began to shrink, Vilb thought, but no. They were sinking, yet that was not quite right either. The Aegis were melting into the cavern floor and where they once stood they left a pool of molten stone with Vilb on a small island at the center.

The voice of Gabulus spoke out: "The Keystone begins this way."

"What way?" cried Vilb, unsettled and unsure.

"And the Aegis… await the Power of M," announced the voice of Gabulus, and as if they had been listening and waiting for just such a moment, the teeming crowd of Aegis who filled the cavern beyond let out a deafening roar.

"Enough!" he cried. I do not remember! I cannot remember anything anymore."

He was exasperated and desperate and wanted only to see the sky and the sun. He sank down again, quickly spent. Vilb. Jonathan. Simon. What did it all mean? Perhaps the Ancients were nothing more than a bad dream he had once, long ago. The past was the past. Once long ago he did desire, he admitted, as they all had, to feel the Power of M. But the Power of M then was nothing more than poetry—a way of talking about the desire for more water, or food, or comfort. Now, faced with it, faced with the unreality of a transformation he had not sought nor did he understand, he hesitated.

"All I know is desert and drought and hopeless failure," he whimpered. He looked down at his body. Bedraggled, he thought, though at the same time he became aware of the warmth coming from the river of amber stone flowing around him. It had swelled and made his island center shrink by half.

"I am no one. No one. I don't want it. I am nothing. Do you hear? I do not want this."

Before Gabulus could respond, the ground beneath Vilb's feet crumbled into molten amber and he sank quickly. He stood wide-eyed as he sank and could think of nothing and could say nothing. Oneira gazed at him expectantly but remained still. At the last he took a quick breath and closed his eyes as the lava swallowed him completely.

∎∎

Vilb opened his eyes. He found himself sitting in a chair, his head pinned so that he could not turn either this way or that. It was as if he saw from the top of a high mountain. He could see the blue rather than the green sky he knew, and it was a blue both deep and wide cut by striations of white, flowing clouds. There was a sea beneath the sky too, far beyond, and it lapped black at the edges of an orange land in the far distance. "Welcome home," said a voice from behind, and he knew

that voice, though he had not heard it for two thousand years. He tried to turn and see for certain who it was that had spoken but he found that he could not turn, or move any part of him. "Don't be too alarmed. Try and stay calm," said the voice.

Vilb heard new sounds behind him. Someone had joined the first voice. There was quiet talk. A grunt. Strange sounds like the wind whispering over the stone and then a thin voice, receding, saying, "Thank you, Dr. Levinthal" and then he was alone with the voice again.

"Levinthal?"

"What's to come will be a bit painful, I'm afraid," and as the voice spoke Vilb felt a sharp pain in the backs of his thighs.

"Just a little bee sting my boy, Ancient medicine. Cruel to be kind and all that. But you have no bees where you come from, eh? No stings? No stingers? It's a wonder that she's made it work this long. Dear God. From what I can see the water cycle has completely broken down. No animals of any kind, except of course for you my boy. The whole place suffers from a catastrophic lack of bio-diversity, but who's to blame for that, eh? Who could have planned for such a thing?" A long pause. "I give them credit. I do. They worked with the material they had and well, did not do a bad job after all." Vilb felt a pat on the shoulder as if the voice stood right behind him, and then it moved away again. "The vegetation nearly gone, yes? Oceans still dead? You wouldn't know about that, though, would you." A long pause. "It won't be long now before you start to eat each other, eh?" Laughter. "Seriously though, I know you're already up to that. Ghastly, really. Quadros Prang is to blame. He's not a moral man. Truly. Martha and Qir should be rewarded for making it work this long. The Board... impressed, to say the least. Frightened of that monster, Simon no doubt, but impressed nonetheless."

The backs of Vilb's thighs began to burn and a quelling calm came over him. A hand from behind was on his shoulder again. The voice was quiet, reassuring.

"No worries, son. You're not really here. I've managed to make an inter-Field connection to your pattern. I thought I might help you along as well as I might from this distance. You've dreamed about this place. It's still here, after so many years. I've kept busy. Slept some of it off, as it were but not so much as those idiots in the Alps! I'm thrilled to be alive. Really, better than new. I can only imagine what you've been through. Awake yourself, in a manner of speaking, after all these years. And now here you are. All in one piece. Our bag of tricks have grown rather sophisticated recently. It's amazing what we can accomplish with enough quiet and enough energy. We're so close now. It's been a long road, but we're so close. So close. And the truth of the matter is this: the last thing the Board needs is a competing em-frame. The world is simply not big enough for two. The biospheric infrastructure can't handle that kind of system conflict. Not yet. Not ever if the truth be told." "Let me keep it simple for you. The future is here. The past is where you are. I need you to block... your em-frame—do not let them bring it back on-line whatever happens. Block the restoration of your system and I will reward you. Levinthal Labs has very big plans for the future. I am most pleased that you will be here to join us." Vilb was at a loss for words. "You can hear me, eh? It's now or never. Yes? Understand?"

Another long pause and Vilb's mind turned over sluggishly. He heard muffled footfalls and quiet voices from behind, and then a quick pat on the shoulder by an unseen hand. Vilb could not respond. He felt pins and needles in his temple, his forehead, behind his ears, at the base of his neck. A shooting pain deep inside his head blinded him for a moment and left him gasping.

"There there. To be expected. Indeed. It will pass. What's next is merely a necessary stage in your development. Once we have your Krebs cycle stabilized we can get your VenQuell numbers up and into Aegis-range, then, well then Little Earth will have its hands full." The voice chuckled lightly, patted Vilb one last time and moved off. From a distance now the voice went on.

"And then there's what everyone's talking about, here and there." In the next moment Vilb felt a hot breath on the back of his neck and perhaps a nose, or a finger caressed the back of his ear as the voice whispered something inaudible.

And suddenly the voice was far behind him again. "You know what I'm saying, eh? Who better than you? You're positively eidetic, my boy, and I'm grateful for that. I am. From you I've received so much coveted information. Believe me. I know that it's all about Restoration there, I know. Restoration this and Restoration that. And it's the last thing I want. Not yet anyway. Believe me. It's all about timing. You help me, and I help you, and we all go back to your home one day and enjoy the beach, eh?" He paused at this. More stinging in his legs, arms, back, neck. Levinthal was warm now, in his ear, confident and confiding.

"I don't trust the mother. I hope you don't." A deep hum filled the room and Vilb felt himself drifting off to sleep even as the voice grew animated, angry even. "Destroy everything. Lay it to waste. We have to start over. I want to forget about all of what they did before, all except Prang. He's dangerous, but useful. Keep him for me. Wait! Better yet--bring him back here, the two of you, with me. We could do something special." He paused again, and this time he stood before Vilb and revealed himself.

"You see?" and Vilb did see. The man was massive, as large as an Aegis only under an ermine robe and shimmering blouse he was a mountain of flesh and blood, of living, vibrant tissue, but not the green of Little Earth. He was pink, like so many of the Consortium Ancients once were. Jonathan remembered it. He too was once pink, but never like Levinthal. The giant man's eyes sparkled and his burnished skin was flush with the abundance of buoyant physical health. He was young. He was powerful. "Return to me and I offer you your body's full restoration and worlds in which to enjoy it. Worlds, my boy. Worlds. Serve me now as you have in the past. Serve me and let me save you. I will requite your loyalty."

Block Simon? Save Prang? Betray Martha?

Even as he considered what the voice had asked of him a feeling of warmth and ease flowed through him, like the feeling he experienced in the east of Little Earth as he floated in the waters of Quadros Prang's hanging garden. But the ease and delight he felt was only the beginning, a prelude to a deeper pleasure, an ecstasy in fact, in which he felt himself far above his body, set free from its fettering confines. Levinthal had truly liberated him and for once he was no longer the flesh puppet of unseen masters, but could see the world from the top from where the masters watched their world, and it intoxicated him.

"You, my boy, will sit on my Board of Directors as a member. There is no higher honor than this. Unexcelled, complete fusion with the power that preserves. I offer you this taste, a mere foreshadowing of what's to come. Finish what we have started."

Vilb suddenly grimaced, his bliss interrupted by a blinding flash of light and a deafening roar.

"Ah yes. I see the time has come. I've been detected and now they're blocking our connection. Well. That's good. It shows that there's a real problem down there. A real problem. But I must say my little incursion into Prang's field was very successful. Far beyond what I thought probable. Very lucky indeed. And I've enjoyed seeing you again, my old colleague, though I remember you looking better." The voice receded behind him. " I wish we could talk longer, I do. So few here know what's going on. But off you go. Until we meet again. It's all coming together. Remember your part, my old friend." The rest was silence.

•   •   •

Vilb opened his eyes and looked around, blinking. He found himself standing once again in the dark cavern, Oneira in front of him, Gabulus beside him, the rank and file Aegis waiting expectantly for... something, some word or command, from him apparently.

Levinthal. The memory of bliss and perfect contentment, of freedom from a decaying body, of conflicted loyalty, all remained in his mind the way a dream leaves its trace after awakening, but even as he recalled his vision, it vanished like an exceedingly rare morning mist. He was left racked by pangs of longing and desire.

Vilb looked around and saw that he could see far into the cavern. His vision had become sharper, or else the cavern had become even more illuminated. He scanned over the heads of the Aegis standing at the ready in their ranks.

Ah, Levinthal!

As the vision passed and the exquisite bliss faded from his senses, Vilb considered it more carefully. Why did Levinthal reveal himself now? Contrary to his boasts, Levinthal's power was not complete—he could not block the Power of M and had placed some, or all, of his hope in Vilb. And others, perhaps? Almost certainly there were others. But whom? Who served Chicago? Others like Vilb? Oneira? The girl, Prav? At the thought of her Vilb's hope rose. No, Levithal did not control the girl. How he knew he couldn't say, but he knew it to be true. The girl was his hope, his salvation.

Levinthal assumed that Vilb would, like his ancestors, like Levinthal himself, desire more and would be seduced by desire. For more life. For ease. For easy ecstasy. It was a fair assumption, Vilb's memories told him that much, but Vilb knew that it was wrong, for Levinthal, in spite of his great power, was re-born as one who had not lived so long or so unbearably as Vilb and the Ubernaki. In this Levinthal had made a most egregious error for Vilb had no desire for more life. He laughed bitterly and the cavern shook with the sound. No desire whatsoever. He was a walking dead man. That much at least was decided. He would not block Simon's Restoration. Far from it. He would do what he could to achieve the Restoration if only to confound and disrupt the return of the Consortium and to crush the Board.

Behind him stood Gabulus and Oneira but now they both had to crane their necks to look up at him. He could see in the reflection of the woman's awe-filled stare that something about him had changed. Her eyes were wide, still full of expectation but now also of fear and awe. Vilb turned away and faced the sprawling crowd of Aegis who filled the cavern. Arcs of electricity began to leap from the head of one Aegis to another until there was a sea of blue electric flame dancing in the air of the cavern.

He could see because he had grown taller than the Aegis. Gabulus approached and stood before him, his head lowered. Vilb could have taken the figure by the shoulders and shaken him into rubble. His body too was different, for it glowed with a jade radiance rather than amber and his fingertips glowed emerald and radiated with a throbbing power. He was like the others, however, in that he was carved in the battle dress of the Aegis.

The air crackled with electricity and heat. All of his pasts seemed small and inadequate to him now, each a petty betrayal that amounted to nothing, to straw. From the beginning he'd been the pawn of Levinthal. And now, the transformation wrought by the *remains* within him, the Power of M.

"The Power of M!" declared Gabulus and a roar of approval exploded into the air around them.

Strange even to Vilb was the profound sense that all he knew, all that he understood, was that he missed Prav terribly and to see her again was his only desire. If this desire fell into conflict with Simon's Restoration, then so be it. And he knew what was next even before the thought rose and revealed itself.

He would save Prav, destroy Quadros, and end the reign of the immortals.

He raised his right hand and a flash of emerald light exploded from his fingertips and the Aegis roared their approval.

The arcs of electric blue went suddenly to emerald and as they touched the Aegis, their marbled bodies turned to jade.

"The Keystone," proclaimed Gabulus.

Gabulus leaned in close and looked up at Vilb, obviously pleased. His verdant eyes shimmered. He had to raise his voice to be heard above the din.

"What is your desire?"

Vilb paused, stunned for a moment, for the question was like a mouthful of tender flesh cooked over a cold fire. He chewed and swallowed and the taste of blood and stone was in his mouth.

"Vengeance," he finally said as if remembering. "And *destruction*."

The Scourge of M

When justice and vengeance become one the Arclight will fail and the land will die.

– The Book of M

I

Now Vilb had another vision, though this one was born of the Power of M rather than the power of Levinthal, and it came to him that he knew the gods of Little Earth as if their minds were one with his own. As far as he knew he had no power to control or manipulate the gods and was entirely unsure if such a thing would be desirable even if he could manage it. Whatever they were, they were the gods, and the reality of that was rather impossible to ignore. He knew them, feared them, had at times venerated them—at least The Martha, and had prayed to Simon on many occasions, for his return, though he knew not what it meant at the time, and for his good graces, and for bounty, and for rain, and… now it all seemed as so much putrescence. And still he could not give himself over to his new vision nor could he shut out the unwelcome noise.

Such as it was as Vilb positioned himself with the Aegis that he could see from the eyes of Quadros Prang, though it was not clear at first from whose eyes he saw, nor did he understand the vision completely. It was the feeling inside him, so familiar, yet so alien, that first gave rise to the thought that his sight and his sensations were not entirely his own.

His first experience of what Quadros himself experienced was of guilt wrapped tightly, fused utterly, to overweening desire. The longing was complete and utter and felt to be a totality almost perfect in its absoluteness. Quadros longed, and had longed, since before the beginning, since his time as an Ancient, for more. In this moment, his longing was for what the other gods had promised and withheld long ago—a new body to replace and restore the one Martha Simons had damaged so long ago. He had sat in his seat, nursed his revenge, proffered obsequiousness when required, and plotted his justice—and throughout all the long years there was no body forthcoming.

It was only some small comfort that the promise of an endless series of new clones had disappointed The Martha and Azo. Quadros enjoyed the fact that the bodies Martha had manufactured for her utopia in the east were simply unsuitable as replacements for herself, or for her lackey, Azo, and so it was that their own nano-supported original bodies would serve them, must serve them, indefinitely no matter how ossified they became. This may have been almost tolerable for the others, but for Quadros the reality of his powerlessness—in the face of so much power—was maddening to the extreme. How he longed to stride across Little Earth as Simon once did so long ago—as a true giant among giants.

Only Qir seemed to have mastered the craft of transporting consciousness from clone to clone, and he had hidden this craft away from all of them in his hide-out in the Transveld. Qir's Millenial Cadre—the little people of Little Earth—like children, but not children. They and their delightful, powerful Palm... ahh, Quadros had to respect it even if he did not fully understand it. But Qir had underestimated Quadros—again. What portion of the Power of M Quadros had mastered would allow him to hack Qir's Cadre, if only he could gain access, and lo! she came to him. He was late in the recognition, and had lost the *remains* before he realized what he had in his power, but then he understood: here was his new body, his liberation from the prison of his chair. There was some risk, however. Quadros knew that he would have to hazard his original body—his long, tortured, incapacitated existence—in order to make her body his own.

Quadros had hoped for more, for the *remains* to finally come into his possession, for they would have provided him a body impervious to decay, to injury, to death—and to unlimited access to the Power of M. A perfect body. An Aegis body. The armor of the Aegis was a mighty prize and how he had let it slip through his fingers left Quadros confounded and in doubt.

They were on his lap, and he let them slip away. The bitterness of his failure was almost too much to bear.

But he had not failed, not completely. He did, in the end, take the girl's body as his own, and though the situation was far from ideal, it was, in the end, a vast improvement to what had come before. The girl channeled power—not the kind he controlled, not the Power of M to make, to summon, to grant, and to deny, but rather, she had Qir's magnificent Palm.

The Palm had disrupted the entire eastern mag-field Quadros had so carefully, so quietly gained control of. Ah the *remains*! He had had them on his lap! The humiliation made him squirm. There could be only one explanation for his failure with the clones… he shook his head. Levinthal. It had to be. He was almost sure of it… but not… entirely sure. It was true that for hundreds of years Quadros's probability scans had foreseen Levinthal's eventual return—and the Board's as well. Now it was almost certain: Levinthal had returned and that almost certainly meant that the Consortium Board had returned as well. This could be a serious problem. Very serious.

If he had returned, then to underestimate him could be disastrous. Levinthal was no rogue presence in the M-field. He had power behind him. Perhaps his own em-frame. And if this were true… Quadros felt weak and lightheaded. If Levinthal had control over an em-frame… a Fourth-Realm em-frame… it meant a shift in the global balance of power.

So much depended on the next few moments. Two thousand years had come to this—he would spring his trap and seize the day, vanquish the other gods of Little Earth and bring war to the Fourth and Fifth Realms and all that remained of the Consortium.

Chicago would have to wait for the time being. In spite of his new body Quadros felt tied to Little Earth. Only Simon's Restoration would provide for the mass exodus Quadros had dreamed of long before. Before anything else, Little Earth must be completely pacified and that meant that the clones and their magic bones had to be wiped out, once and for all. He could not leave a viable enemy to his flank when he pressed his attack on the north.

Soon he would press his attack. Soon. First, he must wait, but his waiting was almost at an end. Soon the spring would slam the door shut and the prey would be between the hammer and his anvil. And he imagined his victory, and it was sweet, and his new body surged with anticipation, and it was good.

Then it was there a quiet whisper interposed into his scheming thoughts. He heard as if from close beside him, but gave it no mind, for he thought at first it was a trick of his powerful new ears. He waved it away and shook his head.

He stood up in the seat of the mag-chair as it silently moved along. It felt good to stretch to his full height in spite of the diminutive size of his new frame. He was no larger than a nine-year old girl-waif, but whatever the size he could move, jump, fling his arms and pound his fists. He could scream and shriek and kick and make his body perform his mind. He was positively drunk with his new found motility.

He heard a voice again, whispering in his ear. He waved it away again and slumped back into his seat. He and his Aegis had far to travel but he could feel the Great City's M-field up ahead and he knew he would soon find the crease in the M-field he sought. It energized him and his hands throbbed. He rubbed the palms together and chuckled.

Yes. Alright. The Millennial Palm. The irony amused him. Qir had perfected the old technology and it seemed to prove what Qir had always said. The quality of the clone must not be compromised. Cellular degradation will be a living death. This proved to be true for Martha, for Azo, and for Quadros especially. But Qir had perfected his sequencing and the Cadre and the Palm were, well, wonderful. Do not underestimate Qir, he thought.

Yes, that's right. The whisper again in his ear, louder this time.

To take Levinthal, Quadros Prang would have to take down Qir first.

Not possible. Quadros waved the voice away dismissively and made his plans: from Little Earth then, to the Transveld. From there to the southern tip of the Fifth Realm, and then north to the Fourth. And to Chicago. That's where real power was exchanging hands. That's where the future of the Greater Earth would be decided. That's where he needed to be. That's where the future would begin.

You are nothing but a child.

Yes, but… I am alive, he thought, and agile. And I have the Power of M at my command.

You control a shadow of power, not Power itself. Look at what you have settled for.

The voice struck him like a blow and suddenly the indignity of his new body dropped him into a black mood of morbid introspection, something he had hoped his new body would have forestalled, yet here it was again. The guilt. The doubt. The dark dread.

Damn them! He almost had the entire Aegis in his power and now only this, this, stuck with… this! He flung his hand against the chair back and banged a knuckle hard. He whined and brought the back of his hand to his mouth. He sucked on the bruise and hopped from foot to foot. Even the sound of his voice mocked him.

Levinthal would laugh in his face should they ever meet again.

If only he had the Aegis behind him. He lusted after them and their power and agility, their size and speed and upward motility. They were remarkable for their consistent quality. Each one a perfection. If only he had the power to usurp the entire Aegis field. But he had that power and he lost it! The *remains* would have made such a thing possible, he thought, and he could not suppress a whine. He had had them in his lap! Stupid! Idiot!

Yes, it's true. You have already been defeated.

The voice was not triumphant, rather, it was resigned, almost burdened with the information and Quadros could not help but listen and consider it in spite of himself.

He looked down at his legs, his small bare feet. His toes. He could move them by command and though there was some pleasure in this, the girl's body was not enough. The Millennial Palm, while a delightful pop-gun, simply paled in comparison beside the Power of the Aegis and the possibility of the Restoration of Simon's New Body.

He sat in his chair and tried to keep still.

He let the mag-chair sink to the tunnel floor and come to a halt. The four amber Aegis stopped alongside and moved to position themselves at each corner of his throne.

Quadros fidgeted in spite of his conscious desire to be still. This lithe body would simply not be still. He exhaled loudly and surrendered to his tapping fingers, jiggling foot and bobbing head.

The clone from the east—certainly awake by now, probably tuned to the *remains* by now. It seemed hopeless. The Martha's clone… still the manipulative bitch she ever was… would almost certainly push for an attack against him, but he knew it already, and he was prepared.

He jumped to his feet. He couldn't sit still for very long. In the past he could sit unmoving for, well, for years at a time. His new flesh surged and screamed with life, it coursed with information, and he had to squirm and bounce and move every few seconds. His very skin seethed with a roaring cascade of bosonic currents. He itched and scratched and jiggled and shook. And the noise of his body! The pounding of the small heart thrilled him even as it drove him to distraction. His hearing was painfully acute. His eyesight was formidable and discriminating.

He had forgotten what it was to live in a body. He found himself weeping and then slowly sobbing for no reason he could understand. It was as if the body simply needed to weep and he could not hold against it. The muscles were too soft. It was all quite humiliating for him and there were times like these when he missed the petrified stillness of his original frame.

Quadros took some pride in the fact that he had finally freed himself of his physical prison—the others had not yet done it, or so he thought. Yet even so, he found his physical freedom less free than he had long imagined it would be.

It was all rather overwhelming really. The girl's body would take some getting used to, that much was painfully clear, and painful was the operative word, for the girl seemed to be in a constant state of bodily distress in spite of her apparent physical buoyancy. Muscles ached. Skin bruised. Nerves were keenly, absurdly sensitive. Her knees were especially susceptible to an agony produced by the slightest impact. In spite of this Quadros could not help but to bump his knees whenever he moved. It was harder than he remembered, this physicality. So vulnerable. So thirsty. So hungry. It had been a hundred years since he had tried to swallow anything. There was simply no pleasure in it. But now his stomach cried out for food constantly. And water. What choice did he have but to feed it?

His stomach jumped and twisted within him as he thought of the clones up ahead, The Martha-clone, the *remains*, the Aegis—perhaps a great many Aegis. How many he had no idea, but it could well be a great many. And then the thought struck him.

This could be his end.

The world tilted and he felt a bile stir in his gut.

He had forgotten nausea.

Horrible and unsettling.

He had to lie down on the tunnel floor. It was cool and still.

You cannot deny that my body is a poor substitute for what you had hoped.

Quadros sucked in a sharp breath.

It was the girl's voice in his ear. He moved his head back and forth to no avail.

How can you show yourself? Claim yourself as yourself?

His chest tightened.

"But the Power of M will obey my command. I have the Palm," he said aloud. He stood up and climbed into his chair.

The Palm is useless to you.

"I think not! They will grovel before me, beg for mercy as they once did."

You will never leave Little Earth.

It was his turn to laugh. In spite of the other gods' best efforts to destroy him had he not taken the Archer's throne even when his control over the Power of M was in its infancy? Had he not imprisoned that simp, Azo? Had he not siphoned the Arclight's power and taken it as his own? Had he not single-handedly brought Little Earth to its knees?

And then there was the wretched beauty of the AkiGazi usurpation of the Gazi and the Ubernaki. He disrupted seventeen hundred years of Martha's sequencing and ridiculous utopia-building. Now they were eating each other! His disruption was pure, unadulterated perfection. It was an obscenity beyond genius.

He spoke out loud to the girl now, flinging his arms about, pacing the tunnel floor. "Now Qir can expect the same. I will set Qir's little minions against their own master. Sooner or later. All will be my toys on my strings. Don't you see? I alone am free. The rest, all of it, all of you are puppets! Even the Aegis. A race of stone slaves." The girl laughed, but not with derision. A sound more like... quiet pleasure.

Quadros winced. He did not understand, and worse, he knew it. All he knew now was that the girl had to be silenced. He could not tolerate her conscious presence in his mind. Yet had he not committed himself to just such a risk when he took the girl's body as his own? He would have to master the girl's frequency and repress any traces of her thereof.

Not possible, my dear Quadros.

"We shall see," he said, and he gathered himself into one corner of his mag-chair, pulled his knees up under his chin and hugged his small legs tight to himself. He closed his eyes, sucked in a breath and held it.

By force of will he tuned his magnetic frequency to an order of awareness in which he could manipulate energy on a scale many orders of magnitude smaller than the waking world of matter's macrocosmic forms. Cells. Atoms. Particles. Vibration—until he reached the deepest bottom, the basso-continuum of existence—where the most basic bosonic pattern flowed and became sub-atomic relations, and then atomic structures, and so on until the basic structure of matter arose as if in response. Here, in this place, the vibratory patterns of self-identity, could be manipulated—as Levinthal had done inadvertently the first time he raised Simon Simons from the dead so very long ago.

Since then, all of the gods of Little Earth had come to realize that as malleable as such vibrations seemed to be, they could never be entirely destroyed, or controlled. Though personality was unreal and impermanent and might be understood to be a manufactured thing, once the sub-atomic pattern had been tuned and made extant, it could not be made extinct. The mystery of impermanence was its permanence. The paradox befuddled Quadros and so limited his power.

Try as he might, he could not find nor quash the girl's mind. It would have to be tolerated. For now.

II

Oneira struggled to keep up with Gabulus and Vilb, though Vilb was no longer recognizable as the Ubernaki man from the east. He had become the Keystone, the Captain of the Aegis. She had to take three steps to their one, and even at a steady Aegis walk it would have left her far behind had she not run hard to keep up. Her breathing came in ragged gasps near the end, but the thrill of what came next kept her going.

Quadros was just ahead Gabulus had said, but she did not need to be told for she could feel it, and now, finally now, Martha would have her long-sought revenge. She thrilled at the chance to be alive, at this moment, in this place, to honor and to serve her genetic legacy. History would finally begin to end as it should have ended two thousand years before. Poor Vilb had struggled with his fate—and had, even now she suspected, not yet made perfect peace with himself. Oneira, on the other hand, embraced it, for had she not always suspected her place in Simon's cosmos, somehow, in her ignorance, known it all along away in the east?

They had traveled far down the Archer's Great Way and at each intersection they passed a phalanx of Aegis. As they passed, the Aegis fell in behind until Oneira could not keep count there were so many following behind. More even than assembled in the cavern now, many hundreds, though it was impossible to know for their ranks disappeared into the tunnel behind and she kept moving forward. Surely the Power of M was behind such an army. Surely it was only a matter of time until the Power of M and Simon's New Body could complete the work He had begun, and was interrupted from, so long ago.

The entire company made a sudden stop and she stumbled into Gabulus, utterly winded.

What was once Vilb stood over her and seemed to regard her, though his face was inscrutable. He was Aegis, but he was more than a head taller than the rest and a verdigris fire burned in his eyes. His form was different than the others now too. His body glowed, or perhaps it vibrated, or both, and it appeared to be something other than solid, as if the stone—or whatever it was—shifted and flowed. Oneira had the sense that Vilb held his shape only tenuously and at any moment he might fly apart. "Is it Quadros?" she said between her gasps for breath.

"Up ahead?" She raised herself at the waist and looked up into his face.

"You must wait behind," he said, but his mouth did not move. His face had become an implacable stone mask that revealed nothing. She shook her head.

"No. He has to... see... me. He has to know that I was the one who did this to him. That I am the one who has defeated him. Nothing less will do. The Martha wants it! Simon... demands it!"

Vilb shook and his chest moved like the surface of water disturbed by a falling stone. He was laughing at her.

"Great Mother. You must remain behind."

Something changed in the figure's face—a look of benign understanding perhaps—and Oneira's eyes grew wide with recognition. "Simon?" She dropped to her knees now and bowed her head.

"No, not yet. I am only a simulacrum. Rise." He held out his left hand and carefully Oneira placed her left hand on the end of his index finger and let him guide her to her feet. "You must stay behind or risk everything that you hope to achieve."

There was a blast from beyond and the tunnel shook around them though the Aegis remained still, waiting for their captain.

"The battle has begun. We meet Quadros in force."

Oneira eyed him.

The tunnel floor shook again and Vilb's chest went liquid for a moment. The entire company of Aegis took a step forward and left Vilb and Oneira one step behind.

We press the attack. Remain behind. With that Vilb turned and strode away from the blast, the Aegis parting as he passed.

May there be no remains, he called out.

The other Aegis took up the call.

May there be no remains.

Now she was alone. Gabulus had gone forward, Vilb back.

She could turn to the Great City and find her predecessor, continue this life, but now as The Martha, though as she considered it, she realized that she had no firm sense that such a gesture would be welcomed—mother's intuition perhaps.

That was not the way to The Martha. Here was the way. Before her. She must be a part of the destruction of Quadros. Who was to stop her? It seemed that she was invisible to the Aegis all around her. They moved steadily forward into the dark of the tunnel up ahead now. Blasts continued to shake the walls and floor.

The Aegis made another stride forward, and then another and she knew then that the only way forward was forward. She took a breath and stepped into the row of Aegis all around her and stood between four figures, each of which could have seen her and taken hold. She waited for a response but there was none. They stepped forward again, but this time Oneira was ready and she moved forward with them, and still they seemed unaware of her presence. She prepared to leap forward again. At that moment the tunnel floor shook and she had to catch herself against the leg of a figure before her. A flash of blinding light came next and a powerful roar deafened her. She fell to the floor, dazed.

When she rose again she moved more slowly. Crawling at first as she found her balance, she scuttled forward. Dust was in the air now and the tunnel floor was strewn with debris, which hurt her knees, hands, and feet. She pressed on. More flashes flashed and distant concussions boomed and shook the earth. Up ahead she could see that the floor was now cracked and pitched. An upheaval.

Her heart raced inside her with the thrill of it. Finally. The battle raged somewhere up ahead, this she could feel and hear, and it was all that she could do to remain calm for her only desire now was to find Quadros and put her own two hands around his neck. Physically he was hopelessly vulnerable, especially against a Quarter-Meson from the east. She could break him into kindling quite easily, and she fully planned to. The Martha within her believed that his Aegis would be completely overwhelmed. His M-field weak. She shook with anticipation. It was simply too good to be true.

Now large pieces of rubble littered the way and made her forward progress more difficult. Worse, avalanches of debris began to rain down with each concussion. The entire tunnel seemed on the verge of catastrophic collapse.

Oneira crawled through a fissure newly opened in the tunnel wall and moved towards what she thought was the opening left by another blasted tunnel, and she was not disappointed.

May there be no remains, she prayed, and she moved forward on her hands and knees towards the noise and the light, her palms tingling. There was another concussion and she found herself pitched onto a precipice overlooking a dark abyss. An emerald fire burned far below. It was as if she were looking at the night sky, not into the bowels of the Earth. Across a ragged chasm she made out a light-filled jagged hole. It was the tunnel running east, or what was left of it.

Well behind her now gaped the blasted tunnel mouth that opened to the west. It remained, though only in a most ragged form. Even so, columns of Aegis continued forward to the edge, one row at a time, and leapt off. As they fell they became a streak of light, like a meteor plummeting towards the emerald fire below. She watched a line of four Aegis step to the jagged edge, leap, and plunge to the bottom of the deep chasm. Just before they reached bottom the four erupted into a great white light, which blinded her and knocked her back. A concussion shook the earth a moment later and Oneira covered her ears and put her head between her knees as rocks tumbled past her from both sides.

Unhurt, she crawled to the edge of the precipice and lay on her stomach and peered down. A blast of noxious, super- heated wind rose from below and blasted her face. She pulled back suddenly gasping.

Quadros was down there. He had to be.

She collected herself and eased forward, over the edge.

Yes. He had to be. She began to climb down, her feet reaching out into the darkness below her looking for purchase.

Step. Step. Step. Reach. She slipped and fell but the way had leveled off and she skittered into an outwash of small, red stone. She shuffled as quickly as she could across this level and dropped down again, deeper into the abyss. There was another flash of Aegis, a blast, and a concussion. Then another. She clambered down quickly, taking risks, placing her hope in the sheer force of her will and her desire.

As if awakening from a dream she neared the bottom and looked up. How she had made it down the rugged chasm wall amazed her, but it was not important. Crucial now was what was before her. She scrambled past an outcropping and then she saw it: a hundred paces beyond lay a wide moat of white magma cutting her off from an island of dark stone. It was at that island that the Aegis continued to fling themselves. In the darkness of the chasm above the Aegis continued to fall and detonate, but around her the ground did not shake and the blasts sounded distant and far less threatening.

Above the island hung an emerald dome, translucent.

The innermost defense of Quadros, she surmised. Above her Oneira could spy another emerald shield against which the Aegis flung themselves and, she realized now, destroyed themselves.

Her heart shriveled inside her and her bowels turned to water.

Quadros seemed quite safe and unharmed.

The thought sickened her and made her desperate. Just then a blast rocked the cavern and Oneira fell from her perch and landed hard on a boulder. She felt her rib crack.

She gasped and sucked in a painful breath, and rolled over. Perhaps his shield would give after all.

Even crawling was difficult but she had to get closer to the dome so she moved slowly, one hand holding her side, the other supporting her across the uneven terrain. She stayed low, though she had no idea if anyone would be watching.

She made it to the chasm's floor and was virtually eye- level now with the magma moat around the dome. Waves of heat rose from its surface and made a shimmering wall of heat between her and the island beyond. Not far. Not that far. She crawled on until the heat from the moat threatened to scorch her. She rolled desperately behind a small boulder for protection. She pounded the earth with one fist in frustration. To go forward would be deadly, yet to give up when she was so close was unacceptable—he was there, she knew it.

Even as she lay there stymied, the floor shook with a powerful concussion and sucked the air out of the chasm. She looked up. Aegis began landing all around her in quick succession. Dozens. Hundreds. She barked an angry laugh. Quadros's outer shield had failed and the Aegis fell through the air as if sliding feet-first down a steep incline, one foot out, one tucked up, both hands out to grab hold if necessary. They were no longer detonating in the air above the dome, rather, they were landing and surrounding it. They continued to fall, silently and gracefully, until they surrounded the edge of the moat many ranks deep. Once again she found herself amid a forest of Aegis bodies.

This was the end of Quadros. She patted the earth in celebration.

Where was Vilb?

Many were scarred by streaks of black. She felt a grim determination among them, something she had not noticed in the tunnel above. They stood for what seemed a protracted moment of silence until Oneira thought that they too had been stymied by the moat, but such was not the case. In the next moment the ranks of Aegis all around her took a quiet step forward, stood, and then another, and then another and another. She rose and followed close behind, using their bodies as a shield from the heat. Her heart raced.

The figures stepped towards the moat again. She moved as close as she dared and watched the forward rows of Aegis step into the molten lava and sink slowly only to disappear. Was this suicide? Was it hopeless? Oneira's heart sank. The next row then stepped forward into the magma, sank slowly and disappeared.

It did appear to be suicide, but it made no sense. Aegis were stepping into the moat from all around its edges and each met the same fate as the other. They slipped away, silently becoming one with the magma.

She moved forward yet again. She had to shield her face and creep up sidelong. She had to see what was happening. It was then she could just make out that the Aegis were filling the moat with their bodies, or somehow cooling the magma, for the surrounding edge of the moat had extended from the shore and a new shore of jade slowly grew out towards the shielded dome beyond. Oneira exhaled deeply. It would take many Aegis to overtake the magma.

"Mother!" a voice called from behind her. It was Gabulus.

He was streaked and burned over most of his figure. "You're not safe here, Mother." Without waiting for a response, Gabulus broke ranks and picked her up in his arms as if she were a child. Together they moved quickly behind the lines of Aegis and he set her down on her feet and then dropped to one knee beside her.

"Forgive me, Mother," and with that he disappeared into the ranks of Aegis moving slowly into the moat.

She lay there catching her breath. Above her was dark and the air was completely still. The earth beneath her hummed expectantly.

The sound of a skittering boulder in the distance brought her back to the east for a moment, to the badlands, to the Pilgrimage. The thought enervated her for an instant. Did it matter that some part of herself was the puppet-master and another part the puppet? Did it make her fate any less purposeful?

But thoughts of Simon filled her mind then and she knew that she had brought herself back for a reason, for a purpose, and it was the most perfect justification the world had given rise to, and no part of her would ever let that die.

In the next moment a flash of emerald burst over the heads of the Aegis and they shone white for a moment, and they did not move.

Something had paralyzed them in mid-step. It could only be Quadros Prang. He still had claws. A moment later the Aegis recovered their verdigris glow and stepped forward in unison. Oneira knew that the final conflagration was near and she looked above her with some trepidation. The jagged remains of tunnels dotted the cavern wall. Perhaps she might still have time to climb out? But going back was impossible and she knew it. Yet going forward meant crawling over a white-hot death.

If crawling over white-hot death meant that her hands would be around Prang's throat, then so be it. She inched her way forward.

Another flash of emerald and the Aegis went still and cold again, but this time they went lifeless for another count, or even two, beyond the first attack. She crept forward now, but carefully, slowly.

Purpose drives us. She moved forward again into the ranks of Aegis, careful to avoid Gabulus. She moved forward easily this time, the heat from the magma having lost much of its potency. The Aegis had succeeded in covering it in a white sheet of marble.

Another blast of emerald lit the air all around her and the Aegis went still. She hurried through a forest of white limbs and made it at last to the edge. She raced sidelong even as the Aegis recovered and finished their task. She moved across in a daze now, suddenly alone, utterly exposed.

Ahead of her was a gossamer dome of white light hovering tenuously above a wide, round ebony foundation. She could make out figures under the dome, but it was too far to see who was there, but Prang must be one of them. He had to be. Oneira's heart pounded in her chest. She stepped onto the island and began to run towards the dome.

After a not too difficult passage over the uneven, loose stone she came face to face against the dome's gossamer shield. She reached out and it was cool and it allowed her passage through.

The ebony floor energized her the instant her feet hit the mirrored surface.

Ahead not more than fifty paces she recognized Prang's throne flanked by three Aegis, two of them white, one of them taller than the others, and the color of jade, the color of the Keystone.

Oneira reeled. It could not be. Had Vilb taken on the *remains* only to betray her? It could not be so yet for an instant the terror of death held her. Would she never feel her hands around Prang's neck?

Two massive hands gripped her from behind. She grimaced in pain but could make no struggle.

She waited for the Aegis to crush her.

"It is I, Gabulus."

"Bring her here," croaked the voice in the chair. Instantly the Aegis lifted her up and carried her swiftly to the crumbled body on his onyx throne. It was Quadros. She recognized him, his acute head on its broken body, the withered skin and the fleshy, bulging eyes. The Martha had done this to him, she had done this to him, two thousand years ago. She remembered and marveled at it.

Quadros turned his chair so that he could peer down onto her. "We meet once again. You've come so far. I'm amazed. I truly, truly am. Now end your assault." Suddenly it became obvious that the old man had been deeply shaken by the Aegis onslaught and he assumed that she was behind it.

From the top of the dais his smaller chair separated and fell silently towards Oneira and stopped before her, but at an angle. It was the only way Quadros could look up at her face.

"Please forgive me and my bad form. Yet even so, I am feeling so very good, you see, and in my good humor even Martha's petty attacks amuse me. Please inform her now that she has my attention."

Quadros began a slow, widening circle around her.

"You're not the first," mumbled the old man, and then glided backward.

She could hear the syncopated thuds of exploding Aegis above him, closer than before.

"You cannot defeat me. Do you hear? I was prepared for this attack."

"This is not my attack," declared Oneira, sensing an opening, a possibility.

"Impossible," Quadros rasped.

"We are all pawns, I assure you," said Oneira, not entirely sure of what she was saying.

"Call off your Aegis!" cried Quadros suddenly, his voice shrill. She felt the floor tremble and the gossamer dome winked in and out. Somewhere in the distance stone cracked.

"Call them off!" Quadros yelled again as well as the shriveled body would allow.

"This is not my attack," Oneira repeated.

"For your help I will return this one to you," said Quadros, and from behind the throne the girl appeared. It was Prav. A white Aegis held her loosely.

"This is not my attack," declared Oneira, her voice stronger now. She played for time. Waited for an opening.

The girl kept her face down. She wore the Easterling's srapi, and her hood was thrown over her face.

"I think he's coming," Prav said quietly, turning her eyes up to the empty cavern above and at this Oneira looked up also. As she peered into the darkness above the translucent dome vanished like a morning mist and a meteor descended from the silence above.

In an instant the streak of light fell among them and an Aegis alighted on his feet not far from where she stood. His landing shook the earth beneath her. It was Vilb, the Captain of the Aegis, the simulacrum of Simon's Body. Oneira seized the moment and leapt across the floor in three large bounds.

She stood before Quadros now, almost within arm's reach.

Quadros quickly moved his chair behind the raised dais even as he cursed and grunted. An instant later the air concussed and a blast of emerald radiance dazzled her and knocked her down. She blinked hard and focused. The other Aegis went white and still.

Oneira struggled forward, grabbed hold of the girl and flung her towards Vilb who awoke quickly from Prang's attack. Vilb's emerald eyes met Oneira's gaze for an instant.

"Why did you not stay behind?"

He moved towards Oneira as if he would scoop her up and take her away, but she moved away.

"No, you have to leave me here. Take the girl. Save the girl. Leave me to kill Quadros. I'll follow you the way I came."

Outside the dome the remaining Aegis silently rose into the air above the dome and disappeared into the dark. Another emerald blast erupted and Vilb shielded his head as if fearing a blow from above. He was alone.

"I cannot stay here."

"Go!" Oneira cried out. "I will kill him!"

"I cannot stay here." But he remained standing, still unmoving, his imperturbable gaze locked on Oneira.

"I remember. I remember."

"Go!"

"I will not forget."

"Go!"

In the next moment he scooped up the girl, leapt into the air and disappeared in an instant into the upper regions of the chasm.

Then it was quiet and she was alone with Quadros Prang.

"I am still young," she said. "And strong."

She turned and moved slowly towards him, prepared to run, to leap if necessary, but Quadros remained unmoving, seemingly locked in place. Oneira smiled grimly and moved forward. At last. At long, long last. Even as she took her first step it became more difficult to lift her second, as if the floor had turned to thick mud. Then it was she felt the burning in the soles of her feet, and she looked down and saw the floor had lost its integrity—it shook and shimmered just like the magma had beyond the dome. She looked up and all at once she knew.

This was death.

Not her first, certainly, but the first she could remember.

Perhaps it was her sequencing, or perhaps it was some deeper nature, but a calm fell about her as she understood her end had come, and she accepted her situation. She looked up and Quadros remained, his chair a victim of the molten floor as well.

It was then one last passion burst inside of her and she drove her legs forward, the molten floor scorching her feet, her ankles, charring her to the bone, and still she moved heavily towards Quadros. His eyes gaped and were wide with fear. His mouth moved but he could make no words form, nor utter any cry. He groaned and his chair made one last desperate pitch as if to turn and flee but it failed, and one corner sank into the mire.

In a moment they would both be swallowed by a lake of white fire. She just had time to struggle the last few steps in and take the sinking Quadros from behind. Her Quarter-Meson's hands went round his ancient neck and she choked and squeezed until she felt the spine snap in her hands. The molten pool took them then, together, in their last embrace, and as she descended, she had time for one last prayer:

May there be no remains.

Return to the Great City

I

Though he dreaded the thought of it, Vilb took Prav to the surface. He had saved her as he promised he would, though Oneira, intent on vengeance, had sacrificed herself in order to end the life of Quadros. Her death left him nonplussed. Had she truly died? What was death, after all? Were there not others like her, perhaps older, perhaps younger? Vilb felt a powerful confusion fog his mind even as he attempted to, at least with his thoughts, mourn his... his... what was she to him? A friend? A distant relation from the Ubernaki east? His wife? One of the gods? His head spun with the bizarre nature of his connection to the woman.

He settled on one stable fact: Quadros Prang was gone.

"We have to get to the Citadel," said the girl, interrupting his thoughts. "But you can't enter in looking... like that." The Power of M was still heavy on Vilb and his Aegis body seemed to shrink even as the strange battle fever that had come upon him cleared. The surface of Little Earth, its arid breeze, its waning sunlight, the dirt under his feet—all of it calmed him and brought him back to himself even as the *remains* seemed to loose their grip and let his conscious mind rise to the surface of his awareness. What had happened felt as if it had happened to someone else and he had been told the story. What he knew was that the surviving Aegis had retreated to the Barrier Ring and the Halo—the few that remained. Many had... had they died, or merely been transformed? Vilb did not know. The survivors quickly left him though with the clear sense that they expected their Captain to meet them at the Throne Room. The Restoration was near at hand. What, or where, was the Throne Room?

Jonathan Simons had never been there. Nor had Vilb. Nor Levinthal. None of the presences that lurked within him understood this, yet he felt the call stronger even than the call to Pilgrimage. Time was running out, that much he knew. A new urgency had crept into him since the defeat of Quadros. The gods would wend the war more directly now, now that the endgame had finally been set in motion by… by Vilb! He shook his head. It was too incredible to be believed.

First he would escort the girl into the city and then, somehow find his way back to the Throne Room, though he did not know the way.

The girl, however, seemed to know just where to go, and she led them on at a brisk clip. They trudged through the arid wastes until they reached the fetid swamps at the outskirts of the city. The tunnel system between the battle and the Citadel had become unsafe since the Aegis battle with Quadros and the girl said that The Martha kept watch. For some reason she thought it best to avoid The Martha, at least for now. The surface was best. For now, she said.

"Perhaps The Martha will send guidance?" asked Vilb, but the girl waved him off.

"We walk." Then she smiled a smile more grimace than grin. "Like we once did."

Vilb nodded, grunted, kept silent.

They walked a great distance until Vilb realized that the Power of M had left him completely as they drew nearer to the city, and soon enough his hands appeared to be the hands of the Ubernaki hermit he once was. It was a relief more than anything else. Some part of him still protested the transformation believing that he had not chosen it, but rather, others had foisted it upon him.

He wrapped his srapi around him tightly and still he felt uneasy, and he clenched his chattering teeth against the air.

"That's the cold you feel," said the girl, though she herself seemed undisturbed by it.

Even here, Vilb thought, even here so close to the Arclight the cold came on. A stiff wind cast up loose stone and set him stumbling for an instant. In the next the calm had returned along with a deep chill. Vilb shivered and his flesh rose. He looked at the girl walking just ahead of him. Her eyes were down as she watched each step of her naked feet pull at the sucking, fulsome mud. Gases like those about the recently dead filled the air and it sent Vilb to retching. The girl, on the other hand, seemed quite at home with it.

"Does the air not make you sick?" Vilb asked, the back of his hand over his nose and mouth. He had to stop to rest but kneeling down gave no respite. The odor hugged the ground more intensely. He rose and did his best to keep going.

The girl gave no sign of having heard. She kept on, her face set grim. It was familiar walking with her, it was the girl he had met in the badlands of the east. But there was something discernibly different about her as well, though as to that Vilb could not say what.

"Little one," said Vilb now, stopping. "I must rest."

The girl took a few more steps as if not hearing, but then she stopped and turned to face him.

"You're not so big anymore," she said. "You look like you used to. How do you feel?"

"Sickened," he said, and gagged on the stench.

"You get used to it," said the girl. "Just take a few deep breaths."

Vilb almost understood his situation now, but he felt far from what had happened to him in the past, or even what had happened to him with the Aegis. It was as if all he had learned from Azo and Gabulus had happened in a dream that was slipping away from him, not that he had awakened. The old questions came back to him now more clearly than ever: were the other gods helping or hindering Vilb on his journey? And would Simon, the Lord of Lords, not speak loudly and clearly so that Vilb might understand more completely His will? He breathed easier now even as his mind unknotted.

"Better?" asked Prav and Vilb nodded slowly. He felt a sudden longing rise up in him for Oneira and felt a cloud of dread descend upon him when he thought of the girl. Did the gods die? Or did they return?

And then he looked at the backs of his own hands. He knew the answer, and it was obvious.

But Quadros is gone. Destroyed.

Vilb could remember the transformation into Aegis and the destruction of Quadros. Of that he was quite sure. Vilb continued to follow close behind the girl and she guided them to a pass that led through a tangled line of jagged hills. "I know this place. I've walked this place many times," she said, but not to Vilb.

"When?" asked Vilb, but the girl ignored him. Beyond the hills the great plateau spread out flat before and below him and at the edge of the plateau he could see San Simon in the distance like a glittering jewel in the desert. He stood and gasped. It was beautiful and harsh in the waning sunlight. The rusted plateau ran ahead to the rim of a wide chasm. Across it lay the black walled city. He could see the Archer's Dome atop the Citadel atop the leveled mountain at the center. On the flanks of the mountain stretched out countless structures. Gray, brown, and white stone in the distance reflected the amber light of the lowering sun and the emerald illumination of the waning Arclight high above.

There it was. He had not seen it from a distance the first time he had arrived. From here it was a stunning monument and a telling proof. The gods had once worked wonders on the face of Little Earth. He choked up at the sight.

"The Great Sewer," said the girl flatly. "Just follow me. You'll get all you want." She trotted off down the descending path that led them towards the city.

The girl was talking now and Vilb was doing his best to follow along, but she had never talked so much, or so quickly. She seemed somehow possessed by a torrent of information and energy, and it poured out of her like a flash flood, not entirely without purpose though not entirely meaningful either. She speculated that by now San Simon was teeming with the AkiGazi from the east. What a feast they would have once they arrived and settled in. But even their starvation would be sated after all. He had seen to that.

"Who had seen to what?" Vilb asked, but she ignored him. She rattled on. "For a time," she said, "the Citadel would be lit by the light of a thousand massive bonfires, but it wouldn't last, no, it could not last. The fuel would not hold out. How could it? Even the resourceful AkiGazi would spend their fuel and the darkness would fall. The Arclight would die. The cold, and the end of Little Earth, would come." She took some strange pleasure in this and a shiver wracked Vilb and he hugged his body. It would take some getting used to, this cold. A distant memory lived in him and warned him that there was no way to grow accustomed to the depth of cold that would grip Little Earth. It was complete. It was absolute. It was a tomb. He was already unbearably uncomfortable and could not imagine anything much colder than this.

And still they trudged along towards San Simon. They were beyond the swamp now and well across the plateau and nearing the great chasm that separated them from the city.

"Martha's Bay down there." Prav went on thinking out loud. She was worried. She had timed it badly, she said, and now it would all be for nothing if she could not find an access tunnel and a functional mag-rail. Unless they traveled as Pilgrims. Took a ferry. She snorted with derision.

Then she paused, turned to Vilb and barked out a grating laugh. They would be traveling as Pilgrims as they had at the beginning, a child two-skin with an Ubernaki savage from the east. It could get very ugly before they found their way to the Citadel, but this seemed to please the girl.

She stopped in her tracks and looked around.

"What?" asked Vilb, pulling up now. She looked up at him.

"You are a wreck. You're a shambles. Look at you. Your face is drawn, lined, haggard. The Martha... shoddy work, after all. You've got no staying power."

"I am what I am," was all Vilb could manage, though he felt stung by the girl's criticisms.

"No matter. Up ahead we'll have to climb down to the water and take a ferry across. Follow the other Pilgrims, what remains of them."

"A ferry?"

"It's a boat. A kind of boat."

"A boat?"

Vilb had heard once about boats though he had never seen one. Jonathan Simons had... taken a long journey on a boat, or perhaps not. Boats belonged to that category of knowledge that housed the likes of the gods, of Simon, of the Arclight. All of his religion was coming true, it seemed, and he shook his head marveling at it. Boats. Arclights. Gods. Aegis.

Simon guide us, Vilb thought.

The girl complained loudly that she hated the wretched surface of Little Earth and she avoided it whenever possible. And this was why. Obviously. She kicked at the rocks in her path. It had never become the garden the others dreamed of. It was rock and more rock. Mountains of rock. Vast plains of deflation. Even the arable soil had to be coaxed to grow anything and would as quickly revert to a near-sterile state as it would produce edible crops. Utterly unsustainable, she cried. What a joke! The so-called gods of Little Earth had failed and walking the surface only made that abundantly clear. What a waste. If only they had listened to him from the beginning.

"To who?" asked Vilb, but once again she ignored him.

And still she could not stop talking. Up they scrambled to a low rise, the girl apparently hopeful that they might find some sign ahead of a way, though she feared that they may have to walk all the way to San Simon.

Something in Vilb hoped it would not be too late. Could it be true? Had the AkiGazi really made it this far south and west? Would they... be allowed to take the city?

The girl urged him to hurry along—her small stomach demanded food and water. Thirst nagged her constantly she said and she scoffed.

The Arclight was failing, she said.

And the long night was falling.

The girl shivered violently for the first time, Vilb noticed.

"I miss my old bones," she mumbled as she trudged. "My old bones had a kind of perfection, did they not? They did. They certainly did. As lifeless as it was it had never felt cold, had ceased to thirst long ago. Eating was unknown to me, though I never stopped feeling hunger for more. Perfect petrification. But now... but now I am a sea of distracting, coursing need."

She said she had forgotten the huge amounts of food and water required to maintain such a fleshy frame, even a small one like the girl's. Even she was exhausted now as well from scrambling over boulders and outwash. She would gladly give the Power of M to anyone who could bring her a mag-chair and its smooth and effortless movement now. Her scraped and bleeding hands stung and throbbed and her burning muscles protested against further movement, yet still they had some ways to travel yet.

Rest was essential, to catch the breath, said Vilb.

"Up ahead," the girl said. "Look. It's an Oasis Arch. Not large, not by old standards at least. It's a piece of The Martha's early work quite obviously. She loved the small, discrete interventions. Make the savages believe in the gods. That was her way. Well, bless her little heart, eh? Wherever she raised an Oasis Arch, a substantial mag-rail station was not far off." They need only find the access port—surely near and by the looks of things far enough from the battle to be in good working order.

Vilb looked up at the Arch in awe. A residual luminous haze clung to the quartz span and a small spring still gurgled somewhere. Ubernaki script, Gazi script and a number of other etchings spanned the arch. Vilb read it out loud as he approached.

Planted here For you by the Lord, Your Simon, to Sustain you through the long night. Eat and Drink, Friend and be filled.

The girl gritted her teeth and let out a murderous moan.

"Tell me what you know of Simon," said Vilb apprehensively. He wanted to draw the girl out and attempt to settle his own mind on the matter.

"I cannot enter the City like this. I would be fed to the AkiGazi without delay," she said.

Vilb had found the water and was drinking noisily beyond a ring of hewn gray slabs of standing stone that surrounded the arch.

"I wish I had skins to fill," he said. "This water is fresh."

He turned on the girl now. "Drink. Drink some and rest for a moment." She shook her head and seemed to be trying to find something in the rocks all around the arch.

Time was running out. They had to hurry if they hoped at all of bringing an AkiGazi army out of Little Earth alive.

The girl looked up one last time at the Ancient writing carved into the stone and stepped towards the weakly glowing M-field beneath the span. She reached out her hand and drew Vilb beside her. His toes tingled and the tips of his fingers throbbed.

"Can Simon save Little Earth?" asked Vilb.

The girl shook her head.

"Then how will we… live?"

"No one will survive the cold that comes. Your only hope is to abandon Little Earth and seek a new home."

"What does this mean?"

The girl shook her head and laughed. "Simon will be your champion and so you cannot fail. He will lead you to victory and to freedom."

"Freedom?" Vilb said, breaking in as if suddenly angered.

"I left my enclave and made a home on the hill to rid myself of such illusions." He stood over the girl now, fuming, wild-eyed, emaciated. He could not last long this way, he knew.

"I took the Pilgrimage because my father took the Pilgrimage," he declared loudly. "I carry the *remains* inside me. I am Jonathan Simons, father of Simon. I am the Keystone. I led the Aegis. I am… I am… "

The girl nodded. "You are a pawn."

Vilb shrunk down at this. "A pawn," he echoed.

"A slave," said the girl. "And you suffer from the disease of your regeneration."

"What is this disease?" asked Vilb weakly.

"Simon's error."

"You talk in circles," he moaned.

"I know you know," said the girl. "Certainly Azo has befuddled you with his history lessons. And so you know the truth of what I'm telling you. You are a pawn of the gods, nothing more. They use you to serve their own ends, and they want to destroy me."

"You?" said Vilb.

"Quadros Prang," the girl said solemnly, and Vilb's eyes went wide. "Yes," she said. "I see you see. Let me be brief. Simon was a machine. This the Jonathan inside you understands, but you must understand it. The Ancients made Simon, and Simon in his rage cursed the rest of us with this unbearable existence as punishment for how he was made. But that is all ancient history. Now is all there is."

"Yet the past is all that we live out in this present," said Vilb, his knees growing weak under him.

"You do not need to understand such things. What you need to do is trust me, and to surrender to me the *remains*. The Power of M is the power of control over this world, and the worlds beyond. Simon controlled it—the gods can shape it—but Simon had perfect control, and only Simon can control it perfectly. You see? I must become Simon in order to save those who I can and take our grievances to he who is the source of all our ills."

Vilb looked down and remained silent.

"You know of whom I speak," said the girl. "Say it."

"Levinthal," he whispered.

"Do you trust me?" asked the girl. She crouched down next to Vilb. She took one of his chapped and bony hands in her own. "Will you trust me?" Vilb put his hand on hers and stood up.

"Quadros Prang?"

"I am not as they have claimed. They lie to manipulate you against the truth."

Vilb's chest fell and he felt unsure if he could move forward. It was all too much to bear, and now the wind blew a cruel, cutting blow that sapped his hope along with his warmth.

"I can take you to warmth," said the girl.

"Lead the way then," said Vilb quietly, and the girl smiled.

"We will complete our Pilgrimage together, eh? As we began it?"

"If you stay here you will die," the girl said flatly.

Vilb nodded. "We cannot stay here." He looked up into the darkening sky. What had happened to him? He felt alone and confused and the girl was no help.

"After the city we will make another, even longer journey together, you and I, and I warn you: the journey will be an arduous one... and there may be flesh eating."

Vilb dropped his chin to his chest and said nothing.

II

They marched on until they reached the chasm's edge. There were a dozen ways down to the bottom and to the village by the bay. They climbed down a long series of stairs quickly along with a great many other folk, including Pilgrims from the east, travelers from the Great City, and denizens on local business.

Vilb was impressed with the vigor of the place. People moved with purpose and speed. Clearly food was plentiful along with water, and it was clear that the basics of life were not the first order of daily business.

The scavengers of this place must have a fine time, Vilb thought. He could imagine living on the remains of what people dropped as they moved from here to there with their wares. He counted well over a dozen people carrying baskets through the crowds. They were heavy laden with fruits and vegetables that he had never seen before, colors and shapes he had never seen before, nor ever even dreamed of eating. There were baskets of red and green, yellow and orange. Spits spun with dripping meats cooked over hot coals that burned steadily. There were rafts of raw materials, bolts of fabrics both fine and coarse, and wicker strands tied in thick bundles as large as a man's waist. Other denizens had cooking pots in their hands, or balanced on their heads, while still others carted large bundles of fuel to and fro. Fire, he thought in awe, must be common here. It was a cornucopia of abundance and he gazed at it all with astounded longing.

The Pilgrims found themselves herded as a group through the village and to the water's edge, towards the *dock* the girl called it. There they could take a floating barge to the other side of Martha's Bay. After another climb they would be in the Great City itself, San Simon. He had been there before, but had come and gone from below, and he remembered it as if it had happened to him in another lifetime. Now, this time, he traveled as himself, as an Ubernaki Pilgrim. As a devotee of The Martha. The Pilgrim's Ingress Guard would guide him and the rest.

"Bow to His Divine Holiness, the Pan-Archer!" a guard barked, and the large group of Pilgrims dressed in colorful srapis along with other trafficers wearing red hooded cassocks of The Martha lowered their heads for a long protracted moment. They shuffled on board, Vilb holding on tightly to the girl's hand. A hundred people or more crowded the ferry and bodies pressed hard against him. "Push in, push in, push in," said a guard's voice, and the crowd grew tighter and Vilb felt suddenly as if he might suffocate and he felt an uncontrollable panic seize him.

"Easy now," said the girl below him, sensing his anxiety. Vilb felt her tug on his hand and he looked down. "Easy now," she said again. "It's okay." The girl smiled and nodded up and Vilb looked behind him and over his head. The ferry was slowly moving away from the dock and out into the bay. The deck pitched unevenly and felt rocked roughly to and fro, fighting the pitch and yaw, and in the next moment he felt sick and felt as if his stomach swam loosely inside him and might crawl up his esophagus soon.

Vilb grunted and kept his eyes on his feet and the many others pressed in around him. He stood that way for an interminable period but finally the ferryman barked out to the dock as they approached and Vilb raised his gaze to the western side of the chasm as it drew near. At its base there sat a village with a dock much like the one behind, just as busy, just as rich with goods. Before long the crowd of Pilgrims disembarked and were herded through the town and to the stair that led to the plateau and to San Simon. Once to the top of the stair Vilb and the girl followed the road that skirted the chasm edge and headed north until the guard ordered them out onto a promontory overlook.

"Behold! By the Power of M the Pan-Archer spans the chasm!" the guard announced.

The girl spoke up now as if an expert. "They say he took a part of a mountain and just dropped it there. I didn't see it, but they say that's what happened," and as she spoke she reached down, pinched an imaginary bit of mountain, swung it around and opened her fingers to let it fall. "He just took it from here, brought it to there, and dropped it. There it is, it filled the chasm," he said. "He made the statue next, but it's all one part of a mountain. And there's a colossus on the other side too, pointing to the beyond... to the Fourth Realm they say." She almost giggled with glee.

"You?" whispered Vilb hoarsely. "You did this? As... Quadros?"

"The Power of M!" she whispered slyly.

They were in the City now and were abandoned at the steps of a low-slung building made of gray slabs of stone massive in their own right, but haphazardly placed. Some had collapsed leaving large, dark caverns, which had become by use a functional part of the building. By necessity as far as Vilb could tell, for there was a frenzy of activity there.

"Now listen to me," the girl said excitedly. "They don't trust... small people... here. Do you understand? Years of training, you see. They've been taught to hate them really. It's because of Qir and his Cadre of infans-terrorists. For hundreds of years he's sent his little bombs into the city. Most inhumanly, I might add. I can't keep up with the repairs."

Vilb stared, only partly comprehending. "Soft-headed," the girl muttered. "Just stay close to me," she said. "I need you."

Vilb looked down at the girl's up-turned face. He nodded. That he could do. He gripped the girl's hand and tried to hold his stomach still.

"Here. This is for you," said a stranger suddenly beside them in the crowd.

"Leave us be," the girl barked, though in his ear it sounded less like a bark and more like a screech.

"And don't thank me," the stranger said. "It's just that I don't need a couple of corpses lying around here. It's bad for business. Come on. We'll get you up out of here." Vilb felt a hand between his shoulder blades gently pushing him along and out of the crowd of Pilgrims. He held on tightly to the girl's hand.

They took a way through gentle hills and their guide led them, along with a bunch of other Pilgrims who followed, for a great distance around the outskirts of the city until they reached a wide way that cut into the heart of it, and came up directly on a wall of black. They walked until they stood almost directly at its base. Vilb stared. It was a polished cliff face that rose above them some fifty men high and blocked out the pale green sky. At the top there seemed to be some kind of broad walkway upon which he had seen earlier the heads of city guards bobbing back and forth, moving between towers placed evenly up and down the length of the wall, and all of it, the wall, the towers, the gatehouses, had been constructed in the same obsidian marble, polished, seamless.

"Isn't it beautiful?" said the girl in a queer voice. Vilb looked down at her and back up at the wall. "The expense was... enormous. Such a drain on the Arclight. Moving mountains, raising colossus—more than one, mind you—and a new wall about the entire Citadel. I thought it would break us but, well, I suppose it did." She giggled again.

Nothing had prepared Vilb for this.

"The Palm could do nothing against such a barrier," the girl crowed proudly and Vilb could discern a strange satisfaction in her tone.

"What's that you're saying there?" the stranger spun around and stood suddenly before them. Vilb recognized the face instantly as Bagnus, servant to The Martha, but he said nothing. The stranger was more interested in the girl and made no sign of knowing Vilb's face. He eyed Prav intently and as if seeing her for the first time he exclaimed, "Here now. You've got a child with you. Now that's not good," and as the voice went on a note of compassion had entered into it. The girl stared back mutely.

Bagnus pulled a bit of rope from under his srapi and quickly wound it around the child's waist. He put the other end in Vilb's hand.

"There now. That's a start." The stranger stood up and faced them both. "Remember old Bagnus the beggar?" They both stared silently at him in response. "By The Martha," the beggar said and he crouched down, his eyes went wide in wonder, looked around, and then took in Prav, close, staring.

"Why do you stare?" the girl demanded even as she pushed the beggar away. He fell backwards and scrambled to his hands and knees and looked her in the eye.

"To make sure. That's all. Bagnus was just making sure." And now the beggar leaned in and whispered. "I was, well, just seeing if you was a child Pilgrim or if you're one of them. You're small like one of them. If you are one well then that would be very bad for begging but very good for Old Bagnus, because The Martha's looking for one like you. So, I got you first, and that's good or else they would come here and shut this part of the wall down before you could chew and swallow." Bagnus had a tight hold of the girl's arm as if measuring her size.

Vilb exchanged a look with the girl and while holding Vilb's gaze she spoke to Bagnus. "There's a rumor that the Pan- Archer is dead," she said. "Is it true?" Vilb coughed. Bagnus dropped her hand and looked as if he had lost his wind.

"Bed-time stories," rasped the old beggar. He drew a wine skin to his mouth and drank deeply. He wiped his mouth with his sleeve and corked the skin before looking up. He handed the skin to Vilb who was grateful for the drink and he too sucked greedily at the old wine skin to quench his burning thirst.

"That's a relief, eh? The wine here works wonders," Bagnus said, and Vilb fixed his form for the first time as he sat himself up. The beggar was round and made a large shadow, and worse, he sounded too congenitally good-natured, and Vilb had begun to distrust him immediately. No one could remain good-natured indefinitely, and he had long ago developed a loathing for those who kept up the pretense. The wine helped, however, and even Prav gulped down the rest and presently Vilb's head cleared and he felt soft and loose for the first time in many seasons.

"Now please leave us be," said Prav and Vilb looked at her, surprised. The beggar was a good thing, was he not? He would help them to find… what… they had come for. And as for that, Vilb could not remember what he had come for.

"I would prefer not to become one with the stinking filth of San Simon… leave us now," declared the girl.

"But…" Vilb managed, not understanding the girl's hostility, but she silenced him with a wave. "In the shadow of my city I will not be afraid," the girl said again in a strange voice and Vilb looked bemused. He was bound to her, that much was certain both in his memory and in his heart and the rope in his hand.

"I've heard the rumors too," Bagnus finally said, "but The Martha denies them. She says Quadros remains," and as he said this he eyed Vilb with a hard stare, rose and took him by the hand to lead him forward.

"Take my advice if you please and don't sleep in the bottom there." He was looking up the face of the wall. "It comes down at any old time you know, and you don't want to be lying here when it does." At the base of the wall ran a deep and wide gutter, as smooth and polished as the wall.

"Yes, very good," Vilb said and followed Bagnus out of the gutter and up onto a wide walkway above it.

"Eating for later," said Bagnus, as if hearing Vilb's stomach. "Follow me." Bagnus pulled Vilb along yet the girl did not follow, at least not immediately. Vilb called after her but she stood for a time and watched the two move away. Finally, as if making up her mind, she jumped out after them and ran to catch up.

Bagnus drew them down the gutter along the base of the wall and here the stone was gray and unpolished. Further along, he turned down a small gutter, and then another, until they reached a round gutter dotted with black holes. Bagnus stepped down and followed the gutter for some ways, carefully navigating the holes at his feet. Up from beneath rose a foul smell and it was here that Bagnus pointed to.

"We've got to get you back down there, lad," he said to Vilb. "I know you. I see you here, and now, you're with one of them, that's obvious enough. Only by Simon's hand could you have made it this far. Eh? The Martha's waiting. She's hoping."

"For exactly what?" asked Vilb quietly.

"Aye, coming from you that I can believe. But this one here." Bagnus gestured to the girl. "Even on a leash she's hurt waiting to happen."

"I am Vilb Solenthay. This is Prav. I serve The Martha. Azo is my patron saint." Vilb turned his gaze on the girl. "She is the scourge of M," he declared baldly.

The girl barked out a laugh.

"Aye, and I respect you for it," said Bagnus. "I do."

Bagnus looked around him as if feeling which way the wind was blowing.

"The Pan-Archer's field is strong around here, anywhere in the City for that matter. It might be hard to remember everything until we get underdown, back with The Martha. You'll know then. Just stick with me." Bagnus bobbed his head as he spoke and leaned in close to Vilb. "She's waiting for you."

The old beggar reached out with both hands and took hold of Vilb's shoulders and turned him around slowly. "You've had a hard time of it out there, no doubt," he said. "I'm pleased to guide you again this time around," the beggar finally said and he thumped himself on the chest. "You have a fine way about you, Vilb Solenthay, I saw that last time you was here."

He looked at the girl now. "And you too," he said still looking at the girl. "You're not from the east, though, that's obvious enough." The girl remained quiet.

"Where's the other... ?" Bagnus's voice trailed off. "The other Pilgrim woman from the east that traveled with you?"

"Oneira's gone," said Vilb. His face went hard and blank.

"Oneira's gone."

"Aye. The Martha mourns your loss as her own." Bagnus bowed his head for a moment. "But hold on to hope, lad," and at this Bagnus swatted Vilb on the back. "You'll see what I mean when we get underdown." He took them in with one final look and then turned and headed off. "Come on," he said and waved them forward up out of the gutters and to a great road that climbed up to a plateau only to turn and run a straight line to the base of a massive black wall. San Simon lay behind it.

They followed the road to the base of the wall and stopped. An entourage approached from the rear and by the sound of it the procession was large.

"Look at this train of Purps and Pilgrims," he said loudly, and moved out onto the road as if he meant to stand and block their way.

The first group of people were five of the largest men Vilb had ever seen. They rose up from where they sat as they approached the wall and continued to glide forward. They rode floating slabs of stone and Vilb thought immediately of Quadros's floating chair. There were other gliding ferries approaching, but they slowed now to placate the beggar's antics.

He hopped and jumped in the road but kept a careful distance away from the lead ferry. Vilb was befuddled by such a sight. The men were three times his size, like massive pyramids, their heads were the pinnacle of a spreading bulk that supported them. Not like the agile Aegis, rather, these men were bulk incarnate and wore great purple folds of fabric that hid the rest of their true size. They stood for only a moment before lowering themselves back to their seats carefully.

To the rear of the ferry stood an even larger figure, but this one was more familiar to Vilb—this one was Aegis. He was white, still and silent. Slowly the ferry slid forward moving just above the polished surface of the road on an invisible current.

"I've got this whole place polarized," whispered the girl. "It costs a fortune but it makes travel for the Purps extraordinarily easy. They're my handy work, by the way."

He could feel the girl clutching at him from behind, hiding perhaps, or excited.

"May your honors enjoy a steady ride," Bagnus proclaimed loudly and he moved to the side of the road and bowed low. The five faces on the barge remained fixed forward and gave no sign to acknowledge the beggar's presence.

The eyes of the Aegis however had been drawn to Vilb and it locked its gaze on him but made no other sign, and no other move. The ferry glided silently on once again and Vilb stared as it passed. Bagnus bowed again deeply. Vilb kept his gaze on the Aegis.

"May Simon Bless the Pan-Archer, and may He shine His face on the House of Prang." Bagnus had his head down but Vilb watched the stone ferry draw even with him. The figures on board were massive. The flesh on their face was pink and round with water. They were taut with fullness. Four on this one, like the other, stone pews, a colonnade that ran around the perimeter of the floating slab, and an Aegis standing above it all to the rear. The Aegis looked to the side of the ferry and fixed Vilb with his stare. Vilb made to raise his arm and wave, to shout out at this familiar face, but the girl grabbed him from behind and hissed in his ear to be still. He froze and watched silently as the last of the procession moved past and disappeared into the wall. Vilb let out a sigh.

"They're so big," he said, genuinely dismayed.

"Aye. Huge. Too big to walk. And it happened all of a sudden. Everything changed. New black wall, the Purps bigger than ever, and the Aegis. Dozens of them. It's a mystery. You just watch out for the Aegis, like I said." And then Bagnus turned and fixed Vilb with a knowing look that surprised him for depths that it suggested in the old beggar. "Millennial Cadre are the small ones, though, eh?" he said, scratching his chin, his gaze dropping onto the girl. "Big things are coming undone right about now," said Bagnus. "The Martha will be anxious to talk with you and will be glad to know."

"To know?" asked Vilb but Bagnus ignored his question.

"It's time we went to see The Martha."

The girl looked up at Bagnus. "You can find her?"

"Aye, Bagnus knows."

"Take us then," said the girl confidently, and Bagnus jumped with delight.

"My new friends!" exclaimed Bagnus, and he grabbed the girl by the shoulders again and shook her roughly. "The Great Mother is counting on you to help her!"

• • •

Bagnus led the way while Vilb led the girl by the leash.

There were to be no untethered children allowed in the city, this Bagnus made clear and so the girl suffered Vilb to lead her by the rope like a child. Bagnus dodged through the crowded road quickly, plunging here, hanging back there, side-stepping when necessary, crashing through if possible. Vilb struggled to keep up. More than once Vilb looked back only to see the rope lead disappearing into a wall of cassocks, the girl somewhere beyond.

"AkiGazi?" Vilb asked quietly once through a particularly thick throng but the girl seemed not to hear him and Bagnus made no response. Perhaps they had not yet come. Perhaps they would not come at all.

They made slow progress across the wide, crowded main roadway. Further along they walked down a lesser obsidian road and left the Citadel's black wall behind them and made for what Bagnus had called the thousand steps.

Up the mountain, Bagnus said.

Once up the thousand steps they came to what Bagnus called the Great Steppe. As wide as the Road above them, and just as crowded, a sea of gray cassocks moved about for purposes the likes of which Vilb could not fathom. Even so, they moved around madly, rushing to get across wide expanses of pavement to gatherings of temples, always in threes, always circled, always surrounding a statue.

"It's the Pilgrim's Progress they call it," whispered Bagnus.

It's what they do. It's why they come. Look over there. You see the white?" Bagnus pointed over the heads of the crowd but Vilb could not see anything but a blur of gray cassocks.

"There's an Aegis over there. Probably Patronius. He patrols up here."

Just then Bagnus dropped to the pavement as if a hand had dropped him from above. Vilb dropped down next to him and pulled the girl down after him.

"Don't lean on that," Bagnus said, and waved him away from a small, stone obelisk as quickly as he could. There were hundreds of them running before them in a straight line that paralleled the edge where the Steppe met the mountain.

"Why not?" Vilb asked.

"That's a Pilgrim's post," Bagnus said, and Vilb left it at that. The girl clung tightly to Vilb's waist and pulled to keep up with Bagnus. It was as if she were fleeing from something. Vilb had to trot to keep up with her.

"What drives you?" Vilb finally called out. He was at the end of his rope.

The girl pointed. "Over there, beyond the roof tops in the distance. Look."

Vilb had seen the light but thought it only the end of season rituals of a way of life he did not understand.

"Bonfires," said the girl, and she kept moving forward, pulling, but then stopped and turned fiercely on Vilb.

"The AkiGazi have entered San Simon, addle-brain. They have answered the call and so they have come. But unlike you, they know their purpose." She pulled again after Bagnus, but called out over her shoulder in the gathering darkness. "There is no more time."

A Most Intimate Interview

I

For Vilb there was no way of knowing whether they had arrived at Casimir's shop or some other jumble of stones in the lower quadrants of the City. Casimir was nowhere to be found but Bagnus was certain of it so they ducked inside and, paying no heed, Bagnus plunged ahead and took them underdown. Bagnus, Vilb and the girl, now trailing, descended stairways and followed long tunnel passages until the air grew stale and the light exceedingly dim. The glow of the tunnel walls had gone out. Except for the small illumination Bagnus carried they would have been in complete darkness.

"The Martha's field is spent," the girl said with some pleasure from the darkness behind Vilb.

"No, no, up ahead. We will find her there. Have faith, little one. She waits for us. She waits."

And as if he had somehow conjured his desire with his words, an ambient amber light emerged before them and soon they were bathed in the warm glow. The air grew cooler and fresh and it was then that Vilb remembered Azo and The Martha and he wondered and dared to hope that both of them waited somewhere in the distance.

After a circuitous journey deep under the Great City Bagnus finally pulled up and waited for Vilb and the girl to gather round him. He ushered them to a small, silver door lit by an emerald point of light from above.

"She's here. Go in. She's waiting for you." Bagnus turned aside. The door opened with a rush of air and Vilb looked at Bagnus.

"My friend, the city will be overrun. They... the AkiGazi... they are a barbarous people.... I have seen it. I have heard tell of it. The people of San Simon will suffer... greatly."

Bagnus nodded, untouched. "Aye, lad. Things change."

"You understand?" Vilb asked.

"Aye, the endgame of the gods," sneered Bagnus.

Vilb stared, befuddled by Bagnus's sanguine response.

"She's the Great Mother," Bagnus said as if in response. There was no trace of derision in his voice.

"She is that." Vilb turned and stepped through the doorway and into the darkness of the chamber.

"Do you remember?" said a voice from inside the chamber, and Vilb knew that voice. He had heard it once before. Vilb walked towards it and an emerald light illuminated The Martha seated in a corner. Like Azo in his cell, Vilb thought. The Martha looked ghastly in the emerald light and Vilb shuddered. Her two thousand year old body was skin and bones, and Vilb thought that her body would not provide even one skin should anyone have the opportunity of harvesting it. She looked as if she had been dead for a dozen circs in the high sun.

Vilb bowed his head. "I've remembered, and I've forgotten again, and I've remembered. What will I do next?"

"It depends on whose field you enter. For now I've tuned my field to protect but not interfere with yours. You are yourself again."

"My... self? What is myself?" asked Vilb quietly.

The old woman seemed to laugh and the girl beside him snorted quietly. "Yes," said The Martha. "My power has grown weak. Quadros overran us here and I could no longer protect my regenerations in the east. Please forgive me." Her voice had grown raspy and it sounded faint and fragile, like a sputtering flame at the end of its tallow.

Vilb shook his head and found that he had to choke back tears that had come upon him.

And then The Martha spoke. She told him of his many years on the hill in the east. And of his Ubernaki childhood. Events. Teachers. His parents. The day his father left on Pilgrimage. His own long retreat to the outlands of his people as a hermit, a gen. All of it and more was there for him at her fingertips.

Yet simultaneously Jonathan Simons was there as well.

He was a regenerated copy—in his case, an exact copy—made from the genetic material of a donating predecessor. He knew that she had regenerated him—that the father who left him was really yet another regenerated copy of himself. That many regens grew in the east—the east was, among other things, a body farm for The Martha and that the east had gone to seed as The Martha's power waned. That even so the regens had developed a culture of their own and returned when they could to San Simon in answer to the gods' distant call.

"Of late, Quadros and Levinthal had made the journey difficult," she said, fatigue in her voice.

Levinthal was awake and serving the Consortium in Chicago and disrupting The Martha's field whenever possible. "Yes, yes," said Vilb. He knew about Levinthal—had a vague memory of… the out and out size of the man, and even Chicago, but perhaps that was Jonathan's memory and not Vilb's.

The Martha went on: many regenerations in the past she had made a deal with Azo to protect her clones against Quadros yet to no avail. Quadros infiltrated her field in the east and perverted her work. Now the entire eastern population had become flesh-eaters, cannibals.

"Good riddance," whispered the girl at Vilb's side, and Vilb sucked in a breath. "And now Levinthal promises to give you life, and abundantly, in trade for your loyalty. He would have you betray me, and forever end the threat of Simon's Restoration. I am weak, but I am not blind."

That was why he was here.

Vilb turned to the girl.

"I remember," he said.

"It's about time," she hissed. They both now turned to The Martha and stepped forward.

"We've come for you, Mother," Vilb said quietly, but she made no move to respond.

Bagnus could not suppress a yelp.

The Martha's voice broke the silence.

"Thank you, Bagnus, for your heart and your kindness. Without you we may not have had this interview today," and Bagnus bowed his head and mumbled. The voice was soft and gentle and familiar, and simply hearing it relieved the tension and fear in Vilb's body and he felt his breathing become easier. A warmth spread from his chest to his extremities and his mind was a blank. Tears sprang into his eyes and the need to lunge into the light and embrace The Martha all but overcame him.

"I just did as you taught me, your honor," Bagnus said quietly and interrupted Vilb's reverie. "We came as quickly as we could," he went on. "I recognized him immediately. The Millennial have arrived in the city," and as he spoke he pushed the girl forward. "She has come from Qir."

"Yes," The Martha said as if seeing her for the first time. "It all happened so fast," Bagnus said. "She's Millennial." "So you have finally come," The

Martha's head fell slightly as she spoke and her face went into shadow. "You dare to show your face to me, here?"

"But do you know who has come before you?" The girl had her hands on her hips. Bagnus was confused and he reached towards the girl but she stepped lightly back and away.

"Sit down," the girl commanded loudly. Bagnus guffawed and snorted and again began to move towards her.

"Bagnus, be seated," The Martha said quietly, her voice suddenly heavy with import.

"Your honor," said Bagnus, "if this little one means you harm then let me dispose of her for you. It would be my pleasure."

"Loyal Bagnus," The Martha said quietly. "The Millennial Cadre will not be disposed of easily by anyone. Sit down and listen to what she has to say to us." And with that Bagnus sank back to the floor beside Vilb.

The girl stood belligerently before the old woman, hands on her hips.

"I know who you are," said the old woman, and she spoke as if she were conceding a defeat. But even then The Martha's emerald eye flashed and her voice stiffened. "I took great pleasure in snapping your neck," she announced and the girl winced and staggered a step back. The Martha chuckled quietly. "You will never change no matter what body you take," she said.

Prav sucked in a breath and bit her lower lip.

The Martha cackled and clapped her hands gently together in mock pleasure. "I see your surprise and it pleases me!" She scoffed and arranged the folds of fabric in her lap haphazardly.

"You remain the fool!" she said harshly and waved as if to wish him away. "Now let me talk to Prav!" she barked.

A tense silence hung between them.

"Prav!" she called again. "I want to talk to Prav!"

The girl's arms went slack and her head fell forward, as if she had fallen asleep on her feet. She took a deep, shuddering breath and let out a low moan.

"Prav! Come forth!" called the old woman as loudly as her thin frame allowed. As she called the chamber began to hum with a soft vibration and the walls and floor and ceiling glowed again with a warm amber light. It was almost as Vilb remembered it in his first visit. The Martha was diminished, but not, it seemed to him, powerless.

Gurgling sounds began to rise from the girl's throat. Bagnus stepped back.

"Prav!" the old woman called again, but this time she sang the girl's name, and the old woman's voice cut right through Vilb. A flood of memories overwhelmed him. Feelings from his chest crowded his throat in an attempt to escape. He coughed and tried to swallow them down but they would not be swallowed.

"Child!" the old mother called again and warmth was in her voice now. Home and safety and all that Vilb had never experienced called to him namelessly. And Jonathan was there in his mind, present and implacable waiting to embrace the old woman, and thoughts of their son, Simon, flashed before him as if he had seen the boy only yesterday. And up from the depths of Vilb's body and mind rose Levithal's presence. The long-suppressed invasive presence, and it clung to the dark regions and refused to be drawn out into the light, but The Martha's light was more powerful than the dark. He dragged at the others like a drowning man, trying to pull them into the abyss with him. Vilb shook. He pushed his chin to his chest to choke himself into silence but he sobbed nonetheless.

The girl's body also shook with the sound of The Martha's voice. She lifted her face, now beaming, to the old woman.

"Mother!" she said. And the sound of the girl's voice was as it was before, out in the east, and to Vilb it had the familiar piping sound of the child he had saved. The corners of the old woman's mouth softened, but only barely and the girl spoke again.

With relief the words poured out of her. "Master Qir has become increasingly distressed about your situation." She paused to let her words find their mark.

The Martha nodded silently and moved her hand.

"Go on."

Prav took a deep breath. "But he is glad to see you well."

With hardly a pause The Martha responded. "You are important to us. The Power of M has brought you here, and we welcome it. I wish it had been sooner."

Prav bowed but made no other reply.

"Erebus," The Martha said, and sounded suddenly at a loss for breath, as if she had exerted herself. The amber glow of the chamber dimmed until only the emerald point shining down on The Martha remained. The fabric around her rustled as she struggled for breath. "We… make… for… Erebus," she managed. "Restoration," came next, and then, "Simon and Little Earth."

Prav raised her right hand, the Millennial Palm toward The Martha and the old woman looked pleased.

"You… Palm?… Here?" she asked slowly.

"It is a gift from Master Qir." With that the girl closed her eyes and stood, palm up, facing the old woman. From her hand waves emerged and flowed to the old woman. She closed her eyes and basked in the waves of energy that flowed from her hand to the old woman. The Martha's entire figure seemed to lift and fill.

Vilb gasped. The Martha's face was suddenly one with Oneira's face. It was true. Oneira and The Martha were one.

In the next moment Prav had lowered her palm and The Martha smiled serenely. Centuries had dropped from her cadaverous body. She looked almost human, barring her titanium facial implant.

The girl turned back towards The Martha. "My master has sent me as a token of his respect for your cause." The girl placed her palms over her heart and bowed.

When The Martha finally responded Vilb noticed that much of her former age had returned, though the old woman seemed the better off for it. "What are your master's demands?" the old woman said with strength.

"My master requests that you aid him in the Restoration and right a great wrong," Prav said flatly. Vilb looked with awe at the girl and felt his connection to her. He reached out from behind slowly with one hand and touched her hand hanging by her side, but only barely, at the tip of her fifth finger. He felt an electric charge leap from her to him and pulled away.

"I am old," The Martha said finally. "And I am weak." She shook her head and lowered her voice to a whisper.

The old woman gathered herself and spoke not so much to the girl anymore, but to the chamber itself, as if she had some wider audience she had now decided to address. She looked over them to the empty space. "Only Quadros moves with power now. He takes all for himself and destroys my work. He will destroy Little Earth on his way to Levinthal! You will suffer as well. And so you believe it now? Now you seek the Restoration? Are you not too late?"

The Martha paused expectantly. Vilb listened intently, waiting for Qir to respond via the girl, or perhaps from the empty space itself. Anything seemed possible. There was a long, crowded silence. Finally the girl spoke.

"My master will meet you at Erebus."

The Martha let out a long held breathe.

"Restoration is our only hope. I'm glad your master agrees with us." The old woman gestured now towards Vilb.

"He is here, finely tuned to the *remains.*" Prav said nothing and The Martha seemed mildly exasperated. "And then there is you," she said, and nodded to the girl and a warmth flowed from her voice for the second time and Vilb felt refreshed and clear-headed.

"We must make our way to Erebus with all mindful speed. Is your master prepared to extend what resources he has to bring Azo from his prison to Erebus?"

"Azo will meet at Erebus," responded the girl.

The Martha's eye flashed one last time and went dark even as the warmth left the chamber. She rose with surprising agility and two attendants appeared and guided her away and a moment later she was gone, out of sight, lost behind a dark door, but not before Vilb heard The Martha's desperate voice inside his mind.

May there be no remains.

II

Two attendants in hooded red cassocks escorted Vilb, Prav, and Bagnus out of The Martha's chamber and into the dark tunnel complex. They followed another long walk of descents, turns and sloping stretches that took them deep, deeper than before, and Vilb felt the earth all around him press into him and his ears began to ring. There were many others walking behind and before them, they were all, apparently, headed in the same direction.

Vilb felt a desultory sadness all around him, as if the many cassocks were in retreat… again, and that a successful outcome was not anticipated. Finally they arrived in a well- lit chamber with vaulted ceilings that rose smooth and white above them. All around the perimeter of the chamber were arched portals opening onto a dozen dark tunnel openings.

Those in the fore moved towards an illuminated archway with Ubernaki script carved overhead: **to ereBus stAtIoN**. Once beyond it Vilb found himself standing on a large platform. They were in a mag-rail station. What must have been hundreds of others in red cassocks milled about, their murmurings thick with trepidation.

The flow of people carried Vilb onto the station just as a mag-rail glided up to the platform. Its doors opened yet no one entered. Vilb looked around and found that the many figures were looking at him, and they gave way for the girl, Bagnus, and Vilb to enter the waiting car.

In the next moment a complete hush fell over the crowd as The Martha entered. As she moved slowly through the throng of acolytes, novices and other servants of The Martha, Vilb began to hear whispers of Restoration. There was quiet sobbing. This was not a celebration, nor a victory, that much was obvious. Hands reached out to touch The Martha's fabric as the red sea of cassocks opened and let her pass. She sat atop a small, square marble slab just large enough for her seated figure and the folds of fabric spilling all around her. Four red- robed escorts walked beside, before, and behind her, one at each corner of the stone. They wore hoods, but the four wore them back and Vilb could see their faces plainly. They were all the same stony face, and they were all the face of Oneira.

They entered the train car and joined Vilb and the others, and the doors closed behind. In another moment the train sped away, humming into the dark tunnel.

• • •

After many uncomfortable and fitful dozings the train stopped and the doors slid open onto a brightly lit station, exactly like the one they had left, only this one was devoid of life.

"Erebus Station!" The Martha said quietly, as if reading her own epitaph. Vilb waited for the rest of them, but they stood there as if frozen. Prav too remained still and Vilb grew anxious to move but before he could be the first to act Bagnus pushed past him and stepped out of the car.

"Well, like I said, no one but old Bagnus to show you in. Follow me."

The Martha then glided forward slowly and stopped beside Vilb. Her one fleshy eye pleaded with him silently and he could see that she was... afraid.

A part of him yearned to reach out to her, to kneel at her feet, and to be warmed by her glow. Yet another part of him, a part of him that he felt some shame in acknowledging, thrilled to see the old crone's vulnerability, and that somehow, up ahead, her just desserts were waiting, and they had long been prepared. Which of his responses represented the truth of the situation? He did not know.

They entered an antechamber just beyond the station and the old woman raised her hand and they stopped. Bagnus dropped to his knees and bowed low before her.

"Rise my child. Rise. I seek no such obeisance here."

"I am sorry for your troubles, Mother," said the old beggar.

"Yes, well. It is to be expected."

"Aye, and worse is on the way," Bagnus whined. "Those monsters must have overrun the city by now. We got out just in time or so I've heard your honor."

"My Loyal Bagnus."

"Aye, your worship."

"Please wait for us in the hall. You must guard our way."

Bagnus hesitated but then finally turned and moved for a door that led out of the station.

"We wait here for Azo," declared the old woman, and with that she went silent and still as a mountain.

Vilb had lost track of time. He stretched out on a slab and napped unsatisfactorily. From somewhere Bagnus had procured them food and water and they ate and slept and ate and slept again. Not long after their third meal, just as Vilb became increasingly unnerved—he had a sense of urgency that the others did not seem to share, or at least, to show—a mag-rail hummed into the station and stopped. The doors opened and an old man draped in the purple silk srapi of the Citadel stepped slowly towards them. Azo had come. He had a furrowed brow and a deep crease in his forehead that was not there before.

Azo stepped onto the station platform on his own two feet and slowly tottered past Vilb as quickly as he might, not looking at him or the girl on his way. He only had anxious eyes for The Martha.

"Quadros has destroyed the Arclight. Our lines have failed." His voice was thick with defeat. The old woman raised a hand and shook her head in an attempt to calm him.

"Look at who has joined us," and with this she pointed to Vilb and nodded to the girl.

Azo shuffled over, one hand dragging his srapi train. He slowly circled them both, looked them up and down and finally stopped before Vilb. He reached up quite suddenly with one hand and grabbed him about the throat. His thumb and index finger seemed to search for something under and behind Vilb's jaw. He found a lump and squeezed hard and it sent a shattering pain through Vilb's head.

"He looks good," said Azo over his shoulder. "Open your mouth," he commanded and Vilb let his jaw relax and fall open. "Not bad. Yes. Good." Azo reached under his srapi and withdrew a milky white crystal cube. He held it in front of Vilb's chest, though he was careful not to let the cube come into contact with him. The cube immediately took on the dusky verdigris of the sky at sunset. Azo moved the stone all around Vilb's chest but finally brought it back to his heart, holding it just above. The cystal was now blood red and throbbing.

"The VenQuell is in the red," he said. A smile tipped the corners of his mouth. At last Azo turned to Vilb.

He looked him in the eye and spoke softly. "I'm proud of you. You've done surprisingly well. I had every confidence, but really, you've done very well indeed." Azo put his hand on Vilb's shoulder. "Well done my good and faithful servant," and he chuckled as he turned away.

A desperate confusion took hold of Vilb. "What am I?" he blurted. He looked at the girl and then Bagnus, but they had nothing for him.

This stopped Azo and he turned to face Vilb again, a shadow across his face.

"You are a pawn that has made it across the board, my boy. You will be crowned with power."

"If we can proceed," said the old woman, now glaring at Azo, and Azo turned to her and returned her stare but made no move. "So proceed!" she barked, exasperation now in her voice.

"What about her?" Azo asked calmly. He looked down at the girl. "What if Quadros…?" He let the unfinished question hang. "It's a dangerous game we're playing. You're bringing him right where he wants you to."

The Martha's face went grim.

"I know. I know."

The Martha left Bagnus and her attendants behind. The smaller company climbed aboard a larger floating slab and made quick progress through dim and deserted tunnels. Vilb walked like the condemned directly behind The Martha's seat and Azo, who walked beside her.

"What of AkiGazi?" The Martha asked.

Azo shook his head. "We are too far west. Even with those beasts they ride on they could not have come so far." He paused. "Quadros has destroyed the Arclight. Little Earth will freeze. All of our work… so much work… I have a thousand bodies I had to leave behind! Such waste!"

"Restoration will change all that," the old woman said quietly, not meeting his gaze.

"I do hope for it… but… I admit to you that I have long dreaded it."

"This time will be different. You see? He will be bound to us, to me, in a way he was not… before."

Azo spoke as if he hadn't heard her. "I have long wished for it and long dreaded it."

"We're close now," said the girl.

Vilb eyed her with dread and fear. Was this Prav or was this Quadros? Could he trust either of them? They made steady progress until they came to a massive open space that rose high above them and all around. An amber light glowed softly but with no clear source. The four moved directly to a bank of doors across the white marble floor.

As they approached a door it slid open and they stepped in, the doors shut behind them and The Martha's floating slab settled to the floor. The four of them were on some sort of lift which rose and carried them up and up with great force before finally stopping. The doors opened and The Martha's stone slab rose and glided out into a foyer. It was dark, square with dark stone all around, smooth and polished, like the ebony walls of the Citadel, or Quadros Prang's palace at Lake Vost. Erebus Control.

"Okay," was all Azo said and he let out a small sigh of relief. The Martha nodded.

Doors opened in one wall and the space inside was even darker, but its darkness was punctuated by emerald points of light. The Martha and Azo moved forward, the girl close behind. Vilb hung back.

"I do not want this," he murmured. "Please do not do this… to me."

The Martha groaned. Azo grew visibly excited. The stone stopped and Azo turned towards Vilb.

"Who is this me you refer to? You were born to this, you and all of your…" and at this he turned to The Martha."

"Enclave," she said quietly.

"You and all of your enclave. Advance," he commanded, and Vilb shuddered, looked around, and had no choice but to obey.

In the next instant Prav was on the floor rocking and moaning.

Azo moved across the room as quickly as he could glancing sidelong at the girl but left her to her rituals. The Martha stayed where she was and put her head in her hands.

Azo stood at a distance looking into the void beyond and Vilb recognized it as the White Room. This was the em-frame. This was the machine that the Ancients had made. It was the source of Simon's power, and the gods themselves. Azo stood within an amber web that had suddenly grown up all around him.

"We're being bombarded here from somewhere," he announced. "We're about to lose field integrity." He stopped and looked over at the old woman. "It's got to be Levinthal."

"Not Quadros?" quavered Martha.

"No. Wait. Wait. No. Not Quadros. We're in a rupture. No field dominates... the girl."

The girl was at the feet of The Martha now, her fists full of the cloth at the old woman's feet. She was breathless and desperate.

"I'm sorry! I'm sorry! Please don't hurt me! Please!"

The girl buried her face in the fabric. "Please make it stop. I want them to stop!"

The old woman sat up straight and seemed to hesitate, unsure.

She turned to Azo. "Levinthal then?" she asked but Azo could not answer her.

"Where is Qir's field?" The Martha demanded, and she sounded desperate. "Why is he not protecting us?" Azo had become a scene of desperate activity. Lines of amber force encircled him, cut through him, blurred the boundaries between his body and the light all around him. Even so Vilb could hear that he struggled to keep up. He grunted and mumbled as he exerted himself. Vilb looked to Azo and back to The Martha and still she did nothing. The girl sobbed and pounded frantically. Vilb's understanding remained hopelessly fractured and all he had left to guide him was his pounding heart.

"It's there," Azo called out after another few moments.

"Critical mass. Oh my word it's beautiful. We have critical mass in the pile." He sounded profoundly relieved.

The Martha turned to Vilb and nodded. "It's now or never. Whom do you serve?"

Vilb stood his ground, nonplussed.

"I serve... I serve..."

"Vilb!" cried the girl suddenly clutching him around his legs. She looked up into his face and he saw the young child he had saved from death so long ago. "You don't have to do this. Please don't do this. Listen to me. Qir wants this because she wants this, but Simon... Simon does not want this. Let him sleep. Let him be."

"Oh my child," said Vilb softly, and Vilb felt Jonathan Simons rise up in him and his painful, distant love of his son, and he clutched the girl to him.

"I'll be good. I promise to be good. Just don't go away! Promise not to go away!"

"I'm not going anywhere, my child."

Prav lurched forward then and grabbed desperately at the old woman's lap and The Martha cooed and stroked her wild hair but the girl kept sobbing hopelessly. "You know what they've done to me!" she cried. "Why did you let them do it? Why? Mother?" She screamed as if in wild torment.

The old woman sat up. "Stop it this instant," she hissed. "You make it much more difficult than it has to be." The old woman tried to grab the girl's wrists but she could not hold on. Prav flailed, broke away from The Martha's ancient grasp and moved backwards slowly, her face twisted in terror, her hands out in front as if warding off a blow. The old woman turned to Vilb. "Simon's Terror," she said flatly.

The wide, round surface of the ascending and descending stone daises glowed warmly with an amber light.

It was hot now in the Throne Room and the air smelled like a dry electrical storm had settled over them.

Just then Azo let out a shriek of dismay. "We've lost field integrity in three... two... No!... one. On my god, we're down."

The lights went out, the console went dark. The girl's sobbing continued punctuated by moans.

Vilb stumbled to her in the dark and his hands found her foot and he took the rest of her in his arms and rocked her. The ragged inhalation of her hopeless sob shook her whole frame and Vilb felt it too and sobbed along with her for the first time in his many lives.

He rocked her gently back and forth in the perfect darkness.

"Can you get us back," the old woman called from the corner and her voice was small and pitiful. Azo merely grunted by way of response.

"This is station wide," he said. "Probably continental." "Then it's Levinthal."

"It has to be," said Azo. "Then we've lost."

"We've lost," echoed Azo.

· · ·

Vilb lost track of time in the absolute blackness of the Throne Room. They waited but he never grew hungry there, or thirsty, so when the power returned it may have been out for an instant, or perhaps many circs. He had no clear sense of the direction or the duration of time. It was dark and then suddenly it was light. He blinked and remembered that the girl was curled up in his arms asleep. He lay her down gently and rose to his feet. Azo too rose and The Martha startled awake.

Vilb heard a familiar voice in his mind and the ringing in his ears stopped. I have released you from all control, it said, you and the girl. Quadros now reigns in her. You only have an instant to choose. If you choose to serve the Restoration, Simon will destroy the world for a second time. If you block him, you will be with me, here, in paradise.

Before Vilb could respond the ringing in his ears returned and he looked around, dazed.

Prav strode to where Azo stood and pushed him back and down to the floor.

"Stay there," she said.

"What is it?" The Martha called over.

"Some other field has him, has them both," said Azo.

The girl was busy tuning the White Room. As she stood in the Qport Vilb knew that she understood its function and how to manipulate it for Quadros had returned. From there he could see the status of the Barrier Ring, the Bosonic Pile and the Halo. All of it. Here was the body of Simon, scattered and disconnected. It needed only to be harmonized into a whole by careful tuning that only the proper tools allowed for—the *remains*.

Vilb understood. *He* and the *remains* were one.

Even as he recognized what he must do, the girl was on her feet and moving to the dais.

The Martha moaned and Azo cursed.

The girl stood before the dais and had to jump up in order to clamber atop. She slipped and sprawled across the stone and left a bright smear of amber behind her as she slid to the center of the smooth surface.

"We're spiking!" Azo cried. "Time please! It's time!"

The ceiling console descended and the girl rolled onto her right side even as the descending surface pressed against her shoulder and wreathed her in amber fire. She brought the palm hard against the flaming surface. In another moment the small body went limp and the bottom and top came together and squeezed out the light and everything else that was between them.

"It has to be Quadros," the old woman moaned. She hovered up close to the dais and then moved towards Azo. The Martha choked back a sob.

Vilb looked at The Martha, then to Azo, and then down at his hands. Just a hermit's hands from the east of Little Earth. Who was he?

The question had to serve as its own answer for the time being, for he found himself lunging across the floor and he leapt with what strength his rigid body allowed for onto the surface of the dias and pushed the girl aside. She fell to the floor with a thud and a cry.

Vilb felt as if the upper and lower surfaces were slowly crushing him and that he would be smeared to a fine film across the world. He had no clear idea of how long he remained there, but finally he heard Azo's voice call out, "Saturation…" and the girl shrieked with rage and The Martha cried out in joy and disbelief.

• • •

Vilb was everywhere and nowhere. From wherever he was, he knew that he could control everything and a compulsion poured through him to bring the sleeping continent to life. He mixed and stirred and commanded the magma in the Halo to circulate faster, and a thousand miles away and two miles down under San Simon a long-closed door opened and magma once barred now poured in and stimulated the sluggish subterranean ring. It was as if his own body had been awakened from a long sleep and the blood and lymph began to flow more vigourously.

A moment later the Barrier Ring surged to life and with that the computational mind of the quantum em-frame sprang to expectant wakefulness and his mind was the stars, and his footstool was Little Earth. In the next moment the Greater Earth's magnetic poles shifted and the Barrier Ring became one with the nanosphere even into space and the furthest edges of the Greater Earth's magnetosphere.

And Vilb controlled it, and it was called Simon.

But he was not alone.

He made it his own until the girl's cries were like a sweet, mournful music to his ears.

It was then he heard a voice he had not heard for two-thousand years.

"I'm down here."

Vilb opened his eyes and a blinding brightness filled the darkness and he blinked hard against the light. He had a body again, and was in a space, and moved in time.

"You've got to breathe," said the voice with some concern.

It was young, like Prav's but not Prav's voice. A child's though, his child's, he was certain of that.

Vilb inhaled deeply and looked around. He found himself a hermit standing alone on a vast plain that curved away in every direction. Overhead a vast, empty blue sky held a scorching sun. It was nowhere he had ever been.

He blinked hard again and forced the world into focus.

He was alone, nearly naked and without food or water but this did not concern him. "Simon!" he called again. He looked calmly around for a moment and saw that the plateau was not so featureless as he had imagined, for behind him was a wide chasm. He walked to the edge and peered in. From a great distance below he heard Simon's voice. That was it. He found an outcropping and began climbing down. Further and further down he climbed. He went deep into the chasm and still the bottom was nowhere in sight but ahead, perhaps closer this time, was the girl's voice. He looked up and saw the sky as a jagged line of blue between chasm walls.

He continued to climb down as fast as he was able.

"Prav?" he called, and he was leaping now from stone to stone in what he once would have considered a mad rush. Now it had become easy, like falling, only he fell lightly and leapt again, and in this way he descended.

Finally a ribbon of dry valley appeared below him and he hurried along until he reached the bottom. He was in deep shade now and a chill wind blew.

From up ahead he heard a child's voice and he set off down the road towards it. His way twisted and turned around outcroppings and boulders leaving him blind to what came next until he rounded a bit of toppled ledge and there stood a child, but it was a boy—a haggard boy, and not Prav at all. No larger than Prav, the boy stood as if waiting for him in front of the black mouth of a cavern.

"Come on!" the boy said, and he jumped excitedly on the balls of his feet. "Hurry!"

"Alright, I'm coming." Vilb trotted now and caught his hand just as he turned to enter the cavern. "I'm here." Vilb looked down at the boy. He had a white shirt on from the old world, and brown trousers and brown shoes. His hair was short and his face pockmarked with scars.

"You're my dad," the boy said and Vilb stifled a sob. He was the boy's father, but he wasn't. He was Vilb, but he wasn't. He was himself, but what is self?

"You're my Simon," said Vilb. "Where's Prav?"

The boy acted as if he had not heard the question. He had Vilb's hand in his and he pulled him into the cavern, tugging to speed them both along. They descended deep into the earth until the light from the cavern opening had been long left behind. In the blackness a point of emerald light emerged and the boy pulled him to it.

"This is where we hide," the boy said as they walked. An ambient green light illuminated their way now and the walking was easy.

"It's a good hiding place," said Vilb, looking around. The cave ceiling disappeared into darkness above. "Is Prav here? Where is she?"

"She's..." and the boy let go and pointed up ahead. "She's waiting for you. Quadros tries to stick her here, but then she gets out again. You know? She's not like me. I'm stuck here."

A rocky wall blocked their path. It loomed up and disappeared into the darkness above.

"Now what?" asked Vilb.

"Look. Right here. There's a door here," said the boy.

"Come on." He stepped forward and there at his outstretched fingers was a doorknob attached to a wide portal with a thick door hewn from oak. Vilb drew his fingertips across the surface. Oak. "Oak," he said. From oak trees. It had been a long time.

The boy was past the door and inside already. "Close the door," he said as Vilb stepped past it. He pushed it shut and felt a latch click in the base of his spine. He tingled and his head throbbed.

"You're here," said the boy. "Finally!" Vilb turned to see the small boy—such a small boy with such small shoulders and sallow skin. His eyes were sunk into his skull and they were lightless and dark. He sat upright, poised even, at a small round table—it's wood, Vilb thought—with his hands clasped before him. Vilb sat down slowly and looked around and placed both hands against the strange, warm surface. The two of them sat in a small cave hardly large enough for the table and two chairs, let alone their bodies. Vilb could touch either side of the cave with outstretched hands. He leaned back and bumped his head. A small... candle... burned in the center of the table. It sputtered and seemed to burn in vain against the dark. "They can't reach me here," said the boy. "None of them can. But if you leave here then they can get you."

Vilb's eyes filled with tears. "Who put you here?" But he already knew. He remembered. The gods of Little Earth had put him here at the scattering, so long ago.

"All of them. You in a way, too." The boy looked down at the table and traced silent figures with his finger. "Quadros. Levinthal. The whole world. Everyone. Everything. History. Time." The boy went silent.

"Quadros?" Vilb asked quietly and the boy nodded, still looking down. "And Qir?"

"I said all of them."

Vilb nodded. "You want Levinthal?" Again the boy nodded, then shrugged, unfolded his hands and put his palms down on the table.

"He's the worst. I hate him the most. All of this is because of him."

"You brought me here?" Vilb shot back, the fullness of his darkness now dawning on his mind. He drew back and bumped his head again.

"Stupid! You have to get even for me! You can be me. You already are me, but now you can really be me. I can feel my whole body waking up. It hurts, you know, but it's… waking up. But first you have to promise. Promise?"

Vilb leaned into Simon. "Promise what? Do you know?"

The boy shrugged and drew a circle on the tabletop and drove his index finger into the center.

"Only if you promise," the boy said. He was sheepish.

Vilb waited. He shook his head. "Promise you what? What do you want me to promise you?"

"Don't let them leave."

Vilb shook his head. "Leave? Little Earth? Who?"

"The whole Earth, stupid. Don't let them leave. They found a way to leave, through me, if they can find me. They want to leave and hurt everyone everywhere. Don't let them do it. Promise me. Don't let them leave. You have to stop them. You have to kill them. That's hard nowadays. You have to rip and tear."

"What are you talking about?"

"Levinthal, stupid. And the Board. They have plans. They've come back. They still want more." The boy paused and looked up. His eyes were brimming before, but now bloody tears spilled down his cheeks and they flowed freely. His eyes were black and blood and water, and Vilb felt penetrated to the core by Simon's gaze.

In those eyes he saw himself and the core of what he was and the answer to his question. What is a self ? A void. An empty cup. He saw that he was a tool and not a purpose, he was a way, but not an outcome. He was a pawn moving into power.

"I remember," said Vilb and he held Simon's stare. "As your dad. I'm sorry. For everything…. I did…. I was…. I am."

"Now I'm helping you. You prayed to me. I heard you. All those years. And now you're here with me. I've tried to help you all along, but it's hard from here. I'm stuck here. It's dark here. I don't like it all alone. I'm glad you're here."

Vilb bit his lip and his eyes swam. He nodded. "I promise."

"You promise?"

Vilb's voice grew dry and hoarse. "I promise to wield the Power of M. For you."

"And?"

Vilb took a breath.

"I promise destruction."

Simon threw his head back and laughed through his bloody tears.

III

Simon remained seated at the table, his hands crossed, his cheeks wet with blood and water as he bade Vilb to go.

"I'll come back," he said quietly, one foot already out of the small cave. "I won't leave you here. Not forever."

The boy made no sign.

"I'll come back. I promise."

Before him a voice cried out: "Come on!" and this time Simon was out in the cavern and moving quickly through the preternatural darkness waving for Vilb to follow. Vilb looked back at the small cell but the door had closed, yet he knew somehow that some part of Simon—the heart of Simon—remained locked behind that oaken door. Vilb turned and scurried off at Simon's simulacrum. Just as he caught up with the boy a vertical cliff rose up and blocked their way.

"Here it is," whispered Simon. "Here is the Power of M."

At the base of the wall he crouched and pointed towards a small hole, difficult to discern in the darkness. The boy crawled forward. "You have to crawl in there. It's right in there."

"Okay."

Vilb dropped quickly to his hands and knees. There was nothing else to do except to crawl into the opening, and he moved forward and stuck his head in the wall, and then his shoulders and then his entire body, but only just barely. The rock pulled at his srapi and dug into his flesh. There was only barely enough room to creep forward. He was on his stomach scrambling along now. His breathing filled his ears and he could hear it growing ragged. Perspiration flowed into his eyes and they burned but he could not wipe them. He crawled on and his knees bled and his fingertips were raw, one was torn. He crawled further still, compelled by desire. Ahead of him waited the fullness of the Power of M. It would be his.

He had to stop and rest and when he did he felt the weight of the world pressing down upon him, humming in his ears. He struggled on. A jagged jog dug into his side and another dug into his skull. To move forward he found he had to pull a knee up and twist onto his back and kick with his heels which allowed for only slow progress, and he had no idea how far yet he had to crawl.

His eyes burned. The darkness was complete. Stone hemmed him in all around. After a few more desperate attempts to move, he could not go forward and he found himself wedged. There was no going back.

A storm of terror came over him and he went mad with the fury to escape. He screamed, he shrieked, he called until he exhausted himself and fell silent.

It was then that he heard a voice calling out, telling him to hold on. He was on the way. Vilb barked out another scream and it seemed the rocks all around took up a vibration in response. A voice called to him and Vilb shouted back. In the next moment he felt hands grip his ankles and drag him feet first out of his dark hole.

Wrong way! he thought, but there he was, squinting in the afternoon light of the long day. An old man stood over him, an Ubernaki by the looks of him. He had a gray srapi, water skins at his side and a sling round his middle. He was thin, painfully so, and tanned by the sun. A thick scruff of whiskers covered his face. The old man crouched over him standing between Vilb and the sun.

Vilb opened his eyes and looked into the old man's green eyes. It was a long and drawn face in which he discerned a curious... hunger.

At that same singular moment it dawned on both men that the face each looked upon was his own. The old man staggered back and Vilb gasped.

In the next moment the earth shook and the cavern wall above him sprayed down a wash of pebble and dust until larger rocks began to fall, and then boulders fell and entire chunks of cliff peeled away and began to lean out and would have fallen and crushed Vilb had he remained where he was, but he did not remain.

The floor under him gave way and Vilb felt himself falling, falling, through the rubble and the dark until the sky grew light and the sun shone overhead and he saw that he was falling to earth. He fell a great distance and came down on his back with a thud and bounce.

He lay there catching his breath and blinking fast in the bright light all around him. In the darkness he could discern what must have been the shadowy figures of Azo and The Martha there before him. He had returned. He lay on his back on the illuminated dias of the Throne Room.

So much confusion had given way to such perfect clarity. He swung his massive feet off of the dais and down onto the floor. He landed with a heavy thud. He was unable to rise to his full height, but instead crouched there in the dark, a glowing body of living marble. Strength surged through him and he looked down at his hands and made them into fists. The Power of M had yet to reach full fruition, yet even now he felt he could topple mountains and swallow seas.

"Lord, command us," said Azo, his head bowed and he trembled.

Vilb looked down at the two of them.

"What of Quadros?" asked the old woman. "Is he gone?"

"He is… in retreat," answered Vilb. "Prav knows."

"Lord, command us," said the old woman, her voice barely bridling her joy.

Vilb closed his eyes and he conjured a vision of the Great City and saw that the AkiGazi were even now pouring in from the north and east. They poured in from the desolate and darkened plains beyond the polar plateau looking for flesh. These creatures—the remains of mischief wrought by Quadros—these twisted beings Vilb would make his New Body Army of the Restoration and he would be their Lord. Together they would set sail for the Fourth Realm before the Arclight failed completely. For now the blood and flesh that covered San Simon pleased him and he gave free reign to the appetites of his minions.

"We leave Little Earth," he said, "and make war on Chicago." But first Vilb would go to where the Aegis had fallen in their battle with Quadros and he would restore them and bring together the scattered remains of the Colossus of Simon. Only then would he make the journey to the Transveld and call Qir forth. Qir's mountain would be left a ruined hole into which Simon would pour the ocean if Qir did not serve. From there a fleet would cross the Girdling Sea and bring Simon's ruin to the Fourth Realm where vengeance would unfold and the bitterest of agonies would be delivered onto the heads of the guilty. There and then the betrayed and the outcast would find Simon's justice.

Vilb was wide awake. He knew now that Levinthal would kneel, or end. And the Consortium Board would be utterly destroyed. Only then and at long last would the Seven Realms be cleansed of the gods of Little Earth.

END OF VOLUME I

Coming from

MERRY BLACKSMITH PRESS

in 2015

2050: A Future History, Volume Two
The Power at the Bottom of the World

2050: A Future History, Volume Three
The Keys to the Kingdom

Visit merryblacksmith.com for details.

www.ingramcontent.com/pod-product-compliance
Lightning Source LLC
Chambersburg PA
CBHW051445260626
47162CB00001B/259